FRIENDS...WITH CONSEQUENCES

JULES BENNETT

ONE NIGHT WAGER

KATHERINE GARBERA

MILLS & BOON

All rights reserved including the right of reproduction in whole or in part in any form. This edition is published by arrangement with Harlequin Enterprises ULC.

This is a work of fiction. Names, characters, places, locations and incidents are purely fictional and bear no relationship to any real life individuals, living or dead, or to any actual places, business establishments, locations, events or incidents. Any resemblance is entirely coincidental.

This book is sold subject to the condition that it shall not, by way of trade or otherwise, be lent, resold, hired out or otherwise circulated without the prior consent of the publisher in any form of binding or cover other than that in which it is published and without a similar condition including this condition being imposed on the subsequent purchaser.

First Published in Great Britain 2023
by Mills & Boon, an imprint of HarperCollins*Publishers* Ltd
1 London Bridge Street, London, SE1 9GF

www.harpercollins.co.uk

HarperCollins*Publishers*
Macken House, 39/40 Mayor Street Upper,
Dublin 1, D01 C9W8, Ireland

Friends...with Consequences © 2023 Jules Bennett
One Night Wager © 2023 Katherine Garbera

ISBN: 978-0-263-31754-1

0223

MIX
Paper | Supporting
responsible forestry
FSC™ C007454
www.fsc.org

This book is produced from independently certified FSC™ paper
to ensure responsible forest management.

For more information visit: www.harpercollins.co.uk/green

Printed and Bound in Spain using 100% Renewable electricity at
CPI Black Print, Barcelona

FRIENDS...WITH CONSEQUENCES

JULES BENNETT

To my parents, who just celebrated fifty years of marriage. You two are the true meaning of happily-ever-after.

One

Nora splashed cold water on her face, closed her eyes, and willed the nausea to cease. She also willed those power tools to stop, but she'd paid a hefty sum to have her cottage renovated both inside and out. Real Estate in Northern California could get pricey and the market was slim right now, so she opted to revamp her entire place instead of dealing with the headache of a move. And considering the work had only begun, she would simply have to live with the early morning start.

Tearing down walls and expanding the back deck were the least of her worries right now. Two thin blue lines stared back at her and Nora didn't know if this new wave of nausea came from morning sickness or the reality of her unplanned pregnancy.

She pulled in a deep breath in an attempt to get ahold of her chaotic emotions. Falling apart now would not change the fact she was having Zane Westbrook's baby. Of all the people she could have had a one-night stand with...

Zane wore so many hats in her life: her best friend's twin brother, her boss, her friend...and now the father of her child.

Nora needed to get into the office, because she never took a day off, let alone showed up late. But there was no way she could face Zane, and thankfully, his brother Cruz was out of the country on business.

How could she ever look either of them in the eye again? The sickening thought that she'd betrayed her best friend by having a one-night stand with his twin overwhelmed her. Cruz trusted her. They'd been friends for years, well before their working relationship had started.

When the guys launched their lifestyle magazine, *Opulence*, she'd been hired as the social media content director. She took her job and their friendships seriously. Though Zane had always been more standoffish, that never deterred her attraction and desire.

She'd fought for so long.

Except for that one night.

Nora cursed herself for being so naive and vulnerable. She had a weak moment that day, coupled with years of Zane fantasies, and they'd ended up tearing at each other's clothes right there in his office. That had been a month ago and she'd managed to dodge that entire area since.

She grabbed her hand towel and dabbed her face before stepping back into her bedroom. Various clothing options lay draped across the foot of her bed, where she'd set them moments ago...before her life changed forever. Suddenly, wearing her green sweater or her blue wrap-style blouse seemed insignificant in the grand scheme of things.

Nora slid a hand over her still-flat belly and had an instant need to protect her baby. This wasn't quite the way she'd envisioned having a family of her own, but she would do everything she could to make sure her child knew love and stability.

She tightened the belt on her silky robe and crossed to her nightstand. She needed to let Zane know she wouldn't be in today, which was so out of character for her. But she never missed work, so she knew one day wouldn't be an issue.

While she didn't like sending Zane the text stating she wouldn't be in, he was her only option since Cruz was not in the US. Even before their night together, she'd tried to keep her distance or at least make sure they were always in a group with other people. Being alone with Zane had never been a good idea, not with the all of those feelings she'd lived with for years. So she'd tried, she'd really tried to dodge temptation.

But that one moment of weakness had caused her to turn to Zane when he'd offered her comfort the day her beloved Clara had passed. Nora had rescued Clara from the side of the road on a rainy night ten years ago. Clara had been the best roommate and confidant.

Nora had thought working would keep her mind off the passing of her rescue pup, but that hadn't been the case. She'd spent the day sobbing with her office door closed because she didn't want to go home to an empty place.

Then Zane had stayed over late as well, like the true workaholic he was.

Zane always treated her like a business associate,

even though he was her boss. The man was too strait-laced and structured with every relationship she'd ever noticed him in. Even if she'd wanted to make a move for him, he'd never given off any vibe that he found her attractive. Maybe he preferred someone taller, with fewer curves, or someone not as loud and outgoing. She wouldn't change who she was, no matter how much she desired a man. Her parents had raised her to be bold, daring, take-charge, and they'd be damn proud of the woman she'd become if they were alive today.

Nora chose not to focus on the negative and sadness in her life. That was no way to live. She'd dealt with many stumbling blocks, but the only way to move forward was to remain positive as much as possible.

After firing off a text to Zane, Nora figured she'd need to go get some hot tea or something else to calm her unrelenting queasiness. The thought of real food nearly sent her right back to the bathroom. Thankfully, the construction crew was outside today, but they would finish up soon and move to the interior.

Was it too early to have the office turned into a nursery?

Nora rubbed her forehead as she padded down the hallway toward the kitchen. She should probably make a doctor's appointment and discuss this life-changing event with Zane before she went choosing paint colors.

A pang of remorse hit her at the fact her own mother wouldn't be here for such a poignant moment in her life. There would be no motherly advice or the bond in helping to choose a name or decorate a nursery. But Nora knew her mother would love this moment and be so excited.

Her cell vibrated in the pocket of her robe and Nora pulled it out to see a reply from Zane.

You're never sick. What's really up?

She stared at the screen, thumb hovering over the keys. How could she reply to that? Not only did she have this secret bomb to drop into his life, she'd also never gotten over their one heated night together. How could she? She'd had dreams of Zane Westbrook for years. Just because his twin, Cruz, might be her very best friend and the brother she never had, and he might even be identical to Zane, never had Nora had brotherly feelings toward Zane. The man had been the star of her wildest dreams since she'd met him.

Cruz had been her absolute best friend and no way would she risk that friendship for a shot at his brother. Not to mention, she absolutely loved her job, so the risks were even higher because her personal and professional lives would be on the line.

Nora had never intended to cross that boundary with Zane. But her emotions had been a jumbled mess and the loss of Clara had crushed her. Still, Nora had insisted on working, but her workday had been a nightmare. By the end, she was an emotional mess.

She should be embarrassed by her actions, but she wasn't. After Zane had wiped her tears away, the only thing she'd felt that night was intense desire. Now that she knew what type of lover Zane was, she only wanted more.

Nora slid her cell back into the pocket of her robe and figured she'd answer Zane later. Right now, she was still trying to wrap her mind around all of the events and combat this nausea. The hammering on her new deck was insistent, but the end result would be worth the headache of living here during renovations.

As she searched her cabinet, she realized she'd forgotten to go to the store for the second week in a row and she had no tea. Now what? She needed to get her queasiness under control so she could do her job. There wasn't a day that went by that she wasn't slammed with work. Which was fine. She loved her job and she loved the mission of the magazine.

She also loved working with the unstoppable duo of Cruz and Zane. She'd thought working for them would get Zane out of her system. Like, maybe he would have been a terrible employer. But the moment she started there, he'd been everything and more. Caring, supportive, strong...sexy. Her desire for him only grew by the day.

Nora grabbed her mug and poured herself some orange juice. Better than nothing, but she didn't know if she had the stomach for the sugar. She padded barefoot toward her home office. Thankfully, this room was on the other side of the house so the construction wasn't nearly as loud, but there would be no escaping the chaos altogether.

As she settled into her plush pink chair behind her brass-and-glass desk, another wave of nausea swept over her. Nora closed her eyes and tried to breathe through it just as her doorbell chimed.

Whoever needed her could check back later. There was no way she could make it if she tried to move now, not with the way the room seemed to be spinning.

Nora pressed a hand to her stomach and leaned back in her chair. This would pass, she just had to wait it out. She hoped like hell this morning sickness didn't go on for weeks or months like in some pregnancies she'd heard of. If only she hadn't been out of tea, maybe that would have helped.

"Nora."

Her eyes flew open and she jolted upright. The sudden movement caused her stomach to roll even more, and she braced her hands on the edge of her desk to still herself. She focused on the figure across the room and a sudden burst of dread consumed her.

Filling her doorway, looking way too damn sexy, stood the father of her child.

Zane stared through Nora's office space and tried to remember why he thought stopping by unannounced was a good idea. He'd only come here in the past with Cruz when they'd helped her move in and get settled or when she'd had them for dinner a few times. He'd never been alone with her, but her absence at work had worried him. Cruz had always been the nurturing twin, but he wasn't available right now so Zane had decided to step up.

Damn it. He could have called. He *should* have called.

Nora said she was sick, which never happened, so he only needed to check up on her. Even though he hadn't been alone with her since their night together in his office, he couldn't just ignore her now.

Yet the sight of her feminine curves wrapped in a silky robe and her strawberry blond hair all in disarray only thrust him back to that night. He recalled exactly how amazing she'd looked after their passionate moment in his corner office. He hadn't been able to look at his desk the same way since.

"What are you doing here?" she asked. "And why did you let yourself in?"

Zane stepped into the room, but the pounding from outside jerked his attention toward the windows, where he tried to see out into her yard. He'd completely forgotten she mentioned having some remodeling done on her cottage. How could anyone get work done with that racket going on?

He couldn't imagine what she was getting done. Her place already seemed so over-the-top to him. She had chandeliers in every room, brightly colored walls, and pictures hung everywhere. So. Many. Pictures. The place seemed much too chaotic for him, but Nora had always been extra with everything...which is why she made the perfect social media manager for his magazine.

"I'm here because I'm worried," he informed her. "And, yes, I let myself in. You didn't respond to my message."

He stopped on the other side of her desk and glanced at the mug full of orange juice, then to her. Her typical pink skin tone seemed a bit pale, which caused another niggle of concern.

"I was on my way into the office anyway," he went on. "And from the looks of things, you really are sick."

He took a second to let his gaze travel over her from head to toe. The briefest of assessments confirmed that Nora looked exhausted and run-down, but he knew better than to voice his opinion out loud. Monday mornings had a reputation for being brutal, but for the first time since he met Nora, she didn't have that bubbly, dynamic personality he'd become accustomed to.

"What's up, and why are you in here working and not in bed?" he added.

Nora curled her delicate fingers around her mug and stared down at its contents. He waited for her to say something, but silence and a thick dose of tension filled the room. Zane fisted his hands at his sides, when he really wanted to circle this desk and lift her into his arms. The need to protect her slammed into him and the foreign concept confused him. The only person he'd ever been protective of was his twin.

Cruz. The heavy ball of dread and guilt Zane carried hadn't lessened any over the past month. He'd crossed the line by sleeping with not only his twin brother's best friend, but also a trusted employee. Any *normal* actions were long gone. He had no clue how the hell to act around her now. Since that night, he'd been a mess, not able to focus and wondering if they'd damaged their own relationship.

Granted, he'd kept her at arm's length for years. He'd had to for his own sanity and out of respect for Cruz. The man truly saw Nora as a sister and always sized up any guy she tried to date. Cruz never thought anyone was good enough for her, which meant Zane had never been able to explore his desire.

Nora let out a little moan and sat back in her seat with her eyes closed, her drink suddenly forgotten. Worry and doubts be damned. He'd merely stopped by to see if she needed anything, and clearly, she needed a keeper because she wasn't taking care of herself.

In an instant, Zane moved around her desk and lifted her into his arms. Her entire body went limp against his as he strode to the plush white sofa across the room. She didn't feel hot like she had a fever, but something had drained her energy and left her weary. She wasn't a drinker, so this definitely wasn't a hangover.

"Tell me what's wrong, Nora."

He was done asking questions and the commotion from outside grated on his nerves and he had no clue how she'd be able to rest with all of that going on. But it was the yawning stretch of silence inside the house that had him growing more and more concerned.

"Do you need to eat something?" he offered.

She shook her head and met his gaze. Those wide doe eyes had always hit him with a punch of lust to his gut. Now was no different...except he'd had her and asking for any type of encore performance was absolutely out of the question. In all their years of working together, he'd been smart in keeping her at an emotional and physical distance. All he could think of now was their intimacy and all the reasons why that had been a mistake.

Cruz had been out of the country for the past month and he had no clue about Zane's night with Nora...he needed to keep things that way. Cruz would be back in a few weeks and Zane didn't want any shift in the way he and Nora interacted.

"I can't eat," she told him. "Just the thought..."

She shook her head again as if she might be sick.

"Why don't you get back in bed," he suggested. "I'll bring your juice and I'll get these workers out of here for the day so you can have some peace and quiet."

"No."

She pressed a hand to his chest and Zane had to grit his teeth and will himself to think of anything else other than the way her curves fit so perfectly against him. He couldn't help her if his mind kept going back to that night, when she'd been so upset and he'd only tried to comfort her. But years of pent-up tension and desire had overwhelmed both of them.

Zane carefully placed her on the couch and stood over her, hands on his hips with worry and confusion consuming him.

"You can't work," he commanded. "You can barely hold your head up. I'll take you to the doctor."

"No."

She scrambled to her feet, clutching her robe when the material parted between her full breasts. When she started to sway, Zane jumped up and gripped her arms.

"You're going to the doctor," he demanded. "Let's get you dressed."

When he started to pick her up once again to get her to her bedroom to change clothes, she held up her hands.

"Wait, just calm down." She pulled in a shaky breath and continued to clutch her robe. "I don't need a doctor. I mean, I do, but not because I'm sick. I—I'm pregnant."

Zane stilled as the room seemed to close in on him.

He misunderstood. He *had* to have misunderstood. But the way she stared at him, with her chin tipped and tears gathering in her eyes, he knew he'd heard correctly and Nora wasn't messing around.

"You're the father, if that's what you were going to ask next," she added.

He honestly didn't know what he was going to ask next because he was still wrapping his mind around the first part.

Zane raked a hand over the back of his neck. "We were careful."

Nora let out a humorless laugh and went back to the sofa. She eased herself down and rested her head on the high arm.

"Not careful enough," she murmured, closing her eyes.

Damn it. Here he wanted answers and instead of helping, he'd opted to grill her when she clearly couldn't even hold her head up. What a jerk.

Fear gripped him at this life-altering news, and he couldn't even imagine how she felt. While he'd never wanted a family, and was quite content being in a committed relationship with his company, he'd heard enough from Nora to know that she did want a family someday... and likely not from her boss.

Zane lifted her into his arms once again, but this time, he headed out into the hallway. He'd been here enough to know the layout and knew which room was hers. Even with keeping a safe distance since they'd met, he did know quite a bit about Nora. If not from her own mouth, then from his brother, who typically spent all of his spare time with her.

Zane had known for a long time that Nora didn't have family of her own and his...well, he had Cruz and that's all that mattered right now. But what would Nora do for support? She only had her work family and her very close relationship with Cruz.

That meant Zane would have to step up and be that man in her life, but there was only so much he could do. She and the child deserved so much better than he could offer them. Oh, monetarily they'd be set for life, but if she wanted any type of emotional bond or connection, there was no way in hell he could be that man.

"You don't have to keep carrying me," she murmured against his shoulder. "I've got morning sickness, that's all."

He didn't like seeing her this way, and he sure as hell didn't like feeling helpless. There was nothing he could do as the control over this situation slipped from his grasp. He prided himself on staying on top of things, making sure his life ran in the neat and tidy order he'd created.

Obviously, no matter how well planned or detailed his world was, he'd let years of need override common sense. Now their night together, which should've always remained a secret and in the past, would be forever out in the open and part of their future.

"I can't go back to bed."

Her words pulled him from his thoughts as he moved through her open living area and down the other hallway leading to her main bedroom. He'd never stepped foot in her room before, but he imagined it was just as bright and feminine as the rest of her home. No doubt she had photos hung all over in there as well, including several selfies with her and her dog. The woman clearly loved pictures.

"You aren't going anywhere else," he informed her as he turned the corner. "And I'll be here in case you need anything."

"Zane—"

He spun around, sliding a finger over her lips. "Not up for debate."

Nora's eyes widened for a fraction of a second, holding him in place. At this point in the quick evolution of their relationship, he truly didn't know who had seduced whom. Maybe touching her now hadn't been his smartest move, but he wouldn't keep arguing this topic.

Without a word, Zane dropped his hand and continued back in the direction he'd been going.

The pounding from the construction crew grew even louder as he got to this part of her house and Zane gritted his teeth. Trying to get any peace here would be virtually impossible. And for someone who already felt bad, someone who was pregnant and needed even more relaxation than normal, this situation was not ideal.

He set Nora down on the edge of her bed and propped his hands on his hips. "There is no way you can rest or work or even think straight with all of that racket going on."

She offered a soft smile, one he'd seen so many times over the years. It was her smile that had pulled him in from the start. She had the sweetest little dimple to the right of her full lips, and he had a really difficult time not staring at that mouth and remembering all the places she'd touched him.

His body stirred and he cursed himself for being vulnerable enough for someone to matter. That right there was why he'd been stony his whole life, why he'd gotten the reputation for being hardened and tough. He couldn't afford to be any other way. He refused to be hurt, and he refused to turn into a heartless man like his father, who'd abandoned everything and everyone around him.

"I hadn't planned on being here while they were working," she retorted. "I would normally be in the office at this time. But my morning sickness won't last forever."

"How long does this last?" he asked, realizing he knew absolutely nothing about pregnancies or children.

Nora shrugged. "From everything I know with friends or books I've read, everyone is different. This could last days or weeks or even the entire pregnancy. And even though it's called morning sickness, it can happen anytime during the day."

Being sick for months sounded like a nightmare. Not to mention months in a home being renovated inside and out. Zane rubbed his palm along his bearded jawline, trying to figure out the best solution. Nora and the baby's health was the most important aspect right now, so their needs had to take priority.

"You'll move in with me."

Nora jerked and her shocked expression paralleled his internal nerves. He hadn't thought about what he wanted to say, the words simply came out. He'd never asked a woman to live with him, never wanted a family at all…not after the hell he grew up with. But this moment was unlike any other he'd ever experienced, which meant he had to think differently than ever before. He also had to care for what was his and not be a deadbeat like his own father.

"I'm not living with you," she countered with a snort. "We're having a baby, not playing house."

Nora's strength and drive had always been one of the things he admired about her most. But he didn't want to get into a verbal sparring match over this. He had to make her see that this was the best solution for the time being. If she moved in with him until he could figure out what the hell to do, then maybe he would have a better grasp on suitable next steps.

No matter what, Zane would be a hands-on dad. He would have his child in his home. Maybe he'd never wanted fatherhood, but here it was, and his child would never, ever lack for stability and protection.

But first, he had to get Nora on his side.

"You're sick," he started. "You've got construction crews surrounding your house, and soon they'll be inside. This is temporary until we can figure everything out."

"I can stay at a hotel."

Damn, she was stubborn. Any other time he'd find that quality sexy, but not when it was directed toward him.

"What would we tell Cruz anyway?" she added. "He's going to hate us."

Guilt gnawed at his gut, but there was no erasing history or escaping the future. While they'd been able to hide their intimacy for weeks, soon that wouldn't be possible.

"He won't hate us." Zane hoped. "But we need to worry about you right now, so get dressed and let's get you moved into my place."

When she only glared at him and didn't volley back an excuse, he took the moment as a win. He had no clue what the hell he'd won, though, because his twin would feel betrayed and Zane was about to have the family that he never wanted.

Two

The only good part about this day was that her nausea had ceased. Maybe if she hadn't felt like death earlier she would have been able to argue her point with Zane back at her place. As things were now, though, she found herself in a lavish spare room on the second story of his palatial estate. Her entire living space could fit into this bedroom, and that didn't even count the adjoining bath.

The drab place really needed some things on the walls. To start with, an updated paint color would go a long way.

"That's the last of it."

She turned as Zane stepped through the doorway carrying her final suitcase. She stared at her matching luggage and nearly laughed. She couldn't even recall what all she'd thrown in there. She'd been so annoyed at Zane for pushing, at herself for caving, and had just started tossing things inside. She did remember the books, though. Reading had always been her outlet in life, and now more than ever, she needed an escape from reality.

"Thanks. Go head on into work," she told him. "I'm fine."

He crossed his arms over his broad chest and leveled her gaze. The intensity of his stare always had a tingling effect on her. How could he hold so much power over her emotions? And that was before the pregnancy. Now? Well, now they were bound for life.

How ironic that the one man she wanted more than anything, the man who was off-limits, would now be an integral part of her life forever? This wasn't how she wanted him or how she wanted to start her own family. Her entire world had just shifted into something completely unrecognizable.

"What?" she asked when he continued to stare.

"You think I can just go into work now like we have nothing to discuss?"

She didn't want to discuss anything. She wanted to just pretend this was normal and not face her emotions, because if she did, she had a very real concern she'd break. And that could never be an option.

Zane emanated strength and power. The man prided himself on control, and she respected and admired him for it. He possessed qualities that made her strive for perfection in her own life. He had an intensity that she couldn't help but be drawn toward.

"Fine," she conceded. "Let's discuss where we can hang some pictures if I'm going to be staying in here. It's rather stark and boring."

Zane's unwavering glare had her shrugging. "What? I'm serious," she added.

"I'm not redecorating and there's nothing about our styles that is the same. Can we focus on the actual issue?"

"I'd rather just get to work," she replied. "I'm not feeling too chatty."

"We have to talk about this, Nora. Everything has changed and we can't pretend it didn't."

Maybe they couldn't, but for now, she needed to focus on the one constant in her life. "Our lives haven't stopped and neither should our work."

Nora crossed the room and grabbed the handle of one suitcase to wheel it away. Before she could turn, Zane's hand covered hers. The jolt she'd always felt before had intensified since their night together. She hadn't even thought it possible to have stronger feelings toward Zane, but her body clearly hadn't gotten that message.

She brought her attention to his and that penetrating stare had her heart skipping. This was absolutely not the time for her heart to become involved. She had enough of a mess on her hands.

Zane had always been the standoffish brother, the quiet, mysterious one. He and Cruz might look identical, but their personalities were on opposite ends of the spectrum.

"Stop avoiding me." He slid his hand up her arm, his fingers curled inside her elbow. "You've avoided me since that night and now you're forced to talk about it."

She pulled away because having his touch right now, or anytime, was a bad idea. She'd taken part in enough bad ideas lately. Now she had to keep her head on straight to figure out how to fix things.

"We don't need to talk about that night," she told him. "We need to move forward and figure out how we're going to deal with Cruz, because I cannot lose his friendship, too."

"Too?" Zane stepped around the luggage and towered over her. "You think you lost my friendship?"

Nora closed her eyes and tried to gather her thoughts. She couldn't concentrate with his piercing gaze on her and that familiar, woodsy cologne surrounding her. And when he got this close, in her personal space, he made her feel so small and delicate. She'd never been labeled as small by society's warped standards, but she'd also never been ashamed of who she was. And Zane had seemed to appreciate each curve. He'd cherished her in ways she'd never experienced with a lover. His hands, his mouth, his body—a night with Zane had far exceeded any fantasy she'd ever had. The way he...

No. She could not keep thinking of that night.

"You're the one who's been dodging me since then," he continued. "You haven't stepped foot into my office and you only want to communicate via text. So who do you think lost a friend?"

There was no mistaking the conviction in his tone. Clearly, she'd tried to push their intimacy to the back of her mind, and in the process, she'd pushed him away as well.

"Is that what we were?" she asked. "Friends? You always avoid me if Cruz isn't around, and when you are around, you're..."

"What? What am I, Nora?"

She closed her eyes. Having him this close, knowing they were alone once again, messed with her emotions and her common sense.

"Too much." Her whispered admission landed between them as she opened her eyes and met his once again. "I never should have slept with my boss."

Zane's thumb stroked the inside of her elbow. "Despite what you think, we were friends before we were in a working relationship. That night shouldn't have happened, but it did. Now we have to move on."

Move on? Did that include her moving into his house? Did that include him touching her like this? Did that include her fantasies of him getting hotter? Because, since he'd unleashed that passionate side all over her, she couldn't help but crave more. Zane's touch kept rolling through her mind, and working or having any type of rational thought had been rather difficult this past month.

"I'm not sure how we can move on when I'm carrying your child."

Zane's lips thinned as he released her. "We need to set some rules."

Of course he'd want to set rules. Zane was the master at rule following…except that one night when he wasn't. Zane had a plan for everything and always played by the book in both his personal and business worlds. That's one way he and Cruz differed. Cruz was more of a laid-back, carefree guy. Perhaps that's why he and Nora clicked so perfectly as best friends. She typically didn't get flustered at life and tried to enjoy the ride… but she wasn't so sure about this ride. The unknowns and worries of starting her family when she wasn't ready terrified her; not to mention the lack of her own mother in her life to learn from and seek advice.

And then there was the fear she had of telling Cruz the truth.

"That night can't happen again."

Zane's words pulled her from her thoughts. As much

as that night shouldn't happen, that still didn't stop her from desiring that very thing. She'd wanted his touch for years. She'd wanted to know how Zane was as a lover. Now that she knew, could she ignore how beautiful and memorable everything had been? For that one night, that one *moment*, her whole world had been absolutely perfect.

"I'll talk to Cruz when he gets back," Zane added. "This isn't something he should hear over the phone, and that will give me a bit to figure out what to say."

"What is there to say?" she countered. "We had sex, I'm pregnant, now we're living together. Even I can't wrap my mind around this pace we're going."

"We're not living together," he corrected, rubbing his hand down his stubbled jawline. "This is temporary, so you can avoid that construction and I can help when you're not feeling well."

"And how exactly is that going to work?" she asked. "You can't stay home all the time and neither can I."

Zane let out a bark of laughter. "I own the company. I assure you, we both can stay here and work if that's what is needed."

There was no way she could stay in this house with him twenty-four hours a day. Hell no. Being here at all set off all sorts of alarm bells, but he did have a point about all the construction and her being sick and needing to rest more. She just hated that he was right and this was her only option.

"I'm not shirking my career." Nora reached for her suitcase once again and wheeled it over to the bed. "I take my job seriously and I'll be going into the office. I just might have to come in late sometimes."

When she started to lift the luggage, Zane was across

the room in a flash, hoisting it up onto the bed. She turned and stared, hands on her hips.

"Are you going to keep hovering?" she asked.

"Yes."

"Then I'm moving back to my place."

A corner of Zane's mouth kicked up. "You'd rather live in that mess than let me help?"

She had to set her own rules and boundaries as he'd mentioned. Her sanity couldn't handle trying to deal with a pregnancy, sickness, and living with the only man she'd ever wanted.

"I'm only staying here because it is the smartest choice for now," she explained. "But I don't need you doing everything for me and I don't need you acting like my big brother."

Zane's dark eyes narrowed, his nostrils flared. Clearly, she'd struck a nerve. Good. He'd been striking her nerves for years.

"I assure you, I don't think of you as my sister," he growled, then took a step back. "I'll let you get settled in, but I'm working from home today. I'll be in the office if you need me."

He turned and left, then shut the door behind him. Nora let out a sigh she hadn't even realized she'd been holding. Nothing had been resolved in their little chat, but what could they say at this point?

She still wanted him. Pregnancy or not, her feelings hadn't changed. Clearly, he thought they'd made a mistake, which actually hurt. For years she'd kept her emotions in reserve, afraid of what would happen if she exposed her truth. Granted, sex could all just be physical and superficial, but not to her. Not with him. Yes, she'd been in a vulnerable position that night, but she'd also known what she was doing.

Nora unzipped her suitcase and wondered just how living with Zane would go, because she couldn't imagine how much self-control she'd have to have to sleep under the same roof as him and ignore that invisible tug of desire.

Zane stared at the layouts for the summer covers. Normally, he approved everything his design department sent his way, but right now, he hated each and every image. Nothing felt right and he had no damn clue how to fix things.

Like the woman in one of his guest rooms.

What now? They hadn't worked through anything other than the fact that she would stay here and she didn't want him hovering. Well, too damn bad. She was pregnant with his child, and despite what she wanted, he would be present in every single aspect of her life from here on out. If she'd gotten pregnant by someone else, he'd still worry about her being so sick, but this was *his* child.

The idea of her carrying another man's child sent a ball of rage bounding through him. He didn't want her to be with anyone else. He didn't care for that mental image of another man touching her sweet curves or driving her to the brink of passion.

But he couldn't have her, not again. There was too much at risk—their friendship, their working relationship, the solid connection between her and Cruz, and his own bond with his twin. So, here he was, at a stalemate with himself.

He couldn't even fathom how Cruz would react. Oh,

Zane had a pretty good idea, considering Cruz had always been territorial with Nora. He would feel as if they'd snuck around, as if they betrayed him, when that was the furthest thing from the truth. Cruz would be upset at first, but he would come around. Zane just hoped that once he did come around, there would be no animosity between any of them.

Thankfully, Cruz was still out of town on business, so that would give Zane time to think. None of this was ideal and he took full blame. He'd hidden his attraction to Nora for too damn long. He'd taken advantage of her when she'd been most vulnerable and now he had to be strong for her. No doubt she was scared, and he knew enough about her childhood and the loss to know her situation hadn't been ideal—something solid they had in common. She'd lost her parents as a teen and Zane had pretty much been raising himself then as well.

Oh, his father had tried reaching out over the past couple years, but his sins couldn't be erased quite so easily and Zane wasn't feeling too forgiving.

One problem at a time.

Zane refocused on the layouts before him on his screen. Business he could control, and that's what he needed right now. All of this outside of *Opulence* would have to be dealt with carefully, so he had to get his head on straight and get his footing back under him. He also had to figure out how to enter into a co-parenting agreement with Nora and pretend that he still didn't want the hell out of her.

Their evening had been too rushed, too frantic. He wanted to take his time with her and explore each and every curve of her body. He wanted to look into her eyes as she came undone, knowing full well he was pleasuring her.

His cell vibrated on his desk and he glanced down to see his brother's name. Zane stilled, not really in the mood to chat, but he had to act like everything was fine or Cruz would know something was up.

Sometimes this twin intuition could be a curse.

Zane swiped the screen and put the call on Speaker. "Hey, how's Costa Rica?"

"I left there yesterday," Cruz stated. "I'm in Puerto Rico for the next couple days, remember?"

Zane rubbed his forehead. "Yeah. It's been a morning. I just forgot."

"What's wrong?"

Of course Cruz would pick up on something in the first five seconds of their call. Zane expected no less.

He shifted in his seat and eased back. "Nothing I can't handle. So, did you find those new models for our fall shoot?"

Even though it was still early in the year, there were still so many things to get done for each installment. They had to line up the fall models and start working on the holiday soon as well.

"A couple with potential," Cruz confirmed. "I'll send you the specs. I actually came across another social media account that I'm thinking about returning to. I'll send you her information as well. Her name is Mila and she's currently in Miami."

Zane and Cruz might be the CEOs of *Opulence*, but they still were very hands-on in every process of the magazine. They'd started out strictly online, more out of boredom than anything. They'd been working on getting back into ranching, something their father had stolen from them, but they'd needed income in the process. They'd tapped into low-key social media accounts to find models, products, and journalists. One thing snowballed into another and their magazine had taken off. The fact they found their talent and related content from "no name" faces online was a huge hit and something that hadn't been done before.

Twelve years later, that's still how they did business. If someone from *Opulence* reached out, you'd better believe you were about to catapult to superstar status.

"Did you see the piece that Annie in marketing wants us to consider for the wedding season?" Cruz asked. "I know we will be cutting it close, but I don't see why we can't pull it off."

"I did. I'll get to that shortly."

"I actually think that would be good for Nora," Cruz added. "She's got an eye for special occasions, and weddings just seem like her, don't you think? And she's going to hate this, but she'd be the perfect model, too. And that's how we'll save time, because she's already in-house."

Something stirred in his gut, something he couldn't quite put a label on. Instantly, the image of Nora in a wedding dress hit him. She'd made no secret about the fact that she wanted a family someday. She had stars in her eyes and would make anyone a great wife.

Not him, but someone.

"Zane?"

His brother pulled Zane back. "Yes, she would be great. I'll make sure she gets the information and mention modeling, but you know she hates attention."

"She's stunning and vibrant," Cruz countered. "All she has to do is put on a dress and be herself."

Zane didn't want to think of her as a bride, so he circled back to business. "When can we expect you back in the office? Or are you just going to keep traveling and meeting beautiful people?"

Cruz laughed. "Hey, you had the opportunity to do this instead."

True. Originally Zane was going to be the one go meet with their prospects, but he'd traveled so much recently, he told Cruz to go ahead. Perhaps if Zane had gone, he wouldn't be in the predicament he was in now staring down the new role of fatherhood.

Would Cruz have crossed the line with Nora when she'd had such a tough day? Would he have taken that friendship to another level?

Another burst of jealousy hit him. No way in hell would he want Cruz with Nora. He shouldn't be so damn territorial, but he couldn't help how he felt. Cruz always said she was the sister they never had, but never had Zane considered her family. Not once. She was...well, Nora. She was part of their inner circle...and now they were truly bound for life.

Zane had every bit of confidence his brother never had any type of sexual feelings toward Nora. Zane never would have made a move if that were the case. But there would still be a hurdle to overcome and an uncomfortable talk to have.

Movement in his doorway caught Zane's eye. *Nora. Of course she would choose this moment to show up.* He jerked upright in his seat and held up a hand to prevent her from speaking. Nora froze and remained in place.

"Cruz, someone just stepped into my office. Make sure you send me all the specs on the new talent and I'll take a look at the other project, too."

"Sounds good."

Zane disconnected the call. "What's wrong?"

"Did you tell him?" she asked.

"No. I'm not going to yet."

Nora pursed her lips and crossed her arms around her midsection. "This doesn't feel right, lying to him like this. He'd never do that to me."

Zane came to his feet and rested his hands on his hips. "He likely wouldn't, but I'm asking you to just let me handle this when he gets back."

When she continued to hold his stare, Zane moved around his desk and figured he better distract her before she got too wrapped up in her thoughts. The best way to handle this was in person. Without a doubt.

"Did you need something?" he asked her. "You're looking better than this morning."

"I feel better." Nora pulled her hair up into some twisty knot on her head and used the rubber band from her wrist to secure it. "I was going to get something to eat, but felt really silly invading your kitchen."

Zane laughed. "Nora, you've been here before. This is no different."

Her head tipped, and in that instant, he flashed to the night in his office when he'd dropped to his knees to remove her heels. Now she stared down with that same tilt, the same heavy-lidded stare…which only meant one thing.

She still wanted him.

"Everything about this is different," she fired back. "I don't know what the protocol is."

The protocol would be for him to keep his distance and treat her like the friend and employee she'd been for years. There was no other option. Getting involved in a personal relationship would only lead to a complete disaster. That family unit was everything she wanted, but it wasn't the life he wanted. There could be no middle ground, and he would never purposely hurt her. Leading her on, making her think there was anything between them, would only be a jerk move.

Zane crossed the office. The closer he got to Nora, the wider her eyes got. Everything about their relationship had shifted. He'd tried so damn hard to keep her in that employee box, to respect her relationship with Cruz. In an instant, years of self-control and willpower had vanished.

He stood within inches of her now. Her mouth parted, her gaze dropped to his mouth. Zane gritted his teeth and clenched his fists at his sides. She still wanted him. Oh, she'd fight it because she didn't want to make things more complicated, but the obvious facts stared him in the face. He had to get a grasp on this situation before things got worse.

"There's no protocol."

He wanted desperately to reach for her, wanted to know if that skin still felt just as silky as he recalled. He wanted to lean in and inhale that sexy scent along her neck. If he rested his hands on that dip in her waist and tugged her close, would she respond as boldly as she had a few weeks ago?

Damn it. One of them had to remain in control. A baby had been thrown into the mix, and they had enough issues on their hands without getting swept up in hormones, lust, and memories.

"You have to stop looking at me like that."

Her attention snapped from his mouth up to his eyes. "Like what?"

Zane propped his hands on his hips and sighed. "You're not naive, Nora."

"No, I'm not," she agreed with a defiant tip of her chin. "But you can't tell me you don't think of that night."

Every touch, every kiss, every single pleasurable moment played over and over in his head like a damn movie. Getting Nora out of his mind would be nearly impossible, but he had to try. Their intimacy might have been unplanned, their night rushed and frantic, but she'd left an impression so deep in his soul...

"It doesn't matter," he countered, needing her to believe what he said. "What matters is getting our friendship back on track, focusing on this child, and talking to my brother. Nothing else can come into play unless we're talking business."

"You think you can live under the same roof as me and not want to see if that night was just a one-time thing or if there's more?"

Oh, she was trying him. Good thing he'd shored up an exorbitant amount of strength and resilience in his younger days because this woman was going to test every last ounce of both.

"I don't think I can. I know it."

Three

Nora truly wished Zane would have just gone into the office. She dodged him after she grabbed something to eat earlier. If she stayed in her room, maybe he would do his work and leave her to do hers. At least she had a large antique desk in the corner of her space, and with the balcony doors open, she also had some much needed fresh air. With a little stretch of the imagination, she could pretend she was on a vacation.

A vacation with a man she wanted to strip down but was totally off limits.

Earlier, she hadn't meant to mention anything about the other night, but every time she looked at him, that's all she saw. His passion, his energy…his hard, well-toned body. How could she ignore the persistent stirrings inside her?

Nora closed her laptop and figured she might as well

grab a book and head out onto her own balcony. Reading always relaxed her. She could escape her own problems and focus on someone else's for a while.

She'd at least thought to grab a few novels from her pile at home. Although she didn't pack enough bras and underwear, she still figured she had her priorities in order. Besides, she could do laundry here.

As she went to her bedside table to choose a book, her cell vibrated in the pocket of her cardigan. With her demanding schedule and workload, she always had her phone within reach.

The second she saw the screen, she cringed. There was no reason to be afraid to answer Cruz's call. He didn't know anything and he was her best friend. If she didn't answer, he'd know something was wrong.

She understood Zane's standpoint that they shouldn't say anything until Cruz was home, but, on the other hand, they were lying to the one man they loved more than anything. Cruz trusted them and she'd been more loyal to him than anyone in her entire life.

With a deep breath, Nora pasted a smile on her face because she knew he'd be able to read her mood in her tone.

"Hey, what's up?"

"I thought for sure I would have heard from you after Zane filled you in on the wedding spread," Cruz told her.

Nora hadn't heard of any such thing, although Zane's mind might not be too focused on work today. She didn't want to throw him under the bus, but she'd definitely discuss the shoot with him after she got off the phone.

"We've been a little busy," she replied, which was not a lie. "Aren't you doing your own thing? Why are you checking in on me anyway?" She dropped her voice to a teasing tone. "I knew you'd miss me being gone this long."

Cruz's laughter filtered through the line. "I actually miss the way you'd grab my favorite mocha on the way into the office, so I guess I miss you."

"You only use me for my coffee runs—I get it." Nora picked up a book and started toward the balcony. "So, how many lovely ladies do you have dinner plans with?"

"It's like you think I find someone each time I travel."

"Don't you?"

She stepped onto the balcony and glanced around at the adorable seating arrangement. A nice sectional surrounded a small fire pit, and off to the other side was a bistro table for two. She had no idea where Zane got these pieces, but Nora highly approved. Maybe she could get the name of the store or website and shop there for her own renovations...and the nursery.

"Nora?"

"What? Sorry," she replied. "I zoned out for a minute."

"Is everything okay?" he asked.

Nora settled into the corner of the sectional and curled her feet to the side. "Nothing I can't handle."

"That's exactly what Zane said to me earlier." Cruz sighed. "Are you two keeping something from me?"

Nora stilled, gripping her phone even tighter. "Why would we do that?"

"I don't know, but if something is going on at the office that I need to know about, just say it."

The office? Nope. Everything was perfectly fine there. The rest of their world? Not so much.

"The office is fine," she assured him, thankful she

could at least tell the truth about something. "Just enjoy your trip and find our next superstars."

"Will do, but ping me and let me know what you think about the wedding idea. I can't believe he got you to agree to model."

Model? She hadn't agreed to anything and had no clue what Cruz even referred to. Were they out of their minds? She wasn't a model, far from it.

Before Nora could ask what the hell he meant by that, Cruz had disconnected the call.

Why didn't Zane come to her and explain this idea? Did he want to try to control her work now? He'd already admitted he would hover, but now he was going too far in volunteering her to model and then not even cluing her in on the big project. She absolutely would not stand for any of this.

If Zane wanted to lay some ground rules, they could start with him not acting like a Neanderthal.

Nora modeling? The whole idea was both laughable and terrifying.

She set her cell and her book to the side and walked back through her room and into the hallway. She had no clue where he'd be, and his house was ridiculously large. Both Cruz and Zane had homes that rivaled a small hotel, yet both men lived alone. She never could make sense of that logic.

Nora went down the hallway and glanced into the rooms. She had no idea which one was his, but she didn't see him anywhere. She wrapped her cardigan tighter around her waist, wondering why he liked his house so cold. Who else was he expecting? Penguins? She should have packed her fuzzy socks and slippers.

When she reached the first floor, she checked his

office only to find it empty as well. Then she stopped. The faintest noise had her moving toward the back of the house. He had to be in the home gym. The clanging of weights seemed to echo as she got closer, and the moment she stepped into the double doorway, she froze at the most glorious sight. How could she not stare at such beauty?

Zane wore nothing but a pair of tennis shoes, gym shorts, and a healthy sheen of sweat. The man had muscles everywhere. Who knew calves could be sexy?

Desire spiraled through her, but before she could make a quick exit with this image seared in her mind, his eyes came up to meet hers in the wall of mirrors.

Busted.

Zane kept his attention on Nora in the doorway. He didn't turn around, didn't need to. Her eyes were huge, her mouth agape, and she looked like she was trying to decide between tackling him or running away.

He always used weights and fitness as an outlet for frustration. If anything warranted an escape, this day had to rank at the top of the list.

"I didn't mean to interrupt," she told him.

Yet, she didn't make any move to leave. Zane set the weights back on the metal frame and turned to face her. He propped his hands on his hips and wondered what had prompted her to seek him out.

Though he wasn't sorry. The way her eyes raked over him only turned him on even more. The dead last thing they needed was heightened sexual awareness. Yet here they were.

"Something wrong?" he asked.

"Yes. Two things, actually."

Wonderful. At this point, what did another issue or two matter? Hopefully, this could be narrowed down to work and he'd have an easy solution.

"Let's have it," he told her.

"Why are you purposely keeping work from me?"

Confused, Zane reached for his bottle of water on the bench. He twisted the cap and took a long drink, trying to process her accusation.

"I'm not keeping anything from you," he replied, screwing the cap back on.

Nora crossed her arms and shifted her stance. Clearly something or someone had set her off, but her anger needed to be redirected. All he'd been doing was trying to figure out how he could be a father, when the notion had never been on his list of goals. Mainly, he'd been having a staff meeting with himself about not getting involved with employees…which had never been a problem until now. He'd let his desire override common sense, but never again.

He'd done so well keeping Nora in that friend/employee zone for so long. He had to circle back and make sure she stayed right where she belonged.

"Then why didn't you tell me Cruz had an idea for me to start planning and working on? And that you wanted me to model for some wedding project?"

Her accusation pulled him from his own thoughts. Just because his personal life imploded, didn't mean his business could.

"Cruz had the idea of you modeling," he countered. "I talked to Cruz this morning, as you know. Then we got distracted and I had other calls and emails. I'm not keeping anything from you."

Though he wouldn't hesitate to pull back if he thought

she was stressing herself or not taking enough breaks. While he knew absolutely nothing about pregnancies, he knew that Nora looked like hell this morning. He had to take care of her even before he took care of his business, which would be quite different from how he ran his day-to-day life. He'd made a commitment long ago to his company, vowing to never have a family after the mess he grew up with.

"I'm not model material."

"Why not?" he asked. "You're striking and curvy, and that's the look we want with this wedding piece."

Did he need to point out the obvious? Nora had a beauty unlike any he'd ever seen. He couldn't imagine a man alive not finding her desirable.

"I never want in front of the camera unless it's for a regular picture." She slid her hands into the pockets of her oversize cardigan. "We have too many beauties available, and those we haven't used yet, for you all to be looking my way. I'm the social media girl, which means I'm behind the scenes."

"Maybe we want you *in* the scene this time," he offered. "There's a time crunch for this project and you're here. I can have everyone come here for the shoot—we'll make it in the afternoon, when you are feeling well."

Nora sighed and stepped into the gym. "It's not the modeling nonsense that had me irritated. Cruz is going to know something is up if I act like I don't know what's going on with my own job. So when he threw that idea at me, I had no idea what he was talking about. I hate lying to him."

She dropped her arms at her sides and let out another frustrated breath. She glanced around the workout room before moving around. Zane recognized her nervous energy and he kept his eyes on her as she seemed to be contemplating her next move. Tension continued to curl inside him and he absolutely loathed that feeling. In all the years he'd known Nora, the only tension he'd had was that of want and need, desire and passion. Now that they'd crossed the proverbial line from their stable working relationship, he didn't know if they'd ever get their footing back under them.

"We should call and tell him what happened." Nora rested her arm on the treadmill and stared across the room. "The longer we put this off, the angrier he will be."

Zane nodded in agreement. There was no doubt Cruz would be upset, but that's why the news couldn't be delivered over the phone.

"He'll be angry no matter what, but let me deal with that," Zane told her. "I know him better than anyone."

"We should both tell him," she countered. "We're a team now, Zane. Whether you like that term or not."

Oh, he didn't. The only team he wanted to be on was one that made *Opulence* larger than the day before. It was the only way to stay alive in this industry, and that meant continually rebranding, reinventing, and recalculating everything you'd done in the past.

If he faced the fact that he and Nora were a team, then he'd have to enter into something deeper with her than he was ready for. He had no clue how this whole co-parenting thing worked, but surely, there was a website or a book or something that would tell him.

Nora nodded toward the weights. "Do you do this every day?"

"Yes."

Her eyes came back to his bare chest and Zane found all his thoughts running together. There were too many emotions, too many red flags waving all around.

"I told you not to look at me like that," he warned.

Nora laughed. "Then put a shirt on. You have everything on display—where else should I look?"

"Anywhere else."

She propped her hands on her hips and raised one perfectly arched brow. "You're saying if I stood here with no shirt, you'd look somewhere else? Unless, of course, you like your women on the smaller side."

Zane found himself crossing to her in two strides. He curled his fingers around her arms and leaned over her until her head tipped back and she had nothing else to focus on but him.

"I don't have a size preference, and I think I made it clear in my office that you are both sexy as hell and desirable. You make me forget every bit of common sense and the outside world, so don't ever doubt your power with this gorgeous body. You'd bring any man to his knees."

"Zane."

When she whispered his name like that, he had an even more difficult time trying to keep his head in the right space. She'd panted his name when he'd lifted her onto his desk and, again, when she'd come undone all around him. Nora was the most passionate lover he'd ever had and the only woman he couldn't get out of his system.

"I can't maintain my control when you look at me like that night." He softened his tone, trying to keep his composure. "You make me remember."

She reached up and slid her thumb along his bottom lip. "You do the same to me."

Everything about her made him want to ignore the alarm bells and ignore the fact they were sneaking behind his brother's back. He wanted to forget she was one of his top employees, but she carried their child now and his role had drastically shifted.

"This can't happen," he murmured.

"It already happened."

Just one taste. Maybe if he leaned in a bit more and grazed his lips across hers, he'd know if his recollection was off or if they were that good together.

Nora continued to hold his gaze, pulling him in even deeper. Zane inched closer and when her eyes dipped to his mouth, he couldn't take another second without her touch.

He covered her lips with his own, opening her to recapture the full experience. Nora swept her tongue against his as she wrapped her arms around his neck. Her body pressed fully against his, from shoulder to thigh. Her hips aligned perfectly with his…just like he recalled.

He gripped her hips and held her right where he wanted as he let weeks' worth of passion consume him and this moment. He'd wanted his mouth on her since that night. He'd dreamed of getting these sweet curves back beneath his touch.

Just another minute and he'd release her. He just needed more.

A chime echoed in the room and pulled Zane from his thoughts and the heated moment. He took a step back, trying to pull in a full breath. But Nora still stared at him, a hunger in her eyes that matched his own.

The ringing echoed once again and he turned to the weight bench where he'd set his phone. And the name on the screen killed the moment, because his father was the dead-last person he wanted to talk to right now.

Four

"That's not going to happen and Cruz is out of town anyway."

Nora stood in the hallway just outside the gym, trying to catch her breath from their heated exchange and not eavesdrop on his personal call. But she was human and couldn't help herself.

"No, Barrett."

Barrett. Zane and Cruz's father. Zane never called the man Dad and had made it clear he wanted no relationship with him. Cruz, on the other hand, had been coming around over the past year or so. Nora knew enough about their past to know the boys' mother had passed when they were around ten. They'd lived on a sprawling ranch and had every intention of taking over when they got older, but after their mom died, their father had given up on life. Nora didn't know all of the details, but the family lost the ranch, thus taking the boys' future and life away. Cruz had opened up to her a couple of times about his past, but she'd seen the pain when he spoke, so she never brought up the topic.

Clearly, Zane had never forgiven his father, but Zane had a harder shell to crack than Cruz. The guys were completely different, yet their identical appearance could be confusing for some. Many of the employees at *Opulence* still couldn't tell them apart, but Nora never had a problem—the way her body reacted to one of them had always been a dead giveaway.

Cruz always seemed like a big brother and best friend all rolled into one. They'd formed a connection instantly stronger than most siblings had.

Then there was Zane. Not only were Nora's feelings for him far from sisterly, she didn't think of him as a best friend, either. If she did, she would feel comfortable telling him all of her secrets and sharing details about her personal life. If Cruz hadn't tied them together, she doubted that he would have ever glanced her way or given her the time of day. With the way he always seemed to keep her in that employee, low-key friend box, she was just as surprised as anyone to be carrying his child.

"You lost that right years ago."

Zane's low voice pulled her back to the moment. She shouldn't still be standing here listening to a conversation that had nothing to do with her. Zane always valued his privacy, something she could appreciate.

A string of curses echoed out from the gym and Nora battled whether she should check on him or leave him be. She didn't know how this was supposed to work with her living here. Were they just to pretend everything was normal? Were they supposed to act like that kiss never happened?

Nora closed her eyes and rested her head against the wall. If Zane's cell hadn't interrupted them, she wondered where they'd be now. Would he have stopped or would he have continued to pleasure her like he had the night at his office? Did he actually find her desirable or did he simply find her convenient?

There were too many questions, too many unknowns. And where did her sudden insecurities come from? She'd never worried what a man thought of her before. Never cared if he found her sexy or perfect enough. She wasn't ashamed of who she was or how she looked. There weren't many people who could say they loved their bodies and were proud of their accomplishments, but Nora learned long ago that confidence carried so much weight for someone's self-esteem.

Yet Zane had managed to crack her steely surface and she wondered if he actually found her attractive or if she was just another—

"Nora."

Her eyes flew open and Zane stood mere inches away. She hadn't heard him step from the gym, but that gaze of his hadn't diminished. The intensity beneath those heavy lids struck her core and heated her all over again. How could just one stare be so potent? How could she see him on a completely different level than his twin when they looked exactly the same?

Because Cruz was a friend and Zane... Zane commanded her attention without saying a word.

"I didn't mean to listen to your conversation." She straightened from the wall and pulled in a breath. "I just needed a minute. I'll let you get back to your workout."

Just as she started to turn, Zane curled his fingers around her elbow and tugged her closer. Nora held her breath as she met those dark eyes.

"This can't keep happening," he all but growled.

"You mean when you kissed me?"

"There were two people in that room," he countered. "But if we're going to figure out this parenting situation, we can't keep getting distracted."

Nora tipped her chin up. "Is that what I am to you, Zane? A distraction?"

His lips thinned as he inched even closer. The need to reach for him, to see if they could pick up where they'd left off moments ago, was too strong. But she didn't know if he had no interest in her or if he'd waged an inner war with himself. Zane held his emotions and thoughts too close to his chest and she couldn't penetrate that tough exterior.

Maybe he didn't let anyone in. Perhaps he had his reasons for being alone and standoffish, but for one night, they'd both been vulnerable to each other. She'd never seen him console anyone or offer her a shoulder to cry on. She'd never had a one-night stand before, let alone with her boss and friend. She wasn't quite sure of the protocol here, but moving in with the man seemed like another wrong move. Yet here she stood, with a plethora of emotions and nowhere to put them.

"You distract the hell out of me," he admitted through gritted teeth. "Working together, now a baby, and you living here is…"

He shook his head and muttered a curse.

"You told me to come here," she fired back. "I can go back to my place or get a hotel during the renovations."

His eyes snapped back to her. "No."

That one-word command sent conflicting feelings spinning through her.

"You can't have it both ways, Zane. I realize people don't deny you anything, but you can't kiss me like that and then get upset about the fact I'm here. This was all your idea."

The way he stood there just staring really ticked her off. How dare he get upset over a kiss they clearly both wanted.

"I'm only here until my renovations are done," she went on. "I'm not here for games, and despite how much I still want you, I won't put myself in that position again."

She jerked her arm from his grasp, hating that she'd just admitted her need. She couldn't undo her words, though, so now she'd just have to deal with it.

"Get back to your workout, Zane."

She moved down the hall and turned the corner, finally pulling in a deep breath once she'd gotten out of his line of sight. He wouldn't follow her; he had too much pride for that – just like she had too much pride to stand around and argue feelings and who kissed whom. All she knew was she couldn't trust her emotions right now. Between the upheaval that used to be her calm life and the unexpected pregnancy, she needed to decompress and take a moment to herself.

Nora headed up to her room and closed the door. A nice bubble bath with one of her books would put her in a better mood. But what would she do about the fact that her lips still tingled and her body still ached? She had no clue what the remedy was, but if she didn't keep her distance, she had a feeling the next kiss would lead to something more.

There weren't enough curse words to fit his mood. Between having his father interrupt the hottest kiss with the woman of his every waking fantasy and then having her throw that kiss back in his face, Zane had no idea where to put his thoughts.

Even when he'd gone back into the gym to finish his lifting, he'd had a difficult time keeping his focus. He'd gone to his office to catch up on emails, but found himself staring at the same subject line for ten minutes.

Nothing had exorcised that woman from his mind and he had nobody to blame but himself.

He hadn't heard or seen Nora since she made her dramatic exit. Part of him wanted to applaud her for being so assertive, but the other part hated how she could stir so many sensations within him. In the years he'd known her, he'd only seen her professional and fun sides. She'd always had a smile on her face, always seemed so full of life and eager to shine her light onto others. She made an excellent employee, and their outside friendship had grown over the years.

Perhaps that's what had gutted him when he'd seen her so upset at the office after losing her dog. Her actions that night had been so out of character and had caught him off guard. He'd let that pent-up passion and years of desire override his common sense. Now Nora and their child were stuck with a man who could offer nothing but a financial commitment.

Zane made his way to the second floor and eyed her door at the end of the hall. Was she in there working? Fuming? Plotting new ways to drive him out of his mind with those sexy curves?

He ran a hand over the back of his neck in a vain attempt to release some tension. He'd have to get into the office to get any work done. Staying here all day would only drive him mad. He'd hang around each morning to make sure she was okay, but once she felt fine, he'd have to remove himself. The only way to get over this roller coaster of hormones would be to get back to the relationship they had before she ever walked into his office that night. The sooner they could regroup and shift their focus from attraction back to business and friendship, the better.

Nora's door opened and she stepped out as he still remained in the hall like some creeper. She jumped when her eyes met his.

"I was just going to go grab something to eat," she told him, closing her door behind her. "I assume you don't care if I make myself at home in your kitchen."

Someone should, because he didn't know how to cook and if it weren't for his chef, who came in once a week, that room would never be used.

"Everything here is yours," he stated. "I don't want to make any of this uncomfortable for you."

She took a step, then another, toward him. Zane didn't move, didn't know what he should be bracing himself for here. Was she still upset over the kiss? Or was she still turned on? Because there was no way in hell she hadn't been affected.

"I didn't mean to snap at you earlier."

She reached out, placing her hand on his arm in a gesture she'd done countless times before, but her touch meant too much now. He wanted more…and that was impossible.

"We both got caught up in the moment again," she went on. "And then your dad called, which clearly didn't help your mood."

Maybe he shouldn't be angry that Barrett had called. The man had very likely thwarted another bad decision.

He'd called to ask if Zane and Cruz would be open to a
dinner at his house, but Barrett Westbrook asked for too
much. After so many years of neglect and selfish actions
by his father, Zane couldn't forgive and forget quite as
easily as his brother.

"Do you want to talk about it?"

That hand on his arm coupled with her sincere question stirred something deep inside him. He wanted nothing to do with deeper emotions; they scared the hell out
of him. Not something he'd ever admit, but he had to at
least be honest with himself. He'd had to shut down that
emotional tunnel from his head to his heart long ago.
Nothing and no one could reopen that channel.

"No."

Nora flinched and dropped her hand. "Despite what's
going on between us, we're still friends. At least, I hope
we are."

Friends. Right. Only he never kissed his friends the
way he kissed Nora, and he sure as hell never slept with
his friends. Was there a label for that narrow swatch between friends and lovers? Because that's where they'd
landed and he wasn't sure which way they would ulti-
mately fall.

"No matter what we are, I won't talk about Barrett."

Her eyes searched his for a moment before she offered
a curt nod and stepped back. That instant wall of divi-
sion slid between them and he knew he'd hurt her feelings. Still, he couldn't go there. Opening up old wounds
and pouring his heart out had never been his style, and
attempting to let Nora into that part of his world would
only pull them closer together...which would give her
the wrong impression. He wasn't ready to share his life
with anyone—he never would be. He didn't need some-

one to talk to when he bottled up memories he never wanted to face.

"Fair enough," she replied. "I'll be in the kitchen. Why don't you send me all the information on that wedding project and I'll make sure the photographer, dresses, and other variables are lined up. I'll even *consider* the modeling gig."

Straight back into work mode. He should love that she went there, but instead, he had an uneasy feeling in the pit in his stomach.

Zane started to reach for her. "Nora—"

She turned to head toward the steps. "Email me."

Frozen in place, Zane watched until she descended the steps and was out of his line of sight. He'd wanted to get back to business between them, right? Isn't that what she'd focused on? What the hell did he have to be angry about when she'd merely done what he'd told her to do?

Zane had never had more conflicted feelings in his entire life. He'd always known what he wanted and had a clear path on how to achieve his goals. But now, with Nora expecting his child and living under the same roof, all he could think about was having her in his bed.

Five

Nora had to admit, working on the heated patio in her house slippers did have some perks. She had dressed for the office from the waist up, with her favorite scoop-neck green sweater and gold hoops. Thankfully, she'd only felt a little nauseous today, so she'd put on makeup, including a bold pink lip. After getting a tall glass of water, she brought her laptop out to the covered patio, where she could overlook the large in-ground pool, which was surrounded by lush plants. Spring would be here soon, but she figured Zane had his pool heated. The attached circular hot tub seemed rather inviting, but she'd read somewhere that hot tubs weren't good for pregnant women. She'd stick with her bubble bath, and besides, this wasn't her house. She couldn't just cozy up anywhere, despite Zane telling her everything was at her disposal.

She had managed to dodge him since last night, when he'd been so damn passive-aggressive. He either wanted her or he didn't. Apparently, he'd waged a war within his own mind, but his mixed signals were driving her crazy.

Keeping her distance would be her best bet. Each time she got near him, her heart kicked up and all she could do was let those memories roll through her mind. That night at the office had been one of the most memorable of her entire life. She couldn't help but want more—any woman would want another chance with the best lover she'd ever had.

The pregnancy complicated things. Living in his house complicated things. Keeping this life-changing secret from Cruz more than complicated things.

Too many variables went into play and her hormones weren't on the list of priorities right now.

Nora scrolled through her email until she found the one from Zane regarding the wedding idea. This could be a wonderful project for them, but she still had no idea why on earth Cruz thought she should be the model. That just didn't make sense. They had far too many other prospects in their queue or even in-house models who would fit this lineup beautifully.

As she read through Cruz's idea, she started making notes of her own. The grounds here at Zane's mountain home would be perfect. Something on the hill with a sunset in the distance would be absolutely breathtaking. He had horses dotting the horizon, various barns around the grounds, and beautiful fields that all looked like something from a movie set. The more notes she took, the more she envisioned herself in the role of model.

She'd hold out the full white skirt of the wedding gown. Her sheer veil would blow in the wind as she clutched a delicate bouquet and stared off into the distance. Her groom would step into the next frame and reach for her hand. Then Zane would—

No. Not Zane. He wasn't the groom of this faux wedding or any other type of wedding where she was concerned. They would have to find someone else for this spread. Her mind wasn't in the right place and she didn't want to have to play a pretend bride. It would hit too close to home that she might never be a bride—specifically not Zane's.

But she wouldn't go down that rabbit hole. Not now—there was too much work to do. Nora fired off several emails to get their art department involved. There were many layers to doing a photo shoot and they were already behind if the guys wanted to crank this out within the next few months. But her job had never been to question their decisions. The tasks they handed her weren't impossible, though some felt like it at times. Once, they'd needed a parachute image and she'd had to find a brave photographer willing to jump out of the plane as well. Nora hated heights, so just the thought of trying to get the perfect shot at the perfect angle thousands of feet in the air had made her knees weak.

After all the emails were sent and deadlines explained, Nora glanced at the clock and figured she had a few minutes before she had to hop on a call. That would give her enough time for a bathroom break and to grab some fruit. Zane had left for the office earlier, so she didn't have to worry about tiptoeing around him.

Just as she started to get up, her cell chimed. She glanced at the screen and contemplated ignoring the message. But she still had a job to do and she had to keep thinking of Zane as her boss and friend because, at the end of the day, he still held those titles.

She swiped the screen to read the message.

I've arranged a doctor to come to the house this afternoon for a checkup. Better to keep this under wraps for now.

She read the message again and the fury within her bubbled to the surface. Who the hell did he think he was just arranging for someone to come here? She had her own doctor and would make her own appointments. And even though they weren't telling people yet, his text sounded like they had some dirty little secret. Nora might not have been ready for a baby, but she wasn't ashamed. Scared, but not ashamed.

Firing back a quick reply, she wanted Zane to understand he wasn't in charge of her life and wouldn't be calling all the shots.

I have an appointment already with my own doctor and I won't be here this afternoon.

If she didn't take a stand now, Zane would try to run her life like his business and make no apologies.

Nora glanced at the time and didn't have much left before her online meeting started, so she'd just have to hope they didn't run too long. She actually had no plans this afternoon, but she would make herself scarce since she told Zane she wasn't available.

Maybe a pedicure or facial would do her good. Some self-care would surely perk her up and give her that boost she needed. She'd been so tired lately between the work and the pregnancy.

Nora sent a quick text to her favorite day spa and set her phone aside as she joined the meeting on her laptop. From the corner of her eye, her cell screen lit up and a quick glance showed Zane's name again. He could just wait. His message wouldn't be about work and she still had a job to do. A job he'd hired her for.

But when he came home this evening, they would certainly have a long talk and lay down some ground rules.

Zane had never missed more work than he had over these past few days. Skipping a couple of days to get Nora settled in, going in late to make sure she didn't need anything, and now leaving early because she'd ghosted his texts. He refused to allow anyone to simply ignore him, especially the mother of his child. He didn't know where this sudden burst of defiance came from, but he had every intention of getting her attention and laying out rules. That was something they both needed and he knew she wanted some rules set in place as well.

The more he thought about her not replying to his messages, though, the more frustrated he became. She claimed she wouldn't be at the house, but he didn't know if she just told him that or if she actually had plans. He knew she'd been on the meeting because he'd gotten a rundown of those in attendance and their discussion, but that had ended hours ago.

Zane pulled into one of the bays of his five-car garage and killed the engine. Nora's car sat in the circular drive, so he knew she was inside. He attempted to gather his thoughts and not just burst inside with his anger blazing. That wouldn't help anything, but she had to know he had certain expectations.

The damn woman drove him out of his mind with want and need, and now the fact that she ignored him had put him a cranky mood. The only person to ever irritate the hell out of him had been his father and, on occasion, Cruz. But now he could throw Nora into the mix.

He didn't want to delve too far into the idea that those closest in his life were the ones who could affect him the most. He didn't want to have trigger points that were easily accessible. Damn it. He wanted control back over his life—was that too much to ask?

Zane attempted to calm himself as he made his way into the house. He had no clue what he wanted to say to Nora, but he had to make it clear that he wouldn't be pushed aside simply because she didn't want to address their situation. She was living here for a reason and that reason was so that he could help her.

The silence of the spacious first floor surrounded him. He'd always come home to emptiness, but this seemed like a different void. He wasn't alone, yet there was still nothing.

Zane headed toward the second floor, and the moment he hit the landing, the clicking of keys echoed from her open bedroom door. He never liked interrupting work, but these were unique circumstances.

He stepped into her doorway and a punch of lust hit him hard at the sight of her sitting on her bed with her legs crossed. She had the laptop propped in front of her on a pillow and that mass of strawberry blond hair piled on top of her head. The cute little glasses perched on the end of her nose gave off that whole naughty librarian image, and he knew just how naughty Nora could be.

Zane pulled in a deep breath, clenched his fists at his sides, and moved into the room as he tried to shift his thoughts from fantasy to reality. Nora's head jerked his way and she eased back from her computer.

"You're home early," she stated, removing her glasses. "At least, I've always known you to stay at the office until late in the evening."

He stopped at the edge of her bed and slid his hands into his pockets to keep from reaching out. The anger from earlier hadn't dissipated, but the way she looked up and met his gaze had him considering moving this conversation to a less intimate room.

"Problem?" she asked.

"Yes. You ignored my messages earlier."

She quirked a brow and closed her laptop before focusing on him again. She shifted her body, flinging her legs over the edge of the bed. He couldn't help but imagine those legs wrapped around him again as he pleasured her. Nora had so much passion inside her and he loved being the one to pull out all of those desires.

Instead of getting lost in those fantasies once again, Zane scooted back as she came to her feet.

"You aren't going to demand I see some doctor I've never met." She poked a fingertip into his chest. "I've made my own appointment and I'll be going to the office. Nobody but the doctor will know why I'm there and nobody knows about us, so throwing your weight around is a really good way to get me out of here."

Zane gripped her finger, gently easing her hand aside, but keeping his hold on her. Those doe eyes flared as she tipped her head up to hold his gaze.

"I want to be part of every step of my child's life," he informed her. "That starts now. I can't exactly walk into a doctor's office in town with you, because then the secret would be out. I can't have anything getting back to Cruz before I can talk to him."

"All the more reason to tell him now," she insisted. "Let me talk to him. He can't stay mad at me."

Zane snorted. "You think I'm going to hide behind you? I'll take care of talking with Cruz on my own time."

She continued to stare back and the silence, coupled with tension, seemed to envelop them, drawing them even closer. Her hand felt so tiny, so delicate in his. And those eyes never wavered, as if she dared him to challenge her again.

Damn, she was something.

"You're making a mistake not telling him now."

Maybe so, but he still knew his brother better than anyone and he had to make the best decision for himself. There had to be something in this situation he could retain control over.

"Will we ever agree on anything?"

Her whispered question shifted his thoughts back to her…and to the hand he still held on to.

Unable to stop himself, he reached to cup the side of her face. She had the silkiest skin with pink undertones, making her blush easily.

"We've agreed on things before," he reminded her. "We're not always at odds."

She tipped her head toward his touch, and the moment her lids fluttered closed, Zane had the urge to close the gap and capture those full lips once again. Nothing about that was a good idea, but that didn't stop his persistent ache.

"Didn't we agree we wouldn't do this again?" she murmured, looking back up at him.

"I'm not doing anything," he countered.

"You can't touch me and expect nothing to happen between us." She covered his hand with her own. "We haven't worked out any details with the baby or work or even Cruz. Getting more entangled would only add to our problems."

"Or we might forget about our problems for a while."

Why was he saying this? He didn't have the time or the mental power to try to keep up with a fling. And who the hell jumped into a fling with a friend, employee, and mother of his child? This pull of attraction consumed him. Just when he thought he'd regained control, something as simple as the look in her eyes or the way she tipped her head or parted her lips pulled him back in.

"Is that what you want?" she asked. "To forget the outside world? Because we tried that once and here we are."

Yeah, he'd tried to console her and assist her in any way he knew how to get her to forget her problems and give her emotional support for losing her dog. Seeing her cry and knowing her heart had broken had ignited inside him something he'd thought he'd buried long ago. For the first time in longer than he could remember, he'd wanted to comfort someone and take their pain away. But that first touch had opened a door they'd both tumbled through.

The one and only time he'd entered into a one-night stand with an employee...

But were they limited to one night? Because this sure as hell felt like something more.

"You seemed angry when you came in," she added.

"I was. I am."

Her lips quirked. "You always get turned on when you're angry?"

He always got turned on near her, but he couldn't keep exposing his thoughts or vulnerabilities. The last thing either of them needed was more confusion regarding the many levels of this relationship.

"Don't ignore me again," he growled.

She let out a soft laugh and took her hand from his to rest flatly on his chest.

"Then don't try to order me around like your assistant. I have no plans to exclude you, but the initial appointment is blood work and basic questions about my health. I can handle that part on my own."

Zane gritted his teeth. He had no idea what took place at these appointments. All he knew was that at some point there would be those little black-and-white photos of his child and he didn't want to miss when that took place. He didn't want Nora to feel abandoned or have her feel like she'd end up a single parent. Maybe he pushed too hard, too fast, but he didn't know any other way.

"Bring your doctor here," he told her.

"You make that sound so simple," she laughed. "You think you can just make anything happen?"

"Money can."

That's why he'd worked so damn hard to get where he was today. He'd gone too long without any financial stability or any way of holding power and control. His father had robbed them all of that foundation. The moment Zane and Cruz had had the spark of an idea for their future and financial freedom, they'd run with it.

"If you want to stay here for appointments, fine," she conceded. "But the doctor will be mine. So feel free to try to make that happen."

Oh, he'd make it happen. One way or another. He'd have to call the office himself instead of having his assistant do it, because every step of this had to be hush-hush. He wished Cruz would get home so he could tell him, but on the flip side, Zane also dreaded that conversation.

"Consider it done," he told her.

With that issue resolved, Zane should leave her bedroom. But they stood so close, with her palm still flattened against his chest and his hand still on her face. He didn't want to step away, let alone leave.

He thought she'd move, but her dark eyes remained locked on to his. Nora had a simple innocence about her that he couldn't help but soften to. But beneath that girl-next-door exterior was a fiery, passionate, strong woman he couldn't get enough of. He had to, though. Not only were they trying to figure out this whole baby thing, they were lying to Cruz.

"Are you staying?" she asked.

"Trying to force myself to leave."

She pursed her lips as her gaze dropped to his mouth. "You should go."

"I should."

Zane slid his hand from her cheek to her neck, then feathered his fingertips down the V of her sweater. She shivered beneath his touch as her lids closed and she dropped her head back. Her fingers curled into his dress shirt and his entire body stirred to life.

"This is a mistake," he murmured, still gliding his fingers along her creamy skin. "Why do you have to be the one I can't stay away from?"

Nora slid her other hand up around his neck as she met his stare and offered a wide smile. "You seem upset over the fact you want me."

"I am."

She quirked a brow. "Then leave."

If she thought he'd back down from a challenge, she didn't know him well at all.

Only, she did know him. For years, she'd been his brother's best friend, his friend, his *employee*. And one night had shifted her role from all of those things to that of his lover. He should walk away, but he knew he wasn't going anywhere.

Six

She'd been irritated just hours ago, but somehow Zane had managed to flip her switch from ticked off to turned on with a few words and a simple touch.

Wait, no. There had never been anything simple about Zane's touch. His stare, the tone of his voice, the way his broad shoulders filled out his designer suits…every single thing about the man sent tingles through her. So how was she supposed to ignore how she felt? Even if she'd stayed at her place, that wouldn't have diminished her want. She'd had an ache for Zane for years, and since the night in his office, her need had only grown to a level she hadn't thought possible.

"I have nothing to offer on an emotional level."

Zane's words penetrated her thoughts and pulled her back to the moment. She released his shirt and looped both arms around his neck. Nora stepped in closer, pleased when his eyes narrowed and his nostrils flared. That muscle in his jaw clenched.

"Do you practice brooding in the mirror?" she asked.

His hands flattened against her backside as he jerked her body flush with his. "I don't practice a damn thing. You drive me crazy."

"Wow, so many compliments."

Zane lifted her, giving her little choice but to pull her arms tighter around his neck. Now she glanced down and there was no mistaking that hunger in his eyes. She'd seen it that night, she'd seen it yesterday in his gym before they were interrupted. So what now?

"You're not going to stop again, are you?" she asked.

"Do you want me to stop?"

Nora closed her eyes and tried to think of what they should do versus what she actually wanted. Clearly, common sense didn't exist when Zane was near. They shouldn't sleep together again, but at this point, what did it matter? They both wanted each other; not having sex wouldn't change that fact.

In lieu of an answer, she gripped his face with both hands and covered his mouth. She'd waited too long since that last kiss and had a hell of a time concentrating on work today.

Finally, though. Finally, she didn't have to hold back. Didn't have to pretend that she didn't want him with a fierce desire unlike any other.

Zane squeezed her backside and turned to sit on the edge of her bed. Nora instantly straddled his lap just as her cell chimed from the nightstand.

"Ignore it," he demanded.

Oh, she had no intention of letting anything disrupt them again. Whoever tried calling her could wait.

Nora reached for the hem of her sweater, only to have Zane's hands cover hers.

"I'll do it."

His fingertips grazed her bare skin as he slid the material up her torso and over her head. He flung the top across the room without a care as his eyes traveled over her. She'd never been tiny and had feminine curves, but the way he looked at her made her feel like the sexiest woman in the world. Clearly, he liked what he saw.

He went to the snap of her jeans and once the denim parted, he laid a hand on her stomach. Just that move had her heart clenching. She didn't know how they would work as parents, but she couldn't worry about that right now...nor could she change the situation.

But she could feel and she could want and she could take.

Nora took hold of his wrist and urged his hand farther down. She didn't want to think about anything else other than his touch and finding out if they were just as perfect intimately as she remembered.

"Nora—"

She covered his mouth with hers as she eased up onto her knees to allow him better access. Maybe she was using him—maybe they could use each other. They were in this uncharted territory together, and for a few moments, they could cling together and find the most basic manner of fulfillment.

Zane slipped one finger into her core and Nora tore from the kiss as a groan escaped her. She clung to his shoulders and tossed her head back, letting Zane work her body.

With his free hand, he reached around and expertly unfastened her bra. She shifted until the garment fell to the floor spontaneously, and a second later, his mouth covered her breast. Nora arched into his touch, completely consumed by everything he gave. Her body started climbing and she bit down on her lower lip to keep from crying out. How could she be so responsive so fast? He'd just started.

Which only proved how potent Zane was and how her body responded so perfectly to his touch.

"Let go," he murmured against her skin. "I want to watch."

That husky, sultry tone of his, coupled with all the ways he'd brought her body to life, had Nora releasing the cry of pleasure she'd been holding in. She didn't want to hold back, not with Zane. Even though they'd only had that one night before now, they shared a connection that went beyond the pregnancy. Their friendship had forged their bond and his compassion had sent her heart flipping out of that friendship zone.

No. She couldn't allow her heart to flip again. She didn't have time for that, and he'd made it clear he wanted nothing to do with feelings.

Nora came undone, and all thoughts vanished as wave after wave consumed her. Zane's hands seemed to be all over her, and she met his gaze as he focused on her release. Beneath those heavy lids, he stared back with arousal, desire, and something else she couldn't quite put her finger on.

The moment her body calmed, Nora eased off his lap and came to her feet. She kept her eyes locked on to his as she finished undressing. In the rushed, frantic state in his office, she hadn't gotten to see him fully, and she wanted that chance now.

Zane stood and trailed a fingertip over the curve of

her hip and to the dip in her waist. "You're so damn perfect."

Not really, but he made her feel that way and that's all that mattered. He made her feel on every single level imaginable, both physically and emotionally.

"I'm also the only one not wearing clothes," she countered with a smile.

He gripped her waist and spun her around, lifted her, then set her on the bed. Damn, if his actions weren't sexy. This entire situation had complication written all over it, but she wanted to hold on to this playful, passionate side of Zane for as long as she could. In a different world, under much different circumstances, maybe they could have something more.

Her mind couldn't even wrap around that concept because a life with Zane would never happen. Even if she wanted a family and to build a fairy tale including a happily-ever-after, he had made his stance perfectly clear.

"Wherever your mind went, come back to me."

Again, Zane's words and command pulled her from her thoughts. She shouldn't get wrapped up in the what-if game. She should focus on the here and now...and the delicious man who had started stripping down to nothing but excellent muscle tone and bedroom eyes.

Whatever he'd paid for that home gym had been well worth the money. She tried to take every bit of him in at once as he kicked the last of his clothing aside. But then he was on her, pressing a hand on either side of her hips and leaving her little choice but to lean back onto her elbows and stare up at him.

"I should have had enough of you," he muttered as he covered her body with his. "But I can't get you out of my every thought. You've ruined me, Nora."

His guttural tone told her he wasn't too happy with how she'd slammed into his life, but, hey, he'd done the same to her. So here they were, trying to figure all of this out together—their feelings and the baby.

But she'd "ruined him." How should she take those words? Had she ruined him for other women or ruined his perfect bachelor lifestyle? What exactly did that bold statement mean?

"Stay with me," he demanded. "Get out of your head and stay right here with me."

Nora slid her hands up his taut arms and over his shoulders as she parted her legs. Zane's body settled perfectly between her bent knees and her arousal started building at the anticipation once again. She should have had enough of him, too, but clearly she needed more. The ache she had deep inside her couldn't be described, so she wouldn't even try.

Zane kept his eyes locked on to hers as he joined their bodies. That instant sensation of everything being absolutely right washed over her. In this exact moment, caught somewhere between a dream and reality, Nora found herself wishing for this to be her life.

The weight of Zane's body on her as he began to move sent a burst of desire through her. Nora slid her legs up around his waist and clenched his body closer to hers. He smoothed her hair away from her face as he continued to hold her gaze. With one hand, he reached back and lifted her leg even higher as he continued to move.

The man knew exactly what he was doing, because those tingling sensations shot all through her. She held on to his broad shoulders as she met his thrusts with her own. Zane braced himself with a hand right next to her head, then leaned down to capture her lips. He consumed her from every direction and she absolutely loved every delicious second.

She bowed against him, taking him even deeper. Zane let out a throaty groan as he rested his forehead against hers. His hips moved faster and the build continued to rise within her. Zane continued to graze his lips over hers, but then traveled down her chin, the column of her neck, and back to her breast again.

Nora cried out as the emotions became too much to hold inside. Zane muttered something she couldn't make out, but it didn't matter. The climax slammed into her and she couldn't hold back another second. Curling her fingertips into his shoulders, Nora held on and let the euphoric sensation consume her.

Zane continued to pump his hips, then he stilled as his entire body tensed and shuddered against hers. Nora forced herself to focus on him, to watch him come undone as she came down off her own high. The man was positively breathtaking, his muscles clenched and eyes shut as he arched and continued to hold on to her thigh.

Nora didn't know how she'd ended up in bed with him again, but she wasn't complaining. Things were already complicated, so another round wouldn't change things.

No, actually this changed everything, because now she realized just how much she wanted him. Maybe she shouldn't, but she was human, with feelings that seemed beyond her control lately. Obviously, Zane wanted her just as much, but he'd made his intentions clear.

She had to be careful or her heart would get broken. She couldn't get attached. She had to protect herself, to focus on her career and her baby...and not ruin her relationship with Cruz.

Another wave of guilt threatened her, but she pushed

it aside. She was allowed to be happy, and an intimate relationship, however temporary, made her more than happy right now. Maybe by the time Cruz came back, she and Zane would have each other out of their systems. She doubted it, but maybe.

Zane's weight shifted off hers as he rolled to his back and eased her over to tuck into his side. The silence in the room threatened to steal the joy of the moment, but she couldn't—and wouldn't—feel ashamed for being an adult with basic needs and going after what she wanted.

"You should move your things to my room."

Nora cringed. Those were not at all the first words she thought he'd say. Actually, she never thought he'd say anything like that.

Nora sat up and stared down at him. "I moved into your house—I'm not living in your bedroom."

Zane shifted, his brows drawing closer together. "Why wouldn't you?"

She couldn't help the laugh that escaped. "Why *would* I? We're not in a relationship. Everything about us is a secret and I'm only here because my place is being renovated. We're not playing house, Zane."

His lips thinned and she really didn't want to have this conversation while naked. Nora slid off the bed and started gathering her clothes.

"If we're having sex, you might as well be in there," he added.

Nora clutched her sweater and whirled around. "You don't want commitment, yet you want me in your room like, what? Your wife?"

Zane sat up, and that passion that had been in his eyes moments ago had been replaced by anger. "I'll never marry, but that doesn't stop me from wanting you. We both just proved again how compatible we are."

"I won't stay in your room so I can just be easily accessible, Zane." This whole conversation irritated the hell out of her. "If you want me in your house, that's fine for now, but I'll stay right here in this room."

When he continued to stare at her, she gathered up the rest of her things and moved into her bathroom. She closed the door and flicked the lock into place. Did he seriously think that, because she had sex with him again, she would just jump at the opportunity he presented her? Like she'd be thankful he wanted more of her?

What a jerk. How could his words be so callous at times and so tempting at other times?

Nora finished getting dressed and decided to contact her contractor. Surely, there was a way to speed up those renovations. Like Zane said, money talked, and she needed to get back to her normal life before she found herself wrapped too tightly in this web of desire.

Seven

Screwing up things wasn't in him, but he'd done a hell of a job since discovering the pregnancy.

No, he'd started screwing up the moment he'd invited Nora into his office and thought he could console her without touching. Because that first touch led to an innocent kiss, which led to not-so-innocent stripping.

He knew better. He prided himself on making smart decisions and keeping a level head in all situations. He'd always said he would maintain control over his own life and not end up like Barrett. He'd never be a half-assed father and ignore his responsibilities or put his own selfish needs above the needs of others around him.

Which meant he had to concentrate here. He had to put Nora and their baby above all else, no matter how damn much he wanted her. Indulging in sex with her epitomized the selfish side of him, the gene Zane had inherited from Barrett that he tried so damn hard to correct.

Zane slammed a hand down onto the edge of the balcony. He'd tried to keep his distance from Nora, but at some point, they were going to have to talk. That's what he'd been trying to do earlier, but she'd turned something inside him. His entire world had been flipped since that one night. Before then, he'd done a good job of keeping his attraction under wraps. He'd dated, nothing serious, and ignored the details when she'd talk about her dates.

Had she been attracted to him before that night? She had to have been or she wouldn't have become such a willing participant.

Attraction was one thing, but anything more would cause even more problems. He'd meant it when he'd told her he had nothing else to offer but financial support... at least for her. He had no idea how the hell to be a father, but he had to at least try. He would never want to make a child feel lost or alone.

He didn't want Nora to feel that way, either. While he'd never planned to have a wife or children, he wouldn't abandon his duties or responsibilities. He just wished like hell he could do more, because she deserved that fairy-tale lifestyle. The vibrant light that had always shined from her had diminished since she'd moved here. She certainly had just as much fire and strength as ever, but he missed her smiles and laughter. Had he stolen those emotions from her?

No doubt, Cruz would pick up on that the moment he got back into town, which was why Zane needed to get to him first.

His cell vibrated in his pocket. Zane eased back from the rail and pulled out the phone, not really in the mood to talk to anybody, but being the CEO of a multibillion-dollar company didn't give him the luxury to ignore calls.

Nora's name popped up on the screen, and he didn't know whether to laugh or be irritated, considering she was across the hall.

He swiped the screen and answered. "Nora."

"I figured calling would be safer than coming to your room to discuss work," she told him.

Again, he didn't know whether to be amused or annoyed. She had a valid point, but on the other hand, he wouldn't mind her coming to his room. Though she'd made it perfectly clear that she had no intention of staying in his house, especially in his bed. He'd been a convenient moment for her, and something about that fact really pissed him off. He'd never wanted commitment before, still didn't, but he also didn't want to be so casual with the woman carrying his child.

"Are you listening?"

Nora's sharp tone pulled him from his wayward thoughts.

"I'm here, but we can meet in the hallway or even go to my office. There's no need to call."

"Oh, there's every need, and I'm already in my pajamas, so I'll stay in my room," she informed him.

What did she sleep in? Something slinky and sexy to hug those curves? Maybe she slept with nothing but the cool sheets gliding over her bare skin.

Zane's body stirred at the mental image and he forced himself to concentrate on her words. He was a professional, damn it. Nora wasn't the first woman he'd slept with, so why the hell couldn't he compartmentalize her? She belonged in the employee/friend box. But due to his lack of self-control and years of growing desire, she now had a new space to fill...mother of his child. Whether he liked it or not, they were bonded for life.

"And then the ostrich will be here for the photo session."

"What? Ostrich?"

Nora's low, throaty laugh spilled through the line. "I knew you weren't listening," she scolded. "There will be white ponies, but no ostriches, though that is a good idea."

There she went being extra again. He wouldn't put it past her to have some obscure bird on set.

"What's this shoot for again?"

"The wedding project you sent to me, remember? I've got everything lined up and I just received confirmation about the photographer and the dress designers. Everything is set for this coming weekend."

Zane rubbed his forehead and turned toward the open doors leading into his bedroom. "And you're still modeling for this?"

Silence answered his question.

"Nora, that's what Cruz requested, and he's spot-on. You'd be perfect."

"I'm not a model—I'm in charge of social media."

"And you do a damn good job," he retorted. "For this particular project, you fit exactly the image we want."

"And what image is that?"

Did her tone drop? Did those words come through with a completely different vibe than the rest of the conversation?

The very idea that she lay in her bed talking to him about business made his attraction grow even stronger... as if he needed that to happen.

"The image we want is a striking woman," he told her, focusing on work as he was supposed to do. "A woman looking forward to her forever and the promise that brings. A woman who embodies power and beauty who is sexy at the same time."

"I don't think Cruz said I was sexy. He's like a brother."

"There's not a man with air in his lungs wouldn't think you were sexy, Nora."

"Zane."

He stared at his open bedroom door through the hallway to her closed door. He only had to take a few short steps and he could be in there. She wouldn't deny him, not when she had the same crushing need.

"I'm stating facts. You're the perfect woman for this project, Nora." He pulled in a deep breath and continued staring at her door, willing her to come out. "You can look at the images first. If you absolutely hate them, we won't use them."

Why had he said that? They didn't have the time to do another shoot, they were already down to the wire as it was. Cruz's idea was brilliant, but had he thought of this even a month ago, they all wouldn't be so crunched for time.

But Zane wanted Nora to be comfortable. More than that, he wanted her to see what everyone else saw…her unabashed beauty and sex appeal.

"Fine."

He blinked, glancing away from her door as her answer came through.

"I'll do it, but I get final say on the shots that will be used."

Zane couldn't help but smile. He would make damn

sure she loved those photos so much that she'd have a difficult time choosing which ones she wanted to use.

"You'll be thanking us later," he promised.

"I doubt I'll be doing that, I—"

A loud crash echoed both through the phone and across the hall. Zane dropped his cell and darted to her room, heart pounding, as he threw open the door.

Nora sat on the floor with a broken teacup in pieces all around her. Her eyes met his as she placed a hand on her nightstand and started to rise.

"Sorry about that," she told him. "I owe you a cup."

"Don't move," he commanded. "You'll cut yourself."

Zane carefully stepped around the shards, though some still crunched beneath his shoe. He reached down and lifted her with one hand supporting her back and the other behind her knees.

"Did you get cut?" he asked, moving to the other side of the room to place her on the chaise near her own balcony doors.

"No, I'm just clumsy." She shoved a mass of strawberry blond curls away from her face and peered up. "I didn't mean to scare you. I'd just finished my tea and was trying to set it on the nightstand. Clearly, I missed."

Scare him? Try terrify. He didn't know if his heart rate would ever get back to normal.

He rubbed the back of his neck, attempting to get his breathing under control.

"Hey." Nora came to her feet and flattened a hand against his heart. "You're fine. I'm fine. The baby is fine. I just dropped a cup and tumbled off the bed trying to save it."

Her calming tone did wonders for his nerves and he had no idea how she could be so convincing. Zane stared into her wide eyes and a stirring sensation wound its way through his chest, way too damn close to his heart.

But then he noticed what she wore…or didn't.

A silky cami exposing a few inches of her abdomen and a pair of little matching shorts had his heart beating erratically for a whole other reason. He'd been across the hall wondering what she wore, and now that he knew, he almost wished he'd never seen her this way.

True, he'd seen her completely bare, and touched and tasted every inch of her, but having her before him in such a seductive, yet almost innocent, manner seemed so much more intimate than sex.

But his thoughts bounced between his attraction to Nora and the flashbacks to his childhood. Another woman, another time.

"You good now?" she asked, clearly oblivious to his thoughts.

No, he wasn't good. A ball of dread formed in the pit of his stomach. Now that he knew Nora was safe, the adrenaline rushed from his system. Zane closed his eyes and forced himself to take a deep breath, then another.

Damn it. Was he swaying?

"Sit down."

Nora tugged on his arm and he pulled his attention from the near panic attack to the chaise as she forced him down. Could this be any more humiliating? He'd stand up and clean the broken cup in just a minute, but he had to get his breathing and heart rate under control.

Of all the times to flash back to his childhood and have this crippling fear…

"Just breathe," she urged. "Slowly, because if you pass out, there's no way in hell I can lift you up."

Zane couldn't help but chuckle. "I'm not going to pass out."

"No, I imagine you're too stubborn for that."

Perhaps, but he'd already embarrassed himself by not being able to control his emotions or reactions over the past several minutes. Nora didn't need to see that the father of her child was actually vulnerable and had a legit fear of losing someone else in his life. This feeling of total helplessness had been the entire reason he'd banned any type of commitment in his life. His mother had passed, and his father had deserted them emotionally, which meant Cruz had been his only family for so long. Allowing anyone else in would only open up a gate he'd closed long ago.

"I'm fine." He blinked, focusing on her worried face. "Promise."

"Why don't you just stay there for a minute," she suggested. "You're finally starting to get some color back to your face. Care to tell me why a broken cup got you so upset?"

Because he still had some pride, Zane stood and placed his hands on her shoulders. Her doe eyes met his as her lips parted in a swift inhale. No way in hell would he share the inner turmoil that had haunted him for years. That darkness inside him had no space here, or anywhere in his world, for that matter.

"I just worried you'd cut yourself," he explained. "That's all. I didn't mean to freak you out."

"I think I'm the one who freaked you out," she countered with a tip of her head. "And I've known you too long. You can't lie to me, but I'll respect your privacy. You should know that I'm a great listener—just ask Cruz."

He didn't want to ask his twin about Nora. For reasons he couldn't explain and didn't want to delve into, Zane wanted to keep his own connection with Nora. He wanted to have his own bond and moments that weren't shared with anyone else. Obviously, they were going to share a child, but he wanted something beyond that. Not a commitment, but moments and memories.

Damn it. Maybe her fall had gotten to his head. His thoughts were all over the place and confusing the hell out of him.

"I'll keep that in mind," he assured her.

When the silence settled into the room once again, Zane realized he still held on to her shoulders. Letting go would be the smart move, and he'd always prided himself on being an intelligent man, but everything about her made him want to hold on.

"We need to get that mess cleaned up."

Her words penetrated the quiet and smacked him with a dose of reality. He couldn't just take her to bed anytime he wanted. That's not why she was here and Nora deserved to be treated better than some random romp.

"Stay here." He dropped his arms and stepped around her. "I'll get it. I still have shoes on."

He needed to concentrate on something other than all of that creamy, exposed skin and her silky pajama set. Why the hell had she packed that anyway? To drive him even more out of his mind?

Zane gathered up the large pieces and grabbed the broom from the utility closet on that floor. Once he was positive there was nothing left for her to cut herself on, he turned toward the chaise, where she sat perfectly posed with a wide grin spread across her face.

"What?"

"I've never seen you actually work."

Gripping the broom in one hand and the dustpan in the other, he held his arms out. "I work every single day, even on my birthday."

Nora tipped her head and snorted. "Not manual labor. I'm surprised you even knew where the broom was."

"I'm offended."

Nora laughed as she came to her feet. "I assume your cleaning lady has just kept you informed of where things are in this enormous place."

"I wouldn't call it enormous," he retorted. "But Charles, who is a man by the way, does communicate often with me. And, considering I built the house, I am fully aware of where things are located."

Nora shrugged and offered a slight nod, her hair falling around her shoulders. "Okay, then. My apologies. I just never expected someone like you to take on any type of domestic role."

Zane moved across the room, propped the broom against the wall and dropped the dustpan, before turning his attention back to Nora. She remained unfazed by the fact that she stood there wearing scraps of silk. Knowing her, she knew exactly what she was doing by making him suffer. His penance for persuading her to move in and trying to get her into his bed with absolutely no promise of commitment.

Yeah, he deserved to be punished for dragging her emotions all over the place. In his defense, though, his had spiraled out of control as well.

"I'm no stranger to hard work," he told her. "You know enough about my childhood and upbringing to know Cruz and I were on our own for a long time."

"You don't have to explain yourself," she told him. "I was teasing you."

Zane swallowed the lump of unwanted feelings. He hadn't faced more of his internal thoughts than he had in these past few days. Nora pulled out so much from him he hadn't even realized he'd buried. Never before had he wanted to justify himself to anyone, let alone a woman.

"It's important you know what type of man I am, considering we're going to raise a child together."

Nora slid her hand along the side of his face. "I know the man you are, Zane. Maybe you're still trying to figure him out, but I know. I wouldn't have slept with you otherwise."

Her audacious statement sent a shock to his core.

"That night wasn't planned," he stated.

"Maybe not that particular night," she agreed, dropping her hand to his chest. "But the attraction had been there for years. At least on my side, so the moment was inevitable."

Oh, hell. Why did she have to go and say that? He'd never been one to back down from a challenge or risky situation, but having such an intimate talk with his brother's best friend put him in a position he'd never been in before. He'd always admired Nora for her bold stance and the fact that she spoke her mind.

Never once did he think she'd been battling an attraction to him. All these years, he'd thought the desire to be one-sided.

She dropped her hand and took a step back, slicing the moment with her actions.

"Which is why staying here is so difficult for me," she went on. "My need for you is stronger than ever, but

I can't just act on that. I have to be responsible and think about Cruz, my career, and our baby. I can't be selfish."

Damn it. Hearing her be so logical made him feel like a complete jerk.

Zane took a step forward, but she held up a hand.

"Nothing else needs to be said. Good night."

He'd been dismissed. Nobody had ever dismissed him before, but Nora's unwavering stare and rapid pulse at the base of her throat were all indicators that her emotions were running just as high, if not higher, than his. He respected her…which was why he found himself leaving her room with more conflicting feelings and turmoil than ever before.

Eight

Nora kept dunking her tea bag in and out of the hot water, hoping to steep her drink a bit faster. She'd thought her nausea had ceased when she'd left for the office an hour ago, but the moment she passed by the break room and smelled someone's microwave breakfast, she nearly lost it right there in the hallway.

She'd made it to her office and closed the door, hoping to cut off that atrocious smell. Thankfully, she had a kitchenette in her corner space, so she could keep the rest of the world out until she regained her composure.

The aroma wafting up from the peppermint tea already had her nausea subsiding.

Her cell vibrated on her glass-top desk. She flashed a glance at the screen and spotted Cruz's name. She certainly didn't feel up for conversation—work or personal—but she still had a job to do and a secret to keep.

No matter how she might be feeling, she had to pretend like everything was perfectly normal.

Normal. She didn't even know what that word meant anymore and had lost touch with it somewhere between sleeping with her boss and moving in with him.

Her only defense was that she'd always wondered what being with Zane would be like and now that she knew, she didn't want to be without. None of that logic made sense, but her needs went beyond physical at this point. Zane did something to her, something that no man had ever done before. He gave her a confidence that she'd never known, which only made her crave him even more.

On a groan, she swiped her screen and propped the cell against her computer monitor.

"Was a video call necessary?" she asked, curling her hands around her mug.

"I haven't seen your face in over a month, so yes." Cruz adjusted his sunglasses and inched closer to the screen. "Are you sick? You look like hell."

"You have such a sweet way with words. It's a wonder you're still single."

Cruz laughed. "You know what I mean. Why are you at the office if you're sick? Go back home to bed."

"I can't stay in bed the entire pregnancy."

The second the words were out of her mouth, she cringed and set her mug back down. Nora closed her eyes and shook her head just as Cruz's jaw all but hit the floor.

"What did you just say?" he demanded.

Damn it. Between the heavy dose of sexual tension she'd been living with and the whirlwind of her emotions, she clearly wasn't thinking straight. She waved a hand, dismissing his question.

"Nothing," she stated. "Forget I said anything."

"Who is he?"

Her heart clenched. She couldn't get into this now via a video chat with Cruz thousands of miles away. Zane had been firm that he wanted to be the one to tell his brother and she wouldn't go against Zane's wishes. That level of respect had to go both ways.

"Let's not do this now," she suggested, forcing a smile. "We can talk plenty when you get home, but nobody knows and I'd like to keep it that way for now."

"Did you tell Zane?"

Considering he'd been there…

"He knows, but that's absolutely it. I mean, I couldn't just keep skipping the mornings at work without telling my boss why."

"Nora, he's more than your boss. He's your friend, too."

Her friend, her lover, her roommate.

"I can't believe he didn't say something to me," Cruz muttered. "Did you ask him not to tell?"

"He thought because you were busy working and this isn't an emergency, it could wait."

An overwhelming layer of shame lay like lead in the pit of her stomach. Never in her life had she lied to Cruz. Their friendship had a connection deeper than most siblings. She told him everything and the one time she actually needed to open up and seek advice, she had to keep her mouth shut.

"How are you feeling?" Cruz asked. "I'm a jerk for giving you hell earlier."

Nora shook her head. "You didn't know and I do look awful. I perk up around noon, so I've still got a while to go."

"Why aren't you working from home?" he asked.

Another lie. She didn't even live in her home right now because of the renovations and Zane's persuasion. She should've stood her ground and either stayed or rented a place for the duration of the construction.

"I've been coming in late." At least that part was truthful. "I actually just got here and made some tea to calm my stomach. So, what's up?"

Cruz laughed and shifted his sunglasses to rest on top of his head. He took a seat in what appeared to be a park or some type of outdoor area with a bench.

"I honestly don't even know now," he admitted. "You threw me a curve I wasn't expecting. I mean, a baby. This is… Damn it. You're going to be a great mother."

Tears pricked her eyes as that pit of dishonor grew. How could she be good at something when everything was based on a lie?

"Why won't you tell me who the father is?" he asked. "Is he a jerk? Is that why?"

"No, no," she assured her friend. "He's a nice guy—it's just that, well…things are complicated."

And that was the calmest term she could use to describe this chaotic mess she'd gotten herself into. Her eyes darted to her desktop. The last time they'd been in an office alone together, they'd been tearing at each other's clothes. Granted Zane's office had been the scene of the most heated night of her life, but still. The mental image of that first time together continued to roll over and over in her mind, but now she had another fiery encounter to add in.

Zane had gone from a one-night stand to her lover. Even though she'd held him off, she wasn't naive. Staying in his home surrounded by all of that sexual tension, in addition to their forged bond, was a recipe for another night of tumbling into bed together.

"If you'd let me in on your secret, I could help."

The concern lacing Cruz's voice touched her heart. He couldn't help her at this point, and if he knew the truth, well, she really didn't know how he would react and that's what terrified her the most. Not only did she not want to ruin their friendship, but she didn't want to come between two brothers.

None of their lives would ever be the same.

"I don't want you to worry about me." She picked up her tea and took a sip, welcoming the peppermint warmth. "All you need to do is find the perfect woman for our fall project."

"I'm actually supposed to be meeting her in a few minutes. I'm early, so I thought I'd give you a call. I did actually have a question for you, but I'll never remember now."

Nora laughed and picked up her cell as she spun in her white leather chair to face the wall of windows behind her desk. A slight wave of dizziness swept over her and she closed her eyes for a moment. Spinning in the chair was another thing she should add to the "do not do while pregnant" list.

"Can your child call me Uncle Cruz?" he asked.

Nora focused on his grin and couldn't help but get a flash of the future with Cruz and Zane playing ball in the yard or teaching the child all about the world of business.

"Absolutely," she promised.

She only hoped Cruz would still want to be part of her life once he discovered the truth. She couldn't stand if she lost him, but she would understand. She'd deceived him, and now she continued to lie. Maybe those things were unforgivable.

Only time would tell.

"What the hell, man?"

Zane sighed as he continued to scroll through and sort his emails. His brother's irritated tone echoed through his cell's speaker.

"Problem?" Zane asked.

"Why didn't you tell me about Nora?"

His fingers stilled over the keys as he jerked his attention toward the phone lying next to the keyboard. What the hell had Cruz heard, and how? Zane sure as hell hadn't said a word. And there was no way anyone could have seen Nora at his house, because he lived on a mountain with a gate at the bottom. He'd demanded privacy when he'd built the place.

"What are you talking about?" Zane replied.

"The baby. She said she's not telling anyone, but it's me. How the hell could she not tell me? Is she feeling okay? She sounds tired."

Zane eased back in his chair and tried to unpack his brother's questions. Cruz's only focus was Nora, which meant he couldn't possibly know who the father was. A sliver of relief slid through him, followed quickly by a rush of shame. His brother only knew half of the truth and not the most important part.

He wouldn't get into this now. Zane still stood by his decision to wait until they could speak in person.

"She's fine," Zane assured him. "She's tired, but that's mostly in the morning. I promise I'm keeping an eye on her."

He'd kept more than his eyes on her, but again, now

was not the time to bring it up. Clearly, Cruz wasn't aware of Nora's living situation, either. Still, he didn't want his brother to know anything. Zane had wanted to reveal the entire truth at once, to have time to explain and have a future plan in place. He never wanted his brother to think that he and Nora were sneaking behind his back, though that's exactly how this looked.

Zane pushed back from his desk and came to his feet. The nerves and guilt wouldn't allow him to remain still. He paced around his desk and rubbed the back of his neck.

"Do you know who the father is?"

Zane cringed, but before he could respond, his brother kept going.

"I asked, but she wouldn't tell me. He better not be some jerk who only slept with her because she was convenient."

As if his layer of guilt couldn't get any heavier. Zane was exactly what his brother had described.

"She said he wasn't a jerk, but if that's true, then there would be no reason for the secrecy."

Oh, there was every reason for the secrecy, but Cruz would have to wait. Zane needed to get out of this dangerous conversation before anything else slipped out.

"When will you be back?"

"Not sure," Cruz replied. "I'm supposed to meet with a potential model this morning, but she's late. I should probably cut my trip short. I hate not being there for Nora."

"No need to cut it short. She'll still be pregnant when you get here."

And Zane needed more time before he crushed his brother's heart and damaged their relationship. Damn it.

Every bit of this situation fell on his shoulders. The lack of self-control, the need to keep her close physically, but at a distance emotionally and all the lies.

He was no better than his bastard of a father.

Commotion filtered through from the other end of the line. "I think my appointment is here," Cruz stated. "I'll call you later, but keep me posted on our girl and take care of her."

Our girl. That vice around his heart squeezed tighter and Zane didn't know if that was the guilt or the fact that Nora had slid into the role of his girl.

"Promise," Zane replied, but his brother had already disconnected the call.

Zane stood on the other side of his desk and stared at his cell, as if he could somehow see his brother and gauge his mood and actions. This entire ordeal had gotten so far out of control, Zane wasn't sure if he'd ever get the reins back. At this point, he was the last person with the power. Nora held way too damn much where his emotions and future were concerned. But it was Cruz who dominated the situation. Every aspect of Zane's relationship with his twin and his relationship with Nora hinged on Cruz's reaction to the complete truth.

How the hell did this pregnancy get out anyway? Why did she tell him when Zane specifically discussed keeping everything a secret until Cruz got home and Zane could speak to him privately?

Anger settled deep within him, yet another layer of his lack of self-control lately. She'd purposely defied him, as if driving him out of his mind with want and need weren't enough.

Working seemed like a nonissue right now. When his entire personal life seemed to be going to hell, he should turn to work, but his mind wasn't on any projects or the next board meeting. All he could think of was talking to Nora and figuring out what the hell was going on. The last thing he needed was the rest of the office to know she was expecting his baby.

Zane ignored all the warning bells and red flags waving as he stormed from his office and headed across the hall.

Nine

"Care to tell me what the hell happened with Cruz?"

Nora glanced up from her computer and relaxed against her cushy chair, meeting the very dark eyes of Zane as he closed, and locked, her office door.

"Well, good morning to you, too. I'm feeling better—thanks for asking."

Zane approached her desk and flattened his palms on the glass. "Don't play games."

"I'm not playing anything."

She shoved her chair back and stood. She'd be damned if she'd let anyone tower over her while spewing anger, especially the father of her child.

"The pregnancy slipped out," she explained. "I didn't mean to say a word, but I wasn't feeling well and he picked up on it. That's all he knows, though."

The muscle in Zane's jaw clenched, his gaze locked directly on to her.

"Believe it or not, Zane. I'm human and make mistakes." She circled her desk and waited until he turned to face her, then pointed a finger in his face. "So don't barge in here acting like some Neanderthal. I'm your employee, not your wife or even your girlfriend."

In a flash, Zane gripped her finger, causing her to stumble against his chest. Nora's breath caught in her throat, not from fear but from arousal. The intensity of his stare, combined with the hard plains of his body and his woodsy cologne, had Nora grappling with why she was angry in the first place.

"You're the mother of my child and living in my house," he countered. "You could be my lover if you'd only give in to what we both want and stop being so damn stubborn."

She jerked her hand away and took a step back. She needed to breathe, needed some space to gather her thoughts.

"You think I'm stubborn?" she retorted, crossing her arms over her chest.

Zane's eyes immediately went to the scoop of her blouse, and that invisible sizzle between them increased. He'd never looked at her like this before, and she would have noticed because she'd been staring at him plenty over the years.

"You're impossible," she went on. "Insist I move into your house, seduce me, then think I'll just hop into your bed but not get attached?"

"I'm not in here to talk about our sleeping arrangements," he fired back. "I'm here to make sure nothing else gets said until I can talk to Cruz. I don't want the office finding out our secret."

"Well, I did just send out a special company-wide newsletter."

Zane's eyes narrowed, his lips thinned.

"Don't make stupid comments if you don't want them thrown back at you," she told him.

He stared at her another long moment before propping his hands on his narrow hips and glancing around the office.

"I can't do this," he murmured, his focus still on the desk. "I can't keep living a lie to Cruz and trying to battle my desire to have you at every waking moment."

Nora remained still, afraid that if she moved, she'd reach for him and they'd end up clearing that glass top of her desk like they'd done with his.

She needed to hear him out, needed to know his thoughts. Above all, she needed to focus.

"You know I can't give you what you deserve, but damn it, that doesn't stop this ache I have for you."

Only his eyes lifted to her and the turmoil staring back at her had her heart clenching. The internal war he waged with himself wasn't something she understood; he wouldn't allow that. But maybe she could help if she knew what he was dealing with.

"Why don't you let me decide what I deserve?" she suggested. "And tell me what has you so desperate to hold on to these fears you keep hidden? I know enough to understand that you and your father don't get along, and I know you lost your mother. Let me in, Zane. Let someone in to help you."

Whatever she'd seen in his eyes vanished in an instant, replaced by determination, as he stood straight up and squared his broad shoulders.

"I don't need help with my past," he growled. "I need to figure out my present and how to make all of this work."

"You mean me? Because you can't have things both ways." She took a step toward him and dropped her arms at her sides. "You can't want me physically and push me away emotionally. If I'm in, then I'm all in."

His lips twitched, his brows drew in just a smidge. She assumed he wanted certain things, but wouldn't go after them for fear of losing control. He would never admit the impact his mother's death and his father's abandonment had on his life. Cruz had hinted that Zane took those tragedies the hardest.

"If we're going to be a united front for our child, then we need to be in all aspects," she added.

His lips thinned. "I'm not looking for commitment."

"Commitment found you."

She wanted to be upset with him, but how could she be when he was clearly broken and didn't even realize it?

"And I'm not asking for a ring on my finger," she went on. "But when I sleep with someone, I'm usually in some type of relationship. I can't keep tumbling into bed with you, because having your child doesn't make us emotionally tied."

Zane stared another moment before nodding. "I understand, and I'm sorry I can't be more for you."

"No need to apologize for being who you are."

Looking for a lifelong commitment from Zane had never been her intention. She wouldn't even know how to work with such permanent feelings. She'd purposely dodged relationships for so long. The pain of losing someone so deeply rooted into your life could make a person hesitant.

But there was still something about Zane. Somehow he'd managed to push beyond her barrier and, while she was afraid, she also couldn't help but have a sliver of hope.

She wouldn't mind seeing where they could go with their commonalities and their sexual tension, but she didn't want to force him to be someone he wasn't and she didn't want him to be uncomfortable.

If he wanted to be with her, truly be with her, then he would have said something long ago. She didn't want a forced relationship—she deserved better. At the same time, she also felt that he deserved better than being trapped. Sex—no matter how amazing—would only take them so far.

Why couldn't Cruz be the father of her baby? That man actually wanted his own family, but he just hadn't found the right woman.

But Cruz had never captured her attention the way Zane had. Other than their physical characteristics, the brothers were nothing alike. Zane had closed himself off from life, afraid to feel anything on a personal level. Cruz, though—he lived his life freely, opening his heart to all experiences. When the right woman came into his life, he would love her with his whole heart.

"I know fatherhood isn't something you ever wanted, so I understand if you need to step back."

She didn't even know where that thought or those words came from. She wanted Zane to be a hands-on dad, but only if he wanted that, too. She wouldn't have her child feeling like an obligation or burden. She might not know a thing about parenting, but she did know about love because she had been so loved by her own parents. If they were alive today, they would no doubt dote all over their first grandchild.

"My child will never wonder if their father loves them or wants to be in their life." He took a step toward her until she could see the amber flecks in his dark eyes. "I'm not stepping back from our baby or from you. We just need to figure out what role I'll be playing in your life."

Yeah, that seemed to be their hang-up. Just five weeks ago, she'd been Cruz's bestie, Zane's friend, and loyal employee at *Opulence*. Now she couldn't even count all the titles she held, but she could add liar and deceiver, which were two she never wanted associated with her name.

"We just need to go back to being friends," she suggested. "We both want different things in life. No matter how strong our chemistry is, nothing will change our visions for the future. So if we focus on building a solid friendship, stronger than before, we can co-parent successfully."

She hoped.

He continued to stare, as if mulling over her suggestion. There really was no other option. They were at a standstill as far as what they each wanted and needed personally. She wanted to see where they could go together, but he didn't. Even before they'd shared that first night, she'd always wondered what a life with Zane would be like. The pregnancy just forced her to bring the topic out into the light.

She never wanted someone to be with her out of obligation. That arrangement would simply be humiliating.

Now that she knew exactly where he stood, she

wouldn't beg or try to trick him into anything. Maybe Zane wasn't the man for her, no matter how much she wanted him to be.

"You're fine with only being friends?" he asked with a quirk of one dark brow.

If he wanted her to plead, he'd be waiting awhile. No matter how much she wanted something, she would never set her pride aside and appear needy. Desperation was not a good look on anyone. But that moment had made her stronger, and she fully intended to carry that strength with her through this journey, no matter what may come.

"Perfectly fine." She smiled and smoothed a hand down her pencil dress. "Which reminds me, we have my doctor coming to the house tomorrow afternoon. Are you still good with two o'clock? There's going to be an ultrasound."

She couldn't wait. She just wanted to see her little baby and start collecting the pictures that would mean nothing to anyone else but her. Would they mean something to Zane, too?

"My assistant already cleared my schedule," he informed her.

"Great. Then if there's nothing else, I'm trying to pin down the location of our shots from the rooftop bar engagement. Our photographer has suddenly gone MIA."

"If you can't find a replacement, let me know. I can take care of it."

She circled her desk once again and settled back in her seat. When she glanced across to Zane, he hadn't moved.

"Was there something else?"

He blinked and shook his head as if she'd just pulled him from a trance.

"I'll let you get back to work."

Only once he crossed her office, unlocked the door, and let himself out, did she finally let go of that breath she'd been holding. She'd wanted him to say they could try for a relationship; that had been the hopeful side of her. But the realistic side had known how he'd respond. Still, she truly did have feelings for him, and she had to admit that this level of hurt at his rejection did sting.

At the same time, she also had to come to terms with the fact that she had to put her baby's needs and stability above all else. The more she thought of her future as a mother, the more excited she became. Yes, this had to be the scariest path she'd ever been on, especially without her parents there to guide her, but there was no turning back, so she might as well embrace her new role.

Nora spun toward her computer and pulled up her emails. She still had a photographer to hunt down and other priorities to address for her job. Daydreaming and fantasizing about her boss and his mad bedroom skills didn't pay the bills.

And real life wouldn't always be this fantasy world. She had a baby coming and a relationship mess to sort through. At some point, she and Zane would have to decide what exactly they were going to be to each other.

Ten

How did one woman make him feel all the things? Aroused, frustrated, foolish.

Zane was almost positive he'd covered the gamut of emotions in the past few days with dealing with Nora. And here he was, once again, at her bedroom door late at night because, clearly, masochism was a new personality trait of his.

He tapped on the door and stepped back with the box in his hand.

Foolish. All of this was absolutely foolish. He was like a child looking for approval.

Not too far from the truth.

The knob clicked a second before the door swung wide. Nora stood there wrapped in another silky number, a robe this time, in a shade of purple that did amazing things to her pale skin.

Her eyes darted to the box in his hand.

"Are we exchanging gifts already? We haven't even had our one-week anniversary yet."

Zane couldn't help the smile that spread across his face. That's the side of Nora he'd always known. The playful, joking, sometimes-snarky side. Was it any wonder she got along so great with his brother? They could have been siblings themselves.

"I hadn't planned on getting you a gift, but I know you need tea in the mornings and your cup broke, so…"

He handed over the box, really wishing he would have just left it at her door for her to find.

"That was your cup I broke." She laughed as she reached for the box. "I should be buying *you* one."

Zane shrugged. "I think you'll like this one better, and I wasn't keeping score."

Nora eyed him a moment before she took the box into her room and set it on her bed. He took a step forward to watch her reaction, but remained in the doorway. Any time he stepped into an enclosed space with her, intense moments ensued, and that's exactly what he needed to be dodging to save his sanity and try to respect her wishes to remain friends.

He leaned against the doorjamb as she lifted the white lid and gasped. Inwardly, he was relieved she appreciated the gesture, but outwardly, he remained calm. No need to show his nerves like some awkward teen with a crush.

Nora lifted the mug and held it up as she turned to face him. Her eyes filled and he couldn't keep his distance. He'd always known Nora to be fun, playful, strong. He hadn't seen her upset since she'd lost Clara, so the tears hit him in a way he hadn't expected.

"Don't cry." He crossed the room and stood next to the bed. "I thought you'd love it."

"Oh my word. I do love it." She glanced from the gift to him. "It's just, this is my first gift with anything that says *mom* on it."

He'd had no idea what to get her, but he'd skipped out of the office earlier and had driven two towns over to a store he'd heard his assistant, Will, mention having the best gift ideas. The boutique had certainly delivered, and thankfully, the clerk had taken pity on him when he claimed he was shopping for a friend and had no idea what to buy.

The white mug had a cursive font in dark blue that read, Best Mom Ever.

"You don't know that I'll be a good mom." She sniffed. "I could seriously suck at this."

A lone tear ran down her cheek and that vise around his heart clenched tighter than ever. Zane slid the pad of his thumb across her smooth skin, wiping away the moisture. He'd thought the mug was a little over-the-top, with a silly, generic saying, but the clerk assured him that any first-time expectant mother would love it. Apparently, she'd been right.

He'd been so damn nervous shopping; that wasn't his forte. But he couldn't exactly send his assistant, considering the circumstances.

"You'll be an amazing mother," he assured her. "The fact that you're concerned about it tells me so, but I've known you for years and worked with you enough to know that you tackle everything head-on. You go into everything with one goal, and that is to succeed. Motherhood will be no different."

"I hope so. I don't want to ruin my baby's life because I have no clue what I'm doing."

A feeling he completely understood.

"I got you a few different flavors of tea, also," he told her, gesturing toward the box on the bed. "I know you need the peppermint, but I also got a chamomile and lavender. If you don't like those, I can get different ones, or more. Just let me know what you want."

"I want you to relax." She offered a sweet smile as she held on to her mug. "I know this is all crazy and scary, but just try to take a breather."

Zane couldn't help but laugh. "Shouldn't I be telling you that?"

Nora shrugged and turned toward her gift. She laid the mug in the tissue paper packaging as she sifted through the sachets of tea.

"I imagine we'll bounce back and forth being each other's support systems," she suggested. "Besides, it's likely more stressful now than ever because the news is still so fresh and Cruz doesn't know the full extent. Once everything is out in the open and we know where we're headed, I think we'll be fine. Not to mention, once I can get back into my house and we both have some normalcy, we can really work on a solid plan."

Getting Nora back into her house had been one of the goals, but he wasn't necessarily looking forward to not having her here. Which was absolutely ridiculous. He couldn't keep her in his home like some pet. She had a life before him and she'd have a life after, only, now, their lives would have to mesh in newer areas.

His ever-pressing attraction and gnawing ache for her would have to be stored in the back of his mind…just as in all the years before. He would have to pull up every ounce of self-control he possessed to keep her confined to the friend zone.

But where the hell would he put all those memories? Every touch, every sigh of pleasure or heavy-lidded gaze, every kiss? Where did he lock all of those away? Because now that he had experienced Nora on a deeper level than ever before, he'd have a hell of a time simply forgetting.

"Are you nervous or excited for the ultrasound tomorrow?"

Zane blinked and realized she'd turned her attention back to him.

"I don't do nervous."

Her lips twitched. "No, I imagine you don't, but even if you did, you'd never admit such a fault."

Hell no, he wouldn't. As if he'd ever tell anyone, let alone the only woman who'd ever captivated him and the mother of his child, that something scared him. He never wanted to be seen as weak or vulnerable, especially to Nora.

Which was why the fact that they succumbed to their attraction the other day still irked the hell out of him. He had to keep his resolve in place and his guard up to make sure that never happened again. Each encounter with Nora seemed to grow more and more intimate. They were well beyond sex and had entered into some territory he'd never been before. That foggy area screwed with his mind and made him question his wants and needs and all of the goals he'd ever set for himself. Suddenly, work wasn't the only thing he worried about, and that scared the hell out of him.

When she stifled a yawn with her hand over her mouth, Zane started for the door.

"I'll let you get back to bed." A bed he wouldn't be sharing ever again. He owed it to Nora—and his very sanity—not to. "I have an early-morning meeting, but I can call in from here if you need me."

Nora shook her head. "Go on in. I'll be just fine."

"You'd never admit if you weren't." He smiled as he tossed her words right back at her.

She slid her hands into her robe and tipped her head, all rolled into one adorable, sexy gesture.

"Never," she agreed. "I guess that's just another way we're so alike."

As if he needed another reason to see their commonalities.

Zane left the room, and closed the door behind him before he ignored her request to just remain friends.

Nora scrolled through images of the sample wedding dresses that she'd been sent and really couldn't focus. Her mind still remained on the sweetest gift Zane had delivered to her door last night. He'd seemed almost shy and unsure, which were not traits she ever attributed to him. She wasn't sure if he'd been cautious about gift giving or if the reality of the pregnancy had hit home.

Either way, he'd been pretty damn adorable. In the span of a few days, she'd seen Zane passionate, vulnerable, and reluctant. For years, she'd really only seen one side, the professional, serious Zane. She had to admit she found each part of him endearing and, well, normal. She'd always assumed he didn't want people to know he had human emotions, because he kept everything so close to his chest.

Nora focused once again on the screen in front of her and tried to envision herself in any of these dresses. To be honest, she'd always thought she'd be in love with the man of her dreams before she ever tried on a wedding dress. So trying to choose three for the bridal store to send over for the day of the shoot was proving to be difficult.

Finally, she selected three completely different gowns and hoped that something would be perfect for the shoot. She also hoped the bridal bouquets being sent would be large enough to hide her face if she held them just right. She still didn't understand why Cruz thought she'd be the best one for this project. She'd never modeled in her life, but she was a hell of a social media mogul. That's where her confidence lay.

Nora glanced at the time. She'd come into the office only one hour late today because, thankfully, her morning sickness hadn't been too terrible. But now she got to leave early for her ultrasound and she couldn't view it soon enough. She just wanted to see the image and hear that heartbeat. Some validation from her doctor that everything looked good would go a long way in easing her nerves.

She shut everything down and was just about to head out the door when her cell vibrated in her hand. She didn't recognize the number as she swiped her screen. Juggling her purse in one hand, she tapped the Speaker option.

"Hello, this is Nora."

"Miss Monroe, this is Sven from Boulevard Bouquet. I apologize for the short notice, but I wanted to call instead of email. I am embarrassed to say that the order of purple roses didn't come in for the photo shoot. We do have a lovely assortment of lavender dahlias and I could still make a dramatic arrangement, but I didn't know if your heart was set on roses."

Considering she wasn't the artistic coordinator on this shoot, Nora wasn't sure what to say, but she was the lead on the last-minute project, so she did have the power to make all decisions.

"Sven, I trust your judgment, as this is your area of expertise," she replied, shutting her office door and then locking it behind her. "How about this. You make up a purple arrangement and bring another one that is wildly vibrant and screams springtime. Sound good?"

"What colors?" he asked.

Nora waved at Cruz's assistant as she headed toward the elevator.

"Let your imagination run wild. The bigger and more extravagant, the better."

Sven gasped. "Oh, this never happens. I promise I will not let you down."

"I have faith in you. Can't wait to see these bouquets."

She disconnected the call and sagged against the wall of the elevator as it descended. Considering she chose three dresses with different features, it was only logical she had a variety with her bouquets as well.

She had no idea how this shoot would turn out, but if Cruz and Zane hated the images, that would be on them. This whole ordeal was their idea. Well, Cruz's idea, but Zane had jumped right on board. They were out of their minds thinking she could be a model. And why choose her? She didn't want to catapult to stardom. Give this opportunity to someone who actually wanted to be in front of the lens.

As the elevator doors opened, she headed for the main entrance and the sunshine. This would be a great day, and all she wanted to focus on now was her appointment and her baby. Worrying about a photo shoot days away would only steal the joy of this moment and she refused to allow anything to rob her of this milestone experience.

Eleven

Zane stared at the black-and-white monitor as he stood next to Nora. The doctor and nurse had set up a make-shift area in his den, and Nora lay on the sofa, her eyes also fixed on the screen.

The nurse maneuvered the wand around on Nora's bare belly and then stopped.

"There's your baby." She pointed to the screen, then tapped another button. "And here's the heartbeat."

The rapid thump-thump-thump seemed to echo through the room, as did Nora's swift inhale.

"Does everything look okay?" he asked, stepping in closer to the screen. "Can you tell the sex?"

"We can't determine the sex this early, but at the next appointment we should be able to give you an idea of the gender if the baby is laying right and you want to know."

He glanced from the image to Nora. "Do we want to know?"

She laughed. "Apparently you do, so that's fine with me."

Seeing that wide smile on her face as she stared at their baby had a roll of emotions balling up inside him. Never in his life did he think he'd be in this position, let alone with Nora.

The wand moved around more and the nurse tapped more buttons as images started to print out. The doctor came over her shoulder and pointed, then murmured something.

"What is it?" Zane asked as panic gripped him. "Is something wrong?"

"Nothing at all." The doctor assured him with a smile. "There are just various angles I like to see and some I want to make sure get printed for you two to keep."

Relief spread through him as Nora reached up and took his hand.

"Stop worrying," she told him. "Everything is fine."

How could he not worry? For years, he'd kept his heart closed off and he was doing a hell of a job keeping himself guarded from Nora as well. But a baby? *His baby?* Only a coldhearted jerk could keep from opening up to a child.

The reality of the situation hadn't hit him until now and the support from Nora's touch eased some of his fears and soothed past wounds. How did she do that? She didn't even know the pain he held deep inside, yet she managed to reach in and comfort him in a way he didn't even know he needed.

All while carrying his child, maintaining her demanding career, and handling stress like a champ.

He was damn lucky this strong, amazing woman was the mother of his child. There was something about Nora that made him believe she could handle any situation and rise above to come out on top. She'd become invaluable in his life over the years and there wasn't a doubt in his mind that she would tackle parenting with as much grit and grace as she did everything else in her life.

Once they finished with the ultrasound, the nurse handed Zane a long strip of photographs, each one with a little peanut-shaped image in a sac. The doctor asked Nora questions and finished up the exam while Zane made the next appointment. After getting Nora's okay, he opted for having it at his home again, considering he wasn't sure who all would know at that point. Even if Cruz knew the truth, Zane still had a business and employees to consider. The CEO's private life didn't need to be fodder for the workplace gossip mill.

The doctor completed his exam and Nora adjusted her clothes. Zane went to the door and waited for them to gather their things. He didn't want to rush them out, but at the same time, he wanted that alone time with Nora. The moment they'd just experienced together had pushed them into another level of bonding that he hadn't expected. Each day that passed, he realized just how much closer they had become.

"I can show you out," he offered.

Once they were ready, he led them down the hall and to the front door. He held the photographs in his hand as he let them out and reset the security code. His cell vibrated in his pocket and he didn't even look as he pulled it out to answer.

His eyes were locked on the image of the life he and Nora had created and he wondered how the hell he'd be the man this child needed. He had no choice and he damn well wouldn't be the father his had been. Zane had every intention of stepping up, even if that meant sacrificing portions of his own life.

"Hello."

"I hope this isn't a bad time."

A call from Barrett never came at the right time, in Zane's opinion, and today of all days. The timing couldn't be worse.

"I'll only be a minute," Barrett promised.

"Fine."

Zane remained in the foyer, still going over each picture of his baby.

"When Cruz gets back into town, I'd like to have you both over. And before you say no, I'm only asking for a few minutes of your time. I know you want nothing to do with me and I know I don't deserve your respect, but I'm only asking for time."

Zane opened his mouth to deny the request, just like always, but he stared at those pictures of his child and something stirred deep inside. He hadn't even met his baby yet, but he couldn't imagine never seeing them or hardly speaking to them. He wanted a solid relationship with his child and wouldn't let anything get in the way.

Granted, he wouldn't drink, himself, and gamble away his entire life. There might be a vast difference between him and his father, but there was also a very fine line.

"I might be able to make it," Zane conceded. "Just text me the information."

Silence greeted him on the other end, and Zane glanced at the screen to make sure he hadn't accidentally disconnected the call.

"Thank you, son."

Barrett's voice cracked on that last word and a punch of guilt hit Zane hard. Other than at his mother's funeral, he'd never seen his father cry or get emotional. The fact that Zane said he might be available was clearly something Barrett hadn't been expecting.

"I need to go," Zane said, then tapped to end the call before sliding the cell back in his pocket.

Damn it. He didn't want to stir up that old emotional baggage, but at the same time, he wasn't the man he'd been just a week ago.

"Everything okay?"

He turned to see Nora in the hallway just outside the den. Leaning against the wall, she had her arms crossed.

"Was that your dad?"

"Barrett," he corrected. "And yes."

"I didn't mean to listen, but I didn't want to interrupt."

Zane sighed and started toward her. He extended the photographs for her to take.

"I don't really know what to do with these or if you want to divide them or make a baby book," he started. "I'm new at this."

She took the images, but never looked away from him.

"Want to talk about the phone call?" she asked, easing off the wall.

"No."

"Are you ever going to open up about your father to me?"

"We've been over this."

She nodded in agreement. "We have, but you can't keep things locked inside."

Zane raked a hand over the back of his neck. He didn't

want to have this conversation again and he didn't need
to face his past, especially in front of Nora.

"I met your dad once," she went on. "Cruz and I actually went to dinner with him about a year ago."

Zane jerked. He'd had no idea.

"Cruz never mentioned it," he murmured.

"Probably because he's trying to mend the relationship and he didn't think you'd approve."

Zane knew Cruz wanted to try to reclaim some relationship with Barrett, but he hadn't heard about the dinner with Nora. He didn't want his brother to feel like he
had to keep secrets.

Damn it. Zane had absolutely no room to complain
or question his twin's actions. Having dinner with their
father was nothing in comparison to the lie Zane had
been holding on to.

"I never knew Barrett before, but he was well-dressed
and charming."

Nora's words cut through his thoughts and Zane studied her. She stared at him, almost as if contemplating
his reaction or trying to read his thoughts.

"I lived with the man for sixteen years and you saw
him for a few hours. I'm sure he was charming for that
amount of time."

Nora blinked and took a step back. "You're right. I
couldn't possibly form my own opinion, and it would
be wrong in comparison to yours."

She stepped around him and started for the stairs.
Zane turned to follow her, but she reached the bottom
step and rested her hand on the banister.

"Listen. You are going to drive everyone out of your
life with the way you are hell-bent on keeping yourself
guarded."

Her eyes bored into his and Zane stilled, unable to look away from that fire.

"You want to keep me at arm's length as well, even though I'm having your baby and I know damn well you want more," she continued. "You better figure out what you want out of life. You can either live it angry or you can *live*. Nobody else can make that decision."

She headed up the stairs, and seconds later, the door to her room slammed. Zane stood in the foyer for about a half second before he followed.

She'd had her dramatic exit, but he was about to make an even more dramatic entrance.

Maybe she'd been too hard on him. After all, she'd had a good childhood and didn't really know what he was going through.

And maybe that's what irked her the most. He had a father here and chose to hold a grudge instead of offering him a second chance.

Her door burst open and Nora whirled around.

"Wh—"

Zane gripped her face and crushed his lips to hers before she could even finish her word. Nora held on to his shoulders and opened, welcoming the passion that she'd been desperately aching for. She didn't want to wait for him to make another move—he'd made the most important one by coming in here and kissing her.

Nora started with the buttons on his shirt but grew frustrated and just gave them a hard yank.

"Whoa, whoa." He stepped back and laughed. "I don't think that's how it works, though your attempt was pretty damn hot."

Nora reached for him again. "I want you out of this shirt. You've been driving me crazy."

Without unbuttoning the rest, Zane reached behind his neck and gathered the material before pulling it up and over his head. He flung the unwanted garment to the side and reached down to lift her up.

Nora let out a squeal as he cradled her against his chest and started toward her door.

"Where are we going?"

"My bed. I've wanted you there for years."

Years? *Years?*

And he was just telling her this now?

"Zane—"

"Not a word," he commanded. "We're not talking about it."

That seemed to be the theme with him lately, but now was not the time to get into a heavy discussion or another argument. She wanted him physically—the rest could be sorted out later...much later. Because her very real feelings had crossed over from superficial to something much deeper.

And that scared the hell out of her.

Zane crossed the wide hallway and stepped into his bedroom, then kicked his door shut behind him. He laid her on the made-up bed and took a step back as he finished undressing. Nora couldn't help but stare at his magnificent form. She'd seen it all before, but she truly didn't think she'd ever tire of such a gorgeous sight.

"I love how you stare at me."

When he stood before her completely bare, Nora offered a smile as she sat up and pulled her thin sweater over her head.

"And I love when you're naked," she admitted.

Zane reached for the waist of her pencil skirt and then started easing it over her hips as she shifted back and forth to help. He'd expertly tugged her panties with the skirt and tossed both pieces over his shoulder. Nora reached for the clasp of her bra between her breasts and rid herself of the final article of clothing.

"I'm positive I love you naked more," he growled, pressing his hands on either side of her hips. "I could look at you all day, right here, in my bed."

Feeling saucy from his heavy-lidded gaze and obvious arousal, Nora tipped her head. "And how does reality live up to the fantasy?" she asked.

In one swift move, Zane gripped her around the waist and maneuvered himself to lie on the bed with her straddling his lap. He smiled up at her as he held her firmly in place with those strong hands on her hips.

"This is the view I would dream of," he told her. "You right there above me, smiling, willing and ready."

Oh, his words sent another burst of need through her. To know that he'd lain right here and thought of her told her that she did have power over this entire situation—and it wasn't just the sex.

Nora flattened her palms on his chest and leaned forward. Her hair curtained his face as she found herself enthralled by that dark stare of his. He might keep his emotions close, but she was starting to read pieces of him. He wanted more with her—he just didn't want to want it.

And if he'd fantasized about her for years, that was more than desiring just a fling, whether he could admit such a thing or not. Maybe they could see where this would go beyond the intimacy and beyond sharing a child. But he would have to come to terms with his feelings and stop dodging everything that spooked him.

"You're frowning, and that sure as hell was not part of my fantasy."

Nora laughed as his words brought her back to the moment. "I'm not frowning," she argued. "I'm thinking."

"None of that here," he ordered.

Zane lifted her slightly, enough for her to hover just above him. A naughty grin spread across his face, which only added to her anticipation and arousal. She shifted enough to merge their bodies, and his groan of delight and clenched jaw were well worth her keeping her focus on him. He filled her so completely, so perfectly, in every single way, and if he'd only see just how good they were together, maybe this could be everything she'd ever dreamed of.

Zane's hands traveled over her hips and up to cover her breasts. He took her in each of his large hands and slowly massaged her flesh as he began to move beneath her. Now she couldn't help but close her eyes as she let the euphoric sensations take over.

"Keep looking at me."

That throaty demand had her snapping her attention back to Zane, who continued to stare up at her. This level of intimacy, achieved by moving with his body while keeping her eyes locked on his, was entirely new and utterly beautiful. What had started out as them ripping clothes off in what she thought would be a quick and dirty session suddenly turned into something meaningful and perhaps even more erotic.

"You're beautiful like this," he murmured, sliding one hand up into her hair to ease her down slightly. "I need more."

Yeah, so did she, but right now, they were talking about two vastly different things.

She knew what he needed, what he wanted. She claimed his mouth as she pumped her hips faster. Nora propped her hands on either side of his head for support as she covered him with her entire body. Zane's hand tightened in her hair as his other one came to clutch her backside and urge her on.

Her body climbed, but she wasn't ready for this moment to end. She wanted to stay right there with him, for as long as he would allow. But she wouldn't beg. He had to come to that conclusion all on his own.

Her body continued climbing and there was nothing she could do to prevent the climax from slamming through her.

She sat back up and cried out as she pumped her hips even faster. Zane reached between their bodies, sliding his fingertip over her core, fully maximizing the burst of sensations spiraling through her.

"That's it," he crooned. "So beautiful."

The release seemed to last longer than usual, but when her body finally calmed, she still had a need for this man and his touch. She stared down at him and the hunger looking back at her gave her another rush of desire and energy.

"You're the one who's beautiful," she told him. "More than any fantasy I've ever had."

And that was the truth. Zane shattered all thoughts of any man that had ever rolled through her mind. He epitomized every single thing good she wanted in her life and in a partner.

She eased her body up slightly, then back down slowly, over and over, as she watched him fight against his own release. His hands fisted the bed covers as he strained against her. Then she couldn't stand it anymore, either. She moved faster now, taking his hands and placing them back on her breasts. She had to have more. Would she ever get enough?

He jerked and cried out as he continued to hold on to her. Another wave swept through Nora and she joined him in their release.

Silence filtered through the room as their bodies ceased trembling.

Nora eased down onto his body, but he shifted and tucked her against his side.

"Stay," he whispered. "We can figure everything out later. For now...just stay."

As if she wanted to be anywhere else.

Twelve

"I used to wonder if Barrett ever cared about us."

Zane hadn't meant to let that thought out, but there was something about the dark that made him feel safer. Like if he couldn't see the world around him, then nothing could harm him.

But even in the dark, he knew full well who lay at his side. She'd stayed. They'd taken full advantage of his open shower outside, off his balcony, which overlooked his property below. Living on a hill surrounded by a forest sure as hell had its perks.

Now they lay in a tangle of sheets and blankets, legs entwined, Nora resting on his arm as she drew a lazy pattern on his bare chest.

She said nothing, likely wanting him to continue talking. He'd never shared his past with any woman before. Hell, he barely talked about things with Cruz. Zane would be perfectly fine if he never spoke of it again.

But Nora's frustrated words about the way he kept his guard up had hit him hard. He had to cope with everything from his past before he could confront his future. His unborn child deserved the best version of himself that he could give.

"When my mom died, I thought the three of us would be a strong, united unit," he went on. "But as the days went by, I quickly realized she was the bond that held us all together, and without her, we just crumbled."

Nora's hand stilled, and her soft breath washed over his skin as she let him get this out. He'd never had any intention of filling her in on those gaps she'd asked about. It wasn't that he didn't think she deserved to know, more that he didn't want to reopen a door he'd sealed shut so long ago.

"Barrett gave up on everything," Zane went on. "Himself first, but then Cruz and I fell in after that. He couldn't even take care of himself, let alone two kids. He gave up on the ranch and that ended up foreclosing. Gambling and alcohol became his life. Drowning out the hurt. At the time, I didn't understand why he didn't care, but as I got older, I realized he'd just checked out of life."

"You lost both parents."

Her words slid through the darkness and collided with his thoughts. He'd known that, but he'd never said the words aloud. How ironic that she'd zeroed in on that turning point in his life and summed it up in a few simple words.

"Cruz and I were scared," he went on. "We didn't know where we'd live or what would happen next. We ended up renting an apartment above a hardware store.

The place had one bedroom that Dad gave to us because half the time, he passed out on the couch. We figured if we wanted anything, we'd have to work for it ourselves. We worked a few hours a week at the store below, but we did odd jobs around the neighborhood, too. Cutting grass, painting, anything that gave us money. We worked anytime we weren't in school. Our grades weren't great, because we didn't have the time to study."

Her hand still on his chest, Nora pushed up and stared down at him. The sliver of moonlight creeping through the balcony doors outlined her perfect silhouette.

"You survived."

Zane swallowed the instant lump of emotion that threatened to consume him. He had survived, but he didn't know what he would have done had Cruz not been there. They'd only had each other, and Zane had never kept anything from his twin, so his deception caused an inner friction Zane had never experienced before.

"That's why you both are so successful," she went on. "You know how to work hard to get what you want. You're not only surviving now, you're thriving."

"Maybe so, but there's always that worry in the back of my mind. One bad business decision or one wrong move could cost us everything."

"Are you worried about our affair and the effect it will have on the office?" she asked. "Because I can find another job."

Zane shot up in bed and covered her hand on his chest. "Like hell you will. You're our best employee and the only one who can handle all of our social media. Yes, I worry what this will look like, but you're not going anywhere. We'd be lost without you."

We. The Westbrook boys wouldn't be nearly as successful with *Opulence* if they didn't have Nora. But he didn't want her going anywhere for selfish reasons. Still, he couldn't admit he was the one who needed her. That would imply too much and confuse this entire situation…confuse him. Because once he said the words, he couldn't take them back. He had to be smart about this, tread carefully, so nobody got hurt.

The stirring of longing and desire he possessed now went beyond his physical needs, but to what end? Could he even trust what he felt, or were years of want and an unexpected pregnancy confusing him?

He'd purposely shut down so long ago, he didn't even know if stronger, long-term emotions could rise to the surface.

"We'll figure this out," he assured her, squeezing her hand. "We don't have to do anything right now but rest."

When she didn't move, Zane wrapped an arm around her and eased her back down to his side. Having her here, in his bed, had been a fantasy; he hadn't been lying. But he'd never thought beyond that. Now he didn't know how to guard his heart and without breaking hers.

"I'm glad you told me," she whispered, snuggling deeper against him.

"Me, too."

Nora turned from side to side in the mirror and couldn't believe that the first time she'd ever put on a wedding dress, it was for a photo shoot. She had to admit that this dress made her feel gorgeous, just as every bride should. But she couldn't get caught up in the dreamlike state the dress evoked. There would be no groom waiting for her out in the gazebo by the pond. Only a photographer, the art director, and Zane.

Thankfully, Maddie the art director had helped her into the dress and touched up her hair after the stylist had left. Maddie seemed to be a Jill-of-all-trades, which was a good thing because she'd really need her help getting into that next dress.

Nora pulled in a deep breath and smoothed a hand down the empire waist of the gown. Her stomach still lay flat, and she honestly couldn't wait until she started to see that bump. She'd heard the little heartbeat, seen the life growing inside her, but she wanted to see that physical change. Oh, she might regret that later when she had to waddle or couldn't fit into her clothes, but right now, she wanted to feel that swell when she covered her belly with her hand.

Nora set aside baby thoughts for now and made her way through Zane's house to step out the back double doors leading to his expansive yard. She bypassed the pool and pool house, following the perfectly placed stone steps to get to the pond.

She clutched the lacy skirt and glanced up to see Zane only a few feet away. She stilled, her eyes locked with his. He wore his typical dark pants and dark shirt, unbuttoned at the top and rolled up on his forearms. But for half a second, she could pretend he waited for her, waited to start their life together and raise the family they'd created.

Zane's eyes traveled over her, and Nora dropped her skirt as she did a slow spin.

When she faced him once again, he'd taken another step closer. He looked nowhere else but at her, and her heart did a flip. Maybe, just maybe…

"Perfection. Absolute perfection."

The clap and declaration from the photographer broke the moment and her thoughts.

"Sven brought the flowers earlier, and I think the vibrant bouquet will be stunning with that lacy, vintage gown. The sun is at a perfect spot along the horizon to make those colors pop and you stand out like the vision you are."

Uneasy with this entire project and the way Zane continued to stare at her, Nora assumed that the quicker she got to the posing, the quicker she could be done. She wished Zane had come inside to see her, that maybe they could have shared a moment alone, but none of this was real and she couldn't let her mind get wrapped up in some playful scene.

Besides, she had to keep her head on straight and her thoughts clear, because this photographer was also trying to make a name for himself with *Opulence*. No need to bring him in on the company secret, not to mention that Maddie was a longtime employee. She would pick up on anything amiss between Zane and Nora before the photographer would.

"Where should I stand?" she asked, gathering her skirts once again.

"Let's get some by the pond first, and then I'll have you change and we'll do the gazebo."

The entire time she followed directions and moved her hands, her shoulders, tipped her head, all of it... Zane's eyes never wavered. With every ounce of her willpower, she concentrated on her poses and the excitement from the photographer and Maddie. They would converse, then change Nora's position again and take more shots. Nora smiled when asked, but when they requested a longing look, her gaze immediately went to Zane. She couldn't help herself. He was just…there.

"Yes, that's it," the photographer said, moving in closer. "Stunning."

"You're going to make a gorgeous bride one day, Nora," Maddie chimed in. "Isn't she, Mr. Westbrook?"

Zane said nothing, and for the first time since she'd met him, she had no idea what he could be thinking. She'd never seen that closed-off expression before, not even on Cruz.

"I think we should have some with her sitting and that lace around her," Maddie stated, breaking through Nora's thoughts.

Nora did as requested and forced herself to keep her focus off Zane. Clearly, something had upset him, but she didn't know what. She thought they'd turned a corner since he opened up to her a few nights ago in his bed. She'd fallen into that same bed every night since.

But maybe he wasn't on the same page as her and perhaps she was naive for thinking he could be.

After several more shots, Nora cheeks started quivering from smiling so much.

"I think you can change into the other dress now," the photographer announced. "I'll get everything set up in the gazebo."

Nora gathered the dress without glancing at Zane or waiting for Maddie's approval. She headed for the house with her ball of emotions and wondered why Zane stuck around if he was just going to be in a surly mood, because that had to be what his silence meant. Wasn't it?

She'd tried to tell both guys this entire ordeal was a terrible idea, but neither would listen to her. She could only assume Zane was having those same doubts now and likely running numbers in his head of how they could scrap this shoot while re-creating the project and staying on track and on budget.

A sliver of her had really hoped he'd see her in a new light as she came out in a wedding gown, knowing she was pregnant with his child. How foolish to think any of this could build a solid future. All she could do now was get through this shoot and, tonight, sleep back in her own bed.

Thirteen

What in the hell had Cruz been thinking, demanding Nora be the star of this wedding shoot? And how ridiculous had it been for Zane to agree?

Zane excused himself from the photographer, who was busy looking through the shots he'd taken. He stepped aside and pulled his cell from his pocket. He had no notion of making a call or checking emails, though there was still plenty of work to be done today. Right now, though, he needed a distraction because he didn't want to talk to anyone or check out the fresh images on the camera screen.

He wanted to erase the image of Nora as a bride for so many reasons. The main ones being that he could never be her groom and he already hated the faceless bastard who would.

"Mr. Westbrook," the photographer called. "I'd like

you to see these so I know if this is the angle you were thinking."

Considering that Zane stopped thinking the second she stepped out as a vision in white lace, he wasn't so sure he'd be of any help.

"You might want to ask Maddie when she comes back," Zane replied as he turned. "She's the art director on this project."

But the young man seemed too eager to show his work and Zane still had to be a professional.

The camera screen slid in front of his face, and Zane endured as the photographer scrolled through image after image. There was no way in hell Zane could choose a favorite, because she looked radiant in each and every one.

Like a dream.

She'd been his fantasy for so long. Even trying to keep everything about her superficial hadn't worked. Somehow Nora had penetrated that protective wall he'd built. She didn't use her words, though. Her actions had slowly embraced every need he'd ever had, and some he didn't even know of. The manner in which she cared for people astounded him. She loved with her whole heart.

Wait. Love? She didn't love him. Well, maybe as a friend, but nothing beyond that.

Their intimate relationship, the baby, and now this wedding project clearly had made his mind a jumbled mess.

"Sir, were you thinking something else? Because we can start from scratch."

Zane realized the photographer likely took his silence for disapproval. Far from it. He had no idea how the hell they'd ever choose what photos to use. Nora might think she belonged behind the scenes, but that woman embodied beauty and shouldn't be kept in the shadows.

A sliver of jealousy threatened to spiral through him at the thought of sharing her in any capacity...which was absolutely absurd. He had no claims on her. She was her own person and could do anything she wanted. Part of him just didn't want her to do anything without him.

"These are perfect."

He finally found the words to assure the young man his work wasn't the issue. No, the issue was Zane's own confused state.

"Here we are."

At Maddie's declaration, Zane turned to see his art director beaming as she carried the long train on Nora's second dress.

If he thought she'd been stunning before, that last dress was nothing compared to this one. The strapless top left her pale shoulders exposed and did amazing things to the swell of her breasts. While the top conformed to her body, the skirt fanned out all around her. He didn't know technical terms for what she wore, but the elegant shape combined with the fun, swirling pattern all over the gown had him wondering if she loved it as much as he did.

Who knew he'd fall in love with a wedding gown?

That better be all he fell in love with. Mentally, he couldn't even fathom opening his heart so wide and freely to another person. He had nothing to offer, not emotionally anyway.

"Isn't this gorgeous?" Maddie all but squealed. "The lavender flowers will be stunning with this, but I think we should also try that bright bouquet to really make this dress pop."

Nora's eyes met his, and everything else fell away. Maddie and the photographer moved toward the gazebo and were chattering away about lighting and angles, but he didn't care about any of that. He only saw Nora.

Slowly, Nora moved toward him and she seemed to almost glide over the cropped grass. She'd pulled her hair up for this one. Some random curls lay against the side of her neck, but kicked up when the breeze passed through.

"I never knew I'd like trying on wedding dresses so much," she admitted with a nervous laugh. "I mean, I've never had a reason to put one on before."

"I hate to tell you this."

Her eyes widened. "What is it?"

He took a step closer, using every ounce of willpower not to touch her as he leaned in to whisper, "You're the most beautiful model we've ever had."

When he eased back, her eyes were still wide and met his.

"Don't act surprised," he added. "You did look in the mirror, right?"

"I did, but I wouldn't go so far as to say 'the most beautiful.' I feel pretty, but—"

"Not pretty," he corrected. "Stunning, breathtaking, a damn masterpiece. Why have we never used you before?"

Nora blinked as if taken aback by his declaration. Maybe he'd been a little extra with his wording, but every bit of it was true, and she should start seeing herself like he did. The most perfect woman he'd ever encountered.

"You haven't used me, because I do my best work in my office," she replied. "And don't get any ideas. I'm no model, though I have enjoyed the day. But I'm not like the women who are vying for the attention of *Opulence*. I don't need a chance at a dream job. I already have one."

He wouldn't argue with her now, but this sure as hell wasn't the last time she'd be in front of the camera, and there was no doubt his brother would agree once he saw these shots.

"If you all are ready," Maddie called. "Oh, let me help you with that train."

"I've got it."

Zane hadn't meant to volunteer himself for the service, but the words slipped out and now he found himself stepping behind Nora and gathering up the yards of fabric.

"Damn, this is heavy. How did you walk in this?"

Nora laughed as she glanced over her shoulder. "I love it, so it didn't seem like work."

Zane stilled as her stare found his and something hit him hard in the chest. Too hard, leaving him too raw and vulnerable.

Love shouldn't be work. He didn't work at loving his brother, he just did.

But the way she continued to stare at him had him wondering if he'd been wrong. Did Nora have stronger feelings for him? Because that would make this entire complicated situation even more difficult to sort out.

"Let's start with the bright bouquet," the photographer announced, breaking the moment.

Nora blinked and turned away, leaving Zane with mounds of material and his thoughts. He didn't want to be in his own head right now, so he better focus on this shoot. Only, this shoot was the entire problem.

He never should have been here for it, but he'd had no idea the impact seeing her in a wedding gown would have on his mental state. It was a damn dress. Why did he have to get so worked up over it? It wasn't as if she was actually getting married.

But when she did...would he go? Would he honestly be able to see her walking down the aisle toward another man?

The next several shots would be taken inside the gazebo, and there wasn't a doubt in Zane's mind these were going to be absolutely as perfect as the last set. He'd just pulled out his phone to give Cruz an update when Maddie came up next to him.

"I know this wasn't planned and it's rather last-minute, but could we get you in some shots?"

Zane jerked his attention to his art director. "Are you out of your mind?"

She laughed and shook her head. "I figured you'd push back at that, but hear me out. You're wearing all black, and if we just get images of you from behind, I think it will really be something special. You look off toward the sunset and Nora can be at your side, your arms interlocked, while she faces the camera."

Never in his life did he think he'd play a faux groom to Nora's bride. Fate had to be mocking him at this point.

"You're the boss," she went on. "But you did hire me for my artistic vision, and that's what I'm seeing."

He stared at Maddie and she tipped her defiant chin. While he appreciated her drive and need for perfection, he wished he weren't on the receiving end of her idea.

"Come on." She patted his arm and gestured toward Nora. "Let's go."

"I didn't agree to this." Yet his feet were moving.

"You didn't say no," she countered. "I've worked with

you guys long enough to know you'll do nearly anything for the perfect spread, and this is it."

As Maddie stopped the photographer and started explaining her plan, Zane stepped into the gazebo. He'd had this built more as a focal feature than to actually use. He never came this far out on the property, never had a reason to.

"What are you doing?" Nora whispered.

"Apparently, I'm the groom."

She stared for a second, her eyes wide, then she burst out laughing. "You're kidding, right?"

"Oh, I wish I was. I'm supposed to keep my back to the camera, though."

She licked her pink-painted lips and clutched the colorful bouquet in front of her. "Well, okay then. Whatever they want. But if you're not feeling this, I can feign a sickness."

"If I'm not feeling what?" he asked, stepping closer. "Like I want to pretend to marry you? Like I don't want to stand beside you? Like this isn't driving me crazy to see you looking this damn gorgeous, but knowing I can't touch you? Oh, I'm feeling everything, Nora."

Her perfectly shaped brows rose and she sucked in a breath. "Zane—"

"We're all set." The photographer stepped into the gazebo and started motioning where Zane should stand. "And Nora, you next to him, but face me."

"Let's change the bouquet," Maddie added. "I think for this simple, romantic look, we need the lavender for a classy feel."

Nora's arm lined up with his and his entire body stirred. Her arm, for pity's sake. She'd been sleeping at his side for days now and they'd done a hell of a lot more than touch arms. But knowing they were out in the open trying to pretend like they were just friends or boss and employee put an entirely different spin on the situation.

Between the photographer and Maddie, multiple orders were given: tilt this way, shift that way, hold the flowers closer to your chin. Basically, Zane stood and stared as the sun crested the horizon in the distance.

"Put your head on his shoulder."

Maddie's direct command had Nora shifting once again. The innocent gesture hit him just as hard as an intimate touch. She trembled and he didn't know if that was from nerves or arousal. Either way, he was here for her.

Between their bodies, Zane slid his hand into hers and gave a gentle squeeze.

"Yes, that's it," Maddie declared. "Holding hands is sweet, endearing, and like a promise all rolled into one. I love it."

The flurry of snaps from the camera and Maddie talking about how these were the best photos yet drowned out any silence.

"I can't believe you didn't pay for that ostrich," he murmured.

Nora snickered. "I tried, but none could get here in time."

He had no doubt she would have truly begged and offered anything to get an ostrich on the set just to get a reaction out of him. But keeping this photo shoot so simple and elegant was exactly the tone Cruz had said he wanted, and Zane had to agree. Still, having Nora pose as the blushing bride made him recall just how gorgeous her glowing skin could be when completely bare.

"What are you wearing under that?" Zane whispered for only Nora to hear.

She laughed, which was the exact response he wanted her to have. He wanted her relaxed and to have fun with this. Even though the whole scenario right now was a bit much, he didn't want her to feel trapped or like their secret was something to be ashamed of. Not the baby, she'd never feel ashamed of their child, but their ongoing affair. Being so close and even touching had to be just as difficult for her as it was for him...maybe more so since she was the one who faced the camera.

"Birthday suit or something lacy?" he murmured.

When she didn't answer, he went another route. "Squeeze once for nothing and twice for lace."

Two squeezes, not that it mattered. Lace or no lace, he'd find her sexy and more than appealing. Would he ever tire of having Nora in his bed? In his life? She added so much to his world he hadn't even known was missing.

He had to be careful. He teetered on a line that he swore he'd never cross, and if he let himself get too vulnerable, she could destroy him. Oh, she wouldn't do so on purpose, and if he got hurt, that would be his own fault for allowing it to happen.

As the photo shoot wrapped up and the sun continued to sink lower, the photographer gathered his things and left. Maddie offered to stay and clean up the dresses and flowers.

"I'm good," Nora told her. "This wasn't difficult to get into. You've put in a great deal of time already. I'll make sure everything gets back to the bridal shop."

Zane approached Maddie. "I'll walk you to your car," he offered. "There are a few things I want to discuss about the project."

Considering he was their boss, he didn't want to seem eager to be in the house as Nora was changing. But he actually did have to discuss some things with Maddie. She didn't need to know that Nora wasn't leaving, that she was temporarily living here. They could keep up the illusion a bit longer, until…

Yeah. Until what? That was the part he still didn't have an answer for.

Fourteen

"This is the room I'd like to have the closet expanded in."

Nora gestured to one of the guest rooms closest to hers in her house. She'd called her contractor to meet to see the progress, get a timeline and have him work on the closet space in the baby's room—though she didn't tell him she was expecting. She wanted to do the designing herself, but she did need the closet much larger to work with her vision.

"Let's see what we have here."

While the contractor took measurements and muttered about a wall being removed, Nora checked her emails on her phone. She had to stay busy. Over the past three days since the photo shoot, she'd done more work than usual. That time with Zane had hit her hard. She'd gotten into her own head, her own fantasy, about how they would live happily-ever-after and raise their little family on his estate.

If she didn't get a grip on reality, she would end up completely shattered.

"It's doable."

Nora shifted her focus to the contractor. "Great. And how soon can I get back in? Realistically?"

He shrugged and slid his tape measure into his pocket. "I'd guess another ten days or so. We haven't run into any issues, but that can always change."

Of course, but ten days seemed like a lifetime and yet so close. She needed to get out of Zane's place. She'd gotten much too comfortable and didn't want to think of his things as her own. But at the same time, she hated to go. She'd never felt more alive, more cherished, than during her time with him.

Would he ever let her in? Truly into his world? He'd opened up about his father and that had been a huge step. She knew that had cost him a great deal of emotional stress, but she had to assume that if he hadn't wanted to tell her, he wouldn't have. They'd shared so much since she'd moved in with him that leaving would be difficult, but would he think so? Would he want her to stay?

"Is that timeline okay?" her contractor asked.

"Oh, yes." She blinked and offered him a smile, realizing she'd gotten lost in her thoughts once again. "Ten days is perfect, and I appreciate you taking on this closet last-minute."

"Not a problem. Get me the paint sample and the lighting fixtures you want and I'll get the room all set for your guests."

Just one guest, and she doubted her baby would care about the paint or the light. Nora still couldn't wait to decorate in there. No matter the sex, she already had ideas for each.

She said goodbye and headed to her car. She had to get back to the office and look over the next set of video clips for their social media campaign launching next month. After that, she had to meet with her immediate team on a few other ideas she'd had for the spring season.

She truly loved her job, and she hoped nothing changed with her status once her truth was revealed to the world. She didn't want any employees thinking she slept with the boss for favors or perks. Thankfully, she'd been with the company for several years and she was always seen with Cruz, not Zane.

Plus, Zane had proclaimed that she was the best at her job and wasn't going anywhere. She hoped that would play out once Cruz discovered the truth. She didn't know if she'd feel freer once the secret was out or if she'd feel trapped in a relationship with her boss and friend who wanted nothing more...while she wanted absolutely everything.

Her day had lasted even longer than she'd intended. All Nora wanted to do was climb the steps, strip out of her clothes, and crawl into bed. She hadn't realized how exhausting it was to grow a human being, but she could have taken a nap at her desk earlier had she not been so swamped with work.

But at least she'd marked several things off her list, and now she had a ten-day timeline for her renovations. She would have to call to get her new furniture delivered, but first she'd wait to make sure her contractor finished on time.

Nora gripped her bag and her keys as she made her

way up to the second story of Zane's house. His car had been in the garage, but she didn't see him downstairs and she hadn't heard anything. Considering that he was a workaholic, which came with the CEO territory, he was likely in his office. Maybe she'd grab a quick shower and change and read or something. She hadn't had a chance to read the book she'd brought, considering that she'd had her evenings occupied.

Not that she was complaining. These nights with Zane had been the best of her life and she wouldn't trade them for anything. Aside from the intimacy, she knew in her heart that something deeper had formed, but could she trust all the emotions swirling around within her?

When she reached the top of the landing, the sound of water running echoed out into the hallway from the room she used to sleep in. Confused, she followed the sound, and as soon as she stepped into the bedroom, she spotted Zane in the adjoining bath, filling the garden tub with bubbles. Candles were lit, and a wineglass filled with juice sat on a tray next to the tub, along with her paperback book.

"Well, this is certainly a welcome sight." She dropped her keys in her bag as she stepped into the bathroom. "Are you taking a bubble bath now?"

"You are," he corrected, shutting off the water. "Perfect timing."

He crossed the spacious bathroom and took her bag as he dropped a kiss on the tip of her nose.

"Where's the real Zane?" she asked. "You've never kissed my nose or run a bubble bath before."

He laughed, returning to her. His hands moved over her skin as he started to undress her. Nora wasn't going to argue that she could do this herself, but she was intrigued as to what he had in mind. Suddenly, she didn't feel so tired anymore.

Strong hands lifted her shirt over her head, then he carefully folded it and placed it on the vanity. He found the zipper on the side of her pencil skirt and eased it down. As soon as she stepped out of it, he folded that piece with care as well and placed it with her top.

"First the tea set and now this?" she asked as he started to remove her bra and panties.

"You've been working so hard and I can tell you're tired."

Nora snorted. "Is that a kinder way of telling me I look haggard? It's because I haven't put on as much makeup lately."

He straightened and took her face between his hands. "You're gorgeous without painting your face. But I can tell you're tired, and I thought you might enjoy just relaxing a bit. I know you like to read or you wouldn't have brought those books. And you can't drink, but I read that orange juice was good for pregnant women."

He took her hand and led her to the tub, but lifted her before she could step in.

She nearly wept as the warm, iridescent bubbles surrounded her. She sank back against the cushy bath pillow and closed her eyes, welcoming the perfect ending to a long, hard day.

"Are you joining me?" she asked, throwing him a glance.

"This is for you," he told her as he took a seat on the stool next to the tub. He held up the book. "Is this one okay?"

"I just bought it, but I love that author."

He glanced at the cover, then read the back before shrugging. "Doesn't sound terrible. Let's get started."

He handed her the juice and then flipped open the cover.

"Wait." She gripped the stem of her glass. "You're reading to me?"

"If you'll relax and just be quiet, I will."

She wasn't sure if she was impressed or still confused, but she wasn't about to ask any more questions. Taking a sip of her juice, she settled back in as Zane's low tone started with chapter one. This was like an audio book mingled with foreplay and very likely shaping up to be the greatest night of her life. He'd put so much thought into her needs and she'd had no idea he'd been planning anything. Here she thought he'd been working in his office.

She'd been dodging him just a bit over these past couple of days, trying to gather her thoughts since the photo shoot. She wasn't sure what answer she was looking for, considering that she didn't fully know the question, but she hadn't come up with anything.

Did she tell Zane her feelings had gotten stronger? Did she lay it all on the line and let him make his own decisions?

Or should she just wait and hope he realized that this could be so much more than temporary? Once their secret came out and Cruz knew the full truth, would Zane feel free to reveal his feelings? He kept everything so close to his chest, but in her own heart, she knew he had to love her on some level. His actions proved that their relationship hinged on much more than friendship and sex. Yes, their baby would always bind them together, but there was more.

Zane paused his reading. "Do women actually look at the size of a man's shoulders?"

Nora shifted her attention back to Zane as she set her juice on the edge of the tub. "Absolutely. And yours are magnificent, by the way."

Zane glanced at the cover again, then back to her. "Better than this guy?" he asked, tapping the image of the male cover model.

"No comparison."

A grin spread across his face. "Good to know."

"Now, keep reading. This is the best gift anyone has ever gotten me."

Zane jerked. "I didn't even buy anything, so I don't think this constitutes a gift."

Nora shifted so she could face him as she rested her arm along the side of the tub. "I don't need anyone to buy me things. I can buy whatever I want. It's the gestures from the heart that mean more than anything."

His brows drew in as he studied her. "You're not like other women I know."

"You're just now figuring that out? We've known each other a long time."

"Maybe so, but I've never spent this much time with you and gotten to know you on this level."

On this level. She wanted to ask what level he was referring to exactly, but she didn't want to ruin the moment with an uncomfortable, yet inevitable, conversation.

"Keep reading," she ordered, settling back against her pillow. "Or join me—the choice is yours."

She closed her eyes once again, waiting for him to decide. The silence in the room seemed to go on forever as she listened for movement or his voice. She wanted him in there with her; there was plenty of room. She wanted to show him just how much she appreciated this night and how he'd thought of everything to make her happy and comfortable.

A man wouldn't go through all of this just for sex. They were already doing that and it wasn't as if he had to beg.

Finally, he shifted. The book fell to the floor with a thunk and the rustling of clothing soon followed. Anticipation and arousal spiraled through her and she opened her eyes to see him stepping into the tub. He sank beneath the bubbles on the other end and extended his legs on either side of her.

Nora smiled and laid her arms along the edge. "I never took you for a bubble bath type of guy."

"I'm doing a great many things I never saw myself doing before you."

She had no doubt he'd done a mental transformation since that night in her office. Neither of them was the same person. They'd started growing together, but would that be enough for something more? She believed so, but Zane still remained so frustratingly cautious.

Maybe now was the time to reveal her feelings. How could Zane make his own conclusions if he didn't have an insight into her true heart? He'd opened himself up to her the other day—now it was her turn.

"I'm pretty sure I'm falling in love with you."

Okay, so she hadn't meant to just blurt that out there, but there wasn't really a great way to ease into that announcement.

And from the silence and Zane's unblinking stare, she had to assume those weren't words he wanted to hear.

"I'm not telling you that to scare you," she added. "I'm sure you'd rather I kept that bit of information to myself, but that wouldn't have been fair to either one of us."

Again, silence. Her heart beat so fast, and she realized she'd chosen the most exposed moment for this reveal. Aside from their obvious state of undress, she'd opened her heart wider than ever before and she knew his still had those cracks from where he'd let her in the other day.

Someone had to bring out the truth so they could move beyond this stalemate and stop dancing around the topic. Now she wished she would have waited until they were wearing clothes, but at least he couldn't just run away.

"I don't know what you want me to say here."

His murmured statement settled between them and she couldn't deny that a tiny piece of her broke. In that perfect dreamlike world, he would have returned the sentiment. But this was reality and she had to accept whatever response he gave. The respect had to go both directions, and she didn't want any man whose emotions she had to pull out.

"I don't want you to say anything if you don't mean it," she informed him. "You need to know where I stand, that's all. I can't lie to you, especially with all we've shared. You deserve the truth."

He continued to stare another moment before easing forward and resting his hands on her raised knees.

"Nora, I can't offer you more."

Pain laced his voice and she knew this cost him. She knew he battled some internal war with himself and had to be torn, especially now that she'd dropped that bold statement.

"I haven't promised anything, for that reason." Those strong hands curled around her knees. "I never want to hurt you and this is exactly what I was afraid would happen."

"I'm not hurt," she countered with a smile. "Love doesn't hurt. I feel fine now that I've told you and now you are free to do what you want. If anything, I feel bad for you for not facing your own feelings, but I can't make that decision for you."

Zane's dark brows drew in. "You're confusing me. You don't want me to tell you I love you in return?"

She wanted nothing more, but she would never beg or force someone into feelings they weren't ready for. She knew what it meant to guard your heart; she'd been doing it for years.

"In a world where everything is perfect, that would happen, but we haven't exactly lived in a fairy tale, have we?" She laughed, but her lame joke didn't go too far, as he still looked just as perplexed. "I didn't mean to ruin this beautiful evening you created for me," she added. "I just couldn't keep that emotion locked away any longer."

He rubbed his hands down her legs and continued to hold her stare. She wanted to know what he was thinking, but his lack of emotions really told her all she needed to know. She just wished he wouldn't be so afraid to take a chance. He'd taken a huge risk years ago when he'd started a business, and each step that propelled him further into success had been risky. Why couldn't he grasp that this moment was no different? They deserved to try, not only for the baby, but also for themselves.

"You didn't ruin anything." He shifted to inch even closer. "The fact you feel that way and you're comfortable enough to let me in is…"

When he shook his head, Nora maneuvered herself onto his lap and wrapped her legs around his waist. She looped her arms around his neck and moved in close, needing him to look her in the eyes.

"Don't say anything else," she whispered. "Let's just enjoy our evening and our time alone."

He looked like he wanted to say something else, but she didn't want him trying to defend his reasoning or saying something only to make her happy. There was no room here for half-emotions or lies. They had enough of that already. All she could do from here on out was be true to herself and how she felt about Zane and their relationship. Everything else would be up to him.

"I don't want you upset," he murmured against her lips as he flattened his palms against her back.

Nora tipped her head up just slightly. "Do I look upset? The father of my child has spoiled me and will do anything to make me happy. Is that love? No, but not saying the words doesn't make you any less caring. We're good, Zane. Promise."

He slid his mouth across hers. Back and forth, enough to drive her completely mad with want.

"You're remarkable. If I could love anyone, Nora, I'd choose you."

A flutter of hope burst through her. She knew Zane teetered on the edge of falling, and all she had to do was make sure she was there to catch him.

Fifteen

Zane had just poured a cup of coffee when Nora padded into the kitchen. She'd piled her hair atop her head and belted her floral robe around her waist. They'd shared a bed last night, but he'd lain awake with her tucked right against his side.

How could he sleep after she'd dropped that proclamation? She loved him? That was never supposed to happen. The oddest thing? He truly believed she was happier after telling him even though he hadn't returned the words.

How did that even work? Love—if that's what she actually felt—had to be the weirdest, most confusing emotion. Why couldn't they just keep on the way they were going? Agreeing to raise their child with the same values, continuing their fling because they enjoyed each other's company, and working together as they had for years?

Was all of that too much to ask?

Now love had entered the mix, and on the coattails of that damn wedding shoot, no less.

The driveway alarm echoed through the house as Nora took a seat at the breakfast table. His stable hands were running a little late this morning, he realized as he glanced at the clock on the wall.

"Do you care to make me some tea?" Nora asked as she rested her head in her folded arms on the table.

Zane crossed the spacious room and slid his hand over her hair, wanting to console her as much as possible. He had no idea what she was dealing with, so all he could do was comfort her the best way he knew how.

"Why don't you go back up to bed?" he suggested.

"I'll be fine." Her words muffled as she remained huddled over the table. "I'm trying to get going earlier, so I thought I'd push myself more today since it's the weekend. Maybe by next week I'll be somewhat back to normal."

He pulled a mug from the cabinet and went to her box of teas on the counter.

"You don't have the flu or a cold. You have morning sickness. Is that something you can just push through?"

"I have no idea," she replied. "But I'm going to try."

He tore open the peppermint pouch and placed the bag into the mug, then glanced back to Nora. She'd sat back up and her eyes were on him now.

"I met with my contractor," she told him. "I'm having him work in one of my guest rooms to get ready for a nursery. So he said the timeline might be just a bit longer. I should be out of here within a couple weeks, though."

He'd known she would leave; that had been the plan all along. But after all they'd shared and after her declaration last night, was that what she honestly wanted to do?

"I didn't think you were in a hurry to go," he replied, resting his hip against the counter.

Nora shrugged and crossed her arms over her chest as she shifted in her chair. She crossed her legs and faced him, and his eyes went to those adorable pink-polished toes. So dainty and so perfect. But she couldn't be perfect...not for him.

"I'm not in a hurry, but it would be nice to get back to my house and start settling into my new normal. We can't keep playing house forever."

Maybe not, but until they knew what they were doing, why couldn't she just stay? He wasn't quite ready to let her go. She'd opened up to him last night, so maybe he should do the same.

"I want you to stay."

Nora blinked up at him as the driveway alarm echoed through the house once again. Damn, he'd have to start cracking down on those employees who lived off-site. They were coming in much too late.

"Why?" she asked.

The kettle whistled, and he grabbed the mug and moved to the stove in the island. He had to be careful with his words, especially after last night. He didn't want to mislead her or give her false hope. He'd been very clear from the start what he could and would offer.

"There's no reason for you to go." He started, but stopped when she let out a snort.

"There's every reason," she corrected. "The fact that we want two very different lifestyles would be the main one. I'm not here just to keep your bed warm, Zane. As much as I love our time together, I deserve more and, frankly, so do you."

He poured the steaming water over the tea bag and then crossed the kitchen to where Nora sat. He placed the mug in front of her, but didn't take a seat. He didn't want to get too relaxed, and he needed to keep the upper hand here.

"I'm just saying that there's no rush for you to go," he went on. "You're clearly still not feeling well and—"

"I'm doing better each morning." She dipped her tea bag and stirred it around the water, all without meeting his gaze. "I'm not asking you, Zane. I'm telling you that I'll be leaving as soon as my house is done."

Now she offered him her unreadable expression and he merely stood above her, not sure what to say next. He didn't want to piss her off or hurt her feelings, and apparently, he was doing both.

"Nora—"

His back door flew open, jerking Zane's attention to the unexpected guest.

"Cruz."

Nora's word came out on a gasp as she came to her feet and clutched her robe.

His twin brother's eyes darted from Nora to Zane, taking in their obvious state of undress.

"What the hell?"

Nora started to take a step, but crumbled. Zane caught her just before she hit the floor.

"Don't move."

Nora blinked up at identical faces, but even in her current state, and with the wave of nausea, she could still tell the difference between these brothers.

. "I'm fine," she assured them. "Just let me get back to my chair."

How embarrassing to be dizzy and move too fast only to fall into a heap.

"I've got you."

Zane lifted her into his arms and started toward the informal living area just off the kitchen.

"This is really silly," she argued in vain. "I can walk. I just moved too fast and got light-headed."

When Zane placed her on the sofa with her legs extended, Nora adjusted the throw pillow behind her and settled in. She really wanted to stand, but her head was still spinning at the fact that Cruz had arrived on scene, unannounced, and clearly confused. She needed to remain still, to get control of her breathing, and deal with everything head-on.

Their time to come clean with him had arrived and she hated that in a matter of moments, their entire relationship would change. As if the morning sickness hadn't made her ill enough, the idea of ruining years of friendships terrified her.

"Are you okay?" Cruz asked, coming to stand beside Zane.

Two sets of worried eyes still held her in place and Nora offered a smile as she nodded.

"I promise, I'm fine. But I would like my tea since my stomach is still a little queasy."

Zane was gone before she finished the sentence and Cruz took a seat on the table before her.

"You look pale," he told her, reaching for her hand. "What else do you need?"

"About two hours and I'm good to go." She laughed

and squeezed his hand. "Stop looking at me like that. I'm not dying—I'm pregnant."

Zane stepped back in with her tea and set it on the table next to Cruz.

"Stay here," Zane told her. "I'm going to talk to Cruz in the other room."

Nora stared for a second before she laughed. "You're joking, right? You think I'm just going to sit here like an obedient dog? Nice try."

Cruz glanced up to his brother. "You both can tell me what the hell is going on, because I doubt Nora came to visit this early in the morning wearing only a robe."

"I've been living here," Nora offered. "My house is being renovated, plus with morning sickness, and—"

"I asked her to move in."

"Why the hell would you do that?" Cruz demanded.

The brothers stared at each other a moment too long and the comfort level in the room plummeted.

"Is that because you're the father of her baby?" Cruz demanded.

The intense silence seemed to wrap them all in an uncomfortable blanket. Nora waited for one of the guys to speak. When the yawning quiet became too much, she swung her legs over the sofa and stood. She braced one hand on each of their shoulders, if for her support or to keep them from ripping each other apart, she didn't know.

"Cruz, we wanted to tell you," she started, her eyes on him. But he wasn't looking at her, only Zane.

"I told her to wait," Zane added. "I didn't want you to find out over the phone or when you were away on business."

The muscle in Cruz's jaw clenched and Nora was

worried he'd haul off and punch his brother, but Cruz typically wasn't one to jump to anger or violence. He took a step back, then another, and his dark stare went from Zane to Nora.

"How long did you all sneak around before this?" he asked, his fists clenched at his sides. "Were you laughing behind my back or just didn't want to clue me in until you absolutely had to?"

"That's not how things went at all," Nora explained.

Zane held up his hand to stop her. "We weren't sneaking and we weren't laughing at you. Nothing happened between us until after you were gone, and it sure as hell wasn't planned."

Cruz stared between them for another moment before raking his hand over his jaw and letting out a bark of laughter. Nora had no idea what could possibly be funny right now, but she also had a hunch he wasn't feeling too humorous. There seemed to be a thread of sarcasm and frustration in that chuckle.

"This is not at all how I had this planned," he finally told them. "I never thought you two would work backward."

Confused, Nora glanced to Zane, whose attention still remained on his brother.

"What the hell are you talking about?" Zane demanded.

Nora reached for her mug, desperately needing the peppermint flavor. At this point, her tea had gone cold, but she didn't care. She welcomed anything that would help soothe the queasiness.

"I've wanted you two together for years," Cruz admitted. "You both danced around each other for so damn long, I took matters into my own hands. Clearly, you guys took off on your own before my plan fell into place."

"What plan?" Zane ground out.

Nora didn't know what the hell he was talking about and she had a sinking feeling this entire situation was about to get worse before it got better. Clearly, she and Zane weren't the only ones who had been keeping secrets. She didn't know why this irked the hell out of her, maybe it was the hormone overload, but she felt her blood pressure rising.

"The wedding shoot," Cruz confessed with a slight grin. "You two think you were hiding your emotions, but I know both of you better than you know yourselves. I figured if I could get Nora into a wedding gown and you overseeing the project in my absence, something might click."

"I don't want a marriage." Zane muttered a curse beneath his breath. "You know that."

Cruz shrugged. "You say you don't, but I also have seen how you look at Nora and how she looks at you."

What had she given away? More importantly, how had Cruz seen something from Zane when she never had?

"So you just thought you'd play matchmaker?" Zane said accusingly. "That's ridiculous."

"No, what's ridiculous is the two of you sneaking around."

"You're the one—"

"Stop!" Nora shouted. "Just stop arguing."

She set her tea back down, held out her hands, and glanced from one brother to the other. There were too many things going on at once, but if she had to find a bright side, at least the bomb from Cruz had taken her mind off her morning sickness.

"We all made mistakes," she started. "I think we're all sorry things happened the way they did, but none of us are trying to be hurtful. Right?"

The guys didn't say a word, so she took that as a yes. They continued to size each other up like fighting dogs, but she knew that anger wouldn't last. They had each other's backs and had been through it all.

"I have to say, I'm surprised you put so much thought into how to push us together," Nora admitted. "But I won't be manipulated into anything. Not a marriage, and not playing house and sharing a bed with a man who doesn't want me."

The more she thought about this entire scenario, the angrier she became. She faced Cruz fully and poked a finger at his chest. "Your plan didn't work. Your brother has no intention of ever marrying, not even to the woman who carries his child, and don't try to push me into a relationship again. I'm good."

Cruz opened his mouth to respond, but Nora turned and faced Zane. "And as for staying here until my renovations are over, I'm fine to return home. I've decided it's best to get back to my world and we can figure out this parenting thing without the sex coming into play."

"Nora, you're upset and not being logical."

"Oh, I'm definitely upset," she agreed. "I'd say we're all upset, but the longer I stay here, the more I'll want what you aren't willing to give. We both have demanding jobs and now a baby to concentrate on. That's more than enough."

When she started to turn away, Cruz slid his hand

around her elbow. Nora glanced over her shoulder and met his dark stare.

"Zane is right," Cruz told her. "You should stay here until that work is done. Or if you don't want to stay here, then come to my place."

Nora eased from his grasp. "I think we all need our individual space right now, and my home is livable. It's just a mess. I'll make it work."

His lips thinned and there wasn't a doubt in her mind he wanted to argue. Nora turned back around and Zane had the same pained look on his face as well.

Too bad. They'd all made mistakes. Each one of them had every reason to be angry, but she wasn't kidding when she'd said they need to take time apart. There was too much hurt between them, and that's not the relationship she wanted with either guy. Despite being upset, she valued both of them and needed them in her life.

"I'm going to go pack my things."

As she started from the room, she wondered which brother would try to follow her and get her to stay. Nothing but silence followed her, and a piece of Nora crumbled. Maybe they had each damaged these relationships beyond repair, and maybe they would never get back to where they were before.

While she loved them both in totally different ways, she still had to look out for herself and her baby. Everything else had to fall in line behind them.

Sixteen

"Care to tell me what the hell is going on with the two of you?"

Zane crossed his ankle over his knee and stared across the living area to Barrett. Reluctantly, Zane and Cruz had come for that meeting Barrett had requested. They'd been there all of ten minutes and Zane was beyond ready to leave.

Nora had left his house four days ago and it might as well have been four months. The days seemed to drag and the damn house was too quiet. Even when he'd gone into the office, he'd pass by her door, which remained closed, and could practically feel the wedge between them.

Same with Cruz. He'd hardly spoken to his brother, yet here they sat in Barrett's modest cottage on the edge of town.

"I understand you don't want to be here," Barrett told Zane, then he glanced at Cruz. "But what is up with you?"

"We're working through some things," Cruz admitted.

Barrett's narrowed eyes volleyed between Zane and his twin. Never before could Zane recall a time when he and his brother were at odds for this long. Oh, they bickered like any other set of siblings, but they never went days without talking. Not only could that destroy their personal relationship, but it could do heavy damage to *Opulence*.

"Tell me."

Zane shook his head. "We'll take care of it on our own time."

Barrett stood before them, propped his hands on his hips, and scoffed. "I might not have been around when you both needed me, but I'm here now. Let me help."

Zane didn't want his help. He didn't want to be here as well, but he couldn't stand to sit at his house in the silence, either. He'd gone with the lesser of the two evils.

"I'm not sure what you could do," Cruz stated, leaning forward on the sofa. "Zane and I both screwed up and managed to damage our relationship in addition to our relationships with Nora."

Barrett's thick brows drew in as he shook his head. "What does Nora have to do with this? Is there some love triangle or something?"

"No, hell no." Cruz raked his hands over his head and sighed. "I tried to fix them up because I thought they were perfect together, but—"

"Cruz."

Zane's sharp word cut off his brother's confession.

Why the hell did they need to clue Barrett in on their business? They could keep everything private and work it out later.

"Let him finish," Barrett stated.

Zane glanced at his brother and Cruz simply shook his head.

"It's Zane's story to tell," he finally conceded. "I made a mistake, he made a mistake, and we've pissed each other off. That's all."

"And Nora is in the middle?"

Barrett took a seat in his recliner and eased back to start rocking. He tapped his hand on the arm as if contemplating his next thought or words.

"You're going to find out at some point," Zane found himself saying. "Nora is pregnant."

The chair stopped and Barrett's brows shot up toward his hairline. "So which one of you is the father?"

"Damn it, not me," Cruz exclaimed. "I've said we're just friends."

"There's a fine line between friends and something more," Barrett explained. "I started out as friends with your mother and then you two came along."

Zane didn't say a word. What could he say? Letting his feelings fester seemed like the next logical step, right? He hadn't had a great relationship with his father in years, he and his brother were pissed at each other for justifiable reasons, and he had no clue where he stood with Nora. She'd moved out, but where did that leave them? Were they back to employee/boss and the friend zone? Just co-parenting? At some point, they would have to talk, but right now, Zane had to work on the relationships right here in this room.

"We need a drink." Barrett rocked upward and came

to his feet. "No alcohol here, but how about some sweet tea or a soda?"

Zane shook his head no and Cruz asked for tea.

Barrett went to the small attached kitchen. Zane stared across the open space at his father and really studied the man as he busied himself playing the host.

His weathered hands, the creases around his eyes, the once-black hair now dotted with white. The years hadn't been kind to Barrett, but he hadn't lived the easiest life. All of his failures and setbacks had been brought on by his own actions. Instead of pulling himself up for his kids after his wife passed, he'd opted to be miserable and selfish, losing himself in the bottle and the world of gambling.

A sizable dose of guilt settled heavily in Zane's chest. Maybe he wasn't so far removed from being exactly like his father. No, Zane didn't have a spouse who had passed, but he'd had an amazing woman walk out of his life…and he'd just let her.

Even though Zane wasn't about to lose himself, there was that part of him that had a better understanding of how someone could self-destruct when their world fell apart. On the other hand, Zane couldn't imagine not being there for his child. He couldn't imagine just letting life pass him by.

Barrett came back and gave Cruz the tea, but he remained on his feet as he stared down at his sons.

"I'm sure neither of you want my advice, but I'm giving it anyway," he started. "I've learned my lesson that life is short and you have to find and create your own happiness. Waiting on someone else to turn your world around will never work. If you have any type of relationship with someone you care about, you'll put in the work to keep it, no matter the cost. I didn't put in the work with the two most important people in my life and I'm still paying for it."

Zane glanced at his twin, who was already looking back at him. They'd both messed up and had hurt each other, but they had a bond like no other.

"I really asked you guys to come here today just so I could see you," Barrett went on. "I didn't know you all had any turmoil going on, and I didn't know I was going to be a grandfather."

Zane jerked his attention back to Barrett.

"I mean, if you will allow that," he quickly added. "I know we're not on good terms, but the fact that you're here tells me you are willing to try to work on us."

Barrett stared for another minute, clutching his own tea and likely waiting on Zane to reply. The room settled in silence as Zane thought over the nugget of information he hadn't yet considered. Not once had he thought of Barrett as being a grandparent. But the look in the old man's eyes held something Zane hadn't seen in so long. Hope.

Maybe the baby he and Nora were expecting could tie them all together. Maybe this would be another layer of healing for all of them.

"I'll talk to Nora," Zane finally stated. "I can't make promises, but I'm not saying no."

Barrett's wide shoulders relaxed and a hint of a smile danced around his lips. "That's all I can ask for."

He took a seat back in his chair and set his tea on an old, worn coaster. "Now, what about the two of you?" he asked, gesturing a finger between them. "Can this be repaired?"

"Of course," Zane replied without thinking. "I'll admit I was wrong and he will, too."

"Will I?"

Zane glanced at his brother, who had a smirk on his face. "You know I hate being wrong," Cruz stated.

"Yeah, well, apologize and move on."

"I'm not apologizing."

Zane sighed. "Me, either."

"Perfect. We're even." Cruz gave a mock cheers gesture with his glass of tea and smiled. "All is right."

Zane knew it would be—at least between him and his twin. As for the relationship with Barrett, Zane had a kernel of faith that things were headed in the right direction. This relationship couldn't be patched up in one day or even one week, but one step at a time would add up. Maybe by the time Nora delivered, he and Barrett would be in a good place.

He just didn't know what place he and Nora would be in, and that entire situation lay directly on his shoulders.

For the past two weeks, Nora had lived through construction, and finally, the crew had left. Her home was all hers now, freshly painted and beautiful. Each room had some type of touch-up or complete overhaul. The deck out back added another level of living space she couldn't wait to enjoy this summer.

She stood in the empty nursery and envisioned a crib and a rocker, a changing table and white shelves full of cardboard books.

Maybe she was still early in her pregnancy, but she wanted everything done and ready for when her baby arrived. Well, the room would be ready—she wasn't so sure about her relationship with Zane.

She hadn't spoken to him or Cruz since she left his house. At some point, she'd reach out, but she was still struggling with all the deceit that had surrounded them.

Her doorbell chimed through her house and Nora stilled. She only knew two people who would show up unannounced. Pulling in a deep breath, she headed down the hall toward her entryway. She glanced down at her clothes and figured her appearance didn't matter. She'd come home from work and put on the most comfortable thing she owned: her old hoodie from college and a pair of leggings.

Nora reached the door and stood on her tiptoes to see out the top window. Then she flicked the lock and opened the door to her uninvited guest.

"Why are you ringing the doorbell?" she asked. "You've never done that since we've known each other."

Cruz slid his hands into the pockets of his jeans and shrugged. "I wasn't sure if you'd care that I used my key, and I wasn't taking any chances that I'd actually be welcome."

He offered her that sheepish grin she'd seen so many times from him....the same grin Zane had worn when he'd given her that box with teas and a new mug.

"Of course you're welcome." She stepped aside for him to enter. "You're my first visitor since the reno project. The crew actually finished up this morning."

Cruz glanced around and made his way through the living area and kitchen. As he passed the new wall of glass doors leading to the new patio, he did a double take.

"This looks awesome, Nora."

Flipping the switch by the door, he turned the exterior lights on, then opened the sliding doors until the entire wall vanished. The crew had put in a sunken firepit with seating all around. A swaying swing hung suspended from the porch's rafters, and a table long enough to feed a small army ran the length of the space. All money well spent.

"They did a remarkable job," he stated again, then turned to face her as she stepped out to join him. "But I didn't come to discuss your renovations."

Nora fisted her hands inside her hoodie. "No, I'm sure you didn't. Why don't you take a seat?"

Cruz went to the swing and sat, then patted the seat beside him for her to join. Nora couldn't deny him. He'd been her very best friend for far too long. Besides, she'd kept a secret from him, so they were on an even field. But she still wasn't happy about being duped.

"Are you feeling okay?" he asked as he eased the swing into a gentle motion.

"I'm good. Glad to be back home."

"Are you really?"

Nora's stomach was tied in knots, and she couldn't lie. There had been more than enough of that going around.

"Honestly, no. I'm not." She shifted until her back was against the cushioned arm of the swing and her legs were stretched out on his lap. "Your brother is infuriating."

Cruz laughed as he rested his hands on her legs. "He can be."

Nora tried to find the right way to explain her frustrations, but first, she had to clear the air.

"I'm sorry we didn't tell you about us," she began. "Well, not that there's an *us*, but you know what I mean. We just didn't think we should say anything while you were gone and we were trying to be private about everything."

Cruz tipped his head her way. "You think you and my brother aren't one unit? I assure you, you are."

"I wouldn't be back home if we were."

Alone in her bed, alone in her thoughts. She didn't realize how much she'd gotten used to a warm body by her side and someone to fall asleep chatting with each night. How could she have gotten so accustomed to the man after such a short time?

"He's confused," Cruz explained. "Probably afraid to admit how he really feels."

"I'm not sure if he's afraid or if he just doesn't feel." That was the hardest part to try to understand and likely accept. "There's a good chance he got what he wanted from me and he's just done."

"Don't say that," Cruz scolded. "You know Zane doesn't use anyone, let alone women."

She rested her head against the back of the swing and knew the truth in her heart.

"He never has before, that I'm aware of." She toyed with the frayed end of one of the strings from her hood. "But what else am I supposed to think? Aside from having a child together, we really connected on a deeper level. I thought he had stronger feelings for me. Clearly, I was foolish for putting myself in this position."

Cruz eased toward her, his hand resting on her knee. The glow from the new exterior lights gave her a perfect view of the compassion staring back at her.

"I don't want your pity," she scolded. "Can we pretend Zane isn't your brother and you're just my friend giving me advice like always?"

He gave her knee a gentle squeeze. "We can pretend anything you want, but the truth is that right now Zane is torn between what he wants and what he thinks he wants."

"That doesn't make sense," she retorted.

"He wants you—that much is obvious. But he's programmed himself to think that he doesn't need anyone."

"I'm positive he doesn't need me or he would've fought for me to stay."

"We were at our dad's house the other night," Cruz informed her, then blew out a heavy breath. "I didn't know what would happen, but I'm pretty sure Dad and Zane are on a path to something better."

Nora dropped her string and rested her hand on Cruz's. "That's great for all of you. What happened to make Zane go there and turn a new leaf?"

"You."

Surprised, Nora jerked slightly. "Me? I didn't do anything other than listen to him talk about your childhood. I gave him some advice, but you know how stubborn he is."

"This baby and your love have changed him," Cruz insisted. "He's not the same man he was when I left."

Nora snorted. "He doesn't love me. Trust me on that one."

"What makes you say that? Because he seems pretty damn protective of you. He's never had a woman live with him before."

"I wasn't living there." Nora pulled her hand away and snuggled it back into the pouch of her hoodie. "My house was torn up and I had morning sickness."

"Is that why you were in only a robe and he was in a pair of shorts when I came by the other day? Because that wasn't just Zane being kind."

Okay, so they had been much more than temporary roommates.

"Regardless, he's made it clear from the start that we aren't going to be more than what we are now. He refuses to open up and let love in."

"Why are you giving him the option?" Cruz demanded. "The Nora I know takes charge of what she wants."

"I told him how I feel. The information is his to do what he wants with it." Her heart still hurt, because that confession had been two weeks ago. "His silence speaks volumes."

"What did he say when he saw you in those wedding dresses?"

Nora popped her head up and narrowed her eyes. "That was pretty damn sneaky of you."

A wide smile spread across his face. The man had no remorse about his little stunt.

"You're not even sorry, are you?"

"Not at all," he admitted. "I bet Zane had no clue what to say when you came out. And I refuse to have regrets, because I saw a couple of the rough shots and I don't know how anyone could edit those to make you look better. You were stunning, Nora. I knew you would be, so there was a method to my madness."

"Oh, you were mad all right. I'm not a model, Cruz, but you all had your fun. I'm retiring."

He chuckled and patted her as he started the swing in motion once again.

"You're a model—you just don't want to be," he retorted. "Sort of like Zane being in love with you when he just doesn't want to be. You're both afraid. But I'm an outsider looking in and I'm telling you that you two are perfect together."

Yeah, well, Zane wasn't having any part of that, so Cruz would just have to meddle in someone else's life.

"Let's forget about me for a bit," Nora suggested. "How did the model search go?"

Cruz groaned and rubbed his forehead.

"That good, huh?"

"Oh, it went fine, but Mila is going to be a handful." Her mind raced through the prospects he'd gone to meet with.

"Mila," Nora murmured. "Oh, is she the one from the Dominican Republic?"

"No. She's from Miami, and I don't know if her attitude or her hair is bigger. She'll be here next month for a trial shoot. We'll see if her ego and mine can get along."

Nora couldn't help but laugh, because Cruz could get along with anyone, so she wondered how this Mila would work out.

She reached out and slid her hand over his arm. "I missed you."

"Yeah, I missed you, too. Now, do you want my help with Zane?"

"Oh, no. You've done enough, and he knows where I stand. The rest is up to him."

Cruz simply stared at her and she could see his wheels in motion. But anything beyond this point was up to Zane. She wasn't begging and she wasn't about to let Cruz play mediator.

Part of her hoped her best friend was right. She hoped Zane did love her and would have enough courage to admit it.

But it was his other words that really hit her hard. She did always go after what she wanted and never let fear stand in her way. So now she had a choice to make.

Wait and see. Or take action.

Seventeen

"Sir. A delivery."

Zane glanced up from his phone, where he'd pulled up Nora's number for at least the twentieth time over the past few days. He didn't know what to say and knew a text wasn't the way to go, but he hated staying silent.

Yet without the proper words, that's exactly what he'd done.

"Just bring it in and set it over there." Zane motioned for his assistant, Will, to put the package on the table near the door. "I'll get to it later."

He typed out the one thing he needed her to know, but didn't hit Send. How could he deliver this over a text message? That wouldn't do at all. He had to see her. He had to fight for what he wanted, no matter the risk or the chances of getting hurt.

"It's rather large," Will added, still in the doorway.

Confused, Zane slid his phone aside and stood. He shouldn't have an order, but that didn't mean anything. Being the CEOs, both he and Cruz would get special deliveries on occasion, often from social media gurus who wanted to capture their attention.

Intrigued, he crossed the office just as his assistant wheeled in a giant image. The canvas stood taller than him and had to be six feet wide. The purple cloth draped over the entire image shielded what it could be.

"I can take it from here, Will. Thank you."

Nora breezed around from the other side of the over-size delivery. She braced her hands on the edge and wheeled it out of the way before offering Will a smile. The young man's brows drew in as he tried to see what was going on, but Nora closed the door before turning to face Zane.

His breath caught in his throat. She looked too damn good, and he hadn't seen her for weeks. Every part of him had wanted to tell her to come back, but what then? What if she came back and he couldn't be the man she wanted...the man she deserved?

She'd put on another one of her fitted, yet classy, dresses, this one in a bold red. Her hair lay as smooth as silk over one shoulder, and she wore a simple pair of nude heels. The woman looked every bit the part of a business exec, but he wanted to know what she wore beneath that dress and if there was any chance in hell he'd ever find out.

"You look good." The words came out before he could think, but he wasn't sorry. "Are you feeling better in the mornings?"

"I'm perfectly fine."

She didn't even look his way as she gave the cloth a yank and revealed the image.

Zane blinked, unable to believe what he was seeing.

"You seemed to love these shots so much, so I chose my favorite for you to keep in here," she explained, as if going over some business plan. "I know I balked at modeling for this, but you were right. I do look great, and we look perfect together."

His eyes ran over the blown-up photo. The pose with her head resting on his shoulder as she smiled sweetly for the camera...

Zane remained still as his throat filled with emotions. He remembered that exact moment with her, but he hadn't seen this shot and hadn't seen the expression on her face...until now.

"You were right about something else, too," she went on.

Now he turned his attention to her as she took a step toward him. Zane remained by his desk, unable to move or even think. He had to concentrate on her words and how perfect she looked in person and in that photo, which seemed to be mocking him.

"I do deserve better than what you were giving me."

Her words penetrated that hazy fog in his mind. He knew she'd come to this conclusion, but he didn't know how he'd feel about it. Right now, a good bit of fear held him captive, but not fear of his emotions. No. This fear stemmed from losing her.

"I deserve someone who will put me first," she went on, ticking off her fingers. "Put our relationship first. I need someone who will take me and my child, because we are a package deal."

Rage bubbled in him. Like hell would any man raise

his child or sleep next to his woman. He refused to believe he was too late. He wouldn't let Nora slip out of his life simply because he'd been too damn afraid to face what was right in front of him.

She had to know the truth. The time had come for him to face his emotions and say them out loud. If he'd learned nothing else from her, he'd learned to be bold and take chances.

"Nora—"

Her sharp gaze cut to him. "I'm not done."

Growing more and more frustrated, Zane crossed his arms and widened his stance as he waited for her to finish. He had a few words to say himself.

"If we're going to co-parent, you're going to have to accept whoever I bring into my life, because you had your chance and—"

In a flash, Zane snaked his arms around her waist. He caught Nora's gasp with his mouth as he kissed her to shut up the nonsense she'd been spewing.

Her body melted against his as she clutched his shoulders. Finally, he had her back in his arms, where she belonged. She opened her mouth beneath his, sweeping her tongue with as much passion as always.

Zane settled his hands on her waist and eased back just enough to catch his breath.

"Did my plan work?" she asked.

"Plan?"

Nora pushed back and that wide smile on her face hit him right in the gut. She was so damn beautiful and everything he thought he didn't need. How could he have been so foolish to ever think he could live without her?

"You think I was just going to let you walk away and

live in misery?" she asked. "I know you're scared of love, but ignoring it won't make it go away."

Zane slid his hands to her back and tugged her again to where he wanted her against his chest. "No kidding. I've been miserable and my house is too damn quiet. Everywhere I look, I see empty walls and find myself wondering what color you'd paint them or where you would put all of those pictures you love. I need you there or we can build somewhere else or, hell, move into your place. I don't care, but I'm not spending another night without you."

Nora's eyes closed as she released a breath. "I'm so glad you said that, because I contacted a Realtor this morning to put my house up for sale."

"What?"

She blinked and refocused on him. "We're raising our family in your house and we're having family get-togethers, and we're going to let your father into our lives and give him that chance he deserves. I want it all and I want it with you. I'd even let you paint our bedroom white."

Zane kissed her once again as his heart swelled with all the emotions. His future, *their* future as a family, seemed to have endless possibilities.

"I'm not taking no for an answer on any of this, by the way," she added.

"I wouldn't dream of telling you no." He glanced toward the intrusive canvas. "Where is that really going? Or do I even want to know?"

She laughed and patted his cheek. "In our house."

Our house. Damn, but he did love the sound of that.

"You know, I was going to come to you," he admitted. "I couldn't find the right words to say."

She quirked one perfectly arched brow. "Is that right?"

Zane released her and went to grab his cell from his desk. The screen was still pulled up from the text he'd never sent. He handed the device over and watched for her expression.

"That's all the words I had."

Her eyes filled as she glanced from the phone up to him.

"I couldn't send it, because that's something that needs to be said in person," he went on.

Zane took the cell from her hands and slid it into his pocket before reaching for her once again. He curled one hand around her waist and cupped her cheek with the other. With the pad of his thumb, he swiped away the single tear that had trickled down.

"I do love you," he confessed. "I didn't realize how freeing that would be to admit, but nothing has ever felt more perfect or right."

She sniffed and let out a watery laugh, throwing her arms around his neck.

"I love you, and I've been waiting on you to say those words to me. I can't believe this is happening." She tipped her head back and dropped kisses all over his face. "I can't wait to tell Cruz."

"Oh, hell," Zane groaned. "He'll think his plan worked and he played matchmaker."

Nora held his face in her hands. "Let him think what he wants. I don't care how we got together, we are now and that's all that matters. But there's one more thing."

"What's that?" he asked.

"Can we get a dog? I'm really missing Clara, and you have the perfect yard for one to run free and—"

He cut her off with a kiss. Spinning her around so he could reach behind her and lock his office door. When he released her, she had a wide smile across her face.

"We can get any dog you want, but I am drawing the line at that ostrich," he told her.

Nora rolled her eyes. "Fine, but if one shows up at our wedding reception, just go with it."

Go with it. He had a feeling that would be the motto for their marriage and he couldn't wait to make it official.

* * * * *

ONE NIGHT WAGER

KATHERINE GARBERA

This book is dedicated to my good friend Joss Wood,
a wonderful writer and also a good person,
who's always there when I need her.

One

Conrad Gilbert didn't look like any beast she'd seen or envisioned. He had the sleeves of his chef's white jacket rolled up to reveal muscly forearms covered in a tattoo that, when the camera zoomed in, seemed to be thorny vines. His hands moved with speed and precision. When he looked up to speak to the viewer, Indy Belmont shivered with sensual awareness which warned her it had been too long since she'd gone out on a date or had a hookup. She wasn't listening to a single word that came out of that perfectly formed masculine mouth.

She wanted to kiss him. She wanted to feel those big arms wrapped around her, with him saying her name in that deep timbre of his that reminded her of long, hot summer nights.

"So what do you think?" Lilith Montgomery, the head of the Main Street Business Alliance and the woman in charge of this endeavor, asked as she hit Pause on the video screen. Leaving Conrad's face zoomed in, looking intently out at Indy.

"Huh?" Indy asked, realizing her father would roll his eyes at the comment. She'd come to Gilbert Corners at the town council's invitation. Her show *Hometown, Home Again* had taken off over the last season and now that Lansdowne was revitalized, her producers had been looking for another town in need of her skills. "Sorry. He's very intense."

"He is. Even as a youth he was. So can you get him to come to town and break the curse?" Jeff Hamilton asked.

Indy smiled and nodded with confidence. They were on the same network, so getting Conrad to come to Gilbert Corners should be easy. Her best friend was from Gilbert Corners and had bought and opened a coffee shop here, and Indy herself wasn't too bad in the kitchen.

"I can get him here. What's this about a curse?"

Lilith shook her head. "It's just sad. Gilbert International closed their main factory, and the very next weekend the three Gilbert heirs were in a horrific car crash."

"One boy-Declan Owen-was left dead and two of the heirs near death. After that the town started drying up."

"When was this?" Indy asked not sure she believed in the curse.

"Ten years ago."

About the time that inflation, combined with the economic downturn, made it hard for small businesses to stay afloat in small towns like this—where college kids went away and didn't come back. She suspected that had more to do with vacant shops on Main Street than a curse. But a curse would make good TV.

"I'd say that curse has run long enough. I can do it,"

she said. Though she had no specific plan. She'd learned that the only way to make things happen was to believe she could do them. "Are we sure getting him to come and do a cook-off in the town is what we need?"

She'd moved to the town of Gilbert Corners eighteen months ago when she'd purchased a failing bookshop and a fixer-upper Victorian house off the main town square. She had done something similar in her hometown after college. She'd started as a YouTuber with a small following, trying desperately to fix up the house she'd inherited as a way to find some peace with the woman she had become. Viewers had responded and she'd ended up with a massive following when the offer to do her own television show on the Home Living channel had come in. That was two years ago, and once she'd gotten the business thriving and the town back on the path to its former glory, she'd needed a new project. Especially since her partner—and the man she'd been crushing on forever—had fallen in love with someone else and married her.

Renovating the Main Street, breaking a curse and getting over her past seemed like a big ask and she knew she had her work cut out for her.

Gilbert Corners was close enough to Boston that it should be a booming commuting suburb but instead it had definitely seen better days.

"It's a start," Lilith said. "Do you think you can do it?"

Indy, who had been called obstinate and been told that she never gave up, wasn't worried about that. "No problem."

She left town hall and walked back across the park where weeds had choked out the once beautiful flower beds. Graffiti covered the base of the statue that honored the four founding fathers of Gilbert Corners who'd helped during the American Revolution. She entered her bookshop, Indy's Treasures, and waved at Kym, the high school student who helped out in the afternoons, as she entered her office at the back.

Conrad Gilbert, celebrity chef known as the Beast. She pulled up his online profile.

He had thick dark curly hair that framed his face. His brows were thick and his eyes were an icy blue. He had a long jagged scar down his left cheek ending at the top of his lip. He wore a chef's jacket but above the collar she saw ink from a tattoo that went around his neck. His arms were crossed over his chest.

Who dares challenge the Beast in his lair?

The words were emblazoned under his crossed arms. She read further and saw that he accepted cooking challenges from across North America to be televised on his show. There was a place to enter information to challenge him. He'd come to the town of the challenger and they would go head-to-head making a famous local or regional dish.

"Yes!"

"Yes, what? I heard you agreed to get the Beast to come to town."

She glanced up as Nola Weston, her best friend and the reason she had come to Gilbert Corners, walked into her office. When Indy had been starting out on YouTube, Nola, her former college roommate and self-taught woodworker, had joined her team. Nola set her mug of coffee on the desk, leaning against it.

"I did. I mean, he's not *really* a beast, and I think it would be good to have a Gilbert to return to town."

"Why didn't you go for Dash? He visits all the time to see his sister at the sanatorium."

"Conrad has a TV show which will get us some national exposure, plus Lilith thought he'd be the easier of the two."

"The Beast, easier? They play it up on TV, but he's a very arrogant and kind of just does what he wants. I'm not sure he'll help you."

"Oh, he'll say yes," Indy said. Nola was skeptical, but Indy was confident. *The Beast's Lair* was a competition show where he accepted the challenges of amateur chefs and if they beat him they were awarded a $350,000 prize. That money would go a long way toward fixing up Gilbert Corners.

She filled in the application and used her grandmother's Low Country Boil recipe, something which she had made a few times on her show for the crew and had gotten rave reviews.

Two days later she heard back from her contact at the network that her application for Gilbert Corners to be featured on *The Beast's Lair* had been accepted.

After closing her email, Indy sat back in the leather chair that had been her grandfather's and started making plans. *Real plans.* They'd need to clean up the park and get the graffiti off the statue, but she was excited… which she told herself had nothing to do with meeting the Beast in person.

"No."

Conrad Gilbert didn't suffer fools or repeat himself. He put down the bottle of garlic-infused olive oil he'd been holding and turned to look at Ophelia Burnetti who was the executive producer on his food television show.

"You can't say no. I've already told them you're coming."

"Well you can tell them I'm not." Conard Gilbert didn't even bother looking up from his bench as he worked on the delicate design for the plating of his latest dish. His new assistant was going to be fired. He hated being disturbed when he was in his test kitchen, and everyone knew it.

"Con, this is happening. Gilbert Corners is close by and we need to fill the vacancy left by the unusable video we shot at the Kentucky Derby."

"It's not unusable."

"The other chef had a meltdown and threw a bottle of bourbon at you. It would ruin him. This place is close, and they want you to film in less than three weeks. It's ideal."

He straightened to his full six foot five inches, giving her a withering stare. She looked back at him nonplussed.

Fuck.

He'd vowed to never return to Gilbert Corners except to visit his cousin Rory. And he didn't want to break that vow now. He hated that place.

"If I go, I'll arrive as the cooking starts and then leave as soon as we are done filming."

"Fine. I only need forty minutes of airable footage. So do that and you're out."

Ophelia left a few minutes later after telling him she'd send the details to his assistant. Conrad followed her out into the main office area where his assistant sat doing something on her cell phone.

"Send it to me," Conrad said to Ophelia, turning to his assistant. "You're fired."

He walked back into the test kitchen, but his mind

was no longer on the dish he'd been creating. It was on fucking Gilbert Corners. He had no happy memories of the town that bore his family's name. His grandfather had been a cold, demanding guardian who'd raised Conrad and his cousins after their parents were killed in an airplane crash as they'd been returning from a ski trip. Conrad had been ten.

He'd never felt like Gilbert Manor was home. He had missed his actual home—the brownstone that had been in his mother's family, where he'd lived with his parents. He'd been loved and treated like their little prince and their deaths had left him empty. His grandfather had taken one look at Conrad and his two cousins when they'd shown up on his doorstep and immediately arranged for them to be sent off to boarding schools. He and Dash, who was like a brother to him, had been sent to the same one.

He reached for his phone and called Dash.

"Gilbert here."

"Gilbert here," he responded.

"Con, how's it going?" Dash asked.

"I have to go to GC."

"You have to? I thought no one dared tell you what to do."

"Me too. But Ophelia isn't scared of me, and we need an episode to fill a programming gap. Why would anyone invite me to town?" Conrad asked.

"You got me. They all think we're bad luck."

"Exactly. Well, I'm going to crush the challenger and then get out of GC. Want to join me?"

"Hell no. I visit Gilbert Corners' care home once a week and that's enough for me."

"How's Rory?" he asked.

Conrad rubbed his face. His scar was a constant reminder of the past but he'd learned to live with it. So much of who he'd been had been lost on that night. But the truth was, he was luckier than Dash and Rory, and he knew it.

He'd often thought that the crash had just brought his true self to the surface. His grandfather had wanted to have a plastic surgeon fix the scar but Conrad had refused. He was tired of playing the old man's game. The scar had reshaped him. And he had no regrets.

"She's the same. Her doctor is retiring. I need to be in GC to talk to the new doctor taking over. When are you going?"

"I'll send the date when I have it," he said. They hung up and he turned back to the bench where he'd been working earlier.

He wanted to smash something at the thought of having to return to Gilbert Corners. It didn't matter that his grandfather had died almost eight years ago; he would always associate that town with the old man.

Ophelia forwarded him the information on his challenger, Rosalinda Belmont. He looked her up and saw that she had recently moved to town and had her own television show *Hometown, Home Again* on the same network his show was on.

He clicked on the promo video of her new program in Gilbert Corners. She had dark hair and a heart-shaped face. She wore glasses in her photo and had a book in her hands. She walked through the bookshop on Main Street in front of a sign that read Indy's Treasures; underneath it was the slogan "Adventure is just one book away."

Conrad never went into a challenge uninformed so he forwarded her information to a private investigator.

He looked down at her big brown eyes, felt something stir inside of him. Part sexual, part curiosity, part something he couldn't define. He just wished he knew what she was up to.

"So...someone was in town asking about you yesterday," Nola said as Indy stopped by Java Juice the next morning. "I don't like it."

"Ha. I'm sure it was nothing. Maybe that wealthy king and queen finally realized where they left me," Indy said as she handed Nola her thermal to-go coffee mug.

"Your sweet parents would be devastated to hear you say that."

"Naw, I promised to cut them in on my fortune once I'm found," she said with a wink. She wasn't too concerned about anyone asking after her. She had nothing to hide.

The morning rush was over and the tables of the coffee shop were filled with the usual suspects. Simone, who was working on her doctoral thesis, Pete, who was planning the next quest for his Dungeons & Dragons group, and then the young moms in the back enjoying some adult conversation while their toddlers played next to them.

Nola prepared Indy's normal order of a large Americano with skim milk. "Would you mind if I put a flyer on your bulletin board asking for some help weeding in the park on Saturday? I want to try to get the park in better shape before the cooking competition. I mean, the town council should do it but..."

"They're busy paying for things like road repair and other community needs."

Indy turned to see Jeff Hamilton behind her. He

smiled at her. "I know, but we need to make this place look nice."

"The park is on the list, but there are so many things that need to be done," Jeff said. "My wife, June, owns the nursery on the outskirts of town. I can talk to her about bringing plants for the bedding. Did you find a sponsor yet?"

"Not yet, I'm still in talks with one of the sponsors I use on my show. But Conrad Gilbert is coming to town on May 1 to film his show. Once I win, we'll have a nice amount of money to put toward it. I'm going to use that to get more people involved. It is a long road but we will get there."

"I'm impressed. How did you convince him to do that?" Jeff asked.

"I contacted his show and challenged him to a cook-off here."

"You did?"

"Yes. I think this challenge will be good," she said.

She wanted everyone to see the beauty she did in Gilbert Corners. She loved the old Victorian architecture that dominated the vacant buildings on Main Street. When she walked down Main Street, she saw so much potential in the town and wanted them to realize it.

She talked to Nola and Jeff about which shop they should renovate next and made some notes before she took her coffee from Nola and left. She opened the bookshop and enjoyed the light foot traffic that came in. She loved the smell of the books and discussing her favorite titles with clients.

She casually brought up Conrad Gilbert with her customers and found out that he'd been considered devastatingly handsome before the accident, spoiled and

arrogant. One of her customers said that he'd acted like
the town of Gilbert Corners was below his social standing. Interesting.

She hadn't thought it would come so quickly, but on
the first of May, she packed up her ingredients and her
courage and headed to Gilbert Manor, following the cob-
blestone road that went over a quaint stone bridge that
spanned the brackish-water river that flowed through
Gilbert Corners.

She was nervous as she hauled her ingredients to the
tent she was directed to. She felt someone watching her.
The figure inside the tent was backlit by the sun. He had
broad shoulders that practically filled the tent frame and
wore a leather jacket. As he moved more across the yard,
she caught her breath as she recognized him. The Beast.

She patted her hair and smoothed her hands down the
sides of the fitted Bardot top she wore before she realized that made her look nervous and stopped.

"Hello there, Mr. Gilbert. It's nice to meet you," she
said.

"Hello, Rosalinda."

She furrowed her brow at hearing her given name
but smiled at him. "No one calls me Rosalind. I'm Indy.
Indy Belmont." She kept talking because he stood there,
sort of glaring at her but not full-on glaring. It made
her nervous.

"What's up?" she asked.

"Why did you challenge me?" he responded.

"Oh, well, I'm not sure if you know it or not, but people in this town believe there is a curse that involves your
family. It's keeping business away and slowly killing the
town," she said. "I have a show where—"

"I know about your show," he said.

"Oh, do you watch it?"

She wasn't nervous now. He was even better looking in person. The scar on the side of his face just added to his appeal, making him look dangerous in a safe-but-sexy way. He was taller than she'd expected as well, and compared to her five foot five inches he was about a foot taller than her.

There was a leashed power in him that made the air around him almost crackle and she felt a shiver down her spine. He looked like a man who took what he wanted. Not that anyone would say no to him. He was watching her so keenly that she was hyperaware of her body and her femininity. She didn't feel threatened or unsafe—just seen. Seen in a way that she hadn't been in a long time.

She pushed her glasses up on her nose and gave him another smile as he stood there, still watching her.

"Want to grab some coffee before we start filming and I'll give you the details?"

"No. Tell me what you know about the curse," he said in a grumbly voice.

"Does this brooding asshole thing work for you?" she asked. Realizing he was just going to keep pushing unless she put a stop to it.

"I prefer to think of myself as laser focused rather than asshole."

"I guess that's in the eyes of the beholder," she said, turning and walking away.

TWO

In person, Rosalinda Belmont was more vibrant than he'd expected. That video hadn't captured her vitality at all. She'd looked slightly rough-around-the-edges. In person she glowed. She had long curly hair which she wore at the top of her head in a high ponytail. She had a curvy figure revealed by high-waisted sailor-style jeans and a plain three-quarter-length-sleeve ballet top.

He was still annoyed with the way she dismissed him.

"She's cute. Actually, this whole town is. Remind me again why you hate it," his sous chef, Rita, said, interrupting his thoughts as she joined him at his bench.

He ignored the comment because it wasn't any of her business and directed her to get the prep done before he moved off to check on the rest of the mise en place for cooking.

He hated this town because it reminded him of who

he had been. How he'd looked down on the townspeople as not being as good as he was. He had hated mingling with them, something his grandfather had reinforced.

The accident had changed all of that, and being back here stirred too much of the man he'd been. He didn't like it.

Conrad was familiar with the setup of the tent as it was always the same and set to his preferences. Ophelia made sure he had a bench where he could work by himself, and that Rita was set to the left side where she could hand him things and be filmed doing her part.

He noticed that Ms. Belmont was chatting with another woman with short red hair and a rounded face. She looked sort of familiar like maybe he'd known her when he'd grown up in Gilbert Corners. But he wasn't interested in renewing any acquaintances; he wanted to do this cook and get out of here.

She glanced over and waved at him before walking toward him. He stood where he was, sharpening the knives he planned to use during the show because he knew a lot of home chefs found that intimidating.

"Sorry for losing my temper with you earlier. I just really don't deal well with…beasts," she said with a flash of a gamine grin that sent a bolt of heat through him.

"No problem. You were right—I was being an ass. Normally my challengers refer to me as Chef Gilbert, not The Beast."

She laughed. A light, tinkling sound that he noticed drew the attention of several of the production crew, which annoyed him.

"Did you need anything else?" he asked, hating that she was a distraction.

"Are you always this brusque?"

He arched one eyebrow. There was something unsettling about her, and he wished it made it easier for him to ignore the attraction between them. But it didn't. He was half aroused from this exchange.

"So that's a yes," she said with a sigh.

"GC brings out the worst in me. I was actually surprised that you wanted to do the challenge here. Why did you?"

"The curse."

He groaned. "Of course. You don't really believe the local legend that if a Gilbert returns then the town will flourish again?" he asked drily.

"Oh, well…yeah. I mean, the publicity from being on your show won't hurt either. I wasn't sure you knew about the curse," she said. "I was hoping we could have lunch after and discuss—"

"Let me stop you there. I'm here for the few hours it's going to take to film this and them I'm gone. There is nothing that interests me in Gilbert Corners."

She tipped her head to the side and narrowed her eyes. "Not even your cousin at the GC Care Facility?"

He shook his head and put down the large knife he'd been sharpening as he leaned toward her, using all of his height and the menace of his scarred face and body to intimidate her. "Is that all?"

She swallowed; he saw her throat work, and she frowned for a minute before putting her hands on her hips. "You're not a very nice man, are you?"

"I don't have to be, I'm the Beast."

"Tell you what, Beast, I'll wager a weekend of having you help out around town that I can beat you at this competition."

"What's in it for me?"

"The gratitude of the people of Gilbert Corners."

He rolled his eyes. "I meant what do I get if I win?"

Her hands dropped and she chewed her lower lip for a moment. "What do you want?"

As soon as she said that, an image of her naked on his bed flashed into his head, but he knew that wasn't something he could say out loud. "You, for one romantic weekend."

He saw a flush move up her neck to her cheeks.

"Me?" she squeaked.

"Yup. Take it or leave it."

He had no doubt that she was going to be dropping her wager faster than a hot dish. She'd made a bold move and he'd countered. He turned back to check the other tools in his chef's kit figuring that was the end of the conversation, but he felt the light touch of her hand on his forearm.

Another jolt of fire went straight through his body making his blood feel like it was flowing heavier in his veins.

"Okay."

"Okay?"

"I accept your wager. Winner gets a weekend. You get romance, I get you volunteering and working around town," she said. "Deal?"

He looked into those large brown eyes of hers and wondered what was so special about this town that she was willing to go through so much to try to get him to come back here. She held her hand out to him. Was it just her show? This felt more important, more personal to her than just a television show.

"Why is Gilbert Corners so important to you?" he asked.

"I hate to see a beautiful town like this abandoned and forgotten. We should be taking care of our past and our history," she said.

That didn't really answer his question. He felt the same way about older city centers and buildings. He hated to see them torn down for new construction and had opened his Michelin-starred restaurant in an old sewing factory in Brooklyn.

"Nice sentiment, but what's in it for you?"

"You're persistent. I like that. I guess you'll have to win the wager if you want to find out," she said.

"You know I've earned three Michelin stars over the course of my career, right?"

She nodded, crossing her arms under her breasts as if to say "so what."

"Just wanted to give you a heads-up that you're probably not winning," he said.

"Or maybe I have a dish that will tame the Beast," she countered.

Interesting. He was going to win the wager and have Indy in his bed for one long weekend.

Indy hadn't expected him to be so overwhelming in person.

His for 48 hours. That sounded…like too much to unpack before she was meant to cook in the Beast's Lair and win.

The way he'd issued what he'd claim had a sent a shiver down her spine. It didn't help matters that her hand still tingled from where she'd touched him. He was solid.

If his eyes had been bright blue in the photos online,

in person, they were even more brilliant. She couldn't stop looking at him. He rattled her.

But. She had a plan. She just had to stick to it. She'd been making *Hometown, Home Again* for three years. After the incident at college, she'd come home and become a sort of shut-in, remote learning and avoiding everyone until her parents had bought a small bookshop and asked her to refurbish the dilapidated building. She'd made YouTube videos as a way of documenting the project at first, but also, she knew, to find her voice again.

At first her audience was small and that was fine. She'd made the videos for herself. But then it had started to grow and the TV offer had come in. For the last few years she'd been fixing up every building in her own hometown. Fixing something so she didn't have to focus on the parts of her that probably could use some work.

If she could revitalize Gilbert Corners and draw in some big developers, it would be another feather in her cap. It was her dream. She liked the bookshop she ran and she got a lot of her ideas for the town from stories she'd read. She saw the potential in Gilbert Corners, and if she had to spend a weekend with Chef Gilbert to get it, she'd do it.

He faced her, raising both eyebrows at her. "Are you sure? I'm willing to let you back out if you want to. Once we start cooking, I won't."

"I'm sure," she said. "I'd never renege. That's not the kind of person I am."

He tipped his head to one side, his gaze moving down her body, awakening things she was just going to ignore. "I can see that."

"Good. So a handshake will seal the deal?"

He hesitated and then reluctantly held his hand out to

her. She reached out, steeling herself to touch him again. The warmth of him enfolded her before his grip did. His hand was bigger than hers and there were calluses on his fingers as they slid along the back of her hand. He held it firmly, professionally, but she still felt that traitorous feminine awareness shiver up her arm.

She pumped their hands up and down and then pulled hers back as if she'd touched a hot poker.

He didn't say anything, just raised his eyebrows again. She licked her lips and then turned to walk back to her cooking station.

"Anything else?" she asked, trying for a calmness that she'd honestly never had. But the chance to get him to stay in town longer than the few hours it would take to cook was perfect. She tried to distract herself from him by thinking of the three things she'd ask him to do.

"Nope. Good luck."

"I have skill. I don't need luck."

"Your ego… I can't wait for this competition to start," she said.

"That eager to be mine?" he asked.

She flushed again and ignored it. "I'm eager to show you off around town. I can't wait to see the excitement of everyone here when you host a spring gala at Gilbert Manor."

"Dream on," he said.

She tried to be cool as she looked at the back bench where she needed to start chopping vegetables to get prepped for the cook-off. Nola raised both eyebrows at her.

"What was that about?"

"I…"

Oh God. Now that she was looking at the ingredients

she'd prepared for her version of a New England clam chowder, she wasn't sure she could win, but she was damned determined to try. She had tested out the dish a few times on her production crew. But they weren't Michelin-star judges. Maybe she shouldn't have made the wager, but she'd always had a problem with impulse control.

Why hadn't see just reasoned with him?

"You?" Nola asked again.

She took a deep breath and then decided to sound confident. The judges of the cook-off were made up of a professional chef from a neighboring town—Tony Elton, town council member Jeff Hamilton, and three randomly selected people from the audience. There was a chance she could win, she told herself. They had mics on, but the production assistant had shown them how to turn them off and on. She double-checked—hers was off.

"Is your mic off?"

Nola looked at hers and flicked it to off. "Yes...but girl, you are worrying me."

"I made a side wager on the outcome of the cooking challenge. And if I win, he has to stay in town for an entire weekend."

"And if he wins?"

She waved her hand toward her friend. "Doesn't matter. I'm not going to lose."

Nola nodded. "Glad to hear it. Either way, you might be in trouble. You don't want to spend a weekend with the Beast."

"Why not?"

Nola looked around to make sure no one was near them, but then still leaned in close, making Indy very worried.

"Rumor has it he's very hard to resist one-on-one. I heard that he goes through a woman a weekend, and they aren't complaining when they leave."

"Nola. He's not interested in me that way," she said, lying to her friend since he'd specifically mentioned a romantic weekend. "He just said that to make me back down."

"Which you didn't. So let's face it, Indy, you're the next delicious morsel on his plate."

She blushed and shook her head again. "Stop it. That's not going to happen."

"We will see," Nola said. "I guess we need to start getting ready to cook, right?"

"Yes."

Nola moved away and Indy looked down at the cooler with her ingredients in it. She hadn't allowed herself to dwell on what would happen if he won. But surely, he knew he couldn't just demand things from her?

Who said he'd have to?

She ignored her inner voice as her eyes strayed over to his cooking station and she saw him with his head down, chopping. He wasn't interested in her. Men seemed to take one look at her and relegate her to the sweet girl next-door. That wasn't the kind of woman a man asked to spend the weekend in his bed. But there was a part of her that wished that was what he'd meant. It would be nice to be the sexy one instead of the smart, reliable one. Just once.

Ophelia waved Conrad and Indy over about forty-five minutes later. The townspeople of Gilbert Corners had come out for the competition which Dash had agreed they could hold on the grounds of Gilbert Manor. The large mansion loomed in the background.

The octagonal tower element at the front elevation made the mansion look welcoming but still grand. The columns and traditional architectural elements on either side of the steps leading to the main entrance added formality to the more laid-back authentic cedar-shingle roof that lent a natural aspect to the mansion and complemented it with an aged soft silver-gray color. There was a porte cochere that the production vans were parked underneath. Locals in attendance had left their cars in the large paved side lot that had always been used for these types of events.

But Conrad knew that no local, save those employed by the Gilbert Manor foundation, had been here since the night of the winter ball that had changed his life and led the town to believe they were cursed.

The classic red brick and Tennessee fieldstone chimney was visible from the backyard where the competition was being held. The audience had entered through a lovely garden gate to the covered rear terrace where Ophelia's team had set up seating for them. There were lattice walls on one side that served as a wind block but let in sunlight.

Conrad had offered to allow Indy to use the outdoor dining area adjacent to the covered lounge, but Ophelia had insisted they use the exact same setup. Stated that the judging would only be fair if they both were using the studio-provided kitchen areas.

"Before we get started, Ms. Belmont, I wanted to make sure you had everything you needed?"

Indy smiled at Ophelia, and he couldn't help noticing the difference between the two women. Ophelia was tall and sleek, carrying herself with a cool sophistication that made Indy seem sort of small-town and…charming. Which just reinforced that his mind was on the wager. He seldom lost a cook-off—in fact, the last time he had, it had been to a master chef who earned his first Michelin star when he was eighteen.

"I think I have everything. One of your assistants showed me how to use the pressure cooker you provided, so I should be good," she said.

He wondered what she was using the pressure cooker for. The cook-off was traditional coastal recipes. He knew that Indy had wanted to do a low country boil, but they had to cook the same dish, so the producers had decided on a traditional New England clam chowder instead. The littleneck clams had been locally sourced from the neighboring town of Calm Bay. There was no time limit on the cook, so she wouldn't be under pressure to get her dish up fast.

He looked over at her and wondered if he should go and give her some advice. He glanced at her bench and made a few notes before realizing what he was doing. He didn't want to spend more time in GC and if he helped her…

"Chef Gilbert?" Ophelia asked.

"I'm good," Conrad said, turning his attention to his friend and away from the tempting Indy. He reminded himself he didn't like anyone associated with Gilbert Corners.

It was just a bit hard since she stood to his right smelling like summer and making him think about what she would look like after he kissed her.

"Great. So, just to run through this. I'll do an intro with both of you and then you will go to your stations.

Don't do anything until the cameraman assigned to you is in position and our director, CJ, will tell you to start. I will bring the judges by and let them ask you questions about your cook as it's going on. Don't worry about anything you say—we will edit the footage later so if you don't want to talk or can't talk, that's fine," Ophelia said.

"What will they be asking?" Indy wanted to know.

Indy was starting to look a little nervous. Conrad almost smiled to himself. He had almost forgotten he was back in Gilbert Corners now.

"Just things like 'what are you doing' and 'how did you come up with the recipe,'" Ophelia said. "Are you ready?"

"Yes."

"As I'll ever be," Indy said, which made Ophelia smile.

"Don't worry, Ms. Belmont, once you start cooking, you'll forget the cameras are there just like on your own show. Let me introduce you both to today's judges and then we'll get the filming going."

Ophelia waved over the local chef, who was one that Conrad hadn't met before, but he'd looked him up and thought he sounded interesting. Jeff Hamilton was his age and they'd met a few times when Conrad had been home on summer break. The locals consisted of three people, with only one person that Conrad had never met before.

After they were introduced, Ophelia checked everyone's mics and then moved to a platform that had been set up. The audience coordinator had already warmed up the crowd and had given them instructions on what to do when Ophelia greeted them. Still, Conrad was surprised by the loud cheers from the locals.

"A love of the traditional and a fierce spirit of competition have brought The Beast back to his hometown and Gilbert Manor. The stakes are high for The Beast. He hasn't lost a cook-off in the last twelve challenges. Will this be his lucky thirteenth win?

"Or will newcomer and local resident Rosalinda 'Indy' Belmont defeat The Beast and send him back to his lair? Let's find out in this traditional *New England Clam Chowder Cook-off.*"

The crowd cheered again and the director called cut. Stepped down and motioned them over to her. "Conrad, go and do your thing."

He stepped onto the platform, crossed his arms and waited for the cameraman to get in place before he glared menacingly into the lens. They did a few different takes and then it was Indy's turn.

"What should I do?" she asked him. "I'm a home cook not a tv chef. I know I have my show and I should be a natural in front of the camera but this is…different."

"I'd say your strength is that charming smile of yours, and your quirkiness. Just smile and feel authentic. Actually…where's Nola?"

"Why?"

"Because you will feel awkward just smiling at the camera—believe me, it takes a bit to get used to it. If she stands behind the cameraman, you can smile at her."

"Thanks," she said.

"No problem. TV is an odd beast."

"Just like you," she quipped.

"Indeed."

He stepped back as she filmed her part. She intrigued him—part of it was that he hated being back on the grounds of the old man's home and seeing so many of the townspeople who were looking at him. Did they resent him for not coming back? They called it a curse, but he couldn't help feeling they blamed all of the Gilberts for the town losing residents and business.

Rubbing the back of his neck, he couldn't help thinking about Indy. Challenging him to break a curse supposedly but he knew there had to be more. And he couldn't wait to find out what it was.

Three

Indy had practiced making clam chowder, but this was different. This wasn't a frame she'd rescued from an estate sale that had languished in an attic for decades that was worn, maybe broken, and needed her care to restore it. This was a bunch of fresh ingredients, and for a moment she felt the beginning of a panic attack.

On her show she was always able to focus on what she was fixing because it was usually just her and a small crew, but here she felt the pressure of the townspeople watching her in real time.

Nola looked at her and took a deep breath, then nodded at her. Indy smiled at her friend and took a deep breath too. She could smell the garlic that she'd chopped a few minutes ago and the smokiness of the grills on the fire that she'd started.

These scents soothed her. She nodded to herself,

blocking out everything but the ingredients on her bench. She was able to start cooking the chowder while the cameramen walked around her station and took different shots. Though Conrad had said that she'd forget the cameras were there, she didn't. But she'd figured out how to make it manageable.

Nola was her cooking assistant and was busily peeling and dicing the russet potatoes she was using in the recipe. Meanwhile Indy was on the clams. Because of the nature of this cook-off and the high stakes, she believed she had the best chance of winning by bringing out the freshness of the clams so she was steaming them in a wine-and-garlic sauce that she would later use to cook the bacon in.

Once the clams were steamed, she pulled them out. She sieved the remaining juice to get rid of any dirt that might have come from the clams. Then she had to shell them, which wasn't that hard since they had mostly all opened during the steaming.

Just as she felt like she was getting into a rhythm, Ophelia came over with a camera. "Ready for me?"

"Sure," she said with a confidence she was starting to feel. This curse-breaking business was more complicated than she'd anticipated. But her cook was going well.

"Is this recipe one of your own?" Ophelia asked.

"No, it's not. But I am bringing some techniques and tastes from my grandmother's lessons. I thought this would be the perfect edge for me to use today."

"Interesting. That accent doesn't sound very New England," Ophelia said.

"No, ma'am, it's not, I'm from Georgia," Indy said.

"So are you bringing any Southern twists to your clam chowder today?"

Indy was. She'd texted her mom that morning and had decided to make some homemade cheddar biscuits that her mom was famous for to go with the clam chowder. "I am. I'm making my mama's biscuits. But also the using the basics I learned cooking low country boil growing up."

"Interesting. Why did you decide to do that?"

"Well the low country boil incorporates many of the same items as the clam chowder, so I thought the flavors might work together. If I'm going to beat the Beast, I needed to have something unique."

"Indeed. I'll leave you to your cooking," Ophelia said.

The director called cut. "That was great. You're a natural on camera."

"Thanks, this is so different from my show. I don't feel natural at all. Do I keep working?"

"Yes. Cut is just for interview part. We'll be bringing the judges through next. But keep cooking. There's a storm advisory and we're hoping to get these dishes finished before the rain arrives."

"How close is it?" Indy had gotten used to the storms that blew through this area off the Atlantic Ocean.

"We've got a couple of hours but not much more."

"Got it. I'll be done in time."

"Great," Ophelia said. "I'm the producer as well as host of this show, so I'm watching the budget. If we don't get this finished today, it'll be expensive to come back."

Ophelia smiled at her as she moved over to Conrad's station. Indy walked over to Nola who was still peeling the potatoes to give her the update.

"A storm's brewing. So chop faster I guess," Indy said.

"Of course there's a storm coming. The Beast is back in Gilbert Corners. It's just like that night ten years ago."

"Stop being overdramatic," Indy said.

"I wish I were. That night of the ball the day started perfect, like today, and then by midnight there was a blizzard. I'm just saying that *perhaps* something is trying to stop you from breaking the curse."

"I thought you didn't believe in it."

"I mean, of course I don't. But you have to admit, the weather's been pretty calm until he showed up."

"Maybe that means we *are* breaking the bad luck of this town. I mean, he's here," she said, moving back to her station to start cooking the bacon. She hadn't thought Nola was as invested in the curse as the others, but it seemed that not just the clam chowder was tradition.

The people of Gilbert Corners were going to read all kinds of bad omens into the storm. It made her realize why Conrad and his cousin Dashiell might not want to live here. But still, she thought, weather wasn't dictated by curses.

She felt someone watching her and glanced over at Conrad. Their stations were close enough for her to see his raised eyebrow and the frown that made the scar on the side of his face more pronounced. She caught her breath at how sexy he looked in his element. He might have been watching her, but his hands were still moving on the cutting board. There was a power in his movements and the way her watched her made her shiver with sensual awareness as he tossed something into his stockpot.

"Get busy," he said to her. "Unless you're that eager to be mine for a weekend that you're going to forfeit."

She realized she was just staring at him. "I'm right on track. Are you worried?"

"No."

She laughed at his comment.

"You should be. Indy is bringing some Southern heat to her dish," Ophelia said.

"Is she?"

"What, don't you think I can bring the heat?"

"Oh you're hot alright," he said.

She wasn't sure what he meant by that. She just went back to cooking, and the words continued drifting in and out of her mind as she tried to concentrate on her recipe. She'd felt a spark between them; she knew he had too. But she'd been trying to convince herself that when he'd asked for a weekend with her, it wasn't really going to be an intimate weekend. Now she wasn't so sure.

Conrad cooked on autopilot, which he knew wasn't a great idea when there were high stakes and a weekend with Indy was on the line, but he was distracted. He could blame it on being back in the one place he'd sworn to never return to, but he knew it was more than that.

Gilbert Manor was the problem.

No one had lived in the house for years, but the trust they'd dumped the inheritance they'd received from their grandfather into maintained the lawn and the house. He felt the stirring of anger, which he had always struggled to control when he was here. He might hate being back here but once he was cooking that all faded.

But he needed the distraction from Indy. She wasn't what he'd expected, and she had rattled him. He knew that he was coarse at times. He justified it by looking in the mirror, reminding himself of the jagged scar and the path he'd been on that had been taken from him in an instant.

But it wasn't the scar on his face that had changed

him from the happy boy he'd been into this man. Gilbert Corners made him morose, and he hated that.

He dumped the ingredients into the stockpot and noticed that Rita was watching him.

"What?"

"You seem…"

He arched one eyebrow at her.

"Never mind."

Well, hell. He was distracted and he couldn't allow himself to be. Not today. He noticed some of the local judges were the Hammond sisters; Martha and Jean-Marie. They'd run the kitchens here at Gilbert Manor. Conrad knew he'd turned to cooking after the accident in part because of them.

"Ladies, it's nice to see you."

"You too, Con," Martha said. "It's been too long since a Gilbert was on these grounds."

"I'm not sure about that," he said drily.

"We've both missed you," Jean-Marie said.

"You two are part of the reason I'm a chef."

"We're flattered," Jean-Marie said with one of those sweet, sad smiles that he sometimes received from people who knew his past.

They asked him some questions about his dish, and he talked them through some of the changes he'd made to the basic recipe. He was using a fusion of Japanese cooking techniques that he'd been enjoying a lot lately and a classic French bisque, which was what the clam chowder was based on.

He couldn't help the soft spot he had for the sisters. The way they'd simply accepted him in their kitchens when he'd been hiding from his grandfather's rages. The way they'd directed him to the garden and told him about the edible plants and explained to him how flavor profiles worked.

Chasing away the last of the lust he'd felt for Indy, the somber feelings that being in this place stirred in him settled as the ladies moved on.

He continued putting in the ingredients and tasting the dish as it developed. Though he was ignoring her, he knew he wanted to win. He wanted her to be his for a weekend. And yeah, he could come back and ask her out, but that wasn't something he'd do. Once he won this wager, Gilbert Corners would see the last of him.

There was something more to Indy than met the eye. That spunky personality, those wide-leg pants and form-fitting blouse. She moved around her kitchen tent in a flurry of movement that was precise, she was a very thorough woman, he realized, wondering if she was like that in every part of her life. The way she'd challenged him, then blushed, touched him and then pulled back.

He wanted her.

He shouldn't be turned on by a woman who lived in Gilbert Corners. But he was. And if his life had taught him one thing, it was that it was unpredictable and there was no guarantee for a long one.

He was going to have her.

"So this is what they pay you for?"

"Dash? What are you doing here?"

"He's a surprise judge," Ophelia said. "The locals were keen to have both of you here for the event."

"No wonder a storm's brewing," Conrad said.

Ophelia just shook her head. "I'm glad you were able to make it, Dash. I'll give you two a moment to catch up and then be back with the cameras."

Dash looked tired. The last ten years had been hardest

on him. Though he'd been unscarred by the crash, he'd been the one to watch Conrad and Rory go through numerous operations and rehab. Rory was still in a coma.

"God, I still hate this place," Conrad said.

"Yeah, me too. I'm really surprised you agreed to do this," Dash said.

He told Dash about the alleged curse as he worked. Rita looked calmer now that he wasn't watching Indy, and their dish was starting to come together.

"So if you win the curse is broken? Or if she wins?" Dash asked.

"I don't think they even know. Folks around this part love a good legend. Apparently, the Main Street Business Alliance is going to use this cook-off to raise the town's profile, and Indy's got a TV show where she refurbishes run-down towns like GC."

"That sounds interesting. But still, I guess you better win."

"I always win."

"Of course you do—you're a Gilbert. I'll leave you to the cooking and go meet your competition."

Dash walked away but he couldn't help thinking about what his cousin had said. He was a Gilbert. The next forty minutes were intense as he finished his dish and the sourdough bread bowls to serve the chowder in. Ophelia told them when to end their cooking and then judges were moved into position at the table. The competition was judged blind, so both his and Indy's workstations had a partition set up as they plated the dishes, and then the servers would come and collect them.

The tables for plating were set back to back and he was very aware of the smell of summer peaches as she moved behind him. He finished and turned to see she was still working, but then she concluded and spun to face him.

"I think that's it," she said, wiping her hands on her curvy hips.

"It is. Now it's in the hands of fate," he said.

"Fate? You strike me as too cynical to believe in fate." She gave him that gamine smile of hers again as she tipped her head to the side to study him.

There was nothing sexual in the pose or the question, but he felt his cock stir. He wanted her. She wasn't his normal type. That dichotomy of confidence and nerves was usually too chaotic for him, but with Indy it seemed to be making him want her more. "I am, but it's right up your alley, isn't it?"

"Maybe," she said with a teasing grin.

"Maybe?"

"Yes. But I don't like the feeling I'm getting from you, that because I believe in fate I'm not grounded."

"I don't think that."

"What do you think?"

"That you believe in breaking curses and magical things. I don't," he said. "But that doesn't lessen you in my eyes."

Hell. This was why he shouldn't be here. Why had he said that?

It was the truth but still…he wished he'd kept it to himself. The sooner this competition was over and he was out of here, the better.

She knew he meant his words as a compliment and took them as one. She wiped her hands on her apron. Nola and Conrad's assistant weren't in this staging area.

It was just the two of them behind the partition as their dishes were taken out to be served.

"What happens now?"

"Nervous?"

"Since this entire thing started," she admitted. "You?"

"Not really."

"Of course not," she muttered. "Can I try yours?"

"Sure. I'm curious about yours as well. I'm not sure about your biscuits."

"Uh, that's my mama's recipe, Beast, so watch it."

He just tore a piece of the biscuit and put it in his mouth. He chewed slowly and she found herself watching his lips and mouth. God, he had a fine-looking mouth. There was something about it that made her wonder what it would feel like pressed against hers.

"Not bad."

"Not bad? They are damned good. Let me try your bread," she said, reached for a leftover piece of the sourdough that he'd carved out in order to make his bread bowls.

The first taste of it against her tongue made her want to moan. It was so good. She loved bread, and this loaf was everything. The texture and the taste were delicious, and she knew they'd complement his soup perfectly. Some doubts about the cheddar she'd added to her biscuits danced through her mind. The cheddar was sharp. Dang.

She glanced up at him.

"Not bad."

He gave a shout of laughter and she smiled when she heard it. "You're something else, lady."

She shook her head. She wasn't. She was just a

woman determined to have the future she wanted. One away from the woman she'd been. So silly, she thought. But Gilbert Corners was her chance to be the woman she was becoming and find her place. Though he'd asked why she needed Gilbert Corners to succeed, she hadn't told him that if it didn't, she'd probably end up back home and back in a life that she didn't want. Staying in Lansdowne hadn't been an option for her. She'd always wanted out. But she'd used her time after college to carve out a path for herself. A path out of Lansdowne. And she wasn't going back.

She could easily see herself following in her mother's footsteps back there. Giving up her dreams to become a wife and mother. Not that there was anything wrong with that, except Indy was pretty sure she'd be crappy at them, and it wasn't her dream.

"Will they announce the winner soon?" she asked. The clouds were thickening around the edges of Gilbert Manor.

"Probably. The storm looks pretty fierce."

"Yeah, it does. I wasn't expecting storms like this when I moved here."

"Why *did* you come here?"

"Nola. She is a whiz at woodworking and joined my show for the last three years. We finished up in Lansdowne and the producers asked us to find another town in need of our help, and Nola suggested Gilbert Corners," she said.

"You're good friends then?"

"The best. We were college roommates and just hit it off. Again fate stepped in to help me out. Maybe you should be scared."

"Of you or of fate? Fate already gave me the finger and I told it to fuck the hell off."

He looked like he could handle anything life threw at him. Not just because of his size and the way he stood, as if it would take a bulldozer to move him. But also because of the confidence he exuded. Nothing seemed to faze him.

"That's an interesting thought. I guess surviving a car accident like yours would make me feel that way too."

He shrugged. "I hope you can take next weekend off because that's the one I'm claiming."

"That will work for me when I win. Glad you're available."

"Still confident after you tried my sourdough?"

"It takes more than a tasty morsel to rattle me."

"Does it?" he asked, leaning closer to her.

She shifted closer, her head tiping back and her eyes starting to close before she realized what she was doing. She stepped back then realized what she was doing. And stood her ground, her gaze meeting his. An electric spark seemed to arc between them, and the hair on her arms stood up. She was transfixed by the look in his eyes and the memories of watching his mouth move as he'd tried her biscuit. Kissing him was a foregone conclusion.

He was the first man she'd met since college who had distracted her. Or maybe it was because he was so closely tied to her future plans for Gilbert Corners that she wanted him. But no, she knew it was that mouth. And those broad shoulders and the tattoos that covered his body.

Conrad Gilbert was temptation incarnate, and no matter the outcome of today's cook-off, she knew that breaking the curse was no longer the reason why she was interested in him.

It was carnal. She'd never thought about lust at first sight. She'd always prided herself on liking men for their humor and their intellect, but Conrad had those as well. It wasn't like he was just a hottie; there was so much more to him. Which was a big red flag.

One of the reasons she'd left Lansdowne was that she didn't want to be her mother. The woman who had fallen head over heels in love and then stopped pursuing her own dreams.

And yes, this was a new century, and there was no reason she had to do that. But Indy knew that when she fell for a guy, she tended to start putting herself second, and she wasn't going to do that again.

Not even to break a curse.

"We're ready for you two now," Ophelia said.

Indy took a deep breath and followed Conrad out into the open in front of the judging table.

"May the best chef win," Ophelia said.

Indy realized she was holding her breath as they waited to hear the results. The plates were taken up to the judges for tasting.

Conrad was announced the winner, and Indy wasn't exactly surprised, though she was a bit disappointed. She had a moment to herself while the eyes of the town were on them, and without thinking, she turned to him with a huge grin.

"Congratulations! I'm sure all of Gilbert Corners is excited that you'll be coming back next weekend to help with the spring renewal project."

She saw the shock on his face, knew there would be a price to pay for her boldness. He could deny it in front of everyone, and there was a moment when their eyes met and she was pretty sure he would.

"That's right. I'll be helping with the spring renewal, and then taking Ms. Belmont away to my lair."

Four

His lair.

She'd be lying if she said those words hadn't been on her mind since he'd issued them. He had been a good sport. The incoming storm had necessitated everyone leaving quickly, including Conrad, who just gave her a hard look and told her he'd be in touch.

What had she been thinking? She'd asked herself that question several times, but the answer was still the same. She'd felt backed into a corner so her impulsiveness had kicked in.

He hadn't been in touch despite saying he would be, and she wasn't entirely sure he'd show up today for the park renewal project she volunteered him for.

So she was the first one in the park with her garden gloves and weeder. If he didn't show up, she was planning to say he'd been here earlier and had to leave.

She groaned at the thought. It was like her dad always said, once a lie is started it can only be kept alive with more lies.

Ugh.

Nola was offering discounted coffee to the volunteers and, good as his word, Jeff had shown up and was directing most of them. Indy went to work on one of the beds near the train station.

She heard the sound of a motorcycle and glanced over her shoulder, relieved as Conrad Gilbert parked his bike, took off his helmet and walked toward her. She almost forgot to breathe as she took in his broad shoulders, skin-tight tee and the slim-fitting jeans that hugged his body like she wanted to. She was glad she had her sunglasses on, so maybe he wouldn't be aware of her checking him out as he walked toward her.

The closer he got though, she started to realize he was still ticked. She brushed off her knees as she stood up, guessing that it would be better to be standing than cowering at his feet when he got to her.

"Hello, Conrad. So nice to see you here today."

He glanced around as if just noticing the townspeople working industriously around him.

"Yeah, I bet. Were you worried I wouldn't show up?" he asked.

She told herself there was nothing sexy about his low-timbered, rough-edged voice, but that was a lie and she knew it. "Yes. Thank you for coming. I know it wasn't what we agreed but I had to do something for the townspeople."

"I swear if you mention the curse, I'm not going to be happy," he said.

He was being a bit of a jerk, and it was time to draw

the line. She needed him back in town of course, but she wasn't going to allow him to bully her. "I won't. But to everyone in Gilbert Corners it's a real thing and we have to respect that."

He made a growling sound, shoved his hands through his thick hair and started to turn away, but Jeff Hamilton stopped him.

"Conrad, I wasn't sure you were going to actually come to town for this. I spoke to your cousin Dash on Friday. Thank you for coming and for suggesting that the Gilbert Trust pay for this."

She watched as Conrad talked to Jeff. She was surprised to learn that he'd arranged the money for this cleanup. The town council had simply said that funding had been found. She had tentatively hoped she'd already broken the curse in their eyes. Of course, she had lost the bet she'd made with Conrad, and she had no doubt he was going to be very demanding of whatever he asked of her.

"I'll help Indy," he said.

"Great," she said, realizing she'd been staring at the two men for too long. "I can use the help on this bed. There's a stubborn—"

"I meant with the organizing. This isn't the kind of thing I normally do," he said, gesturing to the ground and the overgrown flower beds.

"I'm glad to have your help on both parts of the project. I can show you what you need to do here. Do you have some extra gloves, Jeff?"

"Here, take mine. On second thought…you probably need some extra-large ones," he said, taking a pair from the canvas tote he carried and handing them to Conrad. Jeff waved and went back toward the main park area.

"I don't do menial labor."

She gave him a look down her nose that never failed to bring even the most recalcitrant person in line. "This is charity."

He growled again.

"You don't scare me. I need your help getting this thick weed out. I'm not strong enough and your T-shirt is broadcasting the fact that you should be."

"Should be?"

"I don't judge a book by its cover," she said.

Then turned and knelt back down on the ground digging the dirt around the stubborn root. A moment later he knelt to the ground next to her. She took a deep whiff of his cologne which had been teasing her memory since he'd left her a week ago.

"Which one?"

"Right here," she said, pointing to the spot. He worked quickly and efficiently, and for someone who'd professed not to do this kind of work, he was actually really good at it. As he worked, she couldn't help but study the thorned-branch tattoos on his arms, and in the sunlight she noticed the scars underneath.

He'd been badly injured. She'd read the newspaper report on his accident when she'd done her research, but seeing the decade-old scars affected her. She almost reached out to touch him, but pulled herself back.

It was interesting to her that he chose to emphasize his injuries with thorns. She'd never be able to wear her pain on her body. She wrapped it deeply inside where she hoped no one would ever notice it. To her, Conrad had made a brave choice.

And the more time she spent with him the more he intrigued her. He was like an attic treasure, she thought whimsically. She had no idea what she was going to un-cover as she pulled him into the light.

He was essentially a stranger, and she didn't want to give him any signals other than she needed his presence to convince the town that the curse was broken.

He noticed her watching him and pushed his sun-glasses up on his head. "What?"

"Not bad for your first time. If you want to start from that end, we can meet in the middle. Once we get this bed weeded, we can replant the rose bushes."

"And if I don't?"

"Do it anyway," she said with a sweet smile.

She turned away but not before she caught the edges of a slight grin on his face.

Conrad refused to admit that he was starting to enjoy himself with Indy. She was funny with her little asides and when she forgot herself, she sang little snippets of Taylor Swift songs under her breath—which she clearly didn't know the words to because she sort of hummed half of the time.

It didn't change the fact that he was still pissed off at her for forcing him to come back to Gilbert Corners, but in her shoes, he might have done the same. And he respected that. Grudgingly but still. He respected her.

He pulled his phone from his pocket and noticed he'd missed a call from Dash. He got up and started to walk away.

"Hey, where are you going?"

"I have to make a call. I'll come back," he said. He wasn't used to explaining himself to anyone, and he didn't particularly like it. He moved down away from the train station and the crowds of townspeople. Some of them seemed genuine curious about him. A few stopped him to congratulate him on the success of his show.

"Con?"

"Yeah, what's up?"

"Just checking to make sure you're okay," Dash said; there was a note in his voice that Conrad hadn't heard in a long time. Something that he remembered from the teenage years before like had changed.

"Why?"

"Saw a picture on social media of you in Gilbert Corners. I'm pretty sure hell hasn't frozen over—"

"Fuck off. You know she told everyone I was coming," he said, but there was no heat in it. He was happy to hear Dash laughing. Something his cousin didn't do very often.

"I do—you just normally don't allow yourself to be manipulated like that."

"Well between her comment and you donating the funds for the project, I couldn't *not* show up."

"I thought that might be the case, but that's why I was vague about either of us showing up to help. So… Indy Belmont?"

"What about her?"

"You like her?"

"I hadn't realized I'd dialed in to your talk radio show, Dr. Dash," Conrad said.

"So that's a yes."

"I'm hanging up now and I'll mention to Jeff that you can't wait to come help next weekend."

He hung up the phone and pocketed it. The accident had changed so much between him and his cousin, but until this moment, he hadn't fully realized what it had taken from them. None of them had been the same after.

Conrad had leaned into his anger as he always did and let that drive him away from Gilbert Corners and their grandfather, but also from Dash. Something he wasn't going to allow to continue.

"Would you like an iced coffee?"

He turned to see Indy standing a polite distance from him holding one of two tumblers toward him. "Figured you might want something before we start planting."

"Trying to butter me up?"

"Is it working?"

"No."

He took the tumbler from her and their fingers brushed. Her hands were cool and unblemished, he noticed, her fingers long with no nail polish. He almost turned his hand to take her fingers in his but she pulled her hand back quickly. She blushed as she tucked her hand into the back pocket of her jeans. There was something innocent about her and he didn't understand it. She was so bold most of the time.

But every time they touched, it popped up.

"So...tell me about you," he said.

She tipped her head to the side studying him. "Why do you want to know?"

"I want to be able to give the police as much information as I can on my blackmailer," he said sardonically. "It's called getting to know someone."

"Oh, you just don't strike me as someone who does small talk."

"You're making me regret asking."

She threw her head back and laughed, and a shaft of desire went through him. On the surface there was nothing about Indy Belmont that should have attracted him, yet here he was getting turned on.

"You know about my show *Hometown, Home Again* so I'm guessing you mean here in Gilbert Corners. I own the bookshop across the way as well as a Victorian house over on Maple. I thought Gilbert Corners would be a nice place to live and work for the next few years," she said.

"Is it?"

"Well, there was this curse…"

He shook his head at her. She gave him a sheepish grin. "Sorry. I love it here. I mean my house needs more work than I expected and the foot traffic in town isn't as lively as I'd like, but I do a good business online, so I'm good. We've already filmed me making over the book-shop and Java Juice. So next up we're focusing on my Victorian house. I've been hunting for authentic pieces from that era to fill the rooms."

"And you're fixing up the town too?"

"Yes, that's what my show is about. Well, I'm trying. I mean, this town should be a weekend tourist destina-tion and no one gets off the train here," she said. "Half the businesses on Main are closing down. I have friends who own their own businesses who I want to open shops here, but right now… I don't blame them for saying no."

He finished his iced coffee and put the tumbler on the ground. "So will you stay here after you finish fixing it all up?" He gestured to everyone working in the park.

"I don't know. What about you?" she asked.

Her answers felt…pat, like she was hiding something. Her show was successful; when he'd gone back home after the cook-off he'd watched a few episodes, getting turned on watching her work in her overalls and mak-ing molding with a table saw. Not what he would have classified as one of his turn-ons but his erection said otherwise. "What about me?"

"Why did you leave Gilbert Corners?" she asked.

He shut down. He might like her and he planned to have her in his bed. But he never discussed his past. "That's not small talk," he said.

"Why not?" she asked in that soft, gentle way that he was coming to like a little too much. If she'd been demanding he would have walked away, but there was a genuineness to the question he wouldn't ignore.

"It's complicated," he said at last.

"Was it because of the accident? I heard your grandfather died right after you'd recovered. That would make it hard to come back here," she said.

She'd given him an acceptable reason for not wanting to be here. He could just smile and nod, but the fact was he didn't want to lie to her. "No. It's because of my grandfather himself. The old bastard made me miserable, and I want nothing to do with anything that he loved."

She stared at him for a moment than nodded. "I'm sorr—

"Let's get these rosebushes planted. Our groundskeeper used to water the ground before planting. I'll get a watering can."

He turned and walked away from her and the conversation. The last thing he wanted to discuss was his grandfather or this damned town. No matter how much Indy turned him on, he needed to finish this up and get out of town.

The sun was hot, and he heard the sound of kids laughing and playing, and all he could remember was how quiet and somber Gilbert Manor had been when he'd first arrived there.

Indy was starting to get a better picture of why the Gilberts had left Gilbert Corners. If Conrad hated his grandfather...maybe the other cousins did as well. But he was gone now and there was no reason for Conrad to stop coming here. Of course she hadn't been able to make herself go back to campus after...well, after. So she knew that a place could often hold memories that logic couldn't help her get beyond.

Except that Conrad looked like someone who didn't have those kinds of issues. Which she immediately chided herself for thinking. She knew better than to judge him based on his life. Everyone had stuff in their past that they were dealing with.

His surly attitude should be all she needed to tell her that he was dealing with something. She'd thought it stemmed from the accident, but now she wondered if the accident was just the tip of the iceberg. She told herself she wanted to help Conrad because he was tied to Gilbert Corners and the alleged curse.

But she knew that was a lie. She wanted to help him because she liked him. As surly as he could be, there was a decent man underneath. And he was hot, which shouldn't have anything to do with it, but there it was.

The first man she'd noticed as a woman in five years *would* be Conrad, wouldn't it? He was difficult but also complex. There was so much more to him that his domineering chef persona. Instead of deterring her, that made her keener to get to know him. He came back with a watering can, and she realized she'd been watching him the entire time.

"Why didn't you dig the hole for the plant?"

"Ah, you kind of sounded like you knew what you were doing," she said.

"Here, hold this," he said, handing her the watering can.

He dug a hole and then tossed the shovel down. "Put some water in. But not too much. We don't want to drown the roots."

"You actually did more than watch your groundskeeper, didn't you?"

"Yeah. The staff were nice to me when I came to live with the old bastard."

"You shouldn't call him that."

"Why not? That's what he was," he said.

She carefully poured in the water and he gestured for her stop. Then he took the rose plant and set it into the hole he'd made.

"Can you hold it upright while I cover the roots?" Conrad asked.

"Yes. Sorry. I don't know why I said that."

He didn't say anything in response, just covered over the roots and then took the watering can and put more water on top of the soil. They planted the other three rose bushes in silence, working together as a team.

She wished she could unsay that thing about his grandfather. That was the problem with being her. She was impulsive all the time. She never thought things through, just blurted them out.

"I was trying—"

"I know you were trying to be nice because that's who you are. But I'm just as much of a bastard as he was. I can't help myself."

He leaned on the shovel and stared at her. "Sorry."

She had a feeling he didn't often apologize and didn't want to make a big deal out of it. "How about I make you some lunch as sort pax?"

"You mean before I take you away for the weekend I won," he reminded her drily.

"Yes. Want to meet me at my place? I walked over," she said.

"Sure, I'll take my bike over after I return the watering can and shovel," he said.

"I'm number 8 Maple Street."

"I'll see you there," he said.

Yikes!

Her house was still not finished; inviting Conrad over had seemed like the right thing to do, but now she was mentally going through it trying to remember if she had any unfinished projects lying around.

She pushed that to the back of her mind. She'd done some good work with the house, uncovering the herringbone wood floors which she'd sanded and then sealed. She was nervous for him to see all the work she'd put into it. For her, this house would be like letting him see her naked…more intimate than he even knew.

She went over to help Nola clean up and then thanked everyone for helping out, deliberately stalling before she walked to her house. When she got there Conrad's bike was in her driveway, but he wasn't. As she got closer, she noticed he was sitting on the Hammonds's front porch talking to Miss Martha and Miss Jean-Marie. He waved at her as she approached and said goodbye to the elderly ladies.

She fumbled with her old skeleton key to open her door and finally got it to work. She opened the door, which she had repaired when she first moved in. The foyer had terrazzo tiles on the floor and the twelve-foot ceilings created an open and cool space. She had a table next to the door where she tossed her keys into a bowl. She toed off her tennis shoes and then turned as Conrad closed the door behind himself.

"There's a bathroom through that door if you want to wash up. The kitchen is down to the left. I'm going to go use the master bath."

He didn't say anything, but she already knew he wasn't chatty. She was curious to see what he thought of her place, but also to learn more about him. He'd mentioned his grandfather, and given that local lore held that it was the *Gilbert* curse, maybe the surly old man was responsible for everyone feeling that way.

She liked Conrad, and there was something about him that she trusted. But at the same time, she sensed the danger in him.

She needed to be cautious. She didn't think he'd harm her, but she knew herself, and there was a very real risk that she'd let herself fall for him. And Conrad Gilbert wasn't the kind of man who wanted women falling for him.

She would do well to remember that. But when she came into the kitchen and found him already assembling ingredients for their lunch, she knew it was going to be harder than she planned.

Five

Her kitchen hadn't been renovated but had a working stove top, which was all he needed. He decided he'd make her some lunch before they left. He had been rude, but that didn't bother him. He knew most people expected him to be—either because he was born with the proverbial silver spoon, or they knew that his moniker of Beast wasn't just a cute marketing one.

But he'd seen real hurt in her eyes and…

He wasn't going to delve deeper than that.

It was safe to say that Indy had horrible eating habits. He found a forgotten stick of butter in the back of a drawer, along with a block of cheddar cheese and generic store brand white bread. Her cabinets revealed no seasonings to speak of, but he found some salt and pepper packets from a local take-out place in a drawer.

"What are you doing?"

"Making lunch," he said.

"Oh well thanks. I am sorry I trapped you into coming today. I just…no excuses, sometimes my mouth just goes off without warning," she said with a grin that made him want to pull her into his arms and kiss her until they were both naked.

He looked back to the kitchen counter. She'd had an underripe tomato and some wilted lettuce in her fridge. Along with leftovers of some rotisserie chicken.

"Chicken salad or grilled cheese?"

"I don't have any mayo," she said.

"Of course you don't. What were you planning to serve me?"

"Subs from Jacob's Deli. They deliver."

He said nothing, just continued going through her pantry and fridge until he had assembled everything he thought he could use. She pulled out one of the stools, sat at the breakfast counter and watched him.

He forgot that he was in Gilbert Corners and focused only on Indy. He wanted to impress her. He admired the work she'd done on her house, and the way that she'd used her determination and kindheartedness to rally the community to make improvements. He remembered the town, and it had taken more than the money that Dash and he had allocated to get them motivated to clean up the park.

He guessed it was all down to her.

"Have you ever done that cooking show where they only give you a few ingredients?" she asked.

"No, I'm not that kind of chef."

"What kind are you?" she asked. "You don't have a restaurant, do you?"

"Not anymore."

"So you had one?" she asked.

"Yes."

"Ugh. Are you seriously going to just answer everything with one word?"

"Probably."

"The next time you do that you have to…"

"What?"

She shook her head. "So how'd you start cooking."

He pretended he didn't hear that. The last thing he wanted to do was get into postaccident Conrad. In fact, there was very little about himself he wanted to discuss. Maybe a sliver of time when he'd been eight to ten years old and life had been good.

"You said you own the bookshop?"

She tilted her head and reached over to steal a piece of cheese she'd sliced for their sandwiches. "I do. I love bookstores. I used to spend all my money at the bookstore in Lansdowne…that's where I grew up. So when I graduated and came back home to 'figure myself out' and it was up for sale, my parents suggested I buy it and run it."

"Did you?"

"Yeah. But the town was dying, so I started making YouTube videos and then invited friends to come to town and help me make over different abandoned shops. I talked Nola into coming to town and opening a bakery. Which she did. Then my parents used their contacts to talk more families into either coming back to town or enticing their kids back. And then I got my show."

"Sounds impressive. Why'd you leave?"

She chewed her lower lip for a second, drawing his eyes to her mouth. She had a full lower lip and a cute little Cupid's bow on her top lip, which he'd noticed when he'd watched her videos. He really wanted to kiss her.

"I could never tell if my success was mine or because of my parents. I have my own show, but a big part of my success was due to my parents' contacts and easy loans were used as an incentive to encourage people to move back and start businesses. Everyone in town made all of that possible."

"So you came here?" he asked. He was only half listening to her. In his mind he was exploring the softness of her mouth, but this was important to Indy and he wanted to know about her.

"Yeah. I need to prove that I can do it without them. I know how that sounds," she said with a little shrug.

"It's cool—I get it." He'd always been all about proving himself to everyone.

"What about you? How'd you become a chef instead of a CEO like your cousin Dash?" she asked.

He could do this, tell her the safe stuff. The simple answer he gave when strangers asked him. "Well I dropped out of college thanks in part to the accident. I was in a medically induced coma and then rehab for most of my junior year, so I didn't go back. I went to Europe and took dishwashing jobs to piss my grandfather off and learned to cook."

"Did you become a chef to tick him off?" she asked carefully, reaching over to steal another piece of cheese from his tray.

"Partially, but not really. I just loved it. I had a really good mentor and once I worked my way up from sous-chef to *chef de partie*, I knew that I was hooked," he said, smiling to himself as he remembered some of the kitchens he'd worked in, and the people. He'd eventually earned a Michelin star and then felt like he'd reached the pinnacle. That was when he transferred control of the kitchen to his sous-chef and started making his TV show.

He saw her put the piece of cheese in her mouth and chew it slowly. Inwardly he groaned. He needed to get laid, either with Indy or someone else. Because he felt like he was one big hormone at this point. He hadn't been this horny since he'd been a teenager.

"What about you? Is breaking curses your passion?" he asked to lighten things up.

She shook her head and her curls bounced around her face as she gave him a self-conscious look. "I'm not sure I actually broke anything."

She was still hiding something. From experience he knew that passion only came when faced with a desperate choice; only then would a person find the thing that they were called to do. For him it had been cooking. For Indy, well she didn't seem like the kind of lady who had ever had to face that choice.

Watching Conrad in the kitchen, he was starting to make more sense to her. At the park earlier today, he'd held himself as a sort of aristocrat in his fiefdom, but here in the kitchen he was different. There was a harmony to him and his movements, and she struggled to keep from staring at him.

Yeah, that was the reason why she couldn't keep her eyes off him. It had nothing to do with the skintight T-shirt and his muscly arms. The choice of thorns wrapping around his body wasn't one she understood. She wanted to ask about them. Why was she hesitating? It wasn't like he'd feel pressured to answer her.

He'd probably never done anything just to be nice,

which was sort of her modus operandi. She wanted to ask him about his past and how the car crash changed him. But that would be intrusive and she wanted to be chill maybe more refrained.

"Do your tattoos have special meaning?"

"Yes."

She waited to see if he was going to elaborate, but it was clear he wasn't going to. "Thorny bushes aren't the typical tattoo, and what's that thing mean?"

She leaned forward across the counter and touched the stylized symbol on his left forearm.

"It's the Celtic symbol for brother," he said.

"Do you have a brother? I thought it was just you and your cousins."

He had finished chopping the cheese and had mashed together some herbs that she hadn't known she owned in a bowl. He reached above her head to the pot rack where she had a frying pan her grandmother had given her when Indy had left home.

"No brother. Dash and I got them together."

"He's your cousin, right?"

He gave her a sardonic look. "You know he is."

"I do. Figured I'd keep asking similar questions and see if you open up a bit."

He took the pan to the sink and washed and then put it on the burner to heat up. "I'm not going to."

He didn't talk while he made their sandwiches and she sort of just stared at his butt until she realized what she was doing. She got up and set places for both of them at the counter. "What would you like to drink?"

"I didn't see anything but milk in your fridge."

"I made sun tea. Let me go and get the pitcher."

She went outside and collected the pitcher she'd set

out this morning before she'd left for the park. The sugar had melted and the tea was that perfect amber color on the cusp of turning brown. It was just the way she loved it.

She came back inside and Conrad had finished the sandwiches and somehow made a salad out of her sad looking lettuce. She filled two glasses with ice and then poured the tea over it and sat down next to him.

"So…"

He turned, arching one eyebrow at her.

"Thanks for lunch."

"No problem. I was mean to you earlier."

"You were?" she wondered when he meant. He was a brusque person and she'd had to push him back in line, but he hadn't hurt her. Not really.

"I was. Now we're square."

"Because you said so?"

"Yeah," he said, before taking a bite of his sandwich.

She turned her attention to her plate and took a taste of the grilled cheese he'd made and almost moaned out loud. It was literally the best tasting sandwich she'd ever had. How had he made this out of her crappy ingredients?

"You like it?"

She was about to gush over the sandwich but then turned to meet his gaze. "Yup."

He waited a beat and then threw his head back and laughed. He didn't say anything else while they finished their lunch, but she felt like something had changed between them. Maybe enough to just ask him to do her a favor?

She didn't think so. Not yet. But they were getting there. He might be a man of few words, but she was coming to realize that he actually said a lot with his gestures. His cooking for her was personal to him; he'd done it to apologize. Underneath the thorns he'd covered himself in was a man who…she wanted to get to know better. She hadn't thought of what would happen if she lost the wager, but it was getting closer to her paying up, and what would be like to go on a date with the Beast?.

"Would you—

"Want to—"

"Sorry," she said. "What was that?"

"Want to go for a ride on my bike?" he asked.

"For the weekend you won?"

"Nah, I'm going to come back next weekend for that since we've wasted half the day."

"That wasn't what we bargained for." But he was asking her to spend time with him, and he was hot and she liked him. She wanted to get to know him better. And he still intended to claim his weekend.

"No, but neither was me showing up in town for spring renewal. So…bike ride?"

No. Yes. Maybe. Somehow the thought of riding on his motorcycle was both exciting and scary. Also, she'd probably have to touch him, like really touch him, not just fantasize about it.

"Lady. It's a yes or no question."

She turned to face him, chewing her bottom lip trying to find the answer.

He reached up and rubbed his thumb over her bottom lip until it wasn't between her teeth. A shiver went through her, they were so close she could see the flecks of green and gold in his blue eyes. He had thick eyelashes and despite his brusque manner, he had kind eyes.

She licked her lips, swallowing hard.

He groaned. "Oh, hell."

Then he brought his mouth down on hers. He wasn't touching her anywhere except grazing his fingers under her chin and his mouth against hers. But she felt him everywhere. The heat that she'd fantasized about when she'd watched him working at her kitchen counter spread through her. She trembled and opened her mouth to his as he deepened the kiss. His tongue brushed over hers. For a minute her body and mind were on the same page. She wanted to pull him closer. To deepen this kiss and she where it led next.

But memories started cascading through her and she was back on that sticky Georgia night. Everything inside her shut her down.

She pulled back and then tried to stand up and move away from him but knocked over her stool and she knew it was too much. Now she'd made things awkward. There was no going back from that.

Conrad sat back on his stool. He shouldn't have kissed her. He'd known that, but he hadn't been able to help himself. She stood across the kitchen, arms around her waist, watching him.

"I'm sorry I read the signals wrong. I didn't mean to make you uncomfortable."

He stayed where he was and did his best to make himself as small as he could. At six-five that wasn't easy, but he just pulled his energy back as much as he could. A flash of memory came to him, of Rory on the night of the accident running to him and Dash, her hair a mess and her dress partially torn, it was the look in her eyes that cinched it for him.

"Did someone force himself on you?" he asked.

He wanted to comfort her and do whatever he could to help her. But he wasn't always great at that. He'd had to take care of the guy who'd done it to Rory and that had led to them leaving Gilbert Manor the way they had.

Her eyes got wider for a second and she nodded. "Yeah, I'm sorry. I shouldn't have leaned in like that. It's been forever and that reaction—my pulling away like that— was way out of line."

He pushed his chair back slowly as she kept talking; he wasn't even listening now as he was pretty sure she didn't know what she was saying. He just went over to her and leaned against the wall next to her. He was enraged that someone would have hurt her as he had been the night he'd seen Rory. "You have nothing to apologize for."

"I do. It's been years. I should be—"

"You are fine. Don't apologize."

She nodded. "It's just I'm still not sure what you want from me, and I can't kiss you—as much as I want to—if it's just from you winning me like a prize. I know I said you could have a weekend of my time…but not like this. Intimacy should be more than a lost bet."

Damn. He liked her. "I agree. I got carried away. From the moment I met you, your mouth has been driving me crazy. For our weekend I was never demanding anything sexual from you. I kind of said romantic to make you back down."

"I never back down," she said.

"I know, that's one of the things I like about you," he admitted.

"Just one?"

"I enjoyed kissing you," he said.

"I liked it too," she admitted with a shy smile. But she knew he wasn't sure what to say next.

"What were you planning for our weekend?" she asked, at last.

"Some free labor. Make you work in my test kitchen as my sous-chef, chopping onions or washing dishes."

"Wow, this is awkward—I don't do manual labor."

He knew she was throwing his words back at him and he almost smiled. "Tough. You lost and you have to pay up."

"Fair enough."

"I liked kissing you, so there's a pretty good chance if we spend more time together, I'll try it again. Should I leave?"

She chewed her lower lip again and then shook her head. "Don't leave like this."

"How about…we go back to what I asked you earlier. Go for a ride with me?"

She licked her lips and then straightened her shoulders. "Yes."

They cleaned up the kitchen and then went out to his bike and he could tell she was nervous. "You don't have to do this."

"I want to ride behind you," she said.

She blushed again and then put her hand lightly on his arm, rubbing her finger over the raised scar tissue there. His blood ran hotter and his cock stirred. He still wanted her. He couldn't believe he was hanging around Gilbert Corners.

He hadn't been able to really come back to this place until she'd challenged him to. For a moment, he wished he were a different man. But he wasn't. So fuck it. Right now he was going to take Indy on a ride. That was it.

The smell of spring was in the air and the sun shone brightly down on them, but there was still a bit of chill to the breeze that blew around them as they stood in her driveway. He noticed the tulips in full bloom around her mailbox and he remembered that his mom had planted them at their house a long time ago. He never let himself think of his parents. It was easier to keep those emotions hidden.

Indy was stirring things up that he'd ignored for a long time. He didn't like it. Conrad had come here intent on reminding her that he was in charge, but after he'd hurt her... After he'd seen himself being the Gilbert he had always been in Gilbert Corners, he'd changed his mind. This place brought out the worst in him, but it didn't have to.

He'd learned a lot about himself after the accident, and the most important thing was that he didn't want to be anything like his grandfather.

He handed her a helmet and she put it on and then he got on the bike and told her to get on behind him. The helmets had microphones in them so they could hear each other.

"Your voice is so intimate," she said.

"Yours is too," he said as she climbed on behind him. She put one hand in the center of his back as she settled herself on the saddle.

He turned on the bike, nudge the kickstand with his foot. He felt her hands on his waist, just lightly holding him, and his cock stirred. But she wasn't pressed against his back. Her body trembled.

"Have you been on a motorcycle before?"

"No. I've always been a scared of them."

"You don't have to do this."

"I have to do it for me."

He turned the bike and drove down Maple, away from town to the winding circular road that would lead them from the past. He didn't want to go toward the manor and his memories there. He wanted this afternoon in the sunshine, with Indy holding carefully on to him and keeping the space she needed to feel safe, to be for them.

He hadn't realized it, but once he'd seen her fear, he'd forgotten his own. There wasn't room to deal with the ghosts of his past or the anger that still dogged him. He wanted to soothe her and show her that she had nothing to worry about while she was with him.

The road was winding and as he accelerated into the turn, he felt her hands soften and then she scooted closer, wrapping her arms tightly around him as he powered out of the turn. Her touch affected him as it always did, setting fire to him like a Scotch bonnet pepper, and he knew that he wouldn't be able to resist her much longer. But he kept it cool, focusing on making this afternoon about her needs. He wanted this adventure for her, as he had a feeling that she limited her adventures to the ones she found between the pages of her books.

They rode for forty-five minutes before he pulled to a stop at the side of the road. Near the outer edges of the land that he and his cousins owned. There was a small brook not too far from here. He wasn't sure why he remembered it now, but he thought that Indy would like it.

Six

Indy hadn't expected to like the bike ride, but something had changed in Conrad once he'd cooked for her. He had seemed to understand that she'd needed some quiet, and the wind blowing past them as he'd driven them along the curving road nearby Gilbert Corners had soothed her.

Her legs were still vibrating from being on the bike when he'd stopped it and gotten off. He'd offered her his hand and now that she stood next to him, she felt awkward again.

He took off his helmet and she did the same. "That fence borders the Gilbert property."

"Y'all sure own a lot of land," she said.

"The trust does now," he said.

"Isn't that you?" she asked, as he offered her his hand

again to cross the water to the other side. They made their way up an incline that wasn't too steep.

"Dash and I provide oversight, but we don't run it," he said.

"Is it a charitable trust?" she asked. "I was surprised when we got the offer to fund the park restoration."

"Were you?" he teased. "I was pretty sure if we didn't act first, you'd be at the offices making a deal."

She smiled at that. "I hadn't thought of it, to be honest. But I have been busy trying to figure out how to break the curse."

He shook his head. "The people in this town need to stop talking about that."

She agreed; curses weren't something that most people talked about. But she could see where they'd think that the Gilbert family and the town that had been named after them might be. "Seems your family had a string of bad luck."

"Yeah," he said.

That was it. He concentrated on the path which was muddy after the spring rains but soon he found whatever he was looking for and led her through some overgrown trees and bushes. He stopped, his broad back and shoulders all she could see, and it wasn't a bad view.

Somehow riding behind him and being more in control of their touching had relaxed something inside her. And of course, Conrad just being so chill about everything, and him accepting her fears in a way she'd never been able to before had helped more than she'd expected.

From where they stood, she saw the flowers blooming in the manicured gardens near where they'd had their cook-off. The octagonal tower with its cupola was visible. It was hard for her to imagine what it had been like to grow up in a mansion.

"This is it. The best view in Gilbert Corners."

She totally agreed, she thought, staring at the way his jeans hugged his butt and then moving her gaze up to the strength of his shoulders. Everything about Conrad was honed to perfection.

He stepped aside and held his hand out to her, drawing her forward to the edge. She caught her breath. Beyond the rolling green lawn of Gilbert Manor she saw the river snaking toward the town, and from here Gilbert Corners didn't look cursed or run-down. The buildings with their Victorian turrets and spires looked picturesque.

"I guess you don't hate everything about the town."

He put his arm on her shoulder and leaned down close so that his head was level with hers. She glanced over at him.

"Tell anyone and I'll deny it."

She laughed. He sounded so surly and annoyed. And she knew that a part of him meant it.

"You dare laugh at the Beast?" he asked with a mock growl.

"If you were really a beast, I doubt I would be laughing, but the truth is, you aren't. I think… I think you hated Lance Gilbert, not Gilbert Corners."

"Still hate, not past tense," he said.

"Why? He's dead," she said, trying to understand where Conrad was coming from. But then, she had only one person she felt anger and hatred toward, and it wasn't a close family member. Would she have found it hard to let go of her anger as well?

"I never got to have it out with him. Never had my say

as an adult. We fought the night of the accident. After I punched that punk—Declan Owen attacked Rory and I broke his nose—grandfather lit into me. I was so angry I went for him, but Dash pulled me away…and we left."

She turned and put her hand on his thick biceps. Feeling this strength in him while hearing his vulnerability. She'd always believed that anger was just the prickly part of a person. The thorns they used to keep everyone at bay, and with Conrad it seemed especially true.

"Did he die before you'd recovered?" she asked carefully.

"Grandfather? No, just before I'd wised up and matured," Conrad said.

"It's hard to think of you as immature."

"Lady, you should have seen me when I was good-looking. I was all ego and confidence. I mean, I thought the world revolved around me."

"You are still good-looking," she said.

"Don't let the stubble and tattoos fool you. This body has some mileage on it."

She shook her head. "That's okay—this one does too. You just can't see it on the outside."

"Damn. Here you go reminding me I still let my ego take the lead."

"We all do. Look at me challenging you and then making a side dare," she said because things were getting too intimate. She was starting to remember how good the first moment of that kiss in her kitchen had been. And that was dangerous.

"That's because you have some big balls, lady."

She blushed but laughed. "I don't, but I like to act like I do."

He smiled down at her. "What else have you promised that you're not sure you can deliver?"

She shook her head. "I'm always sure I'll deliver—I'm just not sure how. I mean, I'm trying to organize the Main Street retailers to put on the spring fling, though I'm really a shy person."

"Your TV show would beg to differ," he said.

"That's different because it's a few close friends and a camera. So not really the entire town. But I need them to work with me."

"So you just power through until you get the results you want?"

She thought about it for a moment, realizing that she had always been like that. "I'm not six-five with a ferocious nickname. Sometimes...well, all the time, I just keep faking it, and usually people believe that I can do all the things I say."

"Even you?"

She chewed her lower lip and noticed his gaze dropped to her mouth and then moved over to the horizon.

"Not all the time, but most of the time."

Conrad was holding on to his control with more strength than he realized he had. He couldn't put his finger on what it was about Indy that shook him and made him want her so badly. The ride hadn't done anything but sharpen his desire for her. But it was the hint of her vulnerability and that feisty spirit that made him want more than just her body.

He'd never needed anyone in his life. He'd made it a practice to keep everyone at arm's length and she should be no different. Given her ties to Gilbert Corners, she should be someone who sent him running in the opposite direction. Instead he had his arm around her shoulder trying to pretend she was just a buddy he was hanging with—except that he didn't have friends like that. He never touched anyone except for casual sex, and that didn't last as long as this.

Since the night he'd punched Rory's attacker, angering Declan enough that he'd chased them down the icy road and caused the car accident, Conrad had kept his hands to himself. The accident had helped. The first few months he hadn't been able to really use his arms and his strength had gone. But as he'd built it back, he'd made a promise to himself to keep his anger in check.

Like Indy with her confidence.

"I do that, too," he said.

"Liar. You don't have to fake confidence."

"No. I have to fake anger. It gives me a buffer and keeps people from actually making me mad."

She turned her head, and he noticed how big her brown eyes were up close. She had thick black lashes and a small birthmark under her left eye. She'd looked so prim and untouchable when he'd first met her that it had been hard for him to see the scars she'd mentioned. But they were there.

Hell, he knew that from dealing with Dash. His cousin had walked away from the car accident scot-free but dealt with more trauma than Conrad did on a daily basis.

"Why do you have to be angry?" she asked. "I didn't get anger the first time I met you."

"You didn't?"

"I mean, you were definitely trying to intimidate me, but you weren't like a bully," she said.

"I'll have to remember that for the future."

She shook her head and a strand of hair that had come free brushed against his arm. It was soft and springy, a light touch, just like Indy herself.

"Why anger?" she asked again.

He wasn't sure he wanted to get that honest with her but at the same time sort of wanted to. "It's easier. When I'm like this, people ask questions."

"Like I'm doing right now. Sorry about that," she said. "You just make me all mixed-up inside. I mean I know I shouldn't be talking so much yet I can't help it."

She took a breath and he knew she was going to keep talking. She was so close, and that botched kiss in her kitchen hadn't satisfied his yearning for her. He leaned in, slowly giving her time to pull away, and took his arm from her shoulders so she wouldn't feel trapped by him at all.

He tried to make himself stop. Told himself if she looked scared, he wouldn't kiss her, but then her eyes closed and he knew he wasn't stopping. Damn his soul, he'd trade anything for just one taste of her. One kiss that ended like an embrace should. He wanted that. Not just for her, but for himself.

"I'm going to kiss you," he said.

"I know," she retorted. "I want you to."

Her words tore through the last of his resistance. He leaned in and this time his mouth brushed hers. Knowing her fear this time, he just stayed there for a second and then her lips parted and he felt her tongue on his. Sliding into his mouth lightly. Like everything about Indy, she moved with a quickness and surety that he wondered if she was allowing her passion to override her doubts.

He opened his eyes and noticed hers were still lightly closed; he angled his head to deepen the kiss because she tasted so good. Addictive. Like the first time he'd cooked a meal that had made him famous. He felt her hands brush against his stomach, then slowly move to his sides. She didn't pull him closer and he kept the space between them, though her fingers were still on him.

He lifted his head. Her lips were moist from his kiss, slightly swollen, and her eyelids fluttered open. She watched him for a long moment. Then sort of nodded, more to herself than to him.

"That wasn't what I expected," she said.

"Me either," he replied. He realized that if he didn't move and leave this spot right now, he was going to be tempted to kiss her again and again until they were both nude. And that felt like it might be more than she wanted. He needed specifics from her, but this wasn't the time for that.

And that wasn't why he'd come to Gilbert Corners. It wasn't why he'd brought her, which also had nothing to do with his reasons for being in GC. But he'd needed to somehow help her past that fear. Kissing Indy had been the only thing he could do after he'd brought her here to the one spot in this area where he'd always felt comfortable.

Up here, it had never mattered if he'd been an ass because he was too rich, too spoiled, too good-looking to realize that he wasn't better than everyone else. Up here, he was enough in his grandfather's eyes. Up here, his parents were still proud of him.

Now he had a new thought for this spot he hadn't visited in over ten years. Up here, Indy thought he was a better version of himself than he'd ever been.

"Ready to go back?"

No.

"Yes, I think so." That was the safe answer. And right now when she was feeling all this chaotic nervous energy, that was the only thing she could do. "Thanks for bringing me."

He didn't say anything, just extended his hand to her as they walked back down the incline toward his bike. They got there and he handed her a helmet, but before she put it on, she said, "That view up there. The way Gilbert Corners looks perfect. I want people to have that feeling when they are in town."

He shook his head. "Perfection isn't what you are looking for."

"Well graffiti sure isn't it either," she said.

"I know. Some happy medium. I like your shop and I like the coffee place, but there are too many abandoned buildings on Main Street. I guess that's why you're filming your show here."

He had a point. She'd been reaching out to businesses, but the uptick had been slow. She knew once she started getting some more of the buildings renovated, she would entice more retailers to town. She wanted Gilbert Corners to match the image in her head. The one she'd create with her television show and her own imagination.

She smiled at him because he watched her with that intense gaze of his. "Now I don't want to sound like everyone on the town council, but I think that's down to the curse."

"Too late—you sound like 'em. But I know what you

mean. Dash and I shouldn't have turned our backs on the town," Conrad said.

"Does that mean you're going to move back here?"

He shook his head. "No. But the trust can do more, and they will. Maybe we can get some more shops open on Main Street and offer incentives for remote professionals to settle in town."

Of course. Despite what he'd said when he'd showed her the town from his favorite vantage point, Conrad didn't want to be part of the town. It wasn't something she understood, but maybe as she got to know him better, she would.

"I think I can help with that when you are ready. I have a lot of contacts from the revitalization we did in Lansdowne."

"I'll make sure to let Dash know."

They drove back to town and he pulled up in her driveway. Once she was off the bike, he nodded toward her and then backed up and drove off.

She knew it was for the best. She hadn't really planned on anything that happened today. She felt exhausted from all the emotions that had been roiling through her from the moment he'd shown up at the park and helped her replant those roses.

Conrad wasn't what she'd expected yet at the same time…he was what she wanted. She shook her head and went inside to call Nola and ask if she could chat.

"Is it a cookies and ice cream chat or a tequila chat?" Nola asked.

"Both?" she said.

"Give me ten minutes and I'll be there," Nola said.

Fifteen minutes later they were both seated on the front porch in the Kennedy Rockers that Indy had restored over the holiday season. They both had a bowl of

Chunky Monkey ice cream, and an opened package of Milano cookies was on the table between them.

"So, um, Conrad Gilbert."

"Yeah. I saw you two working together. What happened? It was pretty busy at the coffee shop so I couldn't really tell what was happening with you guys."

She didn't hesitate to tell Nola everything. This woman was like a soul sister. From the moment they'd met they both sort of got each other.

"He left just like that?" Nola asked after Indy finished.

"Yeah. I mean I didn't ask him to stay. I don't know that I wanted him to stay," she said, taking a big spoon of ice cream, hoping that it would numb her mouth and maybe give her brain freeze so she could think of anything other than how it had felt to kiss him or to hold on to his back as they'd ridden on his bike the way his back had felt pressed against her chest. Her breasts felt fuller when she remembered that adn she hadn't washed her shirt when she got home because the scent of his aftershave lingered on it.

"Maybe he knew that and that's why he left," Nola said. "But he's usually all growly on this TV show. But he's different in person. Not like he used to be, but not like he is on TV either."

"I mean sort of, but it's more of a bluff, I think. But there is a part of him that's almost sweet."

"He sounds like a decent guy which makes sense because Dash is super nice too. I heard old Lance was a piece of work but that was from the factory workers who he fired. So who knows?"

"Maybe. How did Conrad and his cousins end up here?" she asked Nola, because if Lance wasn't a great person, then where did that innate kindness come from?

"I can't really remember the details because I was a

kid, but Conrad's and Dash's parents were killed in a
plane crash. They were brought here to live at Gilbert
Manor. They went to our school for like two weeks. I was
in third grade and they were in fifth. That's all I know.
Rory was in my class. She was so shy but very sweet."

Indy looked over at her friend, wishing she knew
more of the story. She was trying to imagine what it had
been like to lose his parents like that. She thought about
what he said about not being able to talk to his grandfather as an adult. What if it wasn't just his grandfather
he wanted to talk to, but also his parents?

"Did you go to that party the night of the accident?"
she asked.

"Yes, it was something else. Declan Owen, whose
family did business with the Gilberts, was drunk and
hitting on Rory, and then something happened and Conrad knocked him out. Lance told Conrad and Dash that
he should disown his grandchildren for causing a scene.
Conrad went after the old man and Dash pulled him off
and said something, I wasn't close enough to hear, but
my mom said it was heated. Then they drove off, going
too fast. Declan went after them. We all heard the crash."

"Where did it happen?"

"Right on the bridge over the river in the middle of
town. The roads were okay, but the bridge had iced over
and they skidded across it. The car rolled several times.
It was horrible."

Indy's heart was racing just from imagining what it
had been like for Conrad in that car. He'd told her the
aftermath, but now she thought she understood him a
little bit better. And the man who'd been so kind to her
that afternoon. Maybe he was trying to treat her the way
he'd never been treated.

Seven

At midnight her phone dinged with a text message. She only had two chapters left to finish in the book she was reading and really didn't want to stop, but glanced at her phone in case it was her parents with an emergency.

Instead it was an unknown number with a New York City area code.

Intrigued, she pulled the phone closer.

UNKNOWN NUMBER: It's Con. Couldn't sleep thinking about you.

She read the message, and then reread it. How was she meant to respond? Had he texted her by mistake? To be honest, it was only the fact that Nola had come over that had allowed her to stop thinking about him. The book had provided a distraction… but to be fair, the hero had taken on Conrad's large frame, scarred face and soft lips.

Indy Belmont: It's Indy, you know that right?

UNKNOWN NUMBER: Yes.

Indy Belmont: Oh, good. Me too. Sorry things got awkward.

She saw the little dots that signaled he was typing and quickly saved his contact information in her phone.

Conrad Gilbert: It was me as much as you. GC makes my skin feel too tight. But I'm finding it hard to think of not coming back there to see you.

Indy Belmont: I wish… I wish I were different.

She dog-eared the page she was on in her book and set it aside, turning on her side to get more comfortable on her bed. Then her phone rang with a video call from Conrad. She hesitated for a second before answering it. She saw what she looked like in the camera and lifted her arm to try to make it a better angle.

But then he could see she wore her Ravenclaw nightshirt. Her hair was down and though it wasn't morning Medusa out-of-control it was a bit frizzy. She was just… well her. If he was still interested after seeing her like this…she'd be surprised.

"Hey. Just figured it'd be nicer to chat. You in bed?"

"Yeah. I am. Give me a minute to…" Whatever she was about to say, it was going to sound ridiculous. So she put the phone down and ran to the other room to get the phone holder she used when she talked to her mom and dad once a week.

She came back in time to see Conrad's camera pointing at the floor as he walked through a long hallway. She set up her phone and then tried to look alluring or sexy, but let's face it, with this nightshirt and hair…it wasn't happening.

He stopped walking and brought the camera back to his face. "I just got home."

It was really none of her business what he'd been doing, but… "What were you doing?"

"Like I said, lady, I couldn't stop thinking about you, so I was in the test kitchen."

"You were cooking?"

He shrugged as he plopped down on something. Then he reached over and clicked on a light and she realized he was in a bedroom. His?

"It's what I do when I start feeling restless," he said.

"I read. A good book sweeps me away from my own thoughts," she said. "Did you cook it all out?"

"I didn't. I wish you were here with me."

She did too. But she wondered if she'd feel the same way if he were in the same room with her. It was one thing to fantasize about being intimate with him, but she had no idea how she'd really react. The kiss outside this afternoon had shaken her to her core, made her hungry for him in a way that she hadn't thought she'd ever be able to feel again.

"Too much?"

She shook her head. "I'm just not sure about the reality of it—I mean you live in the city and I live in a place you hate."

"Ah, I thought you meant who'd be on top," he said.

Immediately her mind went to what that would be like. Her on his lap, his hands on her body, her hands on shoulders or maybe his chest.

"Con. I'm not sure this is a good idea."

He sighed. "What would be a good idea."

"I'm not sure. I do owe you a weekend, right? We need to talk about that."

"What if I call it off and we date."

"Date?"

"It's this thing where two people who like each other meet up—"

"Ha. I know what a date is—I meant it more as surprised. You don't strike me as a dating kind of guy."

"What kind of guy do I strike you as?" he asked.

"The hooking up for a hot night kind," she said.

"Well okay, I can be that if you want."

"No. I want you…" she trailed off, trying to think of what she wanted from him. *Everything.* But at the same time, she wasn't sure how that would work or if she'd even be able to be intimate with him.

He gave her a rakish smile. "I want you too, but I suspect that's not what you meant."

"It is," she said. "I just don't know."

"You want intimacy," he said.

"I do. I'm pretty sure you don't," she said.

"I called you at midnight, lady. Fuck, that seems intimate to me."

"Sorry. It's easier for me to deflect than admit what I want from you."

"I know," he said. "So about my weekend."

"With me cutting veggies in your kitchen?"

"Or something else."

"Like what?"

He thought it over for a few minutes. "You could come to the city and I'll show you around my neighborhood and then I'll cook you dinner."

"Okay. I can take the train in," she said.

"I can send a car for you."

"No thanks. Where do you live?"

"On Bleecker in an old brownstone mansion that was my parents'. It takes up half the block." He hesitated, a wistful note in his voice. "I'm lucky it stayed in my mother's family. I'll text you the address."

"Nola told me that your parents were killed in a plane crash. That sounded so awful."

"Nola Weston?"

"Yes. Do you remember her from school?" she asked him. This weekend agreement was dangerous because he was making her think of him in a way that was safe. It was okay to kiss him and let him dominate her dreams, but in reality, she knew he'd dominate her life. And she was on her way to something bigger.

"Not really, but she was friends with Rory," he said. "I don't have any friends in Gilbert Corners."

"You do now," she said.

"You?"

"Unless you don't like me."

"I'm calling you at midnight... I think I like you."

She wrinkled her nose at him. "Sounds like you're not sure."

"Lady, if you were here with me, you'd know how much I *like* you."

There was a note of raw desire in his voice that sent heat down her entire body, her breasts felt fuller and her niples hardened. She shifted her legs under the sheets

and wished she and Conrad were in the same room. She
had enjoyed kissing him. He'd stirred to life desires that
she'd told herself she didn't miss, and until this moment
she'd almost believed that lie.

But there was no way she could deny that she wanted
Conrad.

He wasn't a man used to denying himself when he
wanted a woman, but Indy was different. She'd shown
him her sass and determination. Honestly, if he'd been
able to forget about her, he would have been…well not
happier per se but it would have made life easier. Instead
he was catching feelings for her. She'd been in his head
and on his palate all night.

He'd showered and masturbated when he got home,
hoping that would level off his hormones and give him
a modicum of relief, but again, no. Indy Belmont was
still in his blood and playing hell with his senses. Nothing he'd created in the kitchen had satisfied him either.

Probably because he had only seen the glimpse of
the woman she was. She'd shown him the spunky, feisty
bookshop owner determined to rejuvenate her town.
She'd given him a taste of her passion when she'd
touched him and kissed him in her kitchen.

He admired her. He wasn't going to deny it. But he
needed her naked in his bed. On top of him and under
him, facing him, her back pressed against him. He
wanted her every way he could have her. He just felt
like if he had her then maybe, he could finish that dish
which danced elusively around him. And then, maybe,
he could stop thinking about her.

She shifted on the bed. He could tell she was wearing
some sort of T-shirt. Her hair was down— not as long

as he'd guessed it was—and it was curlier. It framed her face and fell only to her shoulders. She had on a pair of horn-rimmed glasses and her heart-shaped face was free of makeup.

Her lips were a natural dusky rose color, and her eyes were big and brown behind the lenses of her glasses, inviting him closer to delve into her secrets. Or was that only his imagination? He wanted her in a way that he hadn't wanted a woman in a long time.

She hadn't responded after he had emphasized how much he liked her. Hell, he had a hard-on and they hadn't been doing anything but talking.

Except talking was all it seemed to take sometimes. Her voice was soft and gentle late at night. Though he knew she lived alone, it seemed she had quieted her voice.

"Did I scare you off?" he asked. Because he didn't figure her for a woman who'd be scared of anything. Especially a man.

"No. I wish I could be some kind of sophisticated woman who knew what to say to that. But I'm not."

"Just be yourself. Did I scare you?"

"No," she said, shaking her head making a few tendrils of her curls bounce around her face.

"Turn you on?"

She chewed her lower lip for a minute and then slowly nodded.

"Good. That's what I was hoping for. You turn me on too."

"Really?" she asked sounding skeptical.

"I'm not a guy to lie."

"Oh, I got that about you," she said. "You have all

these upper-crust manners some of the time, but most of the time you walk around as if you own the world."

"Don't I?" he asked, teasing her.

She shook her head. "No, dear beast, you don't."

Dear beast.

He had felt like one ever since that night ten years ago. Not the car accident but who he'd been before it. The way he'd turned away women who he'd deemed not pretty enough for him, hurting more than one according to overheard comments later in the evening. Then he'd beaten that punk after he'd attacked Rory. Screamed at his grandfather.

But he'd never felt at home with the name. He'd wore it because he'd known deep in his soul that there was something savage about him. Even with his money and manners, there had been something monstrous about him since the moment his parents had died.

"If I did, would it be easier to claim you?" he asked her.

She laughed, and it was a loud full-bodied sound that made his dick even harder. "I've given you the wrong impression of me if you think there is anything easy about me."

He smiled but it was getting harder to keep things light. No, there was nothing easy about Indy. She was complex and intricate. A nice person but not a pushover. Sexy and shy. She was so many differing things at the same time, and all it did was heighten his need to claim her as his own.

"I remember you bullying me into coming to the spring renewal even though I won."

"Bullying!"

"You weren't about to take no for an answer."

"You're right about that. But I just pushed because you're big enough to take it."

"I am big enough," he said, the words coming unbidden. They were his truest desire in this moment. His voice had even dropped a level and sounded husky to his own ears.

"Is that what you want?" she asked, her own voice slightly trembling.

"More than anything," he admitted. He had no problem with honesty. His problems lay with other things like commitment.

"Why?" she asked. "I googled you earlier. You date some really hot women."

"I don't date," he said. Knowing that he could say he just fucked them. She wouldn't understand it. He was different with her. Actually, he was different because of her, he realized.

"Then what is this about?"

"I thought it was about winning a bet," he said.

She tipped her head to the side, eyeing him for a long minute, and he let her. He had no illusions about the man he was. He might not like all the parts of himself, but he knew ever since he'd woken up in the hospital that he'd tried to be better. To do better. He was never going to be anyone's idea of a white knight. He didn't want to be. He just wanted to be the best of who he was.

Ofttimes that was a beast.

Today…he'd seen someone else when he'd taken her for a ride on his bike. He'd seen a man that he didn't know and wasn't sure he wanted to. But with her, that man was lurking in his skin.

She wanted to ask him more about why he didn't date but wasn't sure that she was ready for the answers. She wanted him, and that was enough to deal with on its own but she also really liked him. A part of her wished she could write him off as a spoiled asshole. He owned that about himself, and that had made her like him even though it shouldn't have.

There were massively overgrown vines around him, blocking her view of who he truly was. But every once in a while, she caught a glimpse of someone who made her heartbeat faster, and not just with lust.

"So did I scare you off?" he asked. His voice had a low graveled whiskey tone that made every sense of her body take notice.

The sheets on her legs felt too heavy and the shirt against her body to thick. She wished for the courage to be naked with him. To find her way into his arms and this time really experience everything he had to give her.

It made her uncomfortable to admit it, even just to herself, but Conrad was the embodiment of everything she'd ever wanted in a man. He was driven and success-ful, a man who commanded respect. He was blunt and asked for what he wanted in a way that made her feel almost superficial in her other interactions with people.

"Lady?"

"Yes?"

"The way you keep licking your lips makes me want to feel your tongue on my skin…" he said, his voice get-ting even deeper. "Did that scare you?"

"No," she said slowly as a moist heat pooled between her legs. She hadn't wanted like this in way too long.

"What are you thinking about?" he asked.

"What it would feel like to lick your chest and then work my way lower," she said.

"Damn. That's…"

"Too much?"

"Not at all. Honestly, I like it."

"I do too," she said.

"I should let you go," he said after a few moments had passed.

"Yes. I have to open the shop in the morning and then my assistant will be in around noon. So I could come see you after that—does that work?" she asked.

"I forgot…" he trailed off.

She arched both eyebrows at him, angling her head to the side. "That I have a life and don't just exist when you want to see me?"

"Indy, you cut me. I just meant I forgot what it was like to run a business. Why don't we do it next weekend?"

"Do you work during the week?"

"I pretty much work in the test kitchen when we aren't filming, developing new menus for the restaurant, but I'm ahead of the game there," he said.

She rolled on her side, starting to get sleepy but reluctant to end the call. It had been a long time—maybe forever—since she'd wanted to just keep talking to someone like this. "How do you develop a menu? I'm not even sure I know what that means."

"Well," he said, punching the pillow behind his head and sinking down onto it. "I start with seasonal ingredients and then see what they inspire. Right now we're working on the spring menu for the restaurant. So I call our suppliers and see what they are going to have—some years the crops vary—and then I talk to my partner and the head chef at the restaurant and we work together to come up with dishes."

"I never realized that cooking was so creative," she

said, her words sleepy. "I'm never going to be able to beat you in a cooking contest."

"No, you're not," he confirmed. "I think I'm putting you to sleep."

"You're not. It's late and I had an exhausting day." It had started with the surprise of Conrad at the cleanup, then their kiss and the bike ride. Nola's revelations and then his call. Her mind was too tired to process everything and she knew she needed sleep. But she didn't want him to go.

"I'll let you go and get some sleep."

She smiled at him, touching her phone screen where his mouth was. She remembered the feel of his lips on hers making her mouth tingle. "I'm so glad you called me."

He looked down at her and gave her that devilish grin of his that sent heat through her entire body.

"I'm glad I did too."

"Good night, lady," he said in that low voice that was straight out of her hottest dreams.

"Good night, dear beast." She realized that no matter how ill-advised it was, she was starting to fall for him.

He disconnected the call and she rolled over on the bed, throwing her arms wide, staring at the ceiling. She liked him. Like really liked him. And he wasn't at all someone she should. He hated this town. And she'd fallen in love with this place the moment she'd seen it. The buildings were solid just neglected and needed some care and new life to them. This place had made her feel like she'd found home.

Gilbert Corners was her future. It felt like there was no place for the two of them to meet except for the contest, and, well, in lust. Maybe that was what she needed.

Actually, she *knew* it was. She needed him to help her get past her lingering fears and finally give into to the desires that thinking about Conrad stirred in her.

And that was enough.

That was more than enough, she thought.

Eight

Conrad looked up from his morning coffee as the doorbell rang at his home in New York City. A few moments later, Dash came into the kitchen.

"Morning."

"Morning," Conrad said as he watched his cousin make himself a cup of coffee before sitting down across from him. Dash took a section of the newspaper that Conrad always had delivered and started reading it.

"Am I supposed to ask why you're here?" Conrad asked after a few more minutes had passed.

Dash didn't answer but put the newspaper down. "No. Can we pretend that this is normal?"

"No."

"Rory's doctor is retiring," Dash said, drumming his fingers on the table.

"You said."

"Well I tried to influence the board to hire a specialist I found who I think might actually help her come out of the coma, but they weren't receptive."

"Can't you move her to wherever the specialist is?"

"He's in Sweden, so it's not ideal for me to continue to see her," Dash said. "And he won't come just to be Rory's doctor."

"Want me to try to convince them?" Conrad asked, putting his own paper down and sitting up taller.

"No. That would just make things worse. Apparently, Gilbert Corners General Hospital which owns and runs GC Care Home doesn't want a Gilbert throwing his weight around."

"They said that to you? I mean, the trust pretty much keeps that place running."

"Which I also pointed out," he said. "That didn't win me any points with them. The board told me they'd let me know when a replacement had been found."

"Fucking hell," Conrad said.

"I know. It's almost ten years that she's been in that damned coma. I don't know what to do. Should I move her? I could probably donate a wing or something at a private hospital."

Dash was looking for solutions, and to be honest, Con knew he didn't have one. He thought about Gilbert Corners and what he'd seen yesterday. "I wonder if you don't take one of the older buildings that's run down in the town and make it into a private facility. Hire your expert to come and work there. Kind of give him carte blanche to set it up."

Dash leaned back, stretching his arm along the back of his chair and looking out the window to the manicured garden. Conrad left his cousin to his thoughts, but the idea made him think a little bit more of what Indy wanted to see in the town. Conrad could open a test kitchen and offer cooking classes. Maybe in part of the old factory. But that wasn't going to help Gilbert Corners. Was he just thinking about himself again? He needed to think bigger and bring in more business.

But did he really want to get more involved?

"Yeah, you know, I like that idea. Thanks, Con."

"No problem. What do you think of me taking over part of the old factory?" he asked.

"And doing what?"

"Maybe put in a test kitchen where I could teach locals to cook, or I could get in touch with some friends I know who have established schools. Just use part of it. Is that dumb?"

Dash shook his head. "I like it. I'll look into it. Your name will probably draw some people from surrounding areas. But you'd have to be in GC. And we both know how much you hate that. Right?"

He shrugged. It was complicated. There was a lot of space. He could put in a filming studio and shoot in GC. Also, his former business partner was always needling him to open another restaurant. Would moving back there be a good thing for him? He'd be in the shadow of Gilbert Manor and memories of his overbearing grandfather which never brought out the best in Conrad. "I don't know."

Dash put his hands on the table and leaned forward. "I'm not going to say no to you, but if you start something and then abandon it, you'll be no better than Grandfather when he closed that factory. We can't go in big and start building stuff only to leave."

"I get it. I wouldn't do that," Conrad said, but he knew there was still a chance he might. Maybe Dash was right.

He shoved his hands through his hair and then sat back. "So it has to be something that doesn't require my name. Let me talk to the television network. Maybe we could partner and use it as off-site place to nurture young talent and rotate different celebrity chefs through a new TV series."

"That's a good start. I think you were right about the town needing our attention, and this is the kind of project that would help the locals. I hate to admit this, but I sort of always lumped the town and Grandfather together."

Conrad had, too, and it had taken Indy to make him realize that the townspeople were actually decent and nothing like his grandfather. "I agree. It's time we made it up to them."

"Never heard you talk like this."

"Honestly, never thought I would. But I met someone recently who is making me see things differently."

"The bookshop girl?"

"She's a woman," Conrad said. Except Indy was so much more than just a woman. She was a temptress, so sweet and sexy making him hunger for her.

"Is she? Want to tell me about her?"

"No," he said. He wanted to keep Indy to himself but then he realized that he did want to talk about her. Maybe Dash would hear something or see something in his comments that would allow Indy make sense to him.

So he told Dash about her. He didn't leave out anything because they were close and had no secrets. They both saw each other for who they were. Conrad might be the Beast and Dash the Prince Charming of the Gilbert family, but they were the same inside.

Deeply protective, defensive, and not afraid to walk away from everything. That bond had been forged at their parents' deaths and hadn't been tarnished through the accident that had shaped their destiny.

Conrad talked through lunch, and they grabbed beers to sit by the pool when he'd finally wound down.

"I like the sound of her. She's not your usual type," Dash said.

"No shit. That's the problem," Con said. "Or am I missing something?"

"Only time will tell. You should think of a relationship with her the same way you do about opening that kitchen in Gilbert Corners. Only do it if you're going to see it through. Otherwise, you'll both end up getting hurt."

The bookshop was busy on Sundays as a rule. Nola set up a pop-up coffee stand in the front of the shop and Indy hosted a children's reading hour between two and three so that parents could browse in her shop or other stores on Main Street.

She'd dreamt of Conrad all night and woken up hungry for him. She couldn't wait for the weekend. It felt like she'd spent most of her adult life waiting for something, and until yesterday, she hadn't realized what it was. She'd frozen a part of herself, afraid she wouldn't find her own path after that horrible date and the attack that had followed. Even Wayne hadn't really been able to handle it.

He'd been her high school boyfriend, and when she'd come back home, she'd tried to date him again. He was safe and he loved her. But she'd never been able to relax with him. She told herself she left her hometown because he got engaged, but she knew it was really to spare herself any residual disappointment.

She knew she'd been lucky to escape with just some scrapes, bruises and a fear of intimacy. She'd punched her attacker Ben so hard in the throat that he hadn't been able to speak for a few weeks. The claw marks on his eyes had taken longer to fade.

The incident had made Indy face the violence within herself, and whenever she saw Ben on campus, she'd felt sickened being near him and an irrational sense of pride at the damage she'd caused him. Eventually she dropped out and started going to online school.

That incident had cemented in her that she had a very large capacity for doing violence to another person. She knew if pushed, she'd react that way. And until last night, she hadn't realized that she also had a lot of passion inside her. She'd shied away from anything that stirred her emotions, wrapped herself in a bubble and faked a friendliness that wasn't true to herself.

But even Wayne, who she'd always trusted, hadn't been able to break through the wall she'd built around herself. They'd worked together on remodeling the bookshop in town and she'd filmed herself doing the job, finding some balance inside herself, and some peace.

Once she and Nola had decided on this path, it had felt right. Like exactly what she needed. She knew she'd sort of lied to Conrad about why she was here. No use mentioning the old boyfriend who was getting married in her hometown. She also knew saying she didn't want to be like her mom had a lot to do with the fact that she'd secretly hoped she *was* like her mom and had found the love of her life.

When Wayne had rejected her, moved on so quickly

and gotten engaged...well, Lansdowne hadn't felt like home anymore. Her producers had suggested they remodel another town and she'd jumped at the chance to be somewhere new.

Gilbert Corners.

She genuinely liked the people here, even the town council when they'd been difficult about her ideas for the park cleanup and the spring fling. She knew a big part of that was the image she had of small towns in her head. It didn't help that she had grown up watching *Gilmore Girls* and then fallen further for small towns viewing *Schitt's Creek*. Those shows had given her a glimpse of something she'd never realized she wanted.

She glanced at her phone. She'd sneakily taken a screen shot of the video call last night, so she opened it after making sure no one could see her and clicked on the saved photo of Conrad.

In the dim light of his bedroom, one side of his features were in shadow. She traced her finger over the jagged scar that disappeared into his beard and zoomed in to look more closely at his eyes, trying to read his emotions. It was hard to say for certain, but she saw passion and need in them. She sighed.

"What are you doing?"

She jumped and screamed. "Nola, you scared me."

"Yeah, I can see that. You seemed lost in thought," she said, craning her neck to see the screen.

Indy quickly hit the button to close the phone and stuffed it into her pocket. "What's up?"

"Thought I'd see if you wanted to take a lunch break," she said. "I stopped by the deli on my way here—the owners want to talk to you about filming its renovations.

They have some good ideas. I took a look around the place and have some photos if you want to look at them."

"Great. I have my eye on the old general store/five-and-ten space. But that is going to be a big job. So the deli might be a nice place to film and get the town involved even more."

She led the way back to the office. After Nola had closed the door and they were both seated, Indy at her desk and Nola in the guest chair, they conference called her producer to discuss options. The production team wanted to meet the next weekend, but Indy had promised it to Conrad, and for the first time since she started the show she decided to keep that day for herself. Everyone was surprised she wasn't available but just agreed on a later date for the in-person talks.

"What are you doing this weekend? I've literally never heard you say no," Nola said.

"I know. But Conrad is taking me to his place in New York and he's going to fix me dinner," she said as Nola handed her a pastrami on rye sandwich.

"That's…wait, when did he do that?"

"Last night. He called me close to midnight," she said.

"Uh, that's interesting. So this thing between you two is more than just a kiss?" she asked.

Indy wrapped one arm around her own waist trying to hold in her excitement. It wasn't as simple as she wished it were. "Honestly, I don't know, and I'm not sure what to expect. Or if I'll even be chill enough to enjoy myself with him. But I want to go."

"I don't blame you. I mean, he *is* hot. All the Gilberts are so beautiful. Why are the rich also pretty? Seems like an unfair distribution of resources to me."

Indy laughed. "He is hot. I haven't been this turned

on by a guy in real life since… Wayne. Which worries me—I don't want to make him into someone he's not just to make myself feel better."

Nola put her sandwich down and came over to hug Indy. "It's okay to give it a few minutes thought, but don't let it overwhelm you. You said you've found yourself again. And I can see that. This move has changed you. It's like…well, like you're the woman I met in the freshman dorm who was ready to set the world on fire."

She hugged her friend back. "I feel like I'm different too. I thought I was back to myself once I got the show and everything, but looking back, I think I was still swimming through life, not really living. Isn't it funny how long everything takes?"

"I mean I thought at twenty-one that's me, done, and here I am at thirty, still single, still working in a coffee shop—"

"You own the coffee shop for one thing, and you're an immensely popular part of our TV show and you have your woodworking," Indy interrupted her friend.

"Career-wise I'm right where I want to be. Romantically… I could get with a couple of guys in town if I wanted to. But just hooking up isn't really doing it for me."

"I've seen that in you lately. But I do think you are living your best life and doing what you love," Indy said.

"Thanks. I think I am too, but we were talking about you," Nola reminded her.

"I'm trying. Every day I feel a little bit closer to figuring out what my best life looks like. I do love the TV show which I thought was a stopgap, but now it feels like what I was meant to do."

"I think it's just being comfortable in your skin," Nola said.

They finished eating their lunch, talking about the latest period drama television series that they'd both binged. After Nola left, Indy couldn't help thinking of what she'd said. Was simply being comfortable in her skin all that she needed?

Dash had stayed most of the afternoon, then left, and Conrad had come to the test kitchen. It was situated in an old warehouse that he'd converted a few blocks from his Michelin starred restaurant La Bête de la Fable. He had done most of his kitchen training in France and all of his recipes were twists on classic French dishes.

Recently though, he'd been leaning more into fusion, which he knew could go either way with the Michelin judges, and the head chef, Lucien, and his partner, Sig, both were wary of doing anything risky. Risk was like second nature to him at this point, but he knew that his livelihood wasn't tied to the success or failure of the restaurant the way his staff's and partner's lives were.

Yet he couldn't help pushing himself. And he was back again trying to find a dish that would help him make sense of Indy. Last night he'd had a different glimpse of her, with her hair hanging down and curling around her face. The dark curls against her lighter skin had made him think of sorrel and mushrooms in a thick cream sauce. There was something so homey and satisfying about that combination.

So he'd start with that as a base. She'd stirred fire and heat in him, so he gravitated toward garlic and maybe some chilies or ginger. He pulled the spices walking through his kitchen pantry and trying to think what else.

She was delicate, and a cream sauce required something else delicate…not chicken, which was too commonplace for Indy. Something more exciting and intoxicating. His mind kept running through ingredients; before he could make his choice the door to the test kitchen opened and Ophelia walked in.

"I was surprised to see your bike out front today," she said. "But glad. We need to talk about the challenge."

She looked understated and sophisticated as always. She wore a pencil skirt and T-shirt that had sequins where her breasts were. He never knew what he was going to get with Ophelia. She loved to experiment with fashion, he had realized a long time ago that her clothes were an indicator of her mood. He just never had been sure what that mood was. .

"What about it?"

"I have been editing the footage. Do you want me to take out the part about you going to the spring renewal? I also found another challenger for you. You free this weekend?" she asked. "The chef who issued the challenge is one the network is thinking of offering a show to, so it would be a nice test run."

Well fuck.

He was tempted to say yes. Maybe it was fate as Indy believed, stepping in to save her from him. But he wanted her, and fate was going to have work harder than this.

"Sorry, but I can't. Leave the spring renewal thing in. I think one of the kids in town put a video of it up on his socials—Dash is monitoring it if you want to add the footage to the end of the show. I'll film with your other guy as well, but just not this weekend."

"You never have weekend plans."

Ophelia and he had spent more than one late night drinking and sharing stories of their pasts. Both of them came from a different world than cooking and restaurants and were glad to have left it behind.

He ignored that.

"I'll let the network know that you'll do a remote pickup for the promos and cook with their guy in a ten-minute spot. That area is famous for fried bologna rolls, so try to plan on doing a take on that."

"Are you serious?"

"Am I ever not?" She paused. "What are you working on, anyway?"

"Not sure yet. Something that's been in my mind and elusive on my tongue. I know the taste I want to achieve, but haven't figured out what's needed yet," he said.

"Good luck with that. I'll send out the shooting schedule tonight so you can prepare. Let me know if you need anything," she said before waving goodbye and leaving.

Yesterday, talking to Indy had made him realize that the hatred he'd been carrying around toward his grandfather had started to wane. Maybe it stemmed from the fact that he'd found a life he liked. Cooking suited him in way that nothing else ever had. And the commercial kitchens he'd worked in had given him a place to rage around as much as he wanted to. They were intense and tempers flared, and words flew but were easily forgiven. He'd found a way to live with his beast in the kitchen.

Now he just had to figure out how to do that outside it. This weekend with Indy…maybe he was taking a step toward that. Inviting her to come and see his neighborhood. Having guests in the house he'd grown up in was something of a gamble. Only Dash visited him there. He didn't entertain, and he knew that he was more himself there than anywhere else. It would be harder to contain his base instincts.

But he would have to.

He didn't want to take a chance on scaring her off, not now when he had her so close. He'd spent the last ten years trying to move on from that horrible night and slowly, small parts of him had, but this was something different.

This was him thinking about a woman, and not just for sex. This was him thinking about a relationship, and though he was a man who didn't allow himself to be afraid of anything, he also wouldn't lie to himself. Something about Indy scared him. He'd used his beastly persona to prevent himself from forming close attachments but none of those things had kept him from starting to care for her.

That felt more dangerous than anything he'd experienced before.

Nine

Indy was surprised when the limo pulled up in front of her house at eight on Saturday morning. Conrad had texted her to ask if she could be ready early, so maybe she shouldn't have been. The driver came to the door and she looked down at her wedge-heeled sandals and the large leather carryall where she'd packed for the weekend on her shoulder and wondered if she was underdressed.

"Ms. Belmont, are you ready?"

"Yes, sir," she said, closing and locking her door behind her.

The chauffeur opened the rear door and she was surprised to find the backseat empty. She'd expected Conrad. But she sat down and scooted into the air-conditioned car. The screen was down between her and the driver and she seemed to remember that proper etiquette dictated the passenger decide if they wanted privacy or not.

She waited until he was seated before leaning forward.

"Is Mr. Gilbert joining us?"

"He asked me to escort you to Gilbert Manor where he's waiting for you."

She leaned back. Obviously, something had changed since last they'd spoken. He had offered to show her around his neighborhood in the city. She sat back as the car drove through the town of Gilbert Corners and then turned left out of town and drove up the winding hills that led to Gilbert Manor.

The main roads had been maintained, but when they turned off them, they became less neat. They drove through Doric columns that supported a marble arch with the name Gilbert on it. The landscaping on both sides of the drive had been maintained, but she could hear the gravel under the tires until they rounded a corner, and the tree-lined drive gave way to a circular solid brick drive that led up to a large portico entrance. There was another man standing at the front door in a dark suit.

Again, not Conrad.

The house was intimidating her a little this time. It wasn't like when she'd been here for the cook-off. She was clearly a guest of "Mr. Gilbert." Not Conrad. Not her dear beast.

He opened the door as the car pulled to a stop and offered her his hand, which she took as she climbed out of the back of the limo.

"Welcome to Gilbert Manor, Ms. Belmont. I am Worthington, head of household. Mr. Gilbert asked that I show you inside to your room."

"I'm not sure I'm staying overnight," she said, though she'd packed for it.

"It's just for the day, so you can freshen up."

She just nodded. The drive wasn't that far, but when she entered the house, she caught her breath and stopped worrying about Conrad and what was going on. The foyer looked like marble to her untrained eye, and the arches she'd seen back at the entrance were mirrored here.

In fact, the entry hall was wide, bigger than her living room and elegantly appointed. There was a grand staircase in the center with hallways that led off in both directions. Worthington told her the history of the house as he led the way up the stairs, but she wasn't paying attention. Instead, her eyes were drawn to the portraiture on the walls. There was a striking resemblance between Gilbert and his ancestors.

Worthington stopped down the left hall in front of a door. "Here is your room. Mr. Gilbert wanted to give you some space. I'll wait outside until you are ready and then escort you to join him in the library."

She went into the bedroom, pulled out her phone and called Conrad.

"Yes."

"What's going on? I thought you hated Gilbert Manor and everything about where you grew up."

"I don't hate it all. This place is probably more directly responsible for who I am than the house I lived in with my parents. Is it too formal? I mean, I would get it if you didn't like it."

She looked around the elegant room with the four-poster bed and Chippendale furniture. She noticed a dress on the bed that looked light as air, all tulle and satin, and she went closer to examine it.

"I don't know. And what's the dress for?" She ran her hand over it. It wasn't the kind of thing she'd ever worn. She never got to walk the red carpet, and she'd never been invited to a ball. This was…too much.

"It's too much for a day date."

"Dinner. We always dress for meals at the manor. Plus, maybe this is what's needed for us to break the curse."

"You said you didn't believe in it," she pointed out.

"I don't, but let's say there is a curse—it probably started the night of the ball and the car crash," he said. "I guess I'll have to leave the ballroom with a gorgeous woman to break it."

Then just left it there. "How about we have this tour and then we see how the day goes?" she said.

"We'll start off slow then. There are some riding clothes in the armoire. Do you ride?"

"Not since Girl Scout camp, and then it was a teth-ered ride."

"Do you trust me to keep you safe?" he asked.

She did. She wouldn't be here if she didn't. "I do. But your head of household mentioned a library. Can I see that before we go riding?"

"Yes. If you want, we can skip riding and have a pic-nic on the terrace next to the library," he said.

"I want!"

"Then come as you are," he said.

She started for the door, but stopped. "What are you wearing?"

"Why?"

"I mean are you in some tux or formal wear?"

"I'll be casual when you get here," he said.

She put her bag on the bed, freshened up her hair and makeup and went out into the hallway about ten minutes later to find Conrad waiting for her.

She looked at his face, with the scar on one side, his hair wild around his head...but his smile was tentative. He wasn't as sure of himself as she'd seen him in the past. Why had he brought her here? What was he trying to show her—more of himself, or was it something he was trying to prove to himself?

She had a feeling that some of his discomfort was rooted in the fact that he wasn't the same man he had been the last time he was here. Like he had said, the night of the ball that started the curse. She wondered if, like herself, Conrad had two lives he was trying to stitch together to make one whole.

For her, it came back to that horrible sexual attack from her date. The two women she was—one before and one after—were slowly becoming one, stronger woman. Conrad from all accounts had been arrogant and very lord-of-the-manor before the accident and then he became the person she saw today. Was he trying to bridge those two pieces?

If so, she wanted to help him find a way. Not that she was an expert.

"I like the place. You make more sense here," she said.

Conrad had given a lot of thought to what Dash had said. He couldn't treat Indy the way he had everyone else in his adult life. Well he *could*, but late last night it had occurred to him that if he did, he'd regret it. There was something about her, and he'd never been a man to walk away from a new experience.

So he'd gone all in. Indy meant spending more time in Gilbert Corners and he needed to wrestle with the demons from his past. While he did think the town belief in a curse was total BS, there was a glimmer of something to it.

That night had really changed his life forever.

He needed to find a way to make peace with it, something that he wasn't sure he could accomplish. Being back in the house had reminded him of memories he'd shoved deep down and covered up. Good memories of running down the halls with Dash and Rory. Planning cookie and pie heists, and helping Worthington by sliding down the banisters so he wouldn't have to polish them.

He smiled as Indy stood next to him. He'd thrown her off by changing their plans at the last minute, which was something he liked to do when he was nervous. He wanted to see if it rattled her. No surprise, the change of venue hadn't.

He liked the grin in her eyes as she called this palatial manor house a "nice place."

"Want the grand tour?" he asked.

"Worthington gave me some of it, but I was distracted," she admitted.

"There's no rush. You did promise me the entire weekend," he said.

"True. Then can we start with the portraits in the entry foyer?" she asked. "Who are all those people? You look like some of them."

She was interested in his past, and he realized he was going to have to crack open and let her see parts of himself. The portraits in the hall were nice, but the gallery above the ballroom would be more impressive.

."Let me show you where we keep the important people," he said, putting his hand on her back and leading her down the hall to the gallery. It was a large balcony with a gold-plated guardrail that overlooked the rotunda that was the ballroom.

The ceiling was a fresco that had been painted in the 1920s by a contemporary painter who had blended the abstract with modern cubism.

"Wow, that's impressive. Is the ceiling supposed to be…actually, I can't make it out? I'm not really good at guessing abstract designs."

He laughed. "Me either. Dash and I decided that the darkish part on this side was where the evil dragons or Pokémon lived when we were kids, and we would battle them around the walkway to the other side where it's lighter. They'd be banished, and we'd win."

"I like it. Is it meant to be a sky?"

"Yes. It's the artist's view of Gilbert Corners' sky in all the seasons apparently. Rory used to know a bunch of facts about it," he said.

"Do you miss her?" she asked.

He didn't like talking about her. But that was why he'd brought Indy here. He needed to see if he could open up. He wanted to let her in. "Yes."

"Do you want to talk about her?"

"No."

She slipped her hand into his and squeezed. A heat spread up his arm then through him and though he'd vowed to take things slow today, he knew he wanted her. Had wanted to pull her into his arms since the moment she'd stepped out of her room.

"That's okay. So who are the people in the portraits behind us?" she asked, dropping his hand and turning to the framed picture.

He stood behind her and put his arm on her shoulder, pulling her back into his body. "This is the first Gilbert family who settled here. They came over from England to help settle this colony."

He kept his arm around her shoulders as he led her circling the rotunda showing her his ancestors through the years, stopping in front of the portrait with him and his parents. He hadn't looked at it in years. In fact, when he and Dash had played up here, they always ignored these most recent pictures.

She slipped her arm around his waist. "Are those your parents?"

"Hmm."

She turned so that her body was pressed to his side as she hugged him. "You must miss them. You look just like your dad, but you have your mother's eyes."

He hugged her back, both comforted and turned on by her touch. He held her and finally lifted his eyes to the painting. He felt his eyes sting as he looked at his mom and dad for the first time in decades. They looked so young. As a child they'd seemed old, but Conrad was almost the age his father had been when he'd died.

God, he missed them.

Indy hugged him tight and then went up on her tip-toes to kiss his cheek. He turned his head and found her mouth with his. Channeling his grief into the one emotion that he felt at home expressing. He didn't move to surround her, even dropped his arm from her shoulder but she stayed where she was.

He felt her hand on his waist tighten as her tongue

brushed over his, and he opened himself to the kiss and the blooming sensuality he felt in her. He kept tight control on himself and turned slightly so her chest brushed against his torso.

She hesitated for a second, then pulled him closer against her as her hands moved down his back to cup his butt and draw him more fully against her.

The blood rushed from his brain, and he stopped thinking and started to give in to the passion, which was never far away when Indy was around. He lifted her slightly off her feet with one arm around her hips and deepened the kiss even more.

Letting loose the tight control he'd been holding on to since the moment he'd seen her today. Desire and lust had been hard to tamp down and he'd surprised himself by how much talking to Indy had just made him want her more.

He would do everything in his power to make her stay with him and to have her in his bed tonight.

She hadn't meant to kiss him, but the pain had been almost palpable when he'd looked at the portrait of him and his parents. And Indy's heart had broken for that little boy. Conrad smiled out of the portrait with innocence and pure happiness. Two things that he no longer had.

She cautioned herself to be careful with him. There was so much hidden inside him that he had just let scab over and moved on. She saw it in him because she felt it inside herself every day. They were both broken—or maybe bent, not broken, but in different ways. She didn't know that their bent pieces could fit together. She was trying to be entirely realistic. Which wasn't how she normally acted. Of course, as he deepened the kiss, lifting her off her feet so that she was leaning fully into his body with his erection growing against her, she realized there was a way that they would fit together very nicely.

But she wasn't sure she was ready to get physical with him. She wanted him, but there was still so much about him she was unsure of. It was only Conrad's sadness that he seemed to allow himself to feel. She suspected he felt something for her but could he express that? As if he somehow was trying to show her what he couldn't say directly.

That was part of it. He was trying to make her feel more comfortable with him. His sadness sort of teased hers out, made the memories start to creep in. Made her remember the reasons why she was hesitating with this man that was so tempting, so intriguing. Despite her doubts it was sort of working and she wanted to just open herself and be vulnerable to him.

No matter that at times that thought scared her.

But she slammed it, pushing the past where it belonged. Far away from this otherworldly balcony surrounded by Conrad's past on one side and his rock-solid, hot body on the other. He tasted so good, like something exotic and addicting. She admitted she wanted more. Of his kisses, of his body, of everything he'd offer her.

She had the feeling deep in her gut that these moments with Conrad were fleeting. That any real chance of him staying with her wasn't realistic. But at the same time, he was offering her something no other man could. A chance to reclaim a part of her femininity that she'd been afraid of for much too long.

He lifted his head, staring down into her eyes, and she wanted to be cool. Wanted to make it seem as if this was just a hot kiss and there weren't a million other emotions rolling through her, but she knew she didn't pull it off when he rubbed his thumb over her bottom lip and gave her a knowing smile.

"I think we've seen enough of my family," he said. "So next stop is up to you. Library or the gardens?" he asked.

She was disappointed at how relieved she was that he'd made this moment normal. But at the same time, this was one of the things that made it hard for her not to fall for Conrad. Her mind was blaring the word *temporary*, but her heart and soul felt this connection that seemed eternal.

"Library first," she said. "I'm going to be fully disappointed if it isn't at least floor-to-ceiling and doesn't have a ladder."

"Oh, you'll have to wait and see," he said, leading her away from the rotunda. Before they stepped off the walkway, she stopped him.

"Is this where the ball was?"

She felt almost as if a curtain had come down between them. He gave her a tight-lipped nod.

"It's so pretty. I bet it looked nice that night," she said carefully. She was backpedaling, trying not to push too hard, but that kiss had blown past the barriers that she'd thought she'd put in place. And even if he was temporary…would it really hurt to ask the hard questions?

"It was. You can see it from here if you look closely— there are a bunch of fiber-optic lights in the ceiling that make it look like twinkling stars," he said.

"Sounds magical," she observed. If she pushed for anything else, he'd shut her out completely. "Like the perfect night for a curse to be born."

"Probably," he said. "I guess that makes my grandfather some sort of evil wizard."

"Maybe, or maybe a jealous witch put a spell on the castle and everyone in it."

"It's a manor house," he pointed out.

"You just said it was magical."

"Did I say that? Seems more like you were the one going for the magic angle."

"Well this is way more castle-like than any house I've lived in," she said.

"I'll allow it."

She lightly punched his shoulder, delighted at the resistance of his solid muscles. She pulled her hand back. "Do you work out?"

He started laughing and shook his head. "Yes. If I don't then I fall into bad habits."

"Like?"

"Indulging your questions," he said.

"I know you count on those kinds of responses to shut me up, but it won't work," she said. "Did your dad grow up here?"

"He did. Dash and Rory's father was his twin," he said.

"When did his mom die?" she asked. "I'm wondering if that's what happened to change your grandfather."

"Don't try to make him human to me."

She took a deep breath. This was pushing in a way that she couldn't justify. She should leave it alone. But she liked Conrad, she wanted him and he was making her think of things that she hadn't dreamed of in a long time. So that meant she was going to have to take a few risks.

But for now she'd leave it.

She was also curious about his grandmother. From all accounts his father was a good, loving man. Which meant at some point, someone in this house had been loving too.

She had a lot of questions, but kept them to herself.

"So the library?"

"Down this way," he said, leading them to the stairs. He put some physical distance between the two of them and she couldn't help wondering if he regretted inviting her here.

But she didn't ask and when they got to the library, she forgot all about that. It was full of floor-to-ceiling bookcases with ladders to reach the top shelves. There were overstuffed chairs positioned in the room and a window seat that overlooked the gardens in the back of the house.

"You do not disappoint, Conrad," she said.

"Stick around. I'm just getting started."

Ten

Conrad wasn't used to second-guessing himself. It just wasn't the way he operated. He moved forward and left regret behind him. But having Indy here wasn't the smartest idea. She stirred fierce emotions like affection and caring. He struggled to deal with them, as he hadn't really allowed himself to care for anyone other than Rory and Dash for a decade. Whether she meant to or not, Indy was making him feel.

She didn't respond to his comment and he was happy enough for that. She moved into the library, which had large French doors that overlooked the patio and then the gardens below. But she didn't move toward them. Instead she went to the bookshelves.

Just given what he'd seen of her shop, he wasn't surprised that she liked books. This wasn't his favorite room in the house and normally he avoided it but he wanted to make her smile. And he had. It was worth the too tight feeling of his skin.

She stood in front of the bookcase that housed some of the oldest and rarest collections of his family's books. There was a genealogy of the Gilberts that went all the way back to a foolscap illuminated manuscript from the late 1400s up to today, which of course was leather-bound. He skipped past his family history to the bookshelf in the corner that had been his father's favorite.

Unless he was drunk, he rarely allowed himself to think of his parents. But seeing their photo today had reminded him of this corner. He stooped down and, on the bottom shelf, pulled out a copy of *The Three Musketeers* by Alexandre Dumas. He held it loosely in one hand, reaching into the space created. He had to feel around for it, but then he caught the braided cord of the hidden book.

He pulled it out just as Indy wandered over to him. He stood up as she approached.

"What have you got there?" she asked.

"*Three Musketeers.* It was my dad's favorite."

"And that?" she asked pointing to the small, bound sheaf of papers held in his other hand.

He lifted it up to show her. "Something my dad and his brother wrote when they were younger. Dash and I found it one rainy summer day. I had forgotten about it until now."

She came closer and put her hand on his arm. The touch went through him like fire and he started to pull away, but then stopped himself. What if Indy wasn't different from other women? What if it was just his reaction to her? What if he was somehow making her into something he needed?

And if that was the case, maybe he should stop trying to see her in a different light. He put his arm around her shoulder and pulled her into the curve of his body. She seemed startled at first and then she put her arm around his waist.

"*The Adventures of Blue and Brown*...not the best title in the world," she said.

"Yeah. Dad and Uncle Hamm were fraternal twins and had different color eyes...so that's where the title comes from," he said.

"Want to read it to me?" she suggested, taking his hand again and leading him over to the window seat.

He followed her, very aware that he wasn't feeling stable. Like he was on the cusp of something. It didn't feel like anger, but anger was his old home and the most comfortable of his emotions. This was different, and he wasn't going to deny that it scared him. She sat down on one side and drew her legs up to her chest before resting her chin on them, watching him.

His chest felt too tight and his body was on fire for her. The touches and this closeness were making it almost impossible to think of anything other than pulling her into his arms. No one would disturb them and making love on the large window seat appealed to him.

"Scoot up. I'll sit behind you," he said.

She nodded and moved forward and after a moment he was seated behind her. His legs cradling either side of her body, her back pressed against his chest, her buttocks right against his cock. He put his arms around her and opened the homemade book.

"'*The Adventures of Blue and Brown* started on a cold, wet Wednesday when the cook made blueberry pie.'"

He read the story to her of two boys scheming to steal

a pie from the kitchen and their misfortune as they got closer and closer and were always foiled by someone or something. They couldn't take a direct route to the kitchens since it went past their father's study and he was working. It ended with them being called down to dinner and their mother giving them both a slice of pie.

He'd never known his grandmother. She'd died when his dad was in high school. But reading this…if he had to guess where his father's kindness had come from, it was definitely her.

"That was fun," she said. "You have a great reading voice. I think you should consider doing some sort of audio thing."

"Yeah?"

"Hmm mmm," she said, turning around so that she knelt between his legs. "Why did you did you bring me here?"

He glanced down at the curve of her neckline where the slight swell of her breasts was visible and then back up to her face. Why? He wasn't entirely sure. But he knew he had to say something.

"I don't know. I want you," he said with blunt honesty. "And you are tied to this town and not a casual person. And I hate this place…so I figured I should try to see if I could like it here."

"Is it working?" she asked.

He wasn't entirely sure of that. "I still want you."

"I want you too," she said. "I've only had sex with one person…before that date that went wrong."

He nodded; that made sense to him.

"Do you want to talk about it?"

"Not really. I wasn't feeling it and said no and he…didn't stop."

Despite what he'd been trying to convince himself of earlier, she wasn't a like any other woman. He knew that. She was passionate and put herself into all things that mattered to her. And that made him want her even more.

The fact that she wasn't casual might be why he wanted her so badly. Why he felt something more for her other than lust, and why he'd brought her here. He might have told himself and acted to the world like he wanted no part of Gilbert Manor or even Gilbert Corners, but the truth was more nuanced than that.

He hadn't been able to admit it until Indy. She was making him see himself and this place in a different way. He wasn't entirely sure he liked it but he also knew he couldn't walk away from her.

"I've had lots of sex and different partners but none of them have been you," he admitted.

She looked into Conrad's big blue eyes and fancied that she could see into his soul. But the truth was more complex than that. He was a man who didn't share himself easily or at all. Since she'd arrived here—actually, since his car had shown up at her house, the day hadn't gone the way she'd expected. She could tell that Conrad wasn't as in control as he usually was.

It was nice to see his guard drop. She hadn't been lying about his gorgeous reading voice; there was a sensitivity to him that he kept carefully hidden. She had a glimpse of it when he'd cooked for her. He was the kind of man who always had his guard up. And hearing how his father and uncle had trodden carefully around their grandfather gave her more of an idea of why he was that way.

He'd been surrounding her while he read, and she had

found that his voice was now as much as part of her as her heartbeat or breathing. She wanted him.

"Is there anything in your sexual health history I should know?"

He shook his head, smiling at her. "No. Nothing at all."

"Sorry, I mean it would be irresponsible not to ask. I know it's not sexy," she said.

"It's not sexy, but your straightforwardness is. And before you ask, I have condoms and I will wear one," he said.

She felt herself blushing but nodded her thanks. She had been planning to ask. They were in a new relationship and still figuring things out. It might not go further than this one day in Gilbert Manor. Neither of them needed the complication of an unexpected pregnancy.

"Great."

"Come on. I want to cook for you in a kitchen that's actually stocked. What's your favorite meal?" he asked, lifting her up and swinging his legs to the floor. He set her on her feet before standing and leading her out of the library.

"Can we come back here later? I didn't get to look at all the books," she said.

"Of course. Favorite meal?"

The hallway they walked through wasn't as formal as the one they'd entered through. She tried to think of her favorite meal, but he was a chef with a Michelin star and a television show, so she wanted to make it sound like a real meal instead of Kraft Mac & Cheese with cut up hot dogs. She tried to remember the best meal she'd had, and it was either her dad's barbecue or her mom's hush puppies.

"It's nothing sophisticated," she admitted.

"It's okay. I like all kinds of food."

She was sure that meant exotic stuff that she'd probably have to force herself to eat. She just wasn't a foodie. "What's *your* favorite meal?"

"Why are you hesitating?" he asked.

She stopped walking and put one arm around her waist. "I don't want to say something else that will just make you realize how much I don't fit in with your life."

He put one hand on the wall behind her head and the other on her shoulder as he leaned in. "I'm the one who doesn't fit. That's why I'm here."

She reached up to touch his face because she'd been longing to do that since he'd stopped reading. "Maybe we fit because we're so different?"

"Maybe. Food is how I…well, how I communicate best. Even Dash has said it and honestly, he's the one person I'm closest to."

"My favorite meals are my dad's barbecue, my mom's hush puppies and boxed macaroni and cheese," she said. "I'm also a fan of fast-food chicken sandwiches. Those foods all connect to my happiest memories. Sometimes it was the aftermath of disappointment but those meals…"

"I get it. Food is love," he said as he started to walk again and she followed him.

"Did I shock you with my basic food loves?"

"No. I like barbecue too and hush puppies. The only food I don't really eat is fast food," he said.

She had a friend in New York who had never had fast food, so that didn't surprise her. She couldn't imagine him eating in that kind of place. "So what are you going to make?"

"I'm not sure yet," he said. "But I've got a few ideas."

"Like what?"

"Something simple."

"Simple?"

"Don't say it like that's an insult. The best meals are simple. Made with fresh ingredients."

"Like those cheese sandwiches you made for us," she said. "I had no idea those ingredients from my fridge could taste that good."

"Yeah, well, this will be better than that," he added.

"I don't see how," she said as he led her into the kitchen and motioned for her to have a seat at the long butcher-block island. There was a stool set up and she realized that he'd planned this.

This was truly Conrad's world and she believed she'd learn a lot about him in here. She told herself that was what she wanted, but she already liked him more than was healthy and that possibly this wasn't her smartest idea.

"I'm thinking a creamy pasta, maybe with a smokey element."

"Sounds great. Where do you keep the pasta? I'll make that."

"I don't have dried pasta," he said. "I'm going to make it fresh. Want to learn?"

She did. "I'm not a very good cook."

"You say that but the biscuits you made at the cook-off were delicious. I think you're better at it than you let on."

"Thanks. I deliberately didn't cook at my best during our challenge and let you win."

He gave a loud laugh and shook his head as she started to pull ingredients together. She knew that she was never going to be at his level but there was something about watching him that made her realize how much passion and joy he brought in the kitchen. Cooking seemed to bring down all of his barriers. It was all she could do to stay where she was and not go and wrap herself around him. She wanted this afternoon to be one of her best memories and hoped that it would be.

Hoped that she could find a way to keep her cool and make the most of her time with him. He had awakened her desire and it was impossible to watch Conrad in the kitchen and not get turned on.

He was seducing her without realizing it. Watching his hands move as he took a bunch of herbs made her want to feel his hands on her skin. This was a slow, sensual seduction of her and her senses.

Food had been the only thing that he could use to distract himself from Indy.

He didn't cook with anyone. But because there were words he knew he couldn't say and emotions he was struggling to show her, cooking for her was the safest way for him to be his authentic self. He wanted her to see him here where he felt the most comfortable in his skin. He was pretty much a nightmare to work for in the kitchen because he had exacting standards, but he wanted to show her how to cook. Wanted to extend that feeling he'd had in the library when he'd held her in his arms and thought about her naked body under his.

He showed her how to measure the flour and make a well for it on the bench and then did the same for his own pasta. They wouldn't be able to eat this much pasta on their own, but he'd give the rest to Jenkins the groundskeeper.

"Next, crack an egg in the middle of the well."

He did it with one hand and turned toward her as he heard her tapping the egg on the side of the counter three times. Then she broke it and poured it into the center. He took the shells from her and tossed them in the sink without looking back.

"Now it's time to get messy. Use your fingers to incorporate the egg and flour."

She started to do it; as the flour and egg got caked on her fingers, he saw her struggle. He moved to stand behind her, before putting his arms around her. He took her hand in his and showed her the right motion. She smelled like summer flowers, distracting him. Her body fit perfectly in the cradle of his. He felt himself hardening. He let his erection brush against her, her hips rubbed against him. His reaction was to get even harder.

He knew she'd been scared by a man, knew that was part of it, but also, he was beginning to think maybe he was punishing himself by putting her off limits. He leaned down and brushed his mouth against her neck. The scent of flowers was stronger here. She turned her hand under his, their fingers meshing together on the table as she rolled her head and looked up at him.

Their eyes met and he realized he'd held off as long as he could. He wanted her. He wanted more than cooking or trying to slowly seduce her. He wasn't a slow seduction sort of man. "Do you want this?"

She nodded.

But he needed to hear her say it. He wasn't going to guess at anything with Indy. She meant too much for him to fuck this up now.

"Yes?"

"Yes," she said.

He lifted her up on the counter and stepped between her legs, spreading them as he did so. He put his hands on the sides of her waist and pulled her forward so that her legs were on either side of his torso. They were eye level like this. She rested her forehead against his and he felt the exhalation of her breath against his mouth and then the touch of her tongue over his lips.

He hardened even more as he took the kiss he'd wanted all day. It was long and deep, intimate, and left no place for either one of them to hide. Her hands moved up his back and he felt one hand in his hair as she shifted forward, wrapping her thigh around his hips trying to get closer to him.

He put one hand behind her on the butcher-block counter and lifted himself up so that he could rub his erection against her center. He lifted his head, realizing he needed more room. He wanted her naked and spread out under him.

"Wrap your legs around me," he said. His voice sounded rough and guttural to his own ears.

She did as he asked, wrapping her arms around his shoulders as well. He turned them and carried her up the stairs to the bedroom she'd put her bag in earlier. She caressed his shoulders as he carried her, and when they were in the room, he set her on her feet and closed the door behind them. He toed off his shoes and reached for her, then pulled her back into his arms.

She went eagerly, her hands going to the buttons of his shirt and undoing them; her fingers brushed against his chest with each button she undid. He let her finish unbuttoning his shirt and then shrugged out of it. He felt her fingers moving over his body. He knew that the tattoos might visually cover it, but with her touch she'd feel the roughness of his scarred body.

He stood still. Normally when he fucked, he did it with his clothes on and standing up, keeping as much of himself hidden from his partner. Making sex into a need instead of a want. But he wanted Indy's bare body against his naked skin. He didn't want to keep anything hidden. .

He wanted to explore all of her and he hadn't thought about how intimate it would be for her to explore him.

Her fingers followed the patterns on his skin, and then she leaned forward and he felt her mouth on his neck. She dropped small kisses all down the column of his neck to his chest. Moving across the front and then under his arm around to his back. Where the worst of the damage was. The nerves of his lower back were shot, and he was numb there, but he almost felt her touch.

She came back around and looked up at him. What he saw in her eyes, he didn't want to hear spoken out loud. So, he lifted her in his arms again, bringing his mouth down hard on hers. Kissing her so deeply that she couldn't think, just feel. Feel him against her. He put her down on the side of the four-poster bed.

He started to come down on top of her, but she scooted back, and he realized she wasn't ready for that. So he undid his pants and then sat down on the bed, with his back resting on the backboard.

"Come sit on my lap," he said.

She nodded and moved forward straddling him. "I'm sorr—

"Don't. There's no need for that between the two of us," he said to her.

Words weren't going to fix either one of them. But maybe sex could. Maybe sex would give them both what they needed. And maybe he would be free of this obsession with her.

Eleven

Nerves and desire warred within her. It was impossible to see Conrad's tattoo-covered body and think of anything other than being in his arms and feeling him inside of her. The top half of his body was heavily muscled; his strength enticed her like nothing else had. The intricate pattern of thorny branches encased him the way she wanted to with her body. She leaned forward, tracing her fingers over the pattern, acutely aware of his thick erection between her legs.

She took her clothes off as she watched him. There were so many times when she had been struck by the similarities between them, but now she celebrated the differences in them. His height and mass against her smaller frame were something she had initially worried about, but he kept himself tightly leashed. There was nothing out of control about him. Which made her feel safe in a way she hadn't realized she needed.

There was something so reassuring about Conrad and his control. He wanted her, but if she changed her mind, she knew that Conrad wouldn't force himself on her. That was freeing in a way that nothing else could be.

She lowered her head and traced the path her fingers had taken with her tongue. He tasted a bit salty and his skin was warm. She heard the ragged intake of his breath as she scooted back on his thighs and moved lower across his torso. His stomach was ridged with muscles and she had to admit, she liked it. Personally she'd never wanted to be muscly or work out, but she was glad he did.

She felt his hand in her hair, massaging her scalp, and then his other arm moved languidly around her, tracing a seemingly random pattern on her back and shoulder and then his touch moved to her collarbone. She held her own breath as his neared her breast. His thumb stroked over her nipple and she felt it harden, and her breasts became heavier and fuller with need. She turned her head. Noticed that thick cock between his legs and shifted around so she could touch it with her tongue as she closed her hand around his shaft.

He arched his hips slightly and she took just the tip of him into her mouth. Then she sucked him in deeper as she stroked him. Her other hand moved to his balls, squeezing them lightly as his thumb continued to rub back and forth across her nipple. She felt his big hand on her butt. First cupping one cheek, and then his fingers lightly tracing between her cheeks. She clenched her pussy as she dampened. His fingers moved lower but still so slowly.

She continued to suck him deeper into her mouth but her attention was torn between his big cock and his fingers on her most intimate flesh. He drew his finger light around the opening of her body and she spread her legs a bit wider but he just still moved around the opening. She squeezed his sac and then took him deeper into her throat, enjoying the feeling of him in her mouth and the way he reacted. His thumb on her nipple stopped moving and he arched underneath her again.

She smiled to herself, enjoying the feeling of having this big man under her control. She moved closer to the side of his body as she could take more of him in her mouth and continue to drive him crazy with lust.

He shifted on the bed and she felt him lift one of her legs to slide between them. His mouth was on her feminine center, parting the folds of her body and finding her clit with his tongue. He flicked it over her; her own mouth went slack on his erection as sensual flames licked through her. She arched her own hips trying to get more of his mouth.

But he just kept licking her, as if he had all the time in the world. She wanted more. But Conrad wasn't going to be rushed. She sucked harder on his cock and his hips started moving under her, just two thrusts before he pulled himself back and free of her mouth. He tumbled her onto her back, his hands coming to her hips to hold her on the bed as his mouth stayed busy between her legs.

"Conrad…"

"Shh…let me give this to you," he said against her skin. She shivered at the heat of his breath against her clit, and the sound of his words resonated within her body, sending a deep shaft of desire through her.

She arched her back, putting her hands in his thick hair and holding his head to her as she lifted herself into the lashings of his tongue. He continued to trace her pussy with his other finger. She couldn't take much more teasing when he pushed his finger up into her body.

She cried out his name as her walls tightened around it, twisting her fingers in his hair and holding him to her body as her orgasm washed over her. His mouth stayed busy between her legs until her thighs fell wide open. She tried to pull him up her body, but he just stayed where he was.

His fingers still inside of her, he turned his head looking up. As their eyes met, she knew that something was happening between them that she wasn't ready for. Not sex. Not the intimacy that came with sharing her body with him, but something else. Something deeper that she felt all the way to her soul.

Something that, if she were honest, she couldn't define. But as she reached for his shoulders and tried to draw him up, she realized that there was a part of her that never wanted to let him go.

Even if he couldn't be hers.

Despite the fact that he was fun and this felt like the start of something new, they were both too damaged for a relationship between them to work. He needed someone who could help reach the innocence he'd lost and she needed…well, when as he kissed her belly button and his hands closed over her breasts, his palms rubbing her nipples and making that slow burn start again low in her body, she wasn't sure *what* she needed. Part of her thought it was him. But the smarter part knew it couldn't be.

Conrad had almost come in her mouth, which hadn't been at all what he'd planned, so he'd pulled himself back from the edge. She'd tasted so good and when she'd orgasmed under his lips, that had again torn at his self-restraint but he had a deep well he drew from to keep himself under tight control. Normally sex wasn't a place where he had to fight with himself, but Indy was different.

She tasted so good. Like a dish that had all the best ingredients and flavors, including that elusive taste of umami. That fifth was heady and addictive. He was starting to crave her and admitted only to himself that he might not ever get enough of her. A smart man would only take this woman to bed once or else risk a life-long obsession to her. So he wanted to make this last.

He needed to make this last.

Wanted to explore every inch of her body and create a memory that would last the rest of his life. Because if this afternoon with Indy had shown him anything, it was that he could find a place for himself back here in GC. The only problem was him. Holding on to past hurts and grudges. He knew he should be the bigger man, but the truth was he still wasn't sure if he could be.

He knew a gentleman would start at her mouth and work down but he hadn't. And he wasn't going to deny himself any part of her body. Right now she was spread out on the bed and he was still between her legs, his hands on her small but ample breasts. He was going slowly, didn't want her to feel trapped by him. He knew he was a big man, so he wanted her to always know that she was the one truly in control.

Her hands were on his torso again, her fingers moving lower. He shifted up next to her on the bed so that he was along her side. He put one arm under her head, lifting her shoulders as he leaned down and took a dark pinkish nipple into his mouth. His other hand traced a pattern on her stomach, rubbing over her belly button as he flicked his tongue against her.

He felt her hand around his erection and knew that he wasn't going to last much longer if she kept that up. He had learned to control his responses to pain, but pleasure…this kind of pleasure was rare. When he had sex, he was legendary for his stamina…which he now realized may have been a complete lie. Her hands on his body were the best kind of aphrodisiac. And he didn't want to resist.

Why was he dragging this out? Why was he denying himself what she was so eager to give him? But the why was right there in the back of his mind. They were dangerous for each other. It felt like they could be each other's salvation or destruction.

She pushed against him and though her touch couldn't budge him, he let her urge him over onto his back and she straddled him, her hands on his shoulders. He fondled her breasts as she did so. Their eyes met and something unspoken passed between them. For himself it was all deep affection and caring. The two things he'd thought he'd burned out of his body with partying and fighting years ago.

But Indy was showing him that he hadn't. She licked her lips and gave him a tentative smile as she positioned herself over his cock. He sat up, forcing her to wrap her legs around his hips, and the tip of his erection slipped into her pussy.

She gasped as he did. Their eyes met again and this time he forced his mind to stop and just enjoy this moment with her. He shifted his hips and pushed himself deeper into her. She was so tight and felt so damned good that his instinct was to roll over and drive himself into her again and again until they were both screaming each other's names as they came. But he took a deep breath and held himself still as she adjusted to his girth.

She kissed the spot where his shoulder and neck met. "Why are you covered in thorns?"

"To keep the pain inside," he said truthfully.

"Why—"

He brought his mouth down on hers to stop the questions, because he would tell her anything in this moment and he knew he'd regret it later. He put his hands on her butt and pulled her hips forward as he fell back on the bed. She kissed him deeply and though she was on top, he controlled the pace of their lovemaking.

He drove his hips up into her and pulled her forward with each thrust, making sure he filled every inch of her each time. She started moving faster and faster against him, and he felt that tingling feeling down the small of his back as his balls got heavier. He thrust up into her, feeling her tighten around him as she pulled her mouth from his and cried out his name in a long moan. He drove up into her again two more times and then came in a massive rush, emptying himself inside her. He continued to thrust a few more times, and then she collapsed on his chest as they both lay still, the afternoon sunshine spilling into the room over the back of her body.

His heart stopped racing and she stayed still on top of him. He stroked her back and felt something close to contentment. He didn't allow himself to dwell on the fact that he was in the one place he'd always hated, because he didn't want those feelings in here with Indy.

He wanted to forget about all of that. But then he felt her fingers on his chest, moving over the old ridges of his scars, and her question came back to him. His thorns. It was his version of a hair shirt. His way of reminding himself each time he looked in the mirror that his control was a cage around the rage and the emotions that he'd never been able to handle.

Her soft touch was showing him that his cage might not be strong enough this time.

Indy's emotions were right at the surface and her barriers were down. She felt like she'd seen something in Conrad's eyes that matched that soul-deep feeling she'd had when they'd been making love. She hated that he had wrapped his body in these thorny branches, and she wanted to understand more.

He'd said he used them to keep the pain inside. "What pain are you holding inside?"

She hadn't realized she had said it out loud until she heard her voice in the quiet of the afternoon. He stopped stroking her back, and because she was draped over him, she felt the tension in his body that hadn't been there a moment earlier. She rested her chin on his sternum and looked toward his face but all she saw was the bottom of his jaw, where there was another ragged scar.

He'd been so damaged physically. That didn't mean that his emotional scars weren't as deep. Given what he'd told her and how he acted, it didn't take Nancy Drew to figure out.

"I don't want to discuss that."

She tried not to let his words hurt her, but they did. She was feeling so open and…caring toward him, she'd expected him to feel the same. "Okay."

Now she felt silly and wanted some space. She pushed against his chest to get up but he put his hands on the small of her back and held her to him. Holding her gently but close to him and she realized that some times Conrad was going to show her how he felt with his physicality instead of his words.

"Don't leave," he said. There was an edge to his voice that she didn't recognize. Something in the tone that made her relax against him.

"Sorry I pushed."

"It's your way."

She laughed at that because it was true. And if she didn't laugh, she might cry. She hated this feeling and yet at the same time it was a relief to know that she could feel some emotions like this again. A part of her had been in hiding since that date rape incident back in college. She knew it could have been so much worse, but it had left her shattered.

She needed a man to talk to so that she didn't have to just hear all these thoughts in her own head. That voice that kept needling and picking things apart until she thought she'd scream.

She wanted to just lie in his arms and enjoy this moment, but she wasn't allowing herself to.

His hands moved again, up and down her back. She swallowed and looked up at him again, and this time he had his head tipped down, watching her. Surprised, she almost dropped her head again, but didn't.

"I'm always going to ask things you don't want to answer," she said.

"I know."

"And?"

"And what? I'll be silent or say something douchey. You know I will," he said.

She smiled. That element of honesty mixed with self-deprecation never failed to make her like him even more. He might be warning her, but he never delivered on the darkness he cautioned her against. Her heart was telling her that was because he was an inherently good man worthy of her affection. But her mind was a little more cynical and wary of being hurt again. In the short time they'd known each other, she'd been more real with him than she had been with anyone in Gilbert Corners, including Nola.

"I do know. You know me too. Why are we both so honest with each other?" she asked.

"Because we know this won't last."

She stiffened with shock at his words. But then they settled in; she'd said as much to herself. He was right. They both knew it. It made her sad to hear it out loud, but as he'd said, he wasn't one to lie. And neither was she. As much as she might have pretended to want to hear something that would soften the truth, she'd have seen through it and been upset if he'd lied to her.

"I know. I wish…"

She trailed off. What did she wish? There was nothing she could say that would be true.

"I wish too," he said, gruffly. "But for now, let's take this day and pretend that we both aren't realists."

She thought about it for a few moments. Could she do that? Why not? As he said, they both weren't going to pretend this was the prelude to forever. They both knew that their lives weren't going to merge together suddenly and magically. Today was a moment they'd have to look back on. Fondly, she promised herself.

"No regrets."

"Never with you, lady," he said, rolling them to their

sides as he pulled away from her. "I'll go shower in another room and meet you back in the kitchen."

She shook her head. "Shower with me. This day isn't going to last forever, and I don't want to waste a minute of it without you."

He nodded in that short way of his. Then sat up and got to his feet before reaching back and lifting her in his arms. "No one's ever carried me before."

He arched one eyebrow at her. "Like it?"

"I do. Makes me feel like a princess," she said.

"Hmm. Too bad you don't have a white knight."

"I do. I have you."

"I'm not a white knight."

"Today you are," she said. She wished they had more than this time together. So she could show him the man she saw behind the thorns that he'd wrapped himself in. Behind the legend and the temper he used to keep everyone at bay. But she didn't, so she'd just push and take what she needed from him while he was here in her arms.

"Today only."

"That's all I need," she said but even as the words left her mouth, she knew they were a lie. She'd prided herself on being truthful, but she couldn't be now. She only had one day with Conrad and she wasn't going to ruin it with the truth.

Twelve

Indy had given up on trying to cook and sat on a stool watching him making pasta, talking about her favorite books. It was as if, by saying they only had this one day, he'd unlocked something in her.

"So what's the book about again?" he asked. She was trying to explain the plot of *A Swiftly Tilting Planet*, the third book in the Madeleine L'Engle *A Wrinkle in Time* series. Which he'd read when he'd been a teenager. He and Dash had read it when Rory did because she liked talking about books. He had a feeling that Rory and Indy would get along great. Or the Rory he had known. She was of course a shadow of the girl he'd known now.

But there was a real woman sitting there talking to him about her dreams and her love of fairy tales and books; it gave him hope that Rory might find that one day. He thought of the trauma from Indy's past that she'd dealt with. God, she was such a strong person. At times he was in awe of that strength in her because it allowed her to be open.

His strength was a fortress he used to keep everyone at bay. Hers was a warm hearth inviting those she chose to come closer and be comforted by it.

He wasn't sure he was worthy of being invited in. God, when was he going to? Today when he was with this woman, who had turned him inside out, he had wanted to celebrate so much of himself—and he still couldn't just exhale and let himself be with her.

She took a deep breath. "I love the sibling dynamics in the book. I'm an only child."

"As am I," he said. "But as you know I was raised with Rory and Dash, so I'm sort of not. I read that series a long time ago. It was okay. If you want a really good science fiction book, you should try *Dune*."

"I have. Oh my gosh, it makes my head hurt when I read it. I have to pay close attention to everything. I really like a book I can just sink into and not have to...well, think so much," she said. "What about you?"

"I don't read that much anymore. I will sometimes put an audio book on when I go for a ride on the bike," he said.

She shook her head, smiling at him.

"What?"

"I'm just picturing you looking like a badass on your bike and listening to *Dune*."

He laughed softly. "I can see your point. What's the best book you've read lately?"

"Hmm...not sure I can pick just one. My go-to is always historical romance."

He hadn't heard of the genre. "What do you love about it?"

She tipped her head to the side, chewing her lower lip which he noticed she did when she was weighing her words. "Part of what I like is just the setting, usually in Regency England, and the lavish balls and all the manors of that time. But the other part is the romance. I mean who doesn't love falling in love."

"Me."

She arched both eyebrows at him. "Is that true?"

"Maybe." To be honest he'd never really thought about love. His adult life he hadn't allowed himself to ever love anyone. But what he'd absorbed from watching others had convinced him that love seemed like the worst sort of emotion. He'd loved his parents and had felt so lost after their deaths.

He'd been in love with himself for his early adult years, thinking he was the only one who mattered until that horrible night with the fight and the crash. After that he'd pumped the brakes. Of course he'd had to. His recovery had taken all of his strength and when he was done, love had been the last thing he'd wanted to find.

"Why?" she asked.

He looked at the workbench where he'd cut the pasta into long strips of tagliatelle, pretending he had to flour them again, but the truth was he found this hard to talk about. Sure, in his head it made a sort of sense. But this wasn't something he'd ever say to anyone. Not even Dash.

"It's okay to tell me, as you said, this is probably the last time we'll be together this way," she said.

"I'm not sure I can. Life just feels saner without love. Even you have to admit that."

"How do you figure?"

"Well, you're here with me, for one, and you had been hibernating in Gilbert Corners before," he pointed out.

"I wasn't hibernating. And just because I'm not out there actively looking for love doesn't mean I don't want to find it someday."

"Someday?"

"Yes. I don't know when it will happen. Just like you don't know that it won't happen," she said.

"I can't imagine falling in love with anyone."

"Why not? Do you think no one can live up to your expectations?"

"Not at all," he said, realizing that Indy would probably come close to any expectation he had for a life partner. "It's more that I can't imagine letting myself be that vulnerable to another person."

She got off her stool and came around the counter to him. She put her arms around his waist and hugged him from behind.

"Oh, Conrad."

He stood there not sure what he'd done to elicit that reaction or even how he was supposed to respond.

He liked the feeling of her pressed along his back and he wanted her again, but he was already too deeply in like with her. He had to start pulling back, so he contented himself with a pat of her joined hands and then turned, breaking her hug.

"Oh, what?"

She chewed her lower lip and looked up at him until their eyes met and she sighed. "You try so hard to keep everything inside, but you can't."

"What do you mean try?"

She shrugged. "You won't like what I have to say."

"As you pointed out, we're not hanging out after today," he said.

"Fine. You have covered your body in thorny tattoos as if in some way those will keep people from getting closer to you or keep you from letting them close, but you reach out to everyone around you all the time."

"How?" he asked.

"With food. You picked a career in the one area that creates a connection between you and everyone. Food is love—everyone knows that. It's just that you cook for strangers so you can control the love. It's not that you don't love love. It's that you're afraid of it."

Indy knew she was pushing him, but it was hard not to. She'd been sitting there watching him cook and realized what she'd known deep in her soul all along. She didn't want this to be their only time together like this. She wasn't someone who needed a man in her life, not that there was anything wrong with that. She'd just always been fiercely independent and shy. And after her assault, she'd gone even deeper into herself.

But she had also found people along the way who she resonated with, and Conrad was a man she *definitely* resonated with. She thought maybe it was because he was so locked away in his thorny vest trying to keep the world at bay with his roar that she was drawn to him.

In her quiet way she did the same thing. But she used a book in her hands to do it.

She watched his face go stony as he brought his arms up to his hips, glaring at her. She might have gone too far.

Who wanted to have their fears pointed out?

"Afraid?"

She was tempted to backpedal. It would be the easiest way to get out of this, except she didn't want out. She needed to know what it was that kept him from wanting more intimacy, because maybe it would help her figure out why the only person she'd taken a chance on was a man who didn't want it.

She knew she was pointing out something in Conrad that she herself felt. Something she didn't want to cop to. He was just blunt enough to maybe give her some insight or...or say something that would hopefully make her stop seeing him in this light. This romantic light that made her believe she could help him. Even though she was pretty sure he didn't want to be helped, and that she didn't have the skills to do it.

"Yup. That's what I said. Listen, there's nothing wrong with being afraid of love," she said.

"Thanks," he said sarcastically. "I guess that's your own fear talking right?"

"You're deflecting," she said.

"You are too."

She leaned back against the wall behind her. "I am. I just... I wish there was some way we could both somehow be different but the same. I sort of want everything to be different so we could have more time together. Like this."

That seemed to relax him. She thought she could see the tension leave his body, and he came closer to her. Reaching out, he stroked the side of her face in a way that almost made her believe he returned her feelings. But then, she already knew he liked her. And liking wasn't enough. Liking wasn't what she was after.

She knew that it wasn't her—Indy Belmont—he objected to as much as it was his fear of being hurt. Though she suspected he wouldn't say it that way.

"Just let this be enough," he said. "I'm really not good at anything long-term. Not even the restaurant."

Not good at long term.

Didn't love love.

He was telling her these things to keep her from getting hurt. To keep her from doing something impulsive and passionate and making a mistake that she'd end up regretting.

"Me either," she said.

"Liar," he countered but not unkindly. "You might want to be, but everything about you and this move to Gilbert Corners says otherwise."

"I don't see that," she said.

"You're trying to break the town curse. You want to bring business to the town—you are fixing it in a way that I think you want to fix me."

She chewed her lower lip. "I didn't say that."

"You didn't have to," he said. "I know I need fixing. I'm not trying to pretend that I don't. That's why I don't do this."

He gestured to the two of them and she got it. He'd said he wasn't into dating.

"So why are you?" she asked.

He shrugged and looked away then turned back to the counter where he had been making pasta. She was pretty sure he either wasn't going to answer or was trying to come up with a falsehood she'd believe. She took a deep breath and knew she could save him by just saying something glib and changing the subject and she almost did.

Almost.

But then she saw the thorny branch that came up from the back of his neck, above the fabric of his shirt, and wrapped around his shoulder just the tiniest bit, and knew she couldn't. She wanted to be the princess who ripped down the thorns and found her way to the prince waiting inside.

"You like me," she said. "You might not want to. You might wish it was just lust and getting laid but it's more than that."

"You're right, I do wish you were like every other woman I've screwed, but you're not. I think that's why I'm hesitating here, which isn't like me. I'm talking about bringing my show and maybe a restaurant to Gilbert Corners, but I'm keeping it from you."

"Why?"

He put his head down and she saw him struggling for the words. It was easier to smash things, she thought, easier to fight than to talk things through. But she needed to know. "Is it because you don't care?" she asked.

He didn't say anything, and she walked around the island and leaned on the other side of the counter. He looked up and she saw some unfathomable emotion pass over his features. For a second it looked like hope and regret mixed together.

"Did you get that from reading a book in your book-shop where you hide from the world?"

She knew he was trying to rile her, but this was too important to let anger come into play. "No. I got that from talking to you. From riding behind you on your bike and walking through this ghost-filled home of your childhood. You might think you are keeping your emotions locked away but you're not. Not to me anyway. I see you."

He put both hands flat on the counter and leaned over so that only a few inches separated them. "You see what you want to see."

No one had gotten under his skin the way that Indy was today. He hated it, and yet at the same time a part of him enjoyed it. He was afraid to admit too much to her, but he had been alone for so long he'd sort of thought life was better that way. But with Indy…it wasn't. She'd awakened something in him that he wanted to explore, but it was becoming increasingly obvious that he couldn't control her or her responses.

Why couldn't she just eat pasta and make love to him again and let this day be a happy memory?

Probably for the same reason that he was trying to make it into one. Both of them were seeing in the other what they needed. Not what the other one did. He needed this one day of happy memories in the place that still haunted him, and she needed a lifetime of happy memories to replace the date that had stolen her innocence from her.

"I see you," she said. "But I'll stop pushing, if you come to town and build your restaurant. I'll keep my distance. I know what it's like to be confronted every day with someone you don't want to see."

She stepped back and went to her stool, sat down on it.

He wanted to be a different man. Wanted to give her this thing she thought she wanted with him. Even though he knew if he did, he'd hurt her. He'd disappoint her and become a regret. This wasn't him guessing or trying to make himself feel better. He wasn't into lying to himself even when it would be easier.

He was difficult and hard to be around. Even Dash had said so, and Dash was the one person on the planet who truly knew him.

"I want to see you. I don't want to hurt you," the words were torn from somewhere deep inside him. A place that he wasn't sure he wanted to acknowledge he had.

"I know."

Those quiet words tore him apart.

"There. You see it too."

She shook her head. "I see us. We have both been pushed past limits that would have broken others, but instead we both took those scars and the pain and made ourselves stronger. I know you need someone who can be light and make you laugh—"

"You do that."

"Until I get like this," she said.

He wasn't sure what she was getting at. "Oh, lady, this is a Conrad problem, not an Indy one."

She shook her head. "Nothing is all your fault. I want to take a chance on us. And I know we had sex and have had what, one and a half dates. So there isn't really an us, but I feel like maybe there could be. I guess…well all of this is me trying to ask you to take a chance too."

Take a chance.

No one had ever said those words to him. He had simply just always done what he wanted and dragged people along with him in his career and he had no real personal life. Could he do what she was asking?

Sure. Of course he could. But could he do it and not hurt her or get hurt himself in the process? Because he wasn't sure he could handle letting down another woman he cared about.

And there were no two ways about that. He had let Rory down, and the consequences had left her in coma. He knew he hadn't been driving, hadn't caused the accident, but that didn't change the fact that he'd exacerbated an already tense situation and made it harder for his cousin.

"Conrad?"

He was taking too long to respond. But he didn't know if he could. How was he going to do this? Since he'd woken up in that hospital bed nearly ten years ago, his life had been about learning to live with the pain, then relearning to walk, then figuring out how to cope with life, then the restaurant, then TV. All solitary prospects, but she wanted him to agree to something else. To try something with her.

"Forget it. So what do we need to do for the rest of this dish? Make some kind of sauce?"

She got up and came around by him. He closed his eyes as the scent of summer flowers surrounded him. She was so close. She wasn't asking him to be perfect or expecting him to meet her needs. He could reach out and take her in his arms and to his bed again. She wouldn't' deny him.

But he'd disappoint her. He'd already done that.

His heart started beating so loudly he could hear it in his ears and he'd be surprised if she couldn't hear it. Fear.

She'd called him on it and she was right.

"I don't want to hurt you."

"I know—it's cool. Forget I—"

"I can't. I can't forget you said it. I hate disappointing you," he said. The rest of the words were stuck in his throat.

"You're not. I pushed. I do that when I care about

someone. I can't promise I won't do it again. You set boundaries, I agreed to them and then I decided I wanted more, not your fault."

He pulled her into his arms and brought his mouth down hard on hers. He held her to him closely; there was nothing tentative about the emotions she stirred inside him, and he tried to show her all the things that he knew he couldn't' say with his kisses. He pushed his tongue deeper into her mouth, and she wrapped her arms around him and clung to him as if she'd never let him go.

The storm of emotions ebbed, leaving him feeling like a battered boardwalk and seashore after a hurricane, still standing but just. Still holding the woman he wanted in his arms. He looked down into her face and realized, like that midnight call he'd made to her, he wasn't going to be able to just limit himself to one day with her.

No matter what he'd said or how smart that would be.

"I'd like to try to see you again."

The words sounded rusty and slow in his head, but she heard them. She touched the side of his face, and he knew that no amount of thorny branches tattooed around his body was going to keep him safe. She was already inching her way in and he had no idea what to do with her.

Thirteen

Indy hadn't really thought through what seeing him again would entail. Dating hadn't been something either of them were regulars at. Their dates had become something unexpected, she thought as she saw him standing in the doorway outside her shop a week later. She'd finished a long day filming over at the deli and then stopped by the shop because it helped her relax to be surrounded by books.

Conrad wore a navy blue suit that made his eyes pop. He had on a dress shirt with no tie, and she could see those thorny tattoos around his lower neck as she finished putting away her stuff for the day and walked toward him.

"Are you sure about this? If the people of Gilbert Corners think I'm cursed, I probably shouldn't be seen here," he said.

"Oh, I'm sure, plus it sounds like fun. Why are you wearing a modern suit? I told you to dress in 1920s' garb."

"I figured I'd leave that to you, doll," he said, pulling her into his arms and kissing her. His kiss swept her away from everything, turning her on and making her want to skip the secret pop-up speakeasy that had opened. She suspected that was why he'd kissed her.

She pulled back, brushing her hands down the flapper-inspired beaded dress she wore, winked at him and said, "Thanks, doll."

He laughed and double-checked the door after she locked it. "So where is this place?"

"That's part of the fun—we have to unravel the clues to find it," she said, taking out her phone and going to the Gilbert Corners app.

"You're on the Main Street Business Alliance—don't you know where it is?" he asked.

"Uh, maybe," she said. She did know because all of the businesses around the town square had chipped in to open the pop-up. But she also wanted to see if they could figure out the clues. This was the first night of the club. Social media influencers and dignitaries from other neighboring towns had been invited as well.

"Good thing I recruited some help," he said, lifting his hand and waving someone over.

She turned to see who it was. She was pretty sure it was his cousin Dash Gilbert, whom she'd never met but had seen a photo of on his company's website. He wore a suit similar to the one Conrad had on, but he didn't look as sexy in it.

"Hello," she said as he joined them.

"Hi. I'm Dash," he said offering his hand.

"Indy," she said. "So we have to follow the clues to find the speakeasy."

"Yeah, the head of the committee doesn't know where it is," Conrad said.

She turned and lightly mock punched his arm. "It's supposed to be secret."

"What's the first clue?" Conrad asked.

"Gluten-free or full fat, this is the place to get your baked goods and start your journey," she read out loud.

"Java Juice. Nola Weston owns it," Conrad said. "Let's go."

"Nola? I think she was friends with Rory?" Dash asked.

"She is. She's my best friend and works on my TV show with me as well," Indy said.

"I hadn't made that connection before this," Dash said. "I can't wait to see her again."

The cousins talked back and forth while Indy looked at her phone and noticed a typo on the next clue, which she jotted down on a feedback page for the committee in her notes app. The map was taking them all around the square and then to the back of the old milliner's shop, which had been out of use since the 1970s and was the easiest to get up to building code and open as a bar.

Conrad noticed she was walking behind him and his cousin and stopped to take her hand so that they were walking together. Dash noticed the gesture and then noticed her noticing and winked at her. She smiled back, taking that as a good sign.

Conrad's tattoos weren't the only thing thorny; he was too. It seemed each date they went on started slow, like they were both trying to figure out what to do. He always pushed her sexually, and not in an uncomfortable way; she loved making love with him, but she had the feeling he was trying to make every encounter between them sexual and she wanted—no, needed—more than that. From his own admission most of his "relationships" in the past had been sexual in nature, and she had a feeling after they'd talked about everything that he had done that to protect himself.

Because she knew she was falling for him, she had to coax him out even though just staying home and making love was one of her favorite ways to spend time with him. Tonight it was as if he'd anticipated it and brought his cousin along.

They followed the clues which lead them along the town square.

"I really like to see the town coming back to life," Dash said. "The council members have done a good job with the park and the business here on Main Street."

"They needed a nudge, but once I convinced them there was a way to break the curse, they got on board," she said.

"By bringing Conrad back here?" Dash asked.

"That's right. Seems I'm the most important Gilbert."

"Well, you were the easiest to get here," Indy said.

Dash started laughing.

"I'm not easy."

"No, you're not."

"Glad you agree. So me coming to town made them think the curse is broken?" Conrad asked her as they got closer to the speakeasy.

"Sort of. They are more inclined to think of it as a thaw. Until we get the factory open and all the businesses on Main Street open again, I'm not sure the curse will be lifted," she said.

"Dash and I are working on the factory in addition to the restaurant space I mentioned," Conrad said.

"What else are you doing there?" she asked. She was surprised and a little hurt that he never mentioned it to her. She'd heard gossip around town of course but she would have liked to have heard it from him. As much as he'd opened up to her, there were still things he kept hidden behind his thorny branches.

"A television studio, which I want to talk to you about. Might be nice to have a production studio here," Conrad said. "In fact, I was planning to talk to you about it tonight before we went on this date."

"I'd love to discuss that more in depth," she told him. Well, that wasn't what she'd expected. He wasn't running away after all. Did this mean he wanted something more permanent?

"I think this is the place," she said. "The password is *Gilbert's a goose*."

"Really?"

"Yes. I know it needs work, but we were out of ideas," she said.

The bouncer let them in, and they weren't the first to arrive. The bar was toward the back and the interior was decorated as a 1920s' club with a dance floor in the middle and a stage at the end where they had a chanteuse singing. Dash volunteered to go to the bar and get drinks for them while she and Conrad found a table.

"So you brought your cousin on our date?" she asked. "Not sure if that's a good sign or not."

"I knew you'd say no to staying in and getting naked with me," he said with a wink. "I wanted Dash to see what you've been doing here in town."

"Why?"

"Because I'm proud of your hard work," he said, then leaned over to kiss her.

She felt a spark go through her and her heart beat faster as her mind was starting to think that pushing for this closeness was going to pay off.

Conrad wasn't sure how he found himself watching his cousin and Indy dance and getting slightly jealous, even though after two absinthe cocktails, Indy had told him that there wasn't a man alive who looked as good as he did in a suit. He knew she wasn't into anyone but him.

Which made him happier than it should have. The plain fact of the matter was the more time he spent with her, the more he realized that there was no way to keep her at arm's length. He had thought that agreeing to this dating thing would potentially bore him and that he'd grow tired of her.

But he hadn't. He was catching feelings and they were strong. Stronger than anything he experienced before and a part of him wanted to growl about it. But when he looked at Indy he just…well he couldn't growl. She made him feel good inside and as much as he'd struggled with believing he deserved this kind of happiness he felt it was right there if he only had the courage to reach out and take it.

"Why aren't you dancing?" Nola asked sitting down next to him. Nola was dressed like a gangster tonight in a pair of wide-leg dark pants with suspenders and a white shirt. She had on a flak cap and her hair had been pulled back to a low bun at the nape of her neck.

"Why aren't you?"

"I have no coordination and the Charleston requires too much thinking."

"Same."

"I doubt that."

"Dash asked Indy and we can't both dance with her," he said.

"So noble."

"That's me."

"Your reputation says otherwise."

He arched both eyebrows at her. "Is there a reason for this?"

She shrugged. "Indy is one of my few friends. I don't want to see her get hurt. That being said, I'm glad to see the Gilberts back in town."

He didn't want to hurt her either. He hoped he wouldn't. "The town is starting to shape up."

"Thanks to your girl."

His girl.

Was he ready for this? Date by date he had been letting her into his life and there were times when he held back because he was afraid. But the truth was, for weeks now he knew that he wanted more from Indy, and from himself.

Neither of them was good at dating, and sitting in a restaurant or going to a movie didn't appeal to them. So they'd had a picnic at his place in the city. Another night Indy insisted they lie on her couch and he read out loud to her from a book of poems by Lord Byron. Then there was tonight, the speakeasy around Gilbert Corners. Two people who were both used to the spotlight when it came to their TV shows guarding their privacy just letting their guards down with each other.

It felt odd to have found a woman who suited him so perfectly. It made him remember the man he'd been before the accident and he didn't necessarily like it. She was putting him in touch with parts of himself he'd ignored for a long time. He didn't know how to move forward. But he sensed that was fear holding him back.

"Indy's the best," he said, but even to his own ears that sounded trite. She was so much more than the best. She'd put her heart and soul into rejuvenating this town. And next weekend he was going to come to town with his TV show and give her the national exposure she wanted.

"She is. So your show taping…do you need any audience members?" Nola asked. "My mom is a huge fan."

He had the feeling this was really why Nola was over here. "I'll put you in touch with my producer. Give me your number."

She pulled a business card out of her pocket and handed it to him. "Thanks. I'm going to ask your cousin to dance so Indy will be free."

He got to his feet but didn't follow Nola. The last time he'd danced with anyone had been that winter ball ten years ago.

The thought had sort of drifted in from nowhere. Maybe it was being back in this place and seeing so many familiar faces all drinking and dancing that was stirring up old memories. Or maybe it was Indy who was nudging him to get some closure with his past. He needed to get out of here and get some air.

But as he turned to go, Indy caught his arm. "Dance with me. Just one dance. We can stand in the corner and sway together if you don't know the steps. I just want to be in your arms."

She looked up at him, her eyes wide and shining with that deep affection that he knew was that emotion…the L-word. The one he didn't believe in and certainly didn't

want to see on her face. The one that should have been
the impetus for him to turn on his heel and walk away
but instead he just nodded.

He wouldn't deny her tonight. She wanted to be in his
arms, and he wanted her there. The music was that old
standard a bit later than the 1920s "The Very Thought
of You," and he pulled her into his arms without thinking of the consequences.

He should have stuck to his guns that day at the mansion; he had known it then, and tonight it was confirmed.
He wasn't going to indulge himself and his emotions.
He knew how dangerous that could be and he had to
end this.

But not tonight, as Indy was in his arms, singing off-
key and messing up the lyrics while her hand stroked
along with the drumbeat at the back of his neck. He held
her closer and knew that he might have never believed in
this kind of relationship, but the truth was, he'd feared it.
Had remembered the closeness of his parents, the way
his grandfather had been so cold and angry after Conrad's grandmother's death.

He'd never wanted to admit he had anything in common with the old man, but had his grandfather kept everyone at arm's length to protect them? Fuck. He really
didn't like the path his thoughts were taking. But his
gut told him that walking away from Indy was going to
be the only way he could keep from following that path
that led to anger. Anger had always been the emotion
that had ruled him and essentially driven his success.
He felt himself falling for her. He'd never let himself be
this open or vulnerable to another person, and he was
afraid that he'd turn into a true beast if he lost her. Noth-

ing could ever fill the emptiness he felt at the thought of not having Indy by his side and in his arms.

The stars looked close enough to touch as Conrad held her hand and walked her home. "The speakeasy was a big hit. Don't you think?"

"Yeah. Everyone seemed to like it," he said.

She glanced over at him; she was a bit tipsy, but not too much. "Not your scene?"

"Not really."

She could see that. He wasn't someone for going out. "It's funny that you've always been in the spotlight but hate it so much."

"I don't think that's funny at all. It's probably because I've always been in it that I don't like it."

"True. So why become a TV chef?"

"I didn't mean to. My producer and partner in the restaurant suggested it after I stepped back from being there full-time. It just sort of happened," he said.

"You are so not a sort-of-happened kind of man," she said.

"You're right. I might hate the spotlight, but I also hate the idea of not being in it," he admitted. "I'm sure you're not shocked that I have a huge ego."

She shook her head. "I'm not, but you're not a humble-brag kind of guy. I think you like success and the kudos that come with it, but is it that you are trying to prove something to yourself...or your grandfather?"

When she'd been dancing with Dash, he'd mentioned that he had rarely enjoyed being in Gilbert Corners, which had added to what Conrad had said about their grandfather. She was glad she'd never met him; he sounded like he must have been difficult.

"Yeah."

That was probably as much of an answer as he was going to give, and she wasn't going to push him for more. Not tonight. Not when the stars were bright and she had Conrad by her side.

She knew she was falling for him. It had been there all the time, but she'd ignored it until tonight when he'd taken her hand and pulled her to his side. She hadn't realized that she'd been searching for—someone to walk by her side. Someone who she could trust enough to be this public with and this intimate with.

But now that she knew it, she couldn't go back from it.

"I saw you talking to Nola."

"She wants to provide coffee and snacks for the TV crew when we come to town, and also doesn't want you to get hurt."

"No one can hurt me," she said.

"Good."

But she knew that wasn't true. She could hurt herself by seeing something in Conrad that might not be there. It was one thing to tell herself that he was starting to come out of his thorny cave, but it was something else for him to do it. Was she actually seeing glimpses of the real man, or was she just making any small gesture seem like it?

Who was he really?

She knew he wasn't a man who liked to fail. Was that why he was here with her? He knew he had nothing to worry about in the kitchen when it came to her. But maybe her challenging him at the mansion had made him want to prove something.

"We haven't really checked in on the dating thing," she said, abruptly.

God, when was she going to have a thought and keep it to herself?

He arched both eyebrows at her the way he did sometimes.

"Well?"

"That wasn't a question, lady," he said.

A little of the tension she was carrying disappeared when he called her lady in that soft tone he used only when they were alone.

"Do you think it's working?" she asked.

"Do you?"

"Ugh."

"Ugh?"

"Conrad, stop doing that. I'm being serious."

He stopped walking and pulled her into his arms. "I know."

She put her arms around his neck and looked up at him. He was a big man with a muscly body who didn't need anyone to protect him, and yet there were moments like this when she saw a flash of vulnerability and she wanted to defend him.

"So?"

"Do we have to discuss this?" he asked.

"I guess not. Did I force you to date me?"

He started laughing and lifted her off her feet. "Lady, you couldn't force me to do anything. I'm here because I want to be here."

Those words put her mind at ease and she wrapped her arms around him and kissed him as he held her. Not the little sweet kisses they'd shared through the night but a deep, passionate kiss, because she was very aware that he hadn't answered her question and that there was a panic building inside her as she fell harder for him.

Was this going to last?

She'd been okay on her own, had planned out a life for herself where she accepted who she was and what was enough. Then Conrad came into it. To be fair, she'd drawn him here.

But all the same, this man who she was kissing with the kind of passion she thought she'd never experience again had changed something in her. Had made her start to dream of a future again and she didn't want to give it up.

And the harder she worked to make sure he felt safe and not chained to her, the more she wanted to wrap him in them as a couple. The more she felt compelled to make him see that they were stronger as a couple. The more she wanted to find a way to make him stay by her side.

Or force him to tell her that he couldn't. She knew that love took time, that she needed to be patient and let things unfold as they were meant to. But she wasn't sure she could do that.

She loved him. She had been trying not to, but she did. And Conrad was... Conrad. She felt that deep well of caring inside him, but he'd had a decade of being on his own and had gotten so used to not caring that she feared if she didn't push him to admit his feelings, he never would.

She'd risked everything on Conrad Gilbert, and she hadn't meant to.

He set her on her feet and they finished the walk to her house in silence. Her mind was buzzing with questions and the need for answers and her body was buzzing for him.

Of the two, she chose the safer option and led him up the stairs to her bed.

Fourteen

Conrad leaned against the wall in the hall outside her bedroom. He didn't want to be in her bed again. He needed to claim her but they were becoming too comfortable. Too much like a real couple. Tonight...well, tonight had been the moment where he had to face himself and admit that he'd let this go on too long.

He pulled her against him, so that her breasts rested against his chest and her hips were nestled against him. She leaned up on her tiptoes, her hands on his shoulders, and he put his hands under her butt and lifted her up so they could see each other eye to eye. Hers were still a bit bloodshot from the drinks earlier, but he saw the seriousness in them. Knew that they both didn't have to say it out loud but were thinking the same thing.

This had to end. He saw what she wanted from him; he wanted it too. But there was too much potential for it to go wrong. For him to actually earn the Beast moniker. Not toward her, but if anything happened to her…it was a chance he just didn't think he could take.

They weren't going to find a way to some sort of Hollywood version of happily-ever-after. That had never been the kind of man he was.

She opened her mouth to speak, but he wanted this last night, this time with her in his arms so he brought his mouth down on hers. Angled his head so that he could kiss her slowly and deeply. He took his time wanting this kiss to be enough to keep him satiated for the rest of his life. Even though he knew one kiss would never be enough.

Her hands moved up his shoulders, her fingers pushing into his hair as her tongue rubbed over his, and then she sucked his tongue deeper into her mouth. She tasted of absinthe and that extra special flavor that he had only tasted when he kissed her. He'd tried to re-create her in a dish, but it wasn't possible.

These feelings that stirred in him when she was in his arms came only from Indy. There was no way to replicate it on the plate or in his life. He knew that.

Fuck.

He turned so that she was between him and the wall before he realized what he was doing and started to step back.

"Sorry. I didn't mean to trap you."

She put her hand on the side of his face, rubbing her finger along his jawline. "I don't feel trapped with you. It's okay."

Those words made him feel—fuck, he wasn't able to think of anything but white-hot passion. He shut down the other thoughts in his head. Hell, he was going to get his rocks off…except when had making love with Indy been about just a long, hard orgasm? It hadn't. It couldn't be. Indy was too deeply embedded in him for sex to be just getting laid.

Which should have been a red flag from the very beginning, but in his arrogance, he'd thought he could control it. Hell, he *was* controlling it.

He brought his mouth down on hers again as his hands swept down her, finding the hem of her flapper dress and then pulling it up her body where it got wedged between the two of them and he left it there, as he could feel the bare skin at the tops of her thighs. He swept his fingers higher to her panties, before pushing them underneath and then slowly sliding the underwear down her legs. He didn't bother tossing it to the floor, just left it at her knees so he could caress her nakedness.

She shifted back and forth, and he realized she was working her panties down her legs as he took one full cheek of her butt in his hands, running his finger along her crack as he deepened the kiss even more. He was hungry for her as if it had been years instead of days since he'd had her.

His erection was full, straining against the zipper of his pants, and he knew if he freed himself he'd be inside her, and he wanted this last time to take forever. He wanted to draw out the passion. So he pulled his hips back and dropped to his knees between her legs. The scent of her arousal enflamed him and made him harder.

His blood felt like molten lava as it flowed through his body. Her hands were in his hair as he parted her nether lips, revealing her clit. He breathed on it, then licked her. She moaned and her hands tightened in his hair.

He opened his eyes, trying to memorize everything

about her in this moment. The dark curly hair that protected her femininity. The birthmark at the top of her left thigh right where her pubic area began. The way her hands lifted from his head and then landed again as he drove her higher and higher.

He drowned all of his senses in Indy. He let every part of her essence sink into his mind. He listened carefully to her breathing and the tiny moans she made, the sounds getting closer and closer to the moment when he knew she'd orgasm.

His own body was on fire, and it was only the fact that he'd had a lifetime of keeping himself in check that he could wait. He wanted this. He liked when she came before him. Liked tasting the passion in her and then driving her wild again in his arms.

Tonight though, it was more poignant, as this was the last time he'd taste her like this. The last time he'd hear her voice getting deeper and her sighs turning into longer moans until her legs flexed as her hips drove forward and she tunneled her fingers into his hair holding him to her as she cried out his name and came in his arms.

He looked up her body, craning his head so he could see her arched against the wall in ecstasy and he knew he'd never forget this moment or this woman. But for the sake of both of their souls he had to leave her after this and never come back.

The energy coming off Conrad was intense, and she couldn't read anything but the lust and desire...but she knew there was more. Something had changed between them. She knew that he must feel it too. If only she still believed in fairy tales, then she would tell herself that this was the beginning of forever.

But she lived in the real world where their past baggage didn't easily disappear, and sometimes the emotional wounds of childhood couldn't be cured with a new love. She slid down the wall, crouching in front of him. He looked at her but he didn't speak, and she could tell from the look on his face that he was in sex mode. She'd seen that passionate intensity too many times to mistake it for anything else.

She reached for the buttons of his shirt and her fingers fumbled with them, making it hard to undo them. The emotions of this moment, the feeling that this might be the last time she was alone with him like this overwhelmed her, and she cursed under her breath before she took the two sides of the shirt and pulled until the buttons burst and his shirt fell open.

She didn't look at him as she pushed her hands into the opening, tried to ignore those thorny branches that encased his torso, feeling the ridges of those old scars. But she couldn't ignore any of it. These were the things that made Conrad the man he was. Made him the man she liked—when was she going to feel comfortable with this admission. The man she loved.

Since he was making love to her like it was the last time, she wanted this. Wanted to admit to herself that she loved him and take this moment and make it into everything she'd ever secretly wanted and always believed she couldn't have.

His pectorals flexed as she ran her fingernail over his left nipple and then down the side of his body. She leaned in closer, biting his nipple and then licking it before following the path her finger hand taken with her mouth.

She took her time over the ridged indentation of his abdomen and then lower where that thin line of hair led to his cock. She saw his erection pressing against the fabric of his trousers and it made her hotter and wetter than his mouth had. She reached down to stroke him through his pants. Then she found the tab of his zipper and started to lower it, but he brushed her hands aside, did it himself. He stood and she frowned at him until he took off his pants and underwear and then sank back down on the floor against the wall.

"Shirts are easier to replace than pants," he said.

She smiled at him. "I'll buy you a new one."

"No need. Just climb on top of me and make love to me, Indy."

He had never called her by her name when they were intimate, and she had the feeling he only did so now because he was planning for this to be the last time. She could just feel it in the air around them.

"Oh, I plan to, Conrad."

He pushed his hands into her hair, jostling the pins she'd used to hold it in the Gibson Girl hairstyle and then his big hand rubbed against the back of her head as he pulled her face toward his. Their lips met and their kiss was deep and intense as she straddled him. She felt the ridge of his erection between her legs and she shifted her hips back and forth to ride it.

He felt so good as his big fingers moved over her intimate flesh. He shifted under her. His hands on her waist lifting her and then his mouth found her breast, suckled at her nipple as he positioned her so that his cock was poised to enter her. She put her hands on his shoulders, looking down at him. His head at her breast, his cock at her entrance, his scared and beautiful body underneath her.

She couldn't breathe from want. Both the physical desire for him and the emotional craving. But then his hands moved to her butt, one finger running along her crack, making her shiver and forget about everything but getting him inside her.

Slowly she lowered herself on him until he was fully seated in her body. He was so big that it always took her a moment to adjust to having him inside her. He lifted his head from her breast and their eyes met and she opened her mouth to say his name. He tangled his hand in her loose hair and drew her head to his shoulder, his mouth finding that spot where the base of her neck met her shoulder and then sucking on her skin as he moved underneath. He drove himself up into her and she moved on him. He held her to him, and they felt like one as they found their rhythm.

She felt her climax building and wanted to prolong it, but it felt too good. *He* felt too good as he moved faster and faster under her and then rolled them over so she was underneath him. Their eyes met and she wrapped her arms and legs around him as he drove even deeper, and she came. Shivers wracked her body and stars danced around her as she cried out his name. He drove into her a few more times before he emptied himself in her and called her name too.

He held his weight off her as he lowered his head, resting it against her breast as the sweat dried on their bodies. She put her arms around him and whispered in her mind the truth that she was no longer denying to herself.

I love you.

She had never thought until this moment that love couldn't make everything okay.

Conrad pushed himself to his feet and offered his hand to Indy. He'd been surprised when she'd ripped his shirt off but he'd liked it. She suited him on even levels that he hadn't revealed to her. She chewed her lower lip as she gathered her clothes off the floor. "Are you staying?"

"Yes."

He had promised himself tonight and he was going to take it. "I could use a shower. Want to join me?"

"How about if we share a bath?" she asked. There was almost a fragility to her as she stood there clutching her dress to her chest.

He didn't remember taking it from her body. Just that need to get her naked in his arms.

"Okay. Let's do it."

She walked into her bedroom and tossed her clothes to the floor as she continued to the bathroom; he tossed his near hers. He had an extra set of clothes stored in his bike. Which he'd get in the morning. He wanted this night to be just everything that day at the mansion had started out as.

That part of him that feared love and the ties that it brought made him want to leave right now. While she was in there running the bath. But that was the coward's way out and he wasn't one.

He also wouldn't do that to her. When he left in the morning, she'd know that he wasn't coming back except to fulfill his promises to Gilbert Corners. Damn, there were times when he hated himself.

It had been a long time since he had. He stood in the doorway and watched her staring at the tub that was filling with water. "My grandfather reached out to me after I left the hospital."

She glanced over at him, her hair falling around her

shoulder on one side as she stood up. "No. What happened?"

"I told him to fuck off."

"Conrad."

"Yeah, he died three months later. I just… I knew I was being a dick but I just wasn't ready to forgive him at all. I didn't know he'd die—in fact I would have put money on him being too stubborn to, but he did and…"

He wanted her to know the worst sides of him. She knew about the fight and how he'd almost killed with his fists the man who'd attacked Rory. When he crossed a line and became an asshole, he did it in a big way.

"It's okay," she said. "I mean for him, reaching out to you was probably enough to make him feel better about everything. He could say he tried. Which might have brought him peace when he was dying."

"Maybe." He didn't care about the past except for how it was making him feel about Indy. He walked over to the tub and got in first as she turned off the taps before taking the side with the faucet.

"You're saying goodbye, aren't you?"

"Am I obvious?"

"Yes. I could feel it on the street. What happened to change your mind?" she asked.

"You."

"Me? I swear to God you better give me more than a one-word answer or else," she said.

His arms ached with the need to pull her into them. He wanted her in his heart and in his life, but he wasn't sure he could do it. Be the man she needed. He had held out the television studio and the restaurant as an olive branch. Look at me and see the good things I'm doing. But he'd done them to impress her. For her.

"Fine, the truth is that I hate who I am in this town—I don't mind being a Gilbert out in the world because it's just my last name. Here it comes with baggage, not just mine but the townspeople's too. I watched you tonight, and you love who you are here. This place—"

"Isn't more important than you," she said interrupting him.

She pushed her legs along the sides of his and gave him a smile that felt a bit sad. "You let your guard down with me. Not all the time, but I saw hints of who you would have been if your parents hadn't died and your grandfather hadn't been who he was and—"

"I hadn't lived my life?"

"Ironic I know. But there is a very sweet man underneath that arrogance and that strength that you use to intimidate people and keep them from getting too close. I thought I saw you trying to let that side of yourself out, but then I accepted that you can't."

He wasn't sure he liked where she was going with this. He hadn't realized how much of himself he'd let Indy see or how observant she'd been. But he shouldn't' be surprised. From the beginning she'd seen past the bluster to the man beneath it.

"That man wouldn't have survived the loss that you've experienced. You need that tough thorny exterior—it's the only thing that's keeping you together and letting you live your life."

"I'm not fragile."

She tilted her head. "Not in the way that most people think of that word, but you do have a softness to you. I think I might be one of a handful of people who have seen it. That's what I saw that I wanted to believe in."

"I'm not two men, lady. I'm one. Both of those parts

of me exist together, the same way that you have your fiercely driven side and that private side. We can't be just one thing and we can't change to please someone else."

She pulled her legs back, resting her head on her knees. "I wouldn't want to change who I am. I like me. I like you too, Conrad. I don't want to change any of you."

"Not even the part that is leaving in the morning."

"Not even that. That's your choice. I don't like it, but I can't change you."

She put her forehead down on her knees hiding her face to him and he saw her shoulders shake and then she lifted her head.

"I wish—

"Don't. You're not a wishing man. You've never lied to me. Please don't start now. If you want to leave, I won't stop you."

He got out of the tub and walked out of the room and out of her life without another word.

Fifteen

Conrad had vacillated between coming tonight and staying away. But the truth was, he missed Indy. He'd regretted leaving the moment he'd done it. He'd thought he was doing what was right for her. He was still uncertain what was right for Indy, but he hadn't had anyone to call his own since his parents had died in that plane crash all those years ago.

Indy had been right when she'd said that he wasn't keeping himself safe with the thorns he had tattooed all over his body, covering the scars of the past and the man he'd been. He'd buried himself in the kitchen, found a world where it was okay to be rude, mean and let his temper fly. As the head chef he was the king and everyone had to obey him. Except that had been a false reality. He'd hidden himself in the kitchen away from the real world and the pain it offered.

He'd refused his grandfather's olive branch because he didn't want to reconcile with the man who'd made so many years of his life hell. He'd wanted the old man to die with that on his conscience. And he had held on to that hate as if it were a real thing. Tied it to the town of Gilbert Corners and walked righteously away.

But Indy with her chaotic energy and good heart had somehow found her way past the thorns and anger he'd always used to protect himself. He'd left her because he thought she'd be safer but that was an illusion he no longer could buy into. Indy was stronger than he was with all of his height and muscles and bad ass attitude. She had a strength to be shown the worst part of humanity and decide to create a safe, happy haven for others.

Her show wasn't just something she'd done to figure out where she wanted to go. That show was the essence of the woman he'd come to love. It was her way of showing the world that even in an imperfect world home was what you made of it. And he wanted to make a home with Indy. She'd shown him she wanted that too. Now he had to do the thing he'd never believed he could. He had to open his heart and trust someone else. It had never been easy...

Until Indy.

So he'd thrown this party in her honor and hoped she'd come.

He wanted her back. Not just for a night or few weekends but forever.

A part of him must have known that when he brought her for the weekend, he'd won. He'd struggled to keep her from seeing too much of who he was. Then pushed her away once she had seen the real man.

He wouldn't blame her if she rejected him. She might

not want him anymore. It had been two weeks since he'd left. Two weeks when he'd pretended that she was nothing and he wouldn't come back to GC.

"Are you going to just stand up here like a creeper?" Dash asked coming up next to him on the balcony.

"Fuck off."

"No. That's not happening anymore. I've let you keep everyone at bay with your reputation and gruffness but that stops now. You're not that man. I'm not sure that you ever were."

"I beat a man in this very house," he reminded his cousin.

"To avenge my sister. Con, you were never the monster that Grandfather painted you as. He thought he saw himself in you, but the truth is you aren't him. You never were." Dash pulled him back from the edge and hugged him.

He hugged his cousin back. "I'm not sure you're right. I hurt Indy and all she did was ask me to be real with her."

"You were protecting her," Dash said.

"Yes. I just don't want anyone else I love to be hurt."

"Who else have you let down?"

"Well Rory. I should have gotten to her sooner," Conrad said.

"It's easy to look at that night now and try to reconstruct it, but she was headstrong and wanted to date Declan. Nothing either of us said would have stopped her from being young and enjoying the ball. The one to blame is Declan who didn't listen when she said no. I wish that weren't the truth. But you're not to blame for what happened."

"I am a lot like the old man," Conrad said at last.

"The old man would never have thought to throw a gala to win back his woman."

"She likes these kinds of big gestures," Conrad said. He'd realized that the only way he was going to have a chance at getting Indy back was to return to Gilbert Corners and become part of the town she loved.

This was the hardest thing he'd ever had to do, but Indy was worth it. It had been hard to convince the Main Street Business Alliance to agree to a gala up here at the manor and keep his involvement quiet from Indy. But he had wanted the entire night to be a surprise for her. Magical, like she'd thought the ballroom was on that long ago afternoon.

So he'd done it. He was opening a restaurant in town in the next six months, and he had talked Ophelia into using some of the space in the old factory as a filming studio for his *Beast's Lair* show and had made space for Indy's *Hometown, Home Again* show to have production space as well. But that all meant nothing if Indy didn't forgive him and take him back.

He knew she cared about him. But second chances weren't something that many people gave when it came to relationships. Would she take a chance on him again?

Hell.

He was going to have to leave the balcony and see if she'd come to the party.

Two weeks passed, and as Labor Day weekend approached, Indy gave up all hope of Conrad coming back to Gilbert Corners. The Main Street Business Alliance was happy with the increase in foot traffic to the town. The old factory was going to be opening up again as a combined retail and entertainment space, which made everyone happy.

In fact, the town of Gilbert Corners was on its way to becoming everything that Indy had thought she wanted. Well, she still wanted it, but she wasn't enjoying it. And tonight felt even worse because she had been invited to a formal charity gala at Gilbert Manor. She hadn't been back there since her weekend with Conrad.

It was hard not to see him everywhere she went. It wasn't like he'd been in her shop but still, she saw him there, imagined his broad shoulders filling the doorway. In fact, every time the bell tinkled and the door opened, she glanced up with some hope in her heart that he'd come back.

But he hadn't.

He wasn't a man to do things halfway. When he'd walked out the door, that was it. She knew it. He'd given her back her hope and her confidence as a woman. She could now look back on dating Wayne and see that she'd used him to hide from having to trust again. She'd called her old boyfriend and thanked him for giving her that. He admitted he hadn't known what to do but had wanted to help her. And Indy appreciated that.

It was only after being with Conrad that she could see how she'd been so focused on the pain and stuck in her fear to really move on. But it was also Gilbert Corners and Nola's friendship that had helped heal her.

"We don't have to go," Nola said as they both were sharing the mirror in the bathroom at the bookshop.

Indy leaned in to put on her eyeliner. "I feel like since it's a thank-you for getting Conrad to come here, I can't not go."

"Yeah, I guess. Not that it did much good."

She shook her head in the mirror and turned to face her friend. "It did so. You don't have to be mad at him because he doesn't want a relationship with me."

"Girl, you're my ride or die—I am always going to have your back," Nola said.

"You're mine," she said, hugging Nola and feeling that twinge of sadness come close to overwhelming her. Turned out she wasn't like her mom. Love had just made her more determined to follow her dreams. She'd had a chance at love and it had walked away. She didn't have to worry about losing herself to Conrad because he wasn't willing to let her in.

Which was totally his prerogative. She knew that and respected it. But she was still mad, and also still in love with him. It seemed one of the great injustices of the universe that love wasn't automatically a two-way emotion. Why had she been willing to take the risk when he hadn't?

She swallowed, forced a smile and finished putting on her makeup. She was going to fake being okay until she was. Fake being happy with breaking the curse even though doing so had brought her heartache. Fake being her best self because that's what both she and the town needed.

"I'm surprised that Dash agreed to have the gala at the manor," Nola said.

"Me too. But it is a beautiful space and really should be used." She steeled herself against going into that ballroom again. Even in her memories she still got turned on from standing on the balcony and kissing Conrad. Those moments were etched in her mind. Maybe she should back out.

"It is. Wow, you look like a princess tonight," Nola said. "I've never seen you this dressed up."

"I was a Southern deb and can look nice," she retorted.

But she had pulled out all the stops tonight ordering a custom gown from the seamstress back in Lansdowne so it would fit her perfectly. The fitted bodice hugged her curves and then flowed out from her waist in a fall of tulle that ended at the floor. Her shoes were Manolo because they were her favorite, and she wore the tiara her mother had given her when she turned sixteen. She also had diamond studs that had been her great-aunt's.

Nola was dressed in a tux with a bright pink tie. She'd died one strand of her red hair a bright fuchsia and had done her eyeliner and mascara heavy. Honestly, Nola always was the most eye-catching person which was one of the reasons why Indy loved her. Nola never hid her light, she let it shine.

And Indy wanted that.

Actually, she'd found that. She might be sad that Conrad couldn't love her, but she wasn't broken or less-than because he didn't.

"Yeah, I didn't mean it bad. It's just I'm used to you in your glasses and cardigan in the bookshop. This is next-level. I feel like a schlub next to you."

"Don't be ridiculous. You always look gorgeous. I have no doubt that people will not even notice me when we both walk in," she said to her friend.

"Ha. Ready to storm the manor?"

"Nothing daunts me—I'm the curse breaker."

Nola laughed and when the Uber dropped them off in the porte cochere of Gilbert Manor, they both linked arms. "Thank you for coming with me tonight."

"Like I said, ride or die," Nola responded.

The foyer was decked out for the party with lights and a string quartet playing Vivaldi's *Spring* from *The Four Seasons*. There were waiters carrying trays with champagne and Nola took two glasses before handing one to Indy.

Indy lifted hers to toast her friend when she felt someone watching her and looked up to see Conrad standing on the landing looking down. She tried to be cool and smile at him, but couldn't. She still loved him, and it was heartbreaking to see him again this soon.

He put his hand on the banister and started walking down it just as she looked up. Their eyes met and his heartbeat became faster, his cock hardened and his mind went blank. God, she was gorgeous.

He'd missed her so much and thought he remembered every detail of how she looked, but he saw now that he'd forgotten about that tiny birthmark next to her ear. And exactly how full her mouth was.

Whatever it took, he was going to win her back. He was the Beast and this was his lair, and he wasn't about to lose, not now when the stakes were so high and he'd found the love he hadn't known he'd been craving all of his life.

He went down the rest of the stairs as she turned her back on him and linked her arm through Nola's starting to walk away.

"Indy."

She stopped, looking back over her shoulder at him, her chin held high as she stared at him.

"Yes."

"Can I speak with you privately?"

She chewed her lower lip, which gave him hope and then she nodded and stepped away from Nola.

Conrad held his hand out to her and led her through the foyer and back up the stairs, toward the balcony over the ballroom. He looked so good in the tuxedo that she was tempted to just pretend that everything was okay. But that was old Indy and she couldn't do that anymore.

She stopped walking and pulled her hand free of his. "What are you doing here?"

"I live here," he said.

"Since when?"

"Since Wednesday. I came back here for you, Indy."

What? Surprise, followed quickly by excitement then doubt. "Why?"

He shook his head. "You have every right to question my motives. Will you come with me to the ballroom, let me explain it to you there?"

She was tempted to say no but knew that was just her lingering anger from the way he'd left. "Yes, but first you have to tell what's going on."

"I…"

For the first time ever he was at a loss for words. That startled her. What was going on? What did he mean he lived here?

"Conrad—"

He put his finger over her lips to stop her speaking, a shiver of awareness went through her and she closed her eyes for a moment steeling herself to be strong.

"You were right. I was pretending to protect myself, using my anger at my grandfather to keep everyone at bay."

She smiled at him. "I'm glad you realized that. You

know you don't have to do that. There are a lot of people who care about you."

"I don't really need *a lot of people* to care about me, lady. I just need you," he said. "I know I messed up, and given your past and the trust you placed in me, I really let you down. That wasn't my intention."

She realized she was holding her breath and reminded herself to believe. This was Conrad and she loved him and she couldn't help hoping that he might have realized he loved her too.

"I know you didn't mean to hurt me," she said.

"Thanks for that. I love you. I'm probably still going to fuck up—that's who I am. But it won't be because I don't care. I've moved back here. I'm living here now. I'm opening a restaurant. And I want the chance to start again. Will you start again with me?"

She wasn't entirely sure she believed her ears but for the love she saw shining in his eyes and the sincerity in his voice. If she knew one thing about Conrad Gilbert it was that he didn't say things to be nice. He loved her.

"I love you," she said. "I don't think I'll be perfect but I'm pretty sure that relationships aren't supposed to be perfect. I think they are just supposed to be togetherness. Someone to laugh with, share fears with and hold in the middle of the night."

Conrad gathered her into his arms lifting her off her feet, before kissing her deeply. In the distance she heard the band start playing and the sound of voices chattering away in the ballroom. Conrad set her down and led her to the balcony of the ballroom.

They entered on the dark cloudy side. "This was the day we met. Remember the storm blowing, the competition and the wager?"

"I do," she said.

He led her around to the lightening skies which were transition to a night sky and the fiber-optic stars began to twinkle. "This is where we are now. A new day, a new beginning. Will you marry me and spend the rest of your life with me?"

She looked up at him, to the scar that ran down one side of his face, his full masculine lips and then lower where the thorny branches of his tattoo were visible, and she leaned in closer, noticing something she hadn't before. There were tiny rosebuds on the branches.

"Did you do this for me?"

"I did Rosalinda. Figured I might as well put you in ink since you were already in my heart."

"Oh, dear beast."

"You haven't answered my question," he reminded her, pulling her into his arms, then resting his forehead against hers.

"Yes. I'll marry you."

He kissed her then and she heard the sound of applause from the ballroom below. When she lifted her head a few minutes later the orchestra was playing and everyone was dancing. She and her beast made their way down the stairs and into the ballroom.

* * * * *

COMING SOON!

We really hope you enjoyed reading this book.
If you're looking for more romance, be sure to
head to the shops when new books are
available on

Thursday 2ⁿᵈ March

To see which titles are coming soon, please visit

millsandboon.co.uk/nextmonth

MILLS & BOON

MILLS & BOON

THE HEART OF ROMANCE

A ROMANCE FOR EVERY READER

MODERN

Prepare to be swept off your feet by sophisticated, sexy and seductive heroes, in some of the world's most glamourous and romantic locations, where power and passion collide.

HISTORICAL

Escape with historical heroes from time gone by. Whether your passion is for wicked Regency Rakes, muscled Vikings or rugged Highlanders, awaken the romance of the past.

MEDICAL

Set your pulse racing with dedicated, delectable doctors in the high-pressure world of medicine, where emotions run high and passion, comfort and love are the best medicine.

True Love

Celebrate true love with tender stories of heartfelt romance, from the rush of falling in love to the joy a new baby can bring, and a focus on the emotional heart of a relationship.

Desire

Indulge in secrets and scandal, intense drama and plenty of sizzling hot action with powerful and passionate heroes who have it all: wealth, status, good looks…everything but the right woman.

HEROES

Experience all the excitement of a gripping thriller, with an intense romance at its heart. Resourceful, true-to-life women and strong, fearless men face danger and desire - a killer combination!

To see which titles are coming soon, please visit

millsandboon.co.uk/nextmonth

OUT NOW!

Available at
millsandboon.co.uk

MILLS & BOON